"What of the waltz?"

There was something intimate in his tone. It worked over her skin, pimpling it with awareness. There went that tugging again, that invisible string that seemed to pull her to him no matter that her head didn't want to go.

As if in a trance, she turned to face him, moved toward him. In a few steps, she was before him again. He stared down at her like a starving man, the fire in his eyes so much brighter than before, seeming to have been dredged up from the very depths of his soul.

She didn't know how the words came, her mouth was so dry. "Put your left hand at my waist."

He did as she instructed. His palm burned through the layers of her clothes.

"Now take my hand in your right."

In a moment, her fingers were in his grasp. "Like this?" he breathed.

She nodded, unable to look away from his face. "Yes."

His fingers flexed on her waist, tightened on her hand. He took a step closer.

She breathed in a deep, shuddering breath. His own scent of spice filled her, made her dizzy with longing. "That's a bit too close for this dance," she managed.

He moved even closer. "And this?"

This time the words barely emerged. "Much too close."

A Good Duke Is Hard to Find

CHRISTINA BRITTON

FOREVER
New York Boston

Copyright © 2020 by Christina Silverio
Preview of *Someday My Duke Will Come* copyright © 2020 by Christina Silverio

Cover design by Daniela Medina. Cover illustration by Judy York. Cover photo by Shirley Green. Cover copyright © 2020 by Hachette Book Group, Inc.

Forever
Hachette Book Group
1290 Avenue of the Americas, New York, NY 10104
read-forever.com
twitter.com/readforeverpub

First Edition: June 2020

Forever is an imprint of Grand Central Publishing. The Forever name and logo are trademarks of Hachette Book Group, Inc.

The publisher is not responsible for websites (or their content) that are not owned by the publisher.

The Hachette Speakers Bureau provides a wide range of authors for speaking events. To find out more, go to www.hachettespeakersbureau.com or call (866) 376-6591.

ISBNs: 978-1-5387-1749-3 (mass market), 978-1-5387-1748-6 (ebook)

Printed in the United States of America

OPM

10 9 8 7 6 5 4 3 2 1

To my husband, Eric, who gave me an engraved pen our first Christmas because he knew one day I'd succeed in seeing my dreams realized. And who is still, nearly a quarter of a century later, my biggest supporter. (Even though I still haven't put a sword with a hidden compartment in the hilt in my books...) I love you, hunny.

Acknowledgments

The Isle of Synne and its romantic misfits are so very dear to me. And I'm beyond grateful to the people who came to love it as much as I do and who worked so hard to bring it into the world.

First and foremost, to my agent, Kim Lionetti. You are my safe port in a storm. Thank you so much for believing in me. And a huge thanks to the entire Bookends team for being wonderfully supportive since day one.

To my editor, Madeleine Colavita, for loving Peter and Lenora (and Lady Tesh!) so very much. Your passion for this little world I've created and your dedication to making it shine make my heart so happy. And to Leah Hultenschmidt, Jodi Rosoff, Daniela Medina, Judy York, Luria Rittenberg, Joan Matthews, and the entire team at Hachette Book Group/Grand Central Forever, for welcoming me into your family. I'm so honored to be on this path with you.

To my fabulous beta readers, Maria, Julie, and Joni, who gave me such incredible feedback. To Hannah, Susannah, Cathy, and the Le Bou crew for cheering me on and helping me work out the kinks. To Lenora Bell for inspiring my heroine's name. And to Jayci for being my rock while I worked through edits. I appreciate each and every one of you.

To all of my family and friends who have offered me their encouragement and support. If I mentioned you all here, it would double my word count! But know that your kind words have helped me in so many ways. I'm so blessed to have you all in my life.

To my sweet pup, Miss Emma, for being my writing companion, and for inspiring Freya.

To my readers. I never thought I would be able to say that, and that I do is truly a dream come true. Thank you from the very bottom of my heart for all the love and kindness you've shown me.

Last (but never least), to my husband and children. Every single day you let me know in words and actions how much you believe in me. I cannot begin to tell you how deeply I love you. Thank you, for everything and more.

A Good Duke
Is Hard to Find

Chapter 1

London, 1817

*A*t first it was a whisper, a breath of sound that crept through St. George's like a mist.

As the gathered guests grew aware of Miss Lenora Hartley's arrival, it became a tidal wave of voices that slammed into her where she stood at the back of the church.

She eyed the churning sea of faces that turned in her direction, dread snaking under her skin. For it was not smiles or curiosity or politeness in their eyes, but pity and an almost horrified glee.

Lenora's gaze snapped to the altar. Lord Landon was not there. A sweep of the area confirmed it. The dread that simmered under the surface transformed to a boiling panic, the ground beneath her feet as unsteady as sand in an outgoing tide. With effort, she kept her serene smile fixed firmly in place, yet her fingers convulsed in the wool of her father's sleeve.

Not again.

Just then there was a burst of movement from the congregation. A woman in pale violet darted into the center aisle and hurried toward her. Margery. Lenora nearly sagged in relief to see her friend. The look in the young widow's eyes, however, had Lenora's panic returning tenfold.

"My dear," Margery said with forced joviality. She leaned forward to kiss Lenora on the cheek. Her next words, whispered hurriedly in her ear, turned Lenora's blood to ice. "Go back to the carriage. Now."

Cheeks trembling to hold her smile, Lenora turned to her father. "Papa, I do believe I've forgotten something in the carriage."

Her father, quite against character, held his tongue. Without acknowledging their guests, he turned and guided Lenora and Margery out. *Hold your head high*, Lenora told herself as they stepped into the light of the bright morning sun. Down the steps—*walk, don't run*—to the waiting carriage. Once safely ensconced within, Margery rapped sharply on the trap door.

"Back to Sir Alfred's house, and hurry," she barked to the startled driver. As the carriage lurched into motion, she grasped Lenora's hands tight, her velvet brown eyes sober in her pale face. "I cannot believe he has done this to you. What a horrid mess."

"Enough of the dramatics, Margery," Lenora's father broke in, his voice like gravel crushed beneath a wheel. "What the devil is going on? Where is Lord Landon?"

Margery's eyes hardened. "Would that I knew, for I'm of a mind to teach him a valuable lesson in being a conniving, despicable snake in the grass."

Lenora's breath left her. Lord Landon must have done something horrendous to induce such wrath from her normally even-tempered friend.

"Damn it, Margery, if you don't tell us what the boy has done this instant, I will turn this carriage around and find someone who can."

Margery looked at Lenora. "I'm sorry, dear heart.

There is no easy way to say this, but he's gone and got himself into a duel."

Silence descended at that thoroughly unexpected pronouncement. Suddenly a wild laugh echoed about the interior. Lenora looked at her father and Margery in turn, only to see they were staring at her in shock. She had made that sound, had she? She flushed hot.

"That cannot be right," she blurted out. "Lord Landon. In a duel." An image of her intended rose up in her mind, cool and calm and not dashing in the least. Again that wild laugh sounded. She clamped a hand over her mouth.

Her father gave her a long look, as if assessing her sanity, before turning back to Margery. "Tell us everything you know, in as concise a way as possible."

It was an order, plain and simple, and not at all gently said. Blessedly Margery was more than familiar with his sharp manners and launched on. "Lord Landon met with Sir Francis Denby in Hyde Park at dawn this morning. Sir Francis was hit in the arm and an artery was severed. He may not survive. Lord Landon ran; no doubt he's halfway to the continent as we speak."

"The blasted idiot," Lenora's father growled.

Confusion and horror warred in Lenora's breast. "What in the world could Lord Landon and Sir Francis have fought over to warrant a duel, of all things?"

The pain in her friend's eyes was acute. "It seems they fought over Sir Francis's sister, Katrina."

Lenora blinked. "But why?"

"Come now, girl," her father snapped. "Even someone as dim as you should be able to figure it out."

His words hung heavy and cruel in the air. As Lenora's stunned brain caught up with the rest of her, a horrified realization hit.

"Do you mean to tell me that Lord Landon and Katrina...?"

Margery nodded miserably. "It appears so. I'm sorry, Lenora."

Lenora fell back against the plush squabs. Was this some type of divine retribution? Three fiancés in as many years had left her. Granted, the first had not wanted to leave.

Pain and guilt flared as she thought of Hillram, before she quickly shut him back into the fathomless box her heart had become.

Even so, a memory had escaped, a creeping tendril that wound about her and would not be ignored. Hillram's face, still and pale as death had claimed him. A sight that would haunt her the rest of her days.

She had been given a year to mourn him before she had been paraded before the single aristocrats of London, a berry ripe for the picking in exchange for their support of her father's political aspirations. An engagement had been made, with Lord Fig. When that man had run off to Gretna Green with his housekeeper, her father had matched her with Lord Landon. Who was now on the run for attempted murder.

Again that mad laugh threatened. She clamped her lips closed and gripped her gloved fingers tight in the silver netting of her gown. Perhaps her father was right, that there was something wrong with her. Why else could she not see an engagement through?

Her father grew alarmingly red and drew himself up, leveling an accusatory stare on Margery. "And you didn't think to warn us before we walked into that nest of vipers at St. George's?"

"The news reached me as you arrived," Margery

countered. "You know I would never knowingly put Lenora in such a position."

He turned furious eyes on Lenora then. "Just as well you're packed. Though it won't be a wedding trip you'll be taking."

"You're sending me away?" He couldn't mean it. They were all each other had for family.

"Of course I'm sending you away." He looked out the carriage window at the passing scenery. "Think of the scandal. Your third failed attempt at marriage? You'll be a laughingstock."

Lenora pressed a fist into her roiling midsection, trying and failing to tamp down on the hurt that surged at her father's words. It was only logical that he would want her far away from London at a time like this, she reasoned. And mayhap there was a silver lining to it all, in that she would finally be free of the unending social whirl her life had become.

She took a deep breath, nodding firmly. "Perhaps it's for the best. I can access my trust in a few years and quietly retire after that."

"You fool," her father spat, turning blazing eyes on her. "If you think this is the end of it, you are mistaken. While you're in the country, I'll be clearing your name as best I can. With luck, I may secure you a husband by the winter. Perhaps," he muttered, "Lord Gregson's heir will be willing to overlook the stain on your name. Or even Viscount Burgess. They both owe me a great deal, after all."

Lenora's mouth fell open in disbelief. "You cannot mean to bring about yet another engagement."

"I can and I will," he said, his voice as icy as she had ever heard it. He leveled a hard stare on her. "I'll give you the rest of the summer, Lenora, to lick your wounds.

At the end of that time you'd best be ready to do your duty and marry where I say you shall. And you'd best do all in your power to keep it from falling through this time around. Or you shall be cut off without a cent to your name."

That devastating proclamation was still ringing through the air when the coach arrived at the townhouse. The servants were ready and waiting, their faces wreathed in smiles. Those cheery expressions were quickly wiped, however, as her father stormed through the front door. "Lock up the house," he ordered, "and don't let a damn person through the door. Unless it's Lord Landon. Then I will be happy to see him so I might wring his damned neck."

He headed for the stairs. Lenora, stunned, watched him go. She willed him to turn back to her, to say one kind thing after the devastation of the day. At the top he finally looked back. Lenora held her breath, hope filling her.

His eyes swept past her to settle on the garlands of roses that decorated the front hall. "And have these damn flowers taken down at once. The smell is making me sick."

As he stalked out of sight, a roaring filled Lenora's ears. He had never been one to indulge in softer emotions. Yet after the upheaval of the morning, his refusal to offer even one kind word made her feel as if she'd been punched. It was several long seconds before that miasma of shock was broken by Margery.

"Please send some of the wedding breakfast up to Miss Hartley's sitting room, Mrs. Clark," she murmured to the housekeeper. "And some champagne as well. We could use something to fortify us."

"Of course, Mrs. Kitteridge," the housekeeper said, rushing off.

Lenora felt a hand beneath her arm, and then she was being guided up the gleaming staircase. She shook her head sharply, trying to regain control of her thoughts.

"You should not have ordered up the champagne," she managed through the fog of shock. "What will the servants think?"

"I think, dear heart, the servants are the very last thing you should worry about."

Of course Margery was right. Lenora's whole world was imploding. In the grand scheme of things, a little champagne in the morning was not of concern.

They made it to her suite of rooms in short order. As Lenora collapsed into an overstuffed chair, she became aware of how quiet it was. This house should be ringing with voices and laughter, the rooms bursting with people, the wedding cake in all its frosted decadence gushed over.

Instead she was locked away in her sitting room, dressed in a creased silver wedding gown and surrounded by trunks full of belongings that now had no set destination, while the food went to waste down below.

As if reading her thoughts, Margery came close and placed a comforting hand on her shoulder. "Shall I help you into something else?"

Lenora looked down at the beautiful dress, created so carefully to her father's specifications. "Yes."

Margery glanced at the bronze traveling gown that hung ready for the wedding trip that would never come. Frowning, she ducked into the bedroom. From behind the door there came the sounds of shifting trunks, lids being opened, then slammed shut. When she reappeared, she held in her hands a well-worn pale green gown with twining green leaves embroidered at the hem. *One of my favorites.* Of course Margery would know it was. Her friend knew everything about her, from what books she read to how she hated tea with a passion.

Well, she knew nearly everything.

Without warning, Lenora burst into tears.

"Oh, darling," Margery cried, rushing forward. Plump arms went around Lenora's shaking form, holding her close. A gentle hand drifted over the intricate braids in her hair. "This is not about Lord Landon at all, or even about your father. This is about Hillram, isn't it?"

Which only served to make Lenora cry harder. If Margery only knew…

Her friend rubbed her back, mistaking her reaction for an admission. "I know you don't like to talk of him. But Hillram wouldn't have wanted you to pine for him all your life. As good as my cousin was, as much as I loved him, your life did not end with his death. Nor did it end with Lord Fig's cowardly elopement. And it will not end with this, either. Lord Landon was simply not the right man. After all," she said, her lips quirking at the corner, "no one in their right mind should have the name you would have, had you married him. Lenora Ludlow, Lady Landon? Really? It would have been a travesty."

For a single blessed moment, Lenora's chest lightened. That mood, however, was brittle as finely spun sugar. The rustle of her wedding dress as she moved, the faint scent of ham and pastries wafting through the house, the muffled clink of glass as the servants went about dismantling the carefully planned breakfast buffet, was enough to bring her crashing back to earth. "I cannot do this again, Margery," she whispered.

"You can get through this," her friend insisted, taking up her hand and pressing it. "You needn't be lonely the rest of your days. You'll make some man a fine wife and find happiness in it, you'll see."

"You've accepted loneliness rather than remarry," Lenora snapped, impotence over her lack of control for the future causing the angry words to spill out.

Pain flashed in Margery's eyes, her fingers releasing Lenora's and going to the gold band cradling her fourth finger. Regret, bitter as gall, filled Lenora that she had unintentionally hurt her friend. "I'm so sorry, Margery," she said. "That was inexcusable."

Margery tried for a smile, though grief dulled her eyes. "I should be the one to apologize. We've both lost the irreplaceable. You loved Hillram as well as I loved my Aaron. I shouldn't have pushed you as I did."

Lenora could only stare dumbly at her friend, trying in vain to formulate a reply. Letting her friend believe she had loved Hillram was one of the greatest betrayals she had ever committed. But her friend would despise her if she knew the truth. And she could not lose Margery.

A soft scratching at the door interrupted them. The housekeeper was there with two maids bearing trays of food and drink. Once the small feast was placed to Mrs. Clark's exacting standards, she turned to Lenora.

"Miss Hartley, please let us know if there is anything else you need."

The pity in the woman's eyes nearly did her in again. "Thank you," Lenora whispered, hugging her arms about her middle as the servants left.

Margery wasted no time now that they were once more alone. Soon the silver gown was sailing through the air to fall in an inelegant heap on the floor, the simple but preferable green dress in its place. Lenora was made as comfortable as possible, surrounded by pillows, her feet propped on a small stool. It was only then her friend went to work on the food, heaping their plates with all manner of decadent dishes, from hot rolls to ham to fruitcake.

"Eat," Margery ordered, pushing an overflowing plate closer to Lenora on the low table between them. "And drink." She pressed a delicate flute of champagne into Lenora's hands. "Drink as much as you can and I shall do the same, for I cannot think of a better way to finish off this horrid morning."

To Lenora's surprise, she did. She drank, and ate, and drank some more. The champagne was sweet and light, tickling her nose, relaxing her muscles. And if she couldn't forget what Lord Landon had done, she at least didn't care quite so much about it.

At the end of an hour, she heaved a sigh and slumped back. "Margery, have I ever told you that you are brilliant? Absolutely brilliant?"

Margery gave her a lopsided smile as she studied Lenora over the rim of her own glass. "I am, aren't I? Either that," she said with a bleary frown, peering at the now empty bottle, "or we have had entirely too much champagne."

"No one can have too much champagne," Lenora declared.

"Very true."

Lenora threw the remains of her drink back and smacked her lips in appreciation. "Why does this champagne taste so much better than any I've had before?"

"It's the company," Margery said, motioning to Lenora with her glass. "No stuffy society matrons, no drunken lords."

In an instant, Lenora's mood darkened. "Society," she spat. "I abhor society." She glowered at the silver dress, still crumpled in the corner, seeing not the fine netting and shimmering silk but an unending line of faces judging every move she made. She lurched upright again. "Do you know, I think my father had the right of it. Leaving this city is a genius idea."

Margery made a face. "This city is horrid."

"You're so right," Lenora exclaimed. "It is horrid, and I'm determined to be off now."

Margery smiled in delight. "Then I shall leave as well. It's no fun without you anyway." Then she frowned. Blinking uncomprehendingly, she upended the empty bottle over her glass, trying to force the last drop out by sheer will. "Where shall we go off to?"

Lenora frowned. "He will want me to return to our country seat. And you know I hate it there even more than I hate this city." The wind taken out of her sails, she slumped back again. If London was exhausting in its never-ending social obligations, her father's house in Kent was the opposite. Cold and austere and removed from any polite society, it was a place of exile more than anything.

Margery's voice suddenly burst into the quiet of the room.

"Let's visit my grandmother instead," she announced as Lenora jumped and tipped sideways. "She was your mother's godmother. Your father cannot say no."

Even in her mind-numbed state, an image of sharp brown eyes and a mountain of snow-white hair flashed through Lenora's head. Along with that came the sound of water lapping at the shore, of pale sand between her toes, of impromptu picnics with Margery and the call of gulls as their companions.

And Hillram. For it was on the Isle of Synne during her

visits to Margery's grandmother that Lenora and Hillram had become such close friends, that he had courted her, had asked her to marry him. And that her life had begun to unravel.

She peered into her empty glass. She had refused to face Hillram's death and the devastation that had surrounded it for so long. And ever since, she had known nothing but misfortune. She lived daily with the disappointment on her father's face, with his angry declarations that she was to blame.

Was it possible that, in closing herself off from remembering Hillram, she had locked something important of herself away as well? Was it the lack of that something that had the following two fiancés running from her as fast as they could manage?

Twirling her glass, she watched as the facets grabbed the light, splitting it into a riot of colors. She could go to the Isle, could revisit those glorious places of her youth, could find again that missing piece of herself. And maybe in doing so, she could forgive herself and finally be free of the guilt that had taken hold of her, trapping her like a fish in a tide pool.

Lenora sat forward. A new energy filled her that had nothing at all to do with the champagne. "Let's do it," she said, reaching for Margery's hand. "Let's go to the Isle."

Chapter 2

*F*inally, after thirteen long years, the last of his debts was about to be repaid.

Peter Ashford paused before the massive carved oak door, listening to the waves as they battered some unseen beach far below the cliffs behind him. The wind kicked up, the air heavy and electric, signaling an oncoming storm. A perfect accompaniment to the churning emotions within his chest, the burn of anticipation deep in his gut. He had waited so long for this moment, could almost taste freedom.

And after he was released from this burden, he could go and collect the pound of flesh that was owed him.

He raised his hand, rapping his scarred, work-roughened knuckles on the polished wood. Almost immediately the door swung open. A dour-looking butler stood in the entrance.

"May I help you?"

"Is Lady Tesh at home?"

The servant's eyes tripped from Peter's too-long hair to his scuffed boots, no doubt cataloguing every crease in his travel-stained clothing. The man's expression became even more shuttered, his lip curling ever so slightly. "And may I ask who is inquiring, sir?"

Peter clenched his teeth tight. No one did haughty like the English, that was certain. Reaching into his coat pocket, he extracted a creamy card, one he'd had made up in Boston at Quincy's insistence. He'd thought it a complete waste of money at the time. He was not the face of their real estate empire, after all—he was more often than not the one to roll up his sleeves and deal with the everyday running of things. What reason did Peter have to carry bits of engraved paper?

As he handed it over, however, he came to see how useful they could be. The butler took the card, glancing down to read the name. He did a double take, his eyes widening almost comically.

"Mr. Ashford?" The man peered at him closely, no doubt looking for some familiarity in the arrangement of his features. "You are the heir, come from America?" When Peter continued to glower at him, the butler flushed a deep red and straightened. "Forgive me, sir, for my impertinence. I'll show you to her ladyship."

As he followed the man, Peter took in his surroundings with a sneer. The place screamed old wealth. From the wood banister stained dark from generations of gliding hands, to the portraits of ancestors from centuries past, there was not an inch of space that did not proclaim this was the home of one of the blessed few. Peter's eyes tightened at the corners. He had no place in this world. And despite his impending title, no desire to be a part of it.

The butler opened a door at the end of the hall. "Mr. Peter Ashford here to see you, my lady," he announced.

Peter stepped past the butler into the room, his eyes immediately searching for and finding its lone inhabitant. At the sight of her, memories assailed him, so vivid and vicious that for a moment he could not breathe.

The acrid stench of a peat fire, the embers low, their glow barely reaching to where his mother writhed on the bed. Tears drying stiff on his cheeks. His mother's low moans. Then a knock, the door swinging open, an elderly woman standing in the narrow, dank hall.

He blinked, shook his head sharply, and focused again on the woman who sat before him. She was the same as she had been thirteen years ago, if a bit older. Yet now instead of careful pity on her face, there was a shock so profound, he feared for a moment she would keel over on the spot.

Which wouldn't do, for he had a debt to repay.

She was the first to speak. "Peter? Dear God, is it you, Peter?"

His nostrils flared as he gave a shallow bow. "Lady Tesh."

In a move he suspected was as foreign to her as dancing a jig in her stockinged feet, she slumped back against the settee, her embroidery falling to the floor in a colorful heap. "It is you," she breathed, staring at him with wide brown eyes. Her gaze swept his face, disbelief and wonder and a strange relief flashing and tangling like threads in her eyes. Beside her a pile of cream-colored fur stirred, two small black eyes peering suspiciously at him.

Unnerved by her lengthy perusal—and by the strangely human glare the ridiculously small dog was giving him—Peter cleared his throat. "You may wonder why I'm here."

At the sound of his voice, her spine snapped straighter, her confusion clearing. "Oh, but what you must think of me." She motioned with one gnarled hand to the seat before her. "Please sit."

He eyed the dainty piece of furniture with trepidation.

He was taller than most, and his years of fighting and clawing his way up in life had lent a bulk to his frame that made the chair seem as if it were fashioned from mere twigs. But Lady Tesh was looking at him in expectation, apparently not at all concerned that her furniture might be reduced to kindling. Slowly, carefully, he lowered himself to the embroidered cushion. The chair gave a low moan of protest under his weight but held firm. He exhaled and turned to the woman.

She stared at him as if seeing a ghost. "I did not think to ever see you again. When I learned that you had gone to America and made your fortune there in real estate, I was so very pleased for you."

Peter raised an eyebrow. She made it sound so simple, as if it had been the natural progression of events. When in reality it had been years of fear and determination and fighting for every cent. He supposed he and Quincy could have abandoned Captain Adams and his family when the Embargo Act had destroyed their livelihood. But he had owed them his very life. And he did not turn away from a debt to be paid.

Thus his reason for being here, in the last place he ever wished to be.

"You've made so much of yourself," the viscountess continued. "As I always knew you would. I did try to write, once we located you. But my letters came back unopened, and I thought for certain you would never return."

"I had always planned to return."

"Had you?" Her gnarled fingers wove about themselves, an agitated tell. "I looked high and low for you after your mother's death, tracked you as far as London. But you disappeared without a trace. I worried so, Peter."

There was a faint note of rebuke in her voice. It dug

at him, loosening the guilt he'd buried deep, bringing it to the surface again. Without her, his mother would have spent her last days in unimaginable pain. Instead she had been made as comfortable as possible. For that, Peter owed the woman before him much more than the paltry sum she had paid to ensure a dying woman's peace.

"There was nothing for me here after she died," he explained gruffly.

Lady Tesh's eyes filled with a deep sadness. "You had me, Peter. I would have cared for you, had you let me."

His heart lurched, letting him know it was not as dead as he had thought it. But no, he wouldn't allow her to get under his skin. He had learned long ago how disposable family was. And that caring only led to misery and heartache.

Even so, it took considerable effort to keep his hard-earned defenses in place. "I did not come here to reminisce, or to think of what might have been. I came today because there is something I had to know."

Her brows drew together, further deepening the lines of her face. "What might that be?"

"All those years ago, when I went to the Duke of Dane for help and he turned me away, why did you come find me?"

Understanding dawned, her expression softening. "You are my brother's grandson. How could I not?"

He slashed a hand through the air. "That's not what I meant. The duke, your nephew, my cousin, turned me from his home after I had come to him begging for help to save my mother's life. He told me in no uncertain terms that if I were to approach another member of the family for money, he would have me arrested. Why, then, did you come find me, to help where he would not?"

Something flared in her eyes, frustration and anger and affection all coalescing. In a moment, it was gone and she sighed, her gaze turned inward to some haunting memory. "No matter what your grandfather and father did, you're still family."

Again that damnable word: *family*. His lip curled. "And so you did it out of some blood duty. How quaint."

She surprised him by letting loose a sharp laugh. "Quaint? Now that is not a word often ascribed to me. Prickly, yes. Meddlesome, surely. But never something so mild as *quaint*. But is that truly all you wanted, to ask me a question that could have easily been answered via letter?" She narrowed her eyes. "I do believe there is another reason you're on the Isle, Peter."

Two reasons, actually. But she need not know that. "You're right. There is another reason I've come to seek you out."

He reached into his coat and pulled out a bag of coins, gold sovereigns every one. It was a fortune, so much more than what she had paid for the morphine and the physician all those years ago. There was the faint sound of clinking metal as he held the sack out to her. Yet the relief he'd expected to feel didn't come, only a hollow kind of sadness that the worth of his mother's life had been reduced to this.

Her gaze transferred to the leather bag. "What are you about, Peter?"

"Take it," he ordered. "It's owed you."

There was censure in her eyes. "Did you think I wanted payment for what I did for your poor mother?"

"I know it's more than is owed," he gritted out as his hand began to tremble. "But there is the matter of thirteen years' interest, after all."

A cloud of understanding fell over her. "And what will you do once I take it, Peter? Will you disappear again?"

"There is nothing to hold me here," he growled, letting the bag drop to his lap before the shaking in his hand drew her notice.

"Isn't there? I am your family—"

A harsh laugh broke free from his throat. "That means less than nothing to me, madam. I owe you for providing my mother with peace in her final days, but there is nothing more between us than that."

She arched one thin white brow. "Very well."

He held out the sack again. Her eyes did not leave his face, and her hands did not leave her dog.

"I never intended for you to repay me, Peter."

Again he dropped the sack to his lap. Anger worked its way through him, into the very marrow of his bones, that she would refuse his attempt to close the door on this chapter of his life for good. It made his voice sharp when he said, "I never asked for your help."

"No, you didn't. Yet you asked for Dane's."

He had. God help him, he had. He'd put aside his pride, had thrown himself on his cousin's mercy. For nothing had been more important than his mother.

And his begging had been thrown back in his face.

"Yes, I did," he replied in a low voice. "And look where it got me. My mother could have been saved had he helped as I'd asked."

Her lips, already thin, pressed so tight they disappeared completely. Sadness flashed in her eyes. "No one act could be more regretted, Peter."

The words were so unexpected, he did not immediately hear the maid arrive with a tea tray. Suddenly it was there before them, and Lady Tesh had placed her pet aside and was preparing a cup.

"How do you take your tea, Peter?"

He stared at her long and hard. "This is not a social call."

"That does not mean we need to abandon all civility. Come now, how do you take it?"

He could see it in the stubborn set to her chin, the steely glint in her eyes, that she would not give this up. "Milk, no sugar," he grumbled.

She smiled, for all the world as if he had done a particularly brilliant sum, and set to work. "You will just have to accept that what I did, I did without expectation of remuneration," she said pleasantly. "A gift, if you will."

He accepted the cup from her, staring down into the opaque depths of the brew. "Nothing is done without expectations attached," he said darkly. "And I will not be indebted to you."

"You are not, and never have been."

"Yes I have!" The words exploded from him, the force of them making the tea slosh dangerously close to the edge of the china cup. A tempest in his hands. "You don't understand. You never will. What it means to have nothing, to have less than nothing. To fight for every scrap. My pride was all I had. And to have to go to *him*—" He broke off, his rage nearly choking him. He drank the tea in one swallow, feeling it burn down his throat into his gut, sending the rage down with it to someplace dark and hidden. He looked back to the cup, to the dregs that clung to the bottom, as if he could see his future in it. "I did it for her. I would have done more if it had meant I'd have her even a day longer."

There was a moment of silence. It closed in on him, that silence, until he felt he was suffocating in it. He had lost control, had let Lady Tesh see a part of himself he rarely showed, even to those closest to him. He set the cup down carefully, more than aware of the burning urge he had to take the damned thing and send it smashing into the wall.

"I can see now you will not take the money no matter what I say," he said, rising, tucking the heavy sack of gold back into his pocket, feeling the emotional weight of it far more than the physical weight. "It is no consequence to me whether you do or not. I have made the effort, and so I will consider my debt repaid in full. Good day, madam." He turned for the door.

"You cannot go, Peter," she called after him. "Your mother, she wanted me to care for you."

He let loose a bitter laugh, not bothering to turn, his boots eating up the distance to the door. "I'm a bit old for looking after, madam. You may consider yourself freed from that particular request. Time has seen to that." He gripped the knob.

"And what of the promise she had you make?"

A punch to the gut could not have stunned him more. And suddenly he was no longer in Lady Tesh's vast, opulent sitting room, but that cramped, drafty attic room again. The paint was peeling and stained, the cracks in the single window stopped with grimy rags. The light was dim, barely reaching to where Peter sat huddled in the corner, his bare toes digging into the rough floorboards as he tried not to cry.

And Lady Tesh, so out of place in her brocade gown and jewels, perched on a rickety stool next to the single, narrow bed. Her expensive skirts dragged in the dust at her feet, her hair, white even then, coming loose from her coiffure after hours of tending. She must have been exhausted, yet she sat forward, arms braced on the dingy sheets, his mother's skeletal hand held with infinite gentleness in her own.

But more powerful than that, his mother's voice, the once strong and ringing tones made brittle with illness. "Take him, my lady," she'd begged. "Take my Peter and care for him."

"Of course," Lady Tesh had soothed.

Panic had filled him. To leave everything he knew, to go with this strange woman who talked with such precise, clipped words, terrified him. "I won't do it!" he'd cried, lurching to his feet.

"Come here, my darling," his mother rasped, her eyes shifting to him, bright with fever. He went to her on trembling legs. When she reached for him, he took her hand in his. Her skin was thin, the bones so delicate, he feared they'd snap.

"You must go with Lady Tesh."

Tears had filled his eyes. He'd dashed them angrily away with a dirty fist. "No—"

"You must, Peter. Promise me you will." When he merely stared at her beloved face, ravaged by illness, she gave a weak laugh. "My stubborn boy," she said, her voice wheezing in her sunken chest. "I'll make you a deal. Give Lady Tesh a month. That's all I ask. If after that you don't want to stay with her, you can leave."

Agony filled him. She knew he would not go back on a promise given. His father had done that enough, his broken promises leaving nothing but destruction and hopelessness behind. He shook his head in mute appeal.

"Promise me!"

Peter had jumped, a gasp escaping him, at the

unexpected desperation in his mother's voice, at the strength in her fingers as they dug into his hand.

"I—I promise, Mama."

His mother seemed to deflate in relief, the pain in her eyes diffused for a moment. Her hands shaking, she'd placed Peter's hand in Lady Tesh's before drifting off into a fitful sleep. As if entrusting him into her keeping.

"You were there," Lady Tesh said now, dislodging the stranglehold the memory had on him. A memory he had not thought of in over a decade. "You remember. I know you do."

"It matters naught," he rasped, pressing his forehead to the door.

"It does matter, Peter," she said softly. "You could stay here for a month with me as you promised her."

He squeezed his eyes shut, fighting against the guilt that dragged at him.

Lady Tesh's arrival in their drafty attic room had given his mother more than relief from the never-ending pain of dying. It had also given her peace. Fear for his future had her holding on to life by the thinnest thread. Lady Tesh had made her feel she could finally let go, that her son would be in safe hands.

He had fled before she was cold in the ground, the idea of being thrust into Lady Tesh's world terrifying him more than anything ever had. Yet the guilt he had carried from breaking the promise to his mother had sat heavily on his shoulders since. Would he ignore the chance to make good on the one thing she'd asked of him?

As if she heard the tortured thoughts swirling about in his brain, Lady Tesh spoke then, letting the axe fall. "It was her final hope for you. You would not want to see it unfulfilled, would you?"

Fury pounded through him. She was purposely using his mother's memory to force him to stay. In answer, he tore the door open and hurried through.

What did she know of suffering, of fighting, of want and heartache? He would never cave to her machinations.

Yet he knew that, to ever find peace, he would be forced to concede.

Damn her.

His neckcloth felt too tight, the fabric strangling the very air from his lungs. He had to get outside to fresh air, where he could breathe and think and figure what his next step might be. But had he gotten lost in this labyrinth of a house? Again that tight feeling, of air being stolen from him. He had to find a way out, to find freedom.

Suddenly there was the front door, looming before him. Relief flooded him as he quickened his step, reached for the handle, pulled it open.

And nearly fell over the two young women on the front step.

Chapter 3

*H*aving a very large male nearly bowl her over on Lady Tesh's front step was certainly not how Lenora had envisioned her return to the Isle. Her world tilted, the stone steps rising up to meet her.

In the next instant, strong, warm hands came about her waist to steady her. A heady scent of spices and coffee assailed her senses, tangy and mouthwatering and reminiscent of sitting before a warm fire in winter, curled up in blankets and comfort.

Flustered, she found her feet and stepped back. Whatever words she would have said to berate or thank the man, however, quickly disappeared into the ether as she caught sight of him.

Goodness, but he looked like a Viking come to life. All broad shoulders and muscles that strained against the confines of his clothes. His hair was golden, hanging in waves to his collar, wild and untamed and sinfully thick. Pale blue eyes glinted under the slash of his brows, almost too beautiful for the harsh planes of his face. A short beard framed his jaw, shining gilded in the faint bits of sunlight that were able to battle their way through the increasingly heavy cloud cover.

She swallowed. Hard.

"I'm very sorry," he said. His voice was deep and rumbling, shivering through her in the most disturbing way.

"No harm done," Margery said beside her. "Isn't that so, Lenora?"

Had she been staring at him all this time? Lenora felt herself flush hot as those cool blue eyes gazed back at her. "Of course, no harm done." And if her voice was a bit breathless, she prayed he would attribute it to her near fall.

Still the man stood there, blocking their path into the house and the blessed escape from the cake Lenora was making of herself. Her face grew hotter, her gaze trapped by those oddly pale eyes.

"Mr. Ashford, your hat, sir."

The butler's voice cut through the moment with all the finesse of a spoon digging through rock. There was a beat of stunned silence.

"You are Mr. Ashford? Mr. Peter Ashford, my cousin from America?" Margery asked, disbelief ripe in her voice.

The man's eyes went glacial. One last long stare and he pushed past them, fairly leaping down the steps.

"Dear me," Margery whispered.

Lenora stared after him, eyes wide with shock. "That man is the Duke of Dane's heir?"

"It appears so," her friend replied.

Mr. Ashford mounted up, kicking his horse into a gallop. Within seconds, he was thundering down the drive and out of sight.

"Perhaps," Margery said faintly, "we'd best find out from Gran what's going on."

They hurried through the house, silent and tense. Their footsteps clattered on the marble floor, echoing about the expanse of the great hall. So that was the man who would become the new duke when the present one passed away. The man who had taken Hillram's place as heir. Lenora's stomach roiled.

They burst into Lady Tesh's downstairs sitting room. The viscountess didn't look up as they entered, her gnarled fingers working thread with impressive ease into her embroidery. "Have you made your decision then, Peter?"

"So that truly was Peter Ashford that we saw leaving just now," Margery said, moving close to kiss her grandmother on her cheek.

Lady Tesh gasped, her gaze flying to her granddaughter. "Oh, goodness. Margery. Whatever are you doing here?" Her sharp eyes swiveled to Lenora, her creased face breaking into a grin. "And Lenora? Well, isn't this a treat? Goodness, child, but how lovely you are."

Lenora moved forward to kiss the viscountess, a familiar warmth spreading through her. Here was the woman she had visited every summer as a child, the woman who had loved her as if she were her own granddaughter. Lenora had not seen her in three long years, not since Hillram's death. She had begun to doubt that her return had been wise. Goodness knew what guilt it would dredge up, how it would pain her to be here again.

Yet perhaps, just perhaps, she would find some happiness and peace in coming back.

"You are looking well, Lady Tesh," she said, taking a seat in a delicate embroidered chair.

"What is this 'Lady Tesh' nonsense?" the viscountess demanded. "We never used to be so formal. Don't tell me your time in London has turned you into some uptight society miss."

A smile crept across Lenora's face. "No, ma'am, it hasn't."

"Good, for I shall not put up with it. You will call me Gran, as you always used to."

"Jasper," she called to the butler, who had followed in their wake, "bring in a fresh tea tray for my granddaughter and Miss Hartley, if you please, with lemonade for my young friend here." She gifted Lenora with a wink. Lenora's cheeks warmed with pleasure as she relaxed back against her seat. Lady Tesh had remembered her aversion to tea. It was a simple gesture, yet there was a feeling of coming home in it.

"I'm sorry we didn't write before showing up unannounced, Gran," Margery said, peeling off her gloves. "It was a...last-minute decision."

"Was it now?" Lady Tesh looked at Lenora. "Why do I have the feeling this has to do with the lack of a ring on your finger, child?"

Lenora's good mood vanished in a moment, the events of four days ago crashing through her. "It is exactly that, I'm afraid."

The lines in Lady Tesh's face deepened. "I'm sorry to hear it." She paused before continuing, her voice pensive, "That is three failed engagements in as many years."

Lenora's mouth twisted. "Yes. My father made certain to point that out as well." *Among other things.* She gave a small shudder, the threat of him disowning her hanging over her head like an axe about to fall. It was an unwelcome, yet necessary, reminder that this was no pleasure visit.

Her thoughts must have shown on her face, for Lady Tesh's gaze sharpened. "And what are your plans on the Isle?"

Ah, yes, her plans. "I'd hoped," she said with a forced

smile, "that I might visit all our old haunts, to remember the good times we had when we were young."

"That sounds splendid, my dear," Margery said with a soft smile. "I need a reminder of those days as well."

Just then a scruffy ball of fur made itself known, jumping down from its spot next to Lady Tesh and approaching first Margery, then Lenora. It sniffed at Leonora's toes a moment before, with all the grace of a queen, it placed a dainty paw on her leg.

"Well, aren't you the sweetest," Lenora murmured, bending forward to pat the dog on the head. The creature allowed it for a moment, bestowing a lick on Lenora's knuckles with a tiny pink tongue, before it pranced back to Lady Tesh, jumping up and settling back against her side.

"This here is Freya," the viscountess explained, giving her pet an affectionate scratch behind its ear.

"Freya?" Lenora said. "What an unusual name."

"She's named for a Viking goddess."

Lenora eyed the small, scrappy creature dubiously. For while it carried itself as regal as royalty, its stringy, flyaway fur was almost comical. Lenora might have laughed. If she wasn't fearful of offending the tiny beast.

She very nearly snorted at that. Worried about offending a dog? Perhaps she had needed this trip to the Isle more than she'd realized.

"I suppose you wish to know all about Mr. Ashford," Lady Tesh said.

"Very much so," Margery replied, sitting forward, her face pulled into tense lines. "I was not aware he was planning on returning to England anytime soon."

"Nor I, until he showed up on my doorstep. He doesn't

mean to stay, only came to pay some debt he feels he owes me."

"Doesn't mean to stay?" Margery demanded. "But he's the heir now. He cannot leave." She sent Lenora an apologetic look. "I'm sorry, Lenora."

Lenora gave her a wan smile. She had only learned of the heir presumptive upon Hillram's death, and the story of how his grandfather, the previous duke's brother, had split from the family. It wasn't often talked of, the remembrance bringing too much pain to those who had been affected by it.

"Oh, pish," Lady Tesh scoffed. "You place entirely too much importance on status."

Margery gave her grandmother a droll look. "This from a viscountess?"

"Yes, well." She waved a hand in the air. "It was not my fault your grandfather fell hopelessly in love with me. He couldn't help who he was." It was said in an offhand manner. Yet Lenora could not miss the softened look in the woman's eyes as they shifted to the large portrait of her late husband that graced the wall above the pink marble fireplace.

"It is not snobbish," Margery said. "His Grace is not well, and when he passes, Mr. Ashford will be the head of that branch of the family."

"Very true. Though I'm not sure he cares a fig for it. I thought to entice him to stay. However," she said softly, giving Lenora a sober look, "perhaps it was for the best he refused. Lenora, dear," she continued, sitting forward, "does it trouble you greatly that Mr. Ashford is on the Isle?"

"Of course not," Lenora reassured her hastily, hoping the lie didn't show. "Why should it trouble me? This is his rightful place, after all."

That seemed to ease some of the worry that had taken hold of the other women. Soon the tea tray arrived and their conversation turned to happier matters. Yet as Lenora sipped absentmindedly at her lemonade, she found she could no longer relax. She had hoped to forgive herself on this trip, to move past that horrible betrayal that had affected everything since. Yet how could she when, instead of thinking of her dead fiancé, her mind was full of thoughts of a tall, burly Viking of a man, with eyes as blue as the stormy sea—the very man who had taken Hillram's place?

* * *

Peter exploded into the hotel room. The door slammed back against the wall, the sound rattling the windows in their frames. "Damn stubborn woman," he growled. Ripping his cravat loose, he flung it to the floor. The leather satchel of money quickly followed, landing with a jarring clang.

"Now why do I get the impression that your meeting did not go as planned?"

Yanking off his jacket, Peter glared at the man lounging in the open doorway. "Go away."

Mr. Quincy Nesbitt chuckled and pushed away from the door, closing it before sauntering into the room. "If you didn't want company, you should have shut your door. Then you could have stormed about and cussed to your heart's content."

Peter threw himself into a chair, busying himself with rolling up his cuffs. If he looked in his friend's eyes and saw the humor that no doubt filled them, he would hit something. Namely Quincy. "I'm not good company. If you wish to keep your face pretty for the ladies, you will leave now."

With an ease born of years of friendship, Quincy came close and sank into the chair opposite Peter's. He crossed one booted foot over a knee and leaned back. "Oh, you don't expect me to ignore this little bit of temper, do you? You're so damned calm and controlled all of the time; this is a real treat."

Quincy was right, of course, damn it. He truly had lost control, something he wished he could lay squarely on Lady Tesh's narrow shoulders. Yet it was not just that woman and her manipulations that had Peter so furious. No, there was one other thing that had added to his frustration, that had pushed him over the edge of reason.

He had a quick flash of a pretty, heart-shaped face, hair gold and glinting in the fickle sun, pale green eyes with the longest lashes he'd ever seen.

He exhaled a tense breath and ran a hand over his face. The woman he'd nearly run over in front of Lady Tesh's house had haunted him all the way back here, distracting him from the very real problem of how he would deal with the older woman's sly reminder of his promise to his mother. But who was she? Her companion, the one with the mousy brown hair, had called him cousin. Was the blonde related to him as well?

He nearly growled. He'd done it again, allowed himself to be distracted by that sweet face. With incredible will, he pushed the image of her down and focused on the matter at hand. "Lady Tesh would not allow me to pay her back."

Quincy's unconcerned ennui faded away in an instant, making way for a sharp watchfulness. "What, not a bit of it?"

Peter shook his head, his nostrils flaring. He motioned to the leather pouch where it lay on the floorboards.

Eyes narrowed in thought, Quincy cocked his head and crossed his arms over his chest. "What now? Are we to get on with the rest of it then and sail back for Boston?"

"I would, and gladly."

"Why do I sense a 'but' in your next sentence?"

Peter rubbed his jaw, scrubbing at his beard with his nails. "The woman had a request. No, not a request. Bloody blackmail, using the last promise my mother asked of me to get it."

"What does she want you doing? Manual labor? Riding through town naked? Slaying a dragon?"

"Nothing so easy, I assure you." Peter sent his friend a frustrated glare. "She wishes me to stay on the Isle as her guest for a full month."

The laugh Quincy let loose was long and loud. Peter watched him in stony silence, unable to find an ounce of humor in the situation. His mother's face flashed through his mind again for what seemed the hundredth time that afternoon, the guilt he'd carried since her death roaring back as well. He had a chance to see her wishes through. Yet it didn't sit any easier on his shoulders than it had when he was a boy.

Finally his friend's chuckles died down. Quincy wiped at his eyes. "Well, you have to give her this; she could not have found a more uninterested houseguest."

"Regardless of my personal feelings on the matter," he gritted, "I cannot take that much time away. Lest you forget, we have a business to return to in Boston."

"We deserve a holiday, I'm thinking, after all the hard work we've put into it these last years. Besides, Captain Adams's children are grown now and more than capable

of handling things, having cut their teeth on the business."
Here Quincy grinned. "And I've a mind to get to know
some of the local ladies a bit better. All those fine, prim
English manners make me wish we'd returned sooner."
He rubbed his hands together, his expression turning
almost feral with anticipation.

"You think with your cock," Peter said with disgust.

Quincy shrugged. "It's never steered me wrong."

Done with the ridiculous turn the conversation had
taken, Peter erupted out of his chair. "I cannot stay for
a month."

"Come now, it's not so bad as that here."

"You don't know what it's like, returning to this place."

Quincy sobered. "But I do," he said quietly. "Or at
least enough of it. Mine was the ear you bent when you
needed a friend on the crossing. The one that listened to
your feverish ravings about your guilt over your mother
when you grew ill." He sat forward, resting his elbows on
his knees. "I know what that bastard Dane did, and why
you hate him as you do. And with good reason. But I
also know what Lady Tesh did. She doesn't seem a bad
sort. And while I think she's mad for wanting your surly
company for a month instead of a bag of gold"—here
he smiled, humor flashing in his black eyes—"you can't
deny it says much about her character."

Quincy was right, of course. Damn him. "So you would
have me cave in to her demand?" he growled, holding on
to his last shred of pride.

His friend leaned back. "If it will take away even a bit
of the guilt you still harbor over leaving England against
your mother's wishes, then I say with complete confidence, yes, you should. Besides," he continued, grinning,
"I've a mind to join you."

Peter stared at him. "You would accompany me?"

"And why the hell not? We can have a grand time, you and I. When you aren't sulking and wreaking vengeance on a dying man, I mean."

Caught between the desire to shake his friend's hand and punch him in the face, Peter decided on the former. Standing, he held out his hand. "We are in it together then."

Quincy followed suit, taking Peter's hand in a crushing grip. "Together." He grinned, flashing a dimple. "Though you may not be thanking me later for it."

Chapter 4

*P*eter expected the shock in Lady Tesh's expression as he stalked into her sitting room later that same afternoon.

The worry that colored it, however, was a surprise. Before he could wonder at it, however, the woman spoke.

"Peter, you're back."

"You ensured that, madam," he snapped. Already the walls of the room were closing in on him. He clenched his jaw. The sooner he saw his damn promise fulfilled, the better.

She motioned to the same delicate chair he'd sat in earlier that day. Yet again he tried his luck with the flimsy piece of furniture. If he was to stay here an entire month, they would have to do something about the seating.

"I admit I did not think I would see you again," she said.

"Then you have no notion of how important my mother was to me."

"I think I do, Peter," she murmured, the kindness in her voice making him squirm in his fragile seat. Yet he could not fail to see that her expression did not reflect her tone. Her lips were pressed tight, her brows knit with either displeasure or worry.

He narrowed his eyes. "Why do I get the impression

that you would rather not have seen me back?" An idea took root. "Are you rescinding your demand? For I don't mind saying that I will be happy to simply hand over the money."

"No," she said quickly. She regarded him with an odd mix of concern and frustration before, with a quickly indrawn breath, her expression hardened. "That is," she continued, her voice firming with each word, "my request for you to stay here a month still stands."

He gave a sharp, dry laugh. "Request? Is that how you see it then?"

She shrugged, apparently unconcerned with his foul mood. "You do not have to accept my offer."

"Don't I?" He shifted, the chair protesting loudly beneath him, and narrowed his eyes as he considered her. "I agree to your *request*, madam. And at the end of the month the promise made to my mother will be fulfilled."

Her eyes narrowed. "Shall we shake on it then?" She held out a hand.

Peter stared at it, at the joints twisted and warped with age. "Not yet," he said. "I would have the terms of this agreement set out before I sign my soul to the devil."

Her hand lowered, her lips quirking in amusement. "The devil, eh? Well, I can't say I haven't been likened to that nefarious creature before."

He frowned. "The terms?" he pressed.

"Yes." She straightened, and her gaze turned cunning. "You are to stay here a month, to sit with me every afternoon and dine with me each evening, to provide your company on outings. And before you think you may be silent and sullen, I will tell you here and now I expect conversation from you. You will be here in mind, as well as body, or you may consider our agreement void."

He considered her faint smile, going over her demands in his mind. "Define how you expect me to provide my company."

Her gaze sharpened, though her features remained placid. "I'm an old woman, Peter," she said easily. "I don't get out much, you know."

"Amuse me," he drawled.

Her smile shifted a fraction. "Oh, you know, the typical pursuits in a seaside town. Trips to the lending library, visits to the modiste, taking the air at some of the more picturesque locales." Here her voice dipped, the words becoming a jumble of incoherency.

Peter tilted his head. "I'm sorry, what was that?"

Her smile slipped entirely then. She flashed him a look of annoyance. "I said, you stubborn man, dinner parties and balls as well."

"Oh, no," Peter declared.

"Oh, yes," Lady Tesh came back. "There is a subscription ball held twice weekly in the assembly hall. I may not dance"—here she looked ruefully at her legs—"but I do so love to join in the fun, watching the young people, indulging in the gossip."

"No," Peter said hotly. "I refuse to attend some society ball, madam."

Lady Tesh let out a laugh at that. "Society ball? Peter, where on earth do you think we are? This is not London, my boy. The balls held here on the Isle no more resemble a grand London ball than I resemble a debutante."

He frowned, refusing to be drawn in. "No balls," he said again.

She pursed her lips. "Four balls. And six dinner parties." When he opened his mouth to speak, she held up a hand. "I insist on you giving in a bit. After all, your poor mother..."

Peter swallowed a curse. The woman was a demon sent straight from hell to torment him. He lifted his eyes to heaven for a moment before returning them to her. "If you insist," he bit out. "But with a minor adjustment. One ball, and two dinner parties."

She shook her head mournfully, though her eyes glittered with triumph. "You really must try to meet me partway, Peter. Three balls and four dinner parties."

"You are deluded. Two balls and three dinner parties. And," he continued when she opened her mouth to argue once again, "I shall even endeavor not to sit in the corner and sulk."

She chuckled. "You strike a hard bargain, my boy. I can see how you became so successful in the wilds of America."

Peter felt his lips quirk in a burst of amusement— mingled liberally with annoyance. "Boston is hardly the wilds of America, madam."

She waved a hand in the air. "A figure of speech, I assure you. Very well. I accept your terms. Now, is there anything else you would like to add to this deal before we put an end to it?"

"Just one. I would have my business partner staying here as well."

"He is welcome here at Seacliff," she said without the slightest hesitation. "Now, shall we shake on it?"

This time when she held out her hand, he took it. Her skin was cool and parchment thin, the bones and swollen joints prominent against the press of his fingers. Peter had the sudden fear that if he gripped too hard, they would shatter. A strange protectiveness surged in him, quickly squelched. If there was anything this harridan did not need, it was his protection.

"It is done then," she said. "When can you move your things in?"

The finality of her tone sent a wave of panic through him. *What have I done?* But it was much too late now. Tamping it down, he responded, "Immediately. My associate and our belongings are in a carriage in your drive as we speak."

"Splendid." She reached for a bell on the small table beside her and rang it with vigor. Immediately the butler appeared in the doorway. "Jasper, please see to the carriage in the drive. And we will need two more bedrooms prepared, as my great-nephew and his friend will be staying with us."

"Very good, my lady."

Great-Nephew. The word jolted him, sending a shiver up his spine. Disconcerted by his reaction to a label he should feel nothing for, he rose abruptly. "I will apprise Quincy that things have been settled," he stated, suddenly desperate to leave her. Before he could depart, however, the click of canine nails on the polished wood floor heralded the arrival of Lady Tesh's pet. The creature entered the room with a prancing step, followed closely by the young woman from that morning.

He sucked in a breath at the sight of her. For she was even lovelier than he remembered. Locks of gilded curls bounced about her shoulders, caressing the long, graceful column of her neck. An overly decorated pale blue gown of some expensive, shimmery material hugged her small breasts and moved in glistening folds with each step she took. Her eyes, with their fringe of thick lashes, settled on him, widening perceptibly. That lush little mouth opened in surprise.

"Oh," she said, the word a mere breath of sound.

Peter could only stare back at her, at a loss as to what he had been about to do.

"My dear, you have returned. And how was your walk?" Lady Tesh spoke into the ensuing silence, snapping Peter back to the moment.

The young lady gave him one last look before gliding toward the viscountess. As she passed him, Peter felt a rush of air, and the faint, sweet scent of summer berries teased his senses. He watched as she placed a kiss upon the older woman's cheek. "The walk was lovely, Gran. I had not realized how much I needed the exercise after such a lengthy trip."

"Gran?" Peter demanded before he could school his tongue. Had his suspicions been confirmed, and this young woman was related to him?

And why did that leave a bad taste in his mouth?

"I'm glad for it," Lady Tesh said to her with a soft smile. "But let me introduce you to our guest. My dear, this is my great-nephew, Mr. Peter Ashford. Peter, this is Miss Lenora Hartley. I was her mother's godmother, and over the years, Lenora has become dear friends with my granddaughter, Margery. She is staying with us for the time being."

Even as a disturbing relief flowed through him at the realization that Miss Hartley was not a relation, another unwelcome bit of knowledge punched him in the gut. *Staying with us?* Which meant this lovely creature, who had invaded his thoughts in the most unwelcome way, was also a guest in this house. "You did not tell me you already had guests, madam," Peter said, his voice sounding strangled to his own ears.

"I can assure you," she said with an amused smile,

"there is plenty of room for all of us. You and your friend will not be crowded in the least."

That, Peter thought as he gazed into Miss Hartley's flushed face, may be true. What it would do to his peace of mind, however, was another matter entirely.

* * *

After her confusing—and frankly disturbing—thoughts about the Duke of Dane's heir, the last thing Lenora wanted to see was that very same man standing in Lady Tesh's sitting room.

She dipped a curtsy, praying her trembling knees held her steady, and shot a quick glance at Lady Tesh. The viscountess was watching her intently, concern, as well as curiosity, mingling on her deeply lined face. As confused as she was regarding the older woman's intentions in inviting Mr. Ashford to stay, she could not deny the man had a right to be there.

"It's a pleasure," Lenora said to him now.

He inclined his head, fixing her with the same intense gaze he had earlier that day. The trembling in her legs spread to the rest of her, making her feel strangely flushed and achy.

What in the world was wrong with her?

"So happy to have met you," she continued in a rush, "and I do hope you enjoy your stay, but I must run. Margery is expecting me, and I'm late as it is, as I was out walking Freya. Freya is quite fond of the copse of trees close to the cliff, you see"—*keep quiet, Lenora*—"and was taking much longer than anticipated. Not that I mind walking her." *Goodness, stop talking!* "No, it is a pleasure to help Lady Tesh out in any way. Though, of course, there are servants aplenty to do the job. Still I felt it imperative I do my part while staying here."

Mr. Ashford was looking at her as if she had dropped to all fours and bayed like a dog. Lenora clamped her lips together and offered him a wan smile.

"Who is Freya?" he demanded.

That was what he took from her babbling? "The dog. Freya is the dog," she replied a bit breathlessly.

Everyone looked down to the creature in question, who promptly sneezed.

"She's named for a Viking goddess," Lenora finished lamely.

"A goddess."

"Yes."

Silence descended. Mr. Ashford continued to stare at Freya, who in turn ignored him with cool unconcern. If dogs could feel cool unconcern.

Lenora wished desperately she were Freya in that moment. For it would be preferable to the confusing jumble of attraction and guilt that she was wading through.

As she opened her mouth to speak again, anything to fill that damnable silence, a sinfully attractive gentleman strode into the room. "The man at the door said I could find you here," he said to Mr. Ashford. "Damn near tackled me when I made to walk off without him, but I do believe I gave him the slip." He grinned and turned to Lenora. His chiseled face transformed, going from boyish delight to heavy-lidded interest in the space of a heartbeat. "Well, hello."

A growl sounded. Lenora turned to look at the dog, but Freya was busy staring at Mr. Ashford, her too-large ears tilted toward him. Had that noise come from Mr. Ashford then?

She was saved from ruminating on it as the dark man with the wickedly sparkling onyx eyes sauntered forward. "Peter," he drawled, not taking his eyes from Lenora, "perhaps you would be so kind as to introduce me to this vision."

Mr. Ashford merely glared at the man, who continued to stare at Lenora as if she were a sweet cake.

It was Lady Tesh who finally spoke. "You must be Peter's business associate."

He gave Lenora a bold wink before turning toward the viscountess. "As my friend is playing the brute, allow me to introduce myself," he said, striding to the older woman and bowing over her hand with an impressive flourish. "I am Mr. Quincy Nesbitt. And you must be Lady Tesh. It's an honor to be a guest in your beautiful home."

"The honor is mine," Lady Tesh replied. Suddenly her eyes sharpened. Which really was saying something, as the woman had the most piercing gaze Lenora had ever witnessed. "Nesbitt? An unusual name, that's certain. You're not by chance related to the Duke of Reigate, are you?"

The man's smooth smile turned brittle, the tightening of his lips and the hardening of his eyes altering him in an instant. Then Lenora blinked and his face smoothed back into its previous warmth. A trick of the light, perhaps?

"Ah, I'm afraid not," he said with a mournful shake of his head. "Though that would be something, wouldn't it?" He chuckled, before letting his dark gaze drift back to Lenora.

Lady Tesh took the hint. "My young friend here that you were flirting so outrageously with is Miss Lenora Hartley."

"Miss Hartley," he drawled, bowing in her direction.

"My granddaughter is also staying with me," Lady Tesh continued. "You will meet her later."

"I look forward to it," he said with a slow smile. His eyes fell to where Freya sat at Lady Tesh's feet. To Lenora's surprise, he dropped to one knee before the dog. "And this tiny creature?"

"That there is Freya. I think you will find she is more mistress here than I am," Lady Tesh replied.

"Well, aren't you a beauty," Mr. Nesbitt cooed, reaching out to scratch Freya under the chin. The dog closed her eyes and let out a low moan.

Lenora choked back a laugh. She had a feeling that the man was more than used to such reactions from females. He was quite the most attractive man she had ever seen, and the most confident as well. And that was saying something, having been acquainted with most members of the *ton*.

Why, then, Lenora thought as her eyes were pulled against their will to Mr. Ashford, was she much more drawn to a great glowering Viking?

The man in question made a rude sound. "Come along, Casanova," he growled. Grabbing his friend by the arm, he pulled him to his feet and propelled him out the door. But not before Mr. Nesbitt gifted her with a parting wink.

"Dear me," Lenora said faintly.

Lady Tesh watched the men leave. "This, I do believe, will be a very interesting month."

Chapter 5

*P*eter scowled at his reflection in the looking glass. Not because he was displeased by what he saw. No, he was more than presentable, despite lacking the necessary evening clothes for dinner in a stately home of the English elite. It didn't matter that his coat was not of the finest wool or of the most fashionable cut. He was clothed and clean; nothing else should matter.

No, what caused his mouth to pull down so deeply at the corners was his concern over what a certain young lady might think of him when she saw him.

His frown deepened. The opinion of a society miss should not matter to him in the least. Nor would it, he vowed viciously, turning away from the glass. His gaze landed on Quincy, who was leaning casually in the doorway.

"Do you enjoy sneaking into my rooms?" Peter snapped.

"I admit," Quincy said with a shrug, "while last time it was entirely your fault, this time I was drawn in by pure curiosity. What, I thought to myself, would the much-too-serious Peter Ashford wear to a viscountess's dinner?"

"My clothing is fine," Peter grumbled, tugging at his cravat. Not failing to notice that Quincy, in his impeccably cut stark black evening clothes and snowy cravat, appeared to be an archangel come to life.

Damn the man.

"I told you back in Boston," his friend continued, "to bring along evening wear. Didn't I tell you?"

Peter was saved from giving his friend a blistering set-down by the timely arrival of a maid. She stumbled to a halt, her eyes going wide as she took in the two of them.

Quincy gave her a courtly bow as she continued to stare mutely. "How may we be of service, miss?"

The girl, who could not have been above sixteen, blushed scarlet. "My pardon, sir. You'll be meeting in the drawing room tonight for dinner, and Lady Tesh has bid me to show you the way."

"And she could not have chosen a more charming guide," Quincy said with a rakish grin.

Peter watched with narrowed eyes as the girl gave his friend a shy, adoring smile and beckoned them to follow her. He moved close to Quincy, pulling him back beyond the girl's hearing.

"Stop it," he hissed.

"Stop what?" The wide-eyed look Quincy gifted him with was so innocent as to be almost comical.

Peter was beyond laughter, however. "The women in this house are not here for your amusement, be they lady or servant."

"Come now, old man," Quincy said with a roll of his eyes. "You know I won't let it go further than a flirtation."

"A flirtation can be just as dangerous," Peter said darkly, motioning toward the maid, who cast yet another awestruck glance back at Quincy.

Quincy waved away his concerns. "You're jealous."

"Jealous?" Peter spat in disbelief.

"Because they prefer me. And how could they not, me being so exotic while you're..." He motioned from Peter's scuffed boots to his overlong hair. "Well, you."

This time Peter did laugh. "You, exotic?"

Quincy grinned. "I took so well to life in America, I'm practically American myself. I reek of the exotic."

Peter snorted. "You reek, but not of the exotic. Just promise me, no more of your outrageous flirting with the women in this house."

"Fine," Quincy said. "But know, you're taking all the fun out of this for me."

They reached the drawing room. And in unison stumbled to a halt. For though Miss Hartley was noticeably absent—damn him for even noticing—there appeared to be an entire harem of women waiting there for them.

"Oh, come *on*," Quincy groaned, sending Peter a long-suffering look.

"Peter, Mr. Nesbitt," Lady Tesh called as they moved forward, "I do hope your rooms are to your liking."

"They are, madam, thank you," Peter said.

"I would like to introduce you to some relations of yours, Peter." She turned to the women who milled around her. "Ladies, this is Peter Ashford and his friend, Mr. Quincy Nesbitt. Gentlemen, this is my granddaughter, Mrs. Margery Kitteridge. You will recall she's staying as well at Seacliff. And these young ladies are Lady Clara Ashford and Lady Phoebe Ashford, the Duke of Dane's daughters."

A ringing started up in Peter's ears. So these were the children of the man who had turned him away when his mother lay writhing in pain. Fury surged through him, turning his vision red at the edges. He had not wanted to meet these women. Yet here they were, looking on him with wide, nervous eyes. He was always so careful, considered every possibility. How had he not seen that, by staying with Lady Tesh, there was every chance he would be meeting socially with the duke's family?

He clenched his hands tight at his sides.

Quincy cast Peter a cautious glance before he smiled his most charming smile and bowed. "It is an honor, ladies."

"Ours as well, Mr. Nesbitt," the elder, Lady Clara Ashford, said with a blush. She seemed to drag her gaze from Quincy with effort before turning her attention to Peter. "It's a pleasure to finally meet you, Mr. Ashford. My father sends his regrets that he was not able to attend this evening. His health prevents him from getting out."

Her voice was pleasant and sweet, though there was a flash of pain in her eyes when she spoke of her father's ailment. His eyes tightened at the corners as he studied the young woman and her sister. They looked on him with an uncertainty that he could fully understand, for here before them was the man who would have sole control of their existence when their father died.

He leveled a look on Lady Clara, one that must have been frightening indeed if her widened eyes were anything to go by. Peter opened his mouth, intending to put the woman in her place, their audience be damned.

"I'm so sorry for being late."

That voice, already so familiar, was like a blow to the head. He swung about, his eyes falling on the newcomer as she hurried into the room. And every intention to lay the duke's daughters low was lost as he gazed on Miss Hartley's sweetly smiling face.

Damn the woman.

* * *

How was it, Lenora thought dazedly as she approached the assembled people, that Mr. Ashford could so thoroughly send her brain packing for parts unknown with one look? Was it because he had essentially replaced Hillram? Or something else entirely, some baffling attraction she could not begin to understand, given how gruff and unpleasant he was? Whatever the cause, it was incredibly unfortunate. Especially as Hillram's sisters were present.

"Lenora," Clara said with warmth, enfolding her in a tight embrace. "We're so happy to see you. It's been too long."

Lenora returned the embrace, overwhelmed by the aching familiarity in the gesture. She had always liked Hillram's sisters immensely, and the fact that she would be able to claim them as her own sisters after her marriage had been a bright spot in an otherwise untenable situation. Yet she'd been dreading this meeting. Undoubtedly talk would turn to their brother, and might-have-beens, and the tragedy of it all. Something she tried to avoid at all costs.

As expected, Clara's eyes were moist when she pulled back, and Lenora felt panic bloom. She had come here to face her guilt over Hillram's death. Yet she found she wasn't ready for the memories just yet. In desperation, Lenora turned her attention to Phoebe. The younger woman had been a freckled imp when last she'd seen her. Now, however, she was a lovely young woman. "Phoebe, look at you," she said. "You're as fine a lady as I've ever seen."

The girl smiled ruefully. "You mean I have finally grown into my looks. And it's about time, I would say."

She gave a small sigh. "But London has done wonders for you. If only we had been sisters, as had been destined, we could have taken on the city together."

"Sisters?" Mr. Ashford's voice was sharp. When Lenora looked at him, the intensity that was always present in his gaze seemed to have increased tenfold. And it was centered unerringly on her.

"Yes," Lady Tesh said, her tone thoughtful. "Lenora was engaged to be married to young Lord Hillram, the current duke's son, before his untimely passing."

"Was she?"

Those two words, said in that deep timbre of his, shivered through Lenora. What was wrong with her? She flushed in discomfort.

"But tell me, Lenora," Clara said, "have you kept up your drawing?"

Lenora winced. "Some," she mumbled.

"She has not," Margery declared, fixing her with a look.

"I have," Lenora denied. It was an old argument, after all, and one they'd had numerous times in the last few years.

"You have not. She has not," she said to her cousin. "Oh, she still draws, and does some fine watercolors. But nothing like she used to."

Mr. Nesbitt spoke up, interest keen in his eyes. "You're an artist, then?"

"Insipid pursuits for debutantes to pass the time," Mr. Ashford mumbled.

There was a pregnant pause. Margery, ever the peacekeeper, laughed lightly. "Perhaps for some. But our Lenora's talent went well beyond a mere hobby. She could draw something as mundane as a rock and make it look like it could jump right off the page."

"Ridiculous," Lenora whispered, her face going hot. Her embarrassment stemmed from more than Margery's praise, however. The censorious stare Mr. Ashford fixed her with had her feeling ashamed somehow that she had ever set pencil to paper.

Blasted belligerent man.

"I remember your paintings well," Phoebe said. "So fanciful and full of life. Why don't you draw like that any longer?"

Lenora looked at the floor. How could she tell these women that it was a kind of penance she had given herself, for the great betrayal her heart had committed?

Lady Tesh patted her arm. "We shall see about you finding that bit of yourself again, shall we?"

A doubtful scenario. For as much as she had come here looking to forgive herself, giving herself up to the vulnerability of creating from her heart was not something she would ever do again.

Margery turned to Clara in the ensuing silence. "Would you mind terribly if Lenora and I came calling during our stay?"

"I would like that above all else," Clara exclaimed. She turned to Mr. Ashford. "Perhaps you could accompany them. I know my father would like very much to meet with you."

Which was the very last thing Lenora needed. To visit Hillram's home, Danesford, and deal with all the emotions it would bring up was bad enough. To do so while Mr. Ashford was with her would be pure torture.

The man, however, seemed equally disturbed by the idea. "I'm sure the young ladies don't need my escort. I'll come another time."

Relief and disappointment fought within Lenora's breast. She held on to that relief with both hands.

Until Lady Tesh spoke up and effectively obliterated it.

"They may not need your escort, my boy, but I will. We shall make a party of it. Say, tomorrow around noon?"

Lenora froze and shot a quick, panicked glance at Mr. Ashford. His face had gone hard. For a hopeful moment, she was certain he would refuse Lady Tesh. But then he said, through teeth gritted tight, "As you wish."

What a peculiar reaction, as if Lady Tesh were forcing him into it. Though what hold Lady Tesh could have over someone like Mr. Ashford, who seemed to hold everyone and everything about him in the deepest contempt, was beyond her understanding.

But that was no concern of hers. Even so, Lenora couldn't shake the thought that Mr. Ashford was here against his will.

Chapter 6

*L*enora never had trouble sleeping at Seacliff. Though the house was several centuries old, a great brick edifice propped like an avenging sentinel over the coastline of the remote island, it had been updated over the generations until it could compete with any of the most modern houses in London. Add to that the placement of her bedroom, a spacious apartment at the front of the house that gave her the rolling lullaby of the sea as her constant companion, and more often than not, Lenora dropped off to sleep the moment her head hit the pillow.

Tonight, however, sleep would not come. It was not her recent abandonment at the altar that kept her mind spinning about like a whirligig, or the upcoming trip to Hillram's childhood home. It was not even due to the storm without, which battered at her window and turned the sea into a great thrashing beast. No, she thought with a sinking feeling in her stomach, she knew precisely at whose door she could lay the blame for her sudden bout of insomnia.

Mr. Peter Ashford.

All through the long evening, she had found, though conversation and laughter were plentiful thanks to Mr. Nesbitt, that she was unable to keep her thoughts or her eyes from Mr. Ashford. He had not been the least bit friendly through the meal or after in the drawing room, frowning mightily at any who attempted to converse with him. His clothing, too, had been given no quarter, his hands pulling and tugging relentlessly on the unsuspecting fabric. By the time Clara and Phoebe had left for the night and the rest had made to retire, his cravat was nothing more than a limp, sad thing dangling from his neck.

Even so, Lenora had felt a constant and undeniable pull toward him. There was no move he did not make that she was not fully and painfully aware of, no sound from him that did not earn the complete attention from her straining ears.

Now the man was even disturbing her sleep.

Several of her father's more colorful bits of vocabulary flew through her head. In a burst of frustration, she let them loose into the dark quiet of her room. She'd hoped to find a modicum of relief with it. But no, the frustration and restlessness that plagued her remained. What was it about him that unsettled her so, that made her body go feverish and aching all at once?

Throwing off her blankets in disgust, she swung her feet to the floor and donned her robe and slippers. Perhaps a cup of warm milk from the kitchens would help.

She made it down to the ground floor quickly, her slippers silent on the polished wood, her single candle throwing wavering golden light over the walls and paintings. The faces of long-dead nobles stared back at her, the dips in light and shadow giving their features a fluid cast, making their eyes seem as if they had come to life. One painting in particular caught her eye, a gentleman draped in brocade fabrics and wearing a powdered wig. It was one she had seen a thousand times before, yet now the man's eyes seemed to watch her with eerie intensity, his fingers tightening on the saber he held in his grip.

Her steps faltered for a moment. Surely her eyes were playing tricks on her. The longer she stared at it, however, the more it seemed to shift and sway. Shaking her head, she let loose a nervous laugh. "You cannot frighten me, my lord," she said to the portrait. She made to turn away. And nearly dropped her candle as a muted thumping echoed about the darkened hall.

Lenora froze, her eyes going wide. "Who's there?" she tried calling out. Her throat closed, the words coming out as more of a sputtering wheeze. Before she could gather her courage to try again, the strange pounding started up again, this time accompanied by a solid bang and a very masculine curse.

Her eyes flew to the door across the hall. It was ajar, a faint glow issuing from behind it. Who in the world could be up and about at this hour? Moving closer, she peered through the opening.

A great hulking shape moved about the space. As she watched, it took up a dainty chair and began moving toward the window with it.

A burglar. The breath left Lenora's body. If she raised a cry, help would not come in time. Hoping to catch the person unawares and debilitate them, she quickly blew her candle out and hefted the heavy brass holder high above her head. She inched into the room, praying with all her might the thief would not turn around.

Just then, however, he did.

"Mr. Ashford," she breathed, falling back a step.

He glowered at her a moment before eyeing the candlestick, still held aloft above her head. "Miss Hartley, what were you planning on doing with that bit of brass in your hands?"

She went hot, bringing the candlestick to her chest and gripping it tight. "I thought you were a burglar," she said, but even to her own ears the excuse sounded weak.

"A burglar." One blond eyebrow quirked. "You thought you could stop a burglar with that? Forgive me, but that is the most ridiculous thing I have ever heard."

The heat in Lenora's face spread down her neck as embarrassment turned to anger. Perhaps it had been foolish. But she would certainly never admit as much to him. "It is not ridiculous in the least."

"Isn't it? A pampered society miss, so slight I could easily lift you with one arm, thinking you have the strength to lay low a burglar with nothing but a candlestick?" His gaze, made a fiery orange in the glow from the single lantern he had propped on a low table, skimmed down her body. Her angry flush transformed into something altogether different, a new heat that sent her mind to parts unknown.

But she would not be cowed by a rude brute of a man who had no more manners than a dog.

Which wasn't the best analogy, she thought distractedly, as Freya was quite the most collected dog she had ever met. Even so.

"My intentions are neither here nor there," she countered. "What I would like to know is, what are you doing here in the dead of night, stealing Lady Tesh's furniture?"

He stared at her before letting loose a sharp laugh. "Stealing? Is that what you think I'm doing?"

"What else would you be doing with that chair?"

"I," he said with precision, turning and walking to a

blank spot against the wall, "am moving it." With that, he placed the piece down and turned to face her. In the deep shadows cast by the lantern, she just barely discerned an agitated tick in his jaw.

"Why in the world are you moving Lady Tesh's furniture?"

"Have you tried being as large as I am and sitting in something that is made like *that*?" He motioned to the chair with a disgusted jab of his finger.

Lenora very nearly dismissed that. A chair was a chair, after all. But something in his voice made her pause, a strange tightness to his words. She took him in, noting the fabric stretched tight over his broad shoulders, how he towered above her. She then turned to peer closely at the offending piece of furniture. For the first time, she saw it as he must. The legs were things of beauty, carved into graceful arcs that flayed outward. Yet they looked to be of no more substance than a twig.

"Ah. Yes, I do see what you mean."

"And so you will understand why I choose to sit in something that will not collapse at a mere breath." He moved across the room where a much sturdier—albeit much rougher and not at all attractive—chair sat waiting. He hefted it and, with impressive ease, placed it carefully down where the other had been, then stood back to look at it with grim satisfaction.

Lenora moved closer and considered it as well, though with far more pessimism. "It's...er..."

The smile fell from his lips. "What's wrong with it?"

Even in the dim light, the faint uncertainty in his eyes was evident. It was a vulnerability she had not expected to see, and it made her heart ache in the strangest way.

A moment later and she called herself ten times a fool.

The man didn't have a vulnerable bone in his body. It must be the light playing tricks with her, as it had with that blasted portrait. "You don't care what I think," she dismissed.

"Yes, I do." His answer was quick, the ring of truth in his voice.

"Oh." She blinked, her cheeks warming under his piercing stare as she turned to truly look at the piece to find something kind to say about it. "It looks...very comfortable," she finally managed.

She thought she heard him exhale. In relief? Surely not.

Regardless, some frozen bit of her heart thawed. Which was not good. Not good at all. She was here on the Isle to come to terms with Hillram's death, not to develop feelings for the man who had taken his place.

A suffocating sense of being closed in fell over her. Suddenly she was intensely aware of the heat from Mr. Ashford's arm where it nearly touched hers, the faint sound of his breaths, that wonderful scent of spices that was uniquely his own. She took a hasty step away from him.

"Well then," she said, pulling her thin robe tightly closed with trembling fingers, unable to look him in the eye, "I'd best be getting to bed." Without waiting for his response, she spun about and hurried from the room.

The gradual but unrelenting absence of light, however, made her realize how foolish her hasty escape attempt was. Letting loose a frustrated breath, she turned back around, embarrassment rising up that she would now have to ask him for a light after her display.

And ran straight into Mr. Ashford's very wide, very firm chest as he exited the room.

She stood there, stunned, feeling like she'd hit a brick

wall. That feeling was intensified as she looked up into his frowning face. What little breath she had retained left her, those harsh features uncommonly beautiful for all their starkness in the flickering light of his lantern. She swayed toward him, her free hand bracing against the broad width of his chest. Immediate heat filled her, radiating through her tightly strung body, pooling low in her belly.

With a low oath, he stepped back. For a devastating moment, she felt the loss of his closeness down to the very marrow of her bones.

"Did you need something?"

His voice rasped through her, jarring in the quiet, bringing her back to her senses.

Her cheeks heated. "I haven't a light, sir. Would you mind?" She held up the candlestick, still clutched tightly in one hand.

He heaved an exasperated sigh. "I'll escort you back to your room. You shouldn't be up and about at this time of night alone."

And the surly brute was back. Annoyance flared at his patronizing tone, the change in her feelings toward him such a relief that she purposely stoked it until it burned bright. "I'm not a child, sir," she bit out, "and am perfectly capable of seeing myself to bed. I certainly do not need your reluctant help."

He stared at her, his eyes wide. Then his gaze softened a fraction, a small smile lifting his lips. The expression changed his looks so drastically that once more Lenora forgot to breathe.

"The princess who roared," he murmured. "Very well, Miss Hartley, I shall light your candle and leave you to your independence." So saying, he did just that.

Lenora watched him go, the small flame of her candle dancing with her shaky breath. With a frown, she headed back for the stairs and her room. For she knew, without a doubt, there was no amount of warm milk that would help her sleep tonight.

* * *

It had been three years since Lenora had traveled up the long drive to Danesford, the Duke of Dane's sprawling estate and Hillram's childhood home. The towering Elizabethan brick house with its sharply peaked gables was the same as it used to be, and had no doubt remained for centuries: an ageless, elegant home. And it would have been hers had she married Hillram. For a moment, she expected him to bound down the front steps as he used to, that wide, open smile on his too-handsome face.

She shook her head, desperate to dispel the image. God, she didn't want to be here.

On the opposite bench, Lady Tesh and Margery talked quietly, sending her worried looks now and again. Lenora could not manage even a smile to ease their minds. She knew, without a shadow of a doubt, that they were worried about her for all the wrong reasons. She was not overwhelmed by grief over a lost love as they thought, but by a horrible guilt over not loving Hillram as she ought to have done. And worse, for wishing for a way out of their marriage before his death.

Matters were not helped by Mr. Ashford. He was seated at her side, his taut thigh pressed into her own, his clenched fist mere inches from her skirt. His proximity had her body drawn as tight as a bow. It did not escape her notice that she had never felt anything even remotely close to this heated, aching awareness with Hillram. A painful realization that sharpened her guilt tenfold.

Relief flared as the carriage finally rocked to a halt. When a footman opened the door, it took all of Lenora's willpower not to leap from the conveyance and out of the tense miasma that currently filled it.

Clara and Phoebe were waiting for them on the front steps. "We're so happy you've come," Clara said with a smile. "Father is having a good day; you could not have picked a better time for your visit."

Even with the hopeful news, Lenora could not help being aware of the unnatural quiet that enveloped them as they moved through the great hall. When last she'd been here, it had been just as silent and heavy with the dark cloud of mourning. Though then it had been made sharp by the stunned grief of a young life cut short. Now the sadness was gentler, waiting for a long life to pass into the next.

They made their way to the rose drawing room, a bright, cheerful room on the ground floor with towering east-facing windows. It was there they found His Grace awaiting them.

Lenora just kept herself from gasping at the sight of him. Gone was the robust man of her memories. In his place was a pale, skeletal man seated in a high wingback chair that made him appear even more shrunken and emaciated.

"Dane," Lady Tesh said, taking a seat at his side. She reached across the space separating them to lay a gnarled hand over his. "It's good to see you, my boy."

He smiled warmly, though his eyes were dulled with pain. "It's good to see you, too, Aunt. Forgive me if I don't rise." He chuckled and turned to their small group. "Margery, it has been too long. How are you?"

Margery smiled. "Very well, cousin. And I have brought Lenora with me as well," she said, placing a gentle hand on Lenora's arm.

"My goodness," the duke breathed. "It truly is you. My girls told me you were here, but I would not believe them until now." He held out a trembling hand to Lenora. "It's good to see you, child. And what a beauty you've become. I only wish Hillram could see you."

Lenora's breath left her at the man's words. Unable to speak, she forced a smile and moved close to grasp his hand and plant a kiss on his sunken cheek.

Lady Tesh motioned to Mr. Ashford. "You remember Peter, of course?"

To Lenora's surprise, the smile left His Grace's face in an instant. He looked on Mr. Ashford with sober eyes. "Peter. Thank you for coming to see me."

Even more disconcerting than the man's reaction, however, was Mr. Ashford's response. He glared so ferociously, Lenora was surprised the duke did not burn up on the spot. In the end, Mr. Ashford inclined his head, but even that seemed reluctantly done.

There was a moment of tense silence. Clara quickly stepped in to seal the breach. She smiled brightly on the assembled guests, indicating the seats before her father. "I've ordered up a light repast," she said as they all settled themselves, "after which I thought perhaps we could leave Father to rest while we take a walk in the gardens. The summer roses are blooming and are looking their finest."

Her cheerful chatter provided much-needed distraction. Soon the majority of the assembled were talking and eating. Yet Lenora could not be easy, for as was becoming frustratingly typical with her, she was horribly aware of Mr. Ashford. Seated where she was across from him, she could not help noticing that he never, not once, let his furious gaze stray from His Grace.

Why did he appear to despise the older man? So intent was she on puzzling it out that the touch of a hand on her arm had her jumping in her seat. She looked up to find the entire party minus the duke on their feet.

"Lenora, are you coming?" Margery asked. When Lenora continued to look at her in confusion, her eyebrows drew together in worry. "We were headed out to the garden," she continued, her voice lowered so the others might not hear, "but we can leave immediately if this is too painful for you."

Lenora flushed, her eyes dropping from the kindness in her friend's gaze. She didn't deserve it. "I would love to visit the gardens," she declared with much more confidence than she felt, turning to join the others. His Grace's voice, however, made her pause in the process of donning her shawl.

"Peter, I wonder if you would stay behind?"

The room went still. Everyone looked at Mr. Ashford with wide, worried eyes. It was then Lenora knew, without a doubt, that the tension she had sensed between the two men had not been fabricated by an overactive imagination. Suddenly every word, every concerned glance, from the people around her took on a new meaning. They all knew what was going on, every one of them. Feeling more an outsider than she ever had here, Lenora followed the rest into the garden, willing herself not to look back as they left the two men behind.

Chapter 7

As the rest of the party trailed out into the gardens, Peter kept his gaze fixed on the duke. The fury and frustration that had taken hold of him upon seeing the man again had not abated, instead only growing. Yet not for the reasons he would have thought.

Thirteen years had done much to Dane, and none of it good. The illness that ravaged him had made him a pale copy of the larger-than-life man Peter remembered. His skin was yellow and almost translucent, like waxed fabric, pulled tight over the bones of his face. His body was skeletal in its thinness, his clothing hanging off his once robust frame.

But it was not the physical changes that were the most disconcerting to Peter. It was the man's entire personality. He was nothing like he had been that long-ago day when Peter had come begging for his mother's life.

The man looked at him now out of eyes glazed with pain, with a sober humility that might have tugged at Peter's heart. If he'd been in possession of one.

Without a word, Peter took a chair across from the duke. He would not be forced to stand before the man like he had as a child.

"I did not expect to see you again," Dane said.

"I cannot imagine why."

But either the man had become obtuse owing to his illness, or willfully ignored the dry sarcasm. A small smile lifted his lips. "I'm glad you've come."

Peter's fingers convulsed around the arms of his chair. "You shouldn't be."

"Yet I am." The smile, a weak thing at best, disappeared from his face. He studied Peter almost mournfully. "I know what you must think of me."

"You have no idea what I think of you," Peter bit out.

The duke sighed and seemed to shrink even more into himself. "No, you are right in that. But I'm happy you're here regardless. For there is something I must say to you."

"You have no right to say anything. You said all there was to say thirteen years ago."

"There is no excuse for what I did. I know that—"

"You know nothing," Peter spat. Feeling trapped in the elegant confines of the chair, he lunged to his feet and stalked across the room.

"I cannot begin to tell you how much I regret my actions," Dane said, his voice thick.

Peter spun about, facing the man. "*You* regret? *You?*" He stalked forward, his boots eating up the space between them until he stood directly before him. "You know nothing of regret. You know nothing of heartache, of seeing someone you love slipping away before your very eyes and not being able to do a thing about it."

"Don't I?"

The words, infused with such misery, cut through Peter's rage like a knife.

"I know pain, Peter," Dane continued. He swallowed hard, his eyes going distant, and Peter knew the man must be thinking of his own son. He'd heard all about the death, of course. How the young Marquess of Hillram had attempted a jump; how the horse had landed wrong, snapping its leg. The duke's son had lingered a short while in acute pain before dying in his fiancée's arms.

He started. Miss Hartley had been that fiancée. She had held that boy as he'd passed from this world into the next. Peter had not put the pieces together until now. And suddenly what had been a mere cold fact was given a horrible realism now that he saw Miss Hartley in his mind's eye, sobbing and grieving over the body of that faceless boy.

Furious at himself for softening even a bit over the death of a man he neither knew nor cared about, Peter returned his attention to Dane. Leaning over, he gripped the arms of the man's chair, forcing him to look him in the eye. "I know exactly why you wish to beg forgiveness now," he hissed. "You are dying, and realize that your actions have forever damned you. You wish to meet your Maker with a clear conscience. I will not give that to you."

Instead of anger or outrage, however, the man nodded, his eyes sunken and mournful in his thin face. "I deserve no less from you. But I will ask forgiveness regardless, though you have every right to refuse it."

"You turned a desperate, frightened thirteen-year-old boy from your door," Peter snarled.

"I did—"

"I came to you begging for help."

"Yes—"

"You were my last hope; my *mother's* last hope."

Grief flared in the pain-dulled depths of the man's eyes. "I would take it back if I could. If I had not been out of my mind with fear over your father's blackmailing—"

His jaw closed with enough force to snap his teeth

together, his eyes widening in what could only be described as horror.

Every one of Peter's senses sharpened. His nostrils flared, and for a mad moment, he felt like a tiger getting its first scent of blood. He leaned in closer. "My father was blackmailing you?"

The duke pressed his lips tight, though he could not stem the desperate fear in his face.

Peter narrowed his eyes. "I have more reason than anyone to hate my father. He was a bastard of the first order, a demon spawned from hell. But even I know the man was far from stupid. He would not have chanced blackmailing a duke, no matter he was the man's cousin, unless there was something powerful to hold over his head."

The man let out a shuddering breath. "It matters naught," he muttered. "It's in the past. Suffice it to say, I did not cry when I learned of his death." His expression turned pleading. "Perhaps that is something we have in common, both having been hurt by his machinations—"

Peter recoiled as if burned. "You cannot manipulate me into feeling a pity for you that you do not deserve, nor granting a forgiveness that I have no intention of giving. I don't give a damn that my father was blackmailing you. No doubt it was deserved, or you would not have considered paying a blackguard like my father money to keep his mouth shut."

When the duke made to speak, Peter slashed a hand through the air, cutting him off. Fixing a hard stare at the dying man, he said, "You will listen to what I have to say now. All you have will soon pass into my hands. I want you to know, here and now, that it will all go to waste. The fields will go fallow, this manor will fall down in ruin. I will not marry, will not produce a child. After I'm gone, the title will revert back to the crown." He took a menacing step closer, letting every ounce of hate that was in his heart burn through. "Everything you now love will be turned to dust before I take my last breath. I wanted you to know that before you died, for you to look on the face of the boy you once damned, and see a man who no longer needs you. And you have no one to blame but your own cold heart."

Dane's face leached of all color. Not waiting for a response, Peter turned and strode for the garden door. He yanked it open, needing fresh air—and nearly fell over Miss Hartley. Again.

Truly, the woman had an uncanny knack for being in the wrong doorway at the wrong time.

* * *

Lenora just managed to avoid Mr. Ashford as he threw open the door and made to storm through. Again? Did the man never look where he was going? She glared up at him, intending to put him in his place. Really, this was getting ridiculous.

The look on his face, however, stopped her cold.

The pale blue of his eyes fairly blazed with a furious fire. His entire being was drawn taut, from the tense lines of his shoulders to the clenched hands at his side. Instinctively her gaze shifted to the duke still seated in the wingback chair behind him.

Her heart stalled in her chest.

Pushing past Mr. Ashford, Lenora hurried to the older man's side. He was as pale as death, deep grooves etching his face. "Your Grace," she said, kneeling beside him and taking up his fingers. They were ice cold. "Your Grace, are you well? Do you wish me to call for Clara? Do you wish for a physician?"

The man seemed to rally at her words. His face cleared and he gave her a trembling smile. Even so, there was something haunted in his eyes, as if his soul had been shredded and was now in tatters. "I'm fine, child," he said, his voice uneven and faint. He patted her hand. "Just a bit fatigued. If you can call for the butler, I'll have him return me to my rooms."

"Of course," she said at once, rushing to the bell pull. As she made certain of the older man's comfort, she was aware of Mr. Ashford standing silently by the garden door. Keeping her countenance calm and pleasant through the ordeal, as soon as the duke was safely out of the room, Lenora rounded on Mr. Ashford.

"What did you do that so upset His Grace?" she demanded.

He looked momentarily taken aback by her vehemence. She advanced on him.

"The duke is a sick man who has experienced more than his fair share of grief," she continued. "I will not have you upsetting him further. He deserves to live out the rest of his life in peace."

In an instant, disdain took over the man's features. "You have no idea what that man deserves," he said through gritted teeth.

The answer so stunned Lenora that she stopped and stared at him. There was a wealth of meaning in those angry words.

"I do not pretend to know what has happened between you in the past," she said slowly, carefully, as if he were a powder keg about to go off, "and I certainly will not pry—"

"Then don't," he said, cutting her off. "I have my reasons, Miss Hartley, for giving that man no quarter. Let us leave it at that. Now," he continued, opening the garden door and moving aside, "shall we join the others?"

So stunned was she by the change of topic that she immediately began moving for the door. As she moved to step past him, however, she stopped. Without a word, she turned and made for the chair Lady Tesh had vacated.

"Have you forgotten something, Miss Hartley? Or do you think I enjoy holding doors for indecisive young ladies?"

The words were said with such condescension that for a moment Lenora's muscles seized in anger. Reaching down with exaggerated care, she grabbed the bag from the floor and held it aloft. "Not that it is any of your concern, but Lady Tesh sent me back for her reticule. Now," she said, hurrying back across the room to stalk past him, "if you'll excuse me."

A sudden hand on her arm had her stumbling to a stunned halt. He paused, looking torn. Then, in a low voice, "That was not well done of me."

She gaped at him. "Is that an apology?"

To her shock, he flushed with embarrassment. "In a manner of speaking."

A surprised laugh escaped her, quite against her will. His eyes flew to her face, hurt plain to see before he shuttered it and dropped her arm like a hot poker.

"Yes, well," he grumbled, clearing his throat and heading out the door.

Mortification boiled up, hot and uncomfortable. Now it was her turn to reach for him. He tensed under her fingers but did not pull away.

"I didn't mean to laugh," she said. "I was merely surprised."

He looked at her, the glower back on his face. "Is that an apology?"

It took her some seconds to realize he was teasing her. She relaxed, her lips turning up in a small smile. "In a manner of speaking."

Reluctant humor flashed in his eyes. As they stood staring at one another, however, his humor was replaced by something else, a warmth that she felt clear to her toes. And then his eyes drifted down to settle on her mouth, and that warmth turned into a fire.

Lenora's mouth went dry, and she unconsciously licked her lips. His eyes widened.

Confused, desperate to bring some normalcy back to the scenario, she rasped, "You can talk to me if you like."

He blinked, his gaze still glued to her mouth. "What?"

How she formed a coherent thought, she would never know. But she did, the words coming in a rush. "About the duke. You can bend my ear if you wish."

At once, his expression shuttered. "You want me to talk to you about the duke?"

She swallowed hard. "If you'd like."

"No."

That was it, one word, sharp and final. And then he was pulling from her grip and storming out into the garden.

Lenora drew in a shaky breath. She could not make sense of him, showing unexpected humor one minute, anger the next. As shock subsided, she expected outrage at his brusqueness to take its place. Yet what she felt was quite different, a softening toward him she had not expected, for he was not all bluster as he pretended to be. The man was getting under her skin.

Something she could not permit.

She hugged her arms about her middle. How she would survive this month with him was beyond her.

Chapter 8

*T*hree days later—exhaustive days trying to ignore Miss Hartley and her soft lips and compassionate eyes—Lady Tesh gathered the small Seacliff party together for an impromptu picnic.

Though *impromptu* might be the wrong word for it. Peter surveyed the lavish spread set up beneath a stand of twisted spruce trees. Nothing other than meticulous planning could have accomplished what he was seeing.

A large, pristine white tent rose up against the brilliant blue sky like a triangular cloud. Beneath it, an elegant wood table stood, topped with all manner of crystal and fine china. At its center were several vases, hothouse flowers spilling from them with colorful abandon. Off to the side, a second table fairly groaned under the weight of the food it held. To top off the ridiculous display, half a dozen bewigged footmen stood at attention.

Peter dismounted from his horse, striding to the carriage as it rumbled to a stop. He threw open the door, helping the dog down, then accepting Lady Tesh's hand as she made to alight.

"I do hope you don't mind a meal out of doors," she said with a too-innocent smile.

He raised an eyebrow as he tucked the viscountess's

hand in the crook of his arm to help her over the uneven ground. To his surprise, she pulled away.

"Mr. Nesbitt may help myself and Margery," she said by way of explanation. "If you could assist Lenora, I would be much obliged."

Quincy was beside her in an instant, responding to the sound of his name on a female's lips no matter that woman was old enough to be his grandmother. He bowed gallantly. "You honor me, my lady," he said with a grin, offering his arm. Soon the three were off across the grass, talking and laughing quietly among themselves, the dog trotting regally ahead, leading the procession.

Leaving Peter alone with Miss Hartley.

With unease, he turned back to the carriage. She peered out at the departing trio, her eyes wide. With almost comical slowness, she turned to look at him.

Peter cleared his throat, stepping forward and holding his hand out to her. She hesitated but a moment before slipping her fingers into his. They both wore gloves, yet the shock of the tentative touch stunned him. Making certain to keep their contact as minimal as possible, Peter guided her behind the others.

It took an inordinately long time to walk the short way to the tents. He was painfully aware of every breath she took, every sway of her body. The space of a foot was no hindrance to the heat of her. It seemed to shimmer in the air between them. It took everything in him to hold his arm still under the tentative touch of her fingers on his sleeve.

No matter how he had wracked his brain over the past days, he couldn't make sense of his body's response to her. She was lovely, yes, and had shown proof on more than one occasion that she possessed far more spirit than he'd thought her capable of.

But that did not explain the way he burned for her, how she preyed on his thoughts, how he was achingly aware of her whenever she was near.

It was with relief that they made it to the luncheon area. Peter released her as soon as he was able. A footman was there before he could blink, pulling a chair back for Miss Hartley. It was only then that Peter saw the only chair available was beside her. He stared at it as if it were the fiery pit of hell.

"Come along, Peter," Lady Tesh said. "Take your seat before we all expire on the spot from starvation." The dog, seated regally in Lady Tesh's lap, seemed to stare at him in faint reprimand.

Pressing his lips tight, Peter moved forward and sank into the chair, all the while painfully aware of Miss Hartley on his right.

"I must say, my lady," Quincy said, "this is delightful. A more elegant picnic I could not imagine."

"Mr. Nesbitt, you are too wonderful. If you don't stop with the flattery, I'll be forced to keep you here against your will when your month's stay is up."

Quincy grinned. "You'll have no reason to keep me here by force, not if you continue to house such lovely guests." He looked at the younger women. Was it Peter, or did his friend's eyes linger a touch too long on Miss Hartley?

Scowling, Peter shot a booted foot out and caught Quincy squarely in the shin. The other man grunted in pain, the smile falling from his face. He glared at Peter, rubbing his leg under the table.

"Are you quite all right, Mr. Nesbitt?" Lady Tesh demanded.

"Just banged my knee, is all," Quincy gritted, turning a tight smile her way.

The excuse seemed to satisfy Lady Tesh. "Do take care," she said, before turning to signal to the waiting footmen to serve. As Quincy drew both the viscountess and Mrs. Kitteridge into conversation, Peter began to feel a peculiar tingling at the nape of his neck. Just then a soft voice sounded in his ear.

"Why did you kick Mr. Nesbitt?"

Against his better judgment he turned to look at Miss Hartley. The shock of her green eyes boring into his had him sucking in a breath. He quickly recovered and scowled. "My friend oversteps himself and has to be reminded at times of his impropriety."

Her brows knit a moment before understanding cleared them. "You think Margery or myself might be in danger from his charms? You may lay those fears to rest. There's no chance of that happening with either of us."

It was said with such certainty that Peter found his mood shifting. Was she thinking of Hillram? Had she loved him so very much that she could never see herself falling for another?

And why the hell did that bother him so damn much?

* * *

After the meal was cleared away, Lady Tesh leaned back and surveyed her guests.

"I imagine you all wish to be off now for some exercise."

Instantly an image filled Lenora's head, of wandering over the rolling hills, her hand tucked into the crook of Mr. Ashford's arm. The longing it brought about nearly undid her. "Surely we could not leave you alone, Gran," she hurried to say.

"Nonsense," the older woman stated. "Getting you all

off is just the excuse I need for a nap. Besides, I've found your old paint things and have had them set up just beyond those trees."

Lenora froze. "My paint things?" At Lady Tesh's nod, she said, panic making her voice a touch louder than she intended, "It would be rude of me to separate myself from the party like that."

"A problem I have already considered," Lady Tesh declared, dismissing her with a wave of her hand. "I've had Margery's things brought as well, and so you may have a companion in your artistic endeavors. Margery," she barked, "why don't you go on ahead, make certain things are set up properly."

"But Gran—" Margery tried, shooting a worried glance at Lenora.

"Enough loitering about," Lady Tesh barked. "I've a mind to speak to Lenora alone, and so you may take Mr. Nesbitt and see to things, as I've asked you."

With reluctance, Margery took Mr. Nesbitt's arm and moved off.

Mr. Ashford made to follow. Lady Tesh's voice stopped him.

"Peter, you may stay, for the proposition I'm about to make includes you as well."

Surely the man would not take such a tone from his great-aunt. But apart from a muscle ticking in his jaw, he made no response as he reclaimed his seat.

Lady Tesh returned her attention to Lenora. "I've a job for you, my dear."

Lenora blinked. "A job?"

"Yes, an important one. You gave me the idea on your first day here, when you mentioned your plan to visit your old haunts."

"Ah, yes." She gave her a sickly smile. After the strain of Danesford, she had conveniently forgotten about her original intention in coming to the Isle.

"If I remember correctly," the viscountess continued, not deterred by Lenora's lack of enthusiasm, "it was the historical places that drew you girls like flies to honey. I've long wanted to compile a record of the family history, and have written out all I can remember. But I lack some- one with the skill to paint the various places around the Isle that the Ashford family is connected with. You, my dear, have just the talent."

"You wish me to paint for you?"

"Very much so."

Lenora shook her head. "Surely Margery can manage it. She has talent—"

Lady Tesh slashed a hand through the air. "Talent, yes. For lovely watercolors that any young lady of breeding can create." She sat forward, her eyes blazing. "What I need goes beyond that, paintings with heart, images brought to life with unsurpassed skill. Only you have that, my dear."

Lenora wrung her hands in her lap, any pleasure she might have received from such praise overshadowed by the pain of her memories. She remembered how it used to be, how art had been an extension of her heart. Yet once Hillram died, she'd given it up. Oh, she still drew. But as Margery had pointed out to Clara, there was something different in it. Only Lenora knew that she had retained the mechanics of her art, but had gutted it of any emotion.

Now, however, temptation stirred, to experience again that deep satisfaction of creating from the very depths of her soul, something she had vowed never to do again. And it frightened her.

She opened her mouth to refuse.

Lady Tesh spoke before she could utter a word.

"It would be a great gift you give me." Her voice warbled, suddenly reed thin. "Especially as I wish to see it finished before I pass from this world. And there is no telling how little time I may have left." Here she paused, her vision going distant and sad, as if she were seeing some melancholy truth only she was aware of. The next moment, her eyes cleared, though the mournful look remained. "Would you do this for me, child?"

Lenora was stunned. The woman was talking of her death as if it was close at hand. Was the viscountess unwell? Lenora looked at her closely, noting the tired cast to her shoulders and the heavy way she leaned on her cane. Sorrow engulfed her. No matter that she did not want to be involved, she would see it through. She owed the woman too much for all the love she had given her over the years.

"Yes," she said, "I'll do this for you."

Lady Tesh straightened, a smile lighting her face. "Splendid," she pronounced, all trace of weakness gone.

Lenora gaped. In the space of a second, she looked as if she had shed twenty years.

"Peter," Lady Tesh continued, swinging her gaze to Mr. Ashford, "I would have you accompany Lenora on her outings."

Lenora opened her mouth to denounce the plan. The very idea of being forced to paint with Mr. Ashford nearby left her feeling cold and hot all at once.

Mr. Ashford, however, was quicker than she in attempting to put a stop to the mad scheme. "I don't believe that was part of the deal, madam."

Lady Tesh merely smiled. "Ah, but you see, I asked

that you provide your company. I did not specify with whom."

Mr. Ashford's typical scowl deepened considerably, frustration and a kind of grudging admiration flashing through his cold blue eyes. "Very well," he muttered with a decided lack of grace.

The whole exchange was confusing in the extreme. Even as Lenora wondered at it, however, she ruthlessly tamped down her curiosity. It was none of her business if the two of them had struck up some bizarre understanding. She would not get involved.

She wouldn't.

Chapter 9

*T*he sight of her easel set up beneath the tree, ready and waiting for her like an old friend, hit Lenora harder than a punch to the stomach. Everything else faded: Margery and Mr. Nesbitt fussing over her things, even Mr. Ashford's arm under her fingers. She took a deep breath, let her hand slip from the crook of his elbow, and stepped up to the easel. Dread snaked under her skin as she considered the blank paper ready and waiting for her.

The scene, the tools, were all so reminiscent of her youth on the Isle. No setting in London had ever affected her to such a degree. Once again temptation swirled. She had never once wanted to reclaim her joy in creating art since giving it up three years ago. Now, however, the desire surged in her with an intensity that stunned her.

But how could she, when she had so broken Hillram's heart?

When she had been the one responsible for his death?

As she continued to stare unseeing at the easel, Mr. Ashford came closer. Not close enough to touch, but she felt it all the same, a kind of electricity that scorched the very air between them, sending rivulets of sensation skittering across her oversensitive skin.

"Do you require assistance?" he asked, his voice deep and uncertain.

"No! That is," she amended with much less force, "I don't believe so." Drawing in a breath, she considered the gathered supplies. Her painting box stood at the ready on a small portable table, already propped open. Water was at hand, her brushes and pencils laid out. Even her smock was there, draped over a low stool. And the view itself was impressive, the valley laid out before her like a blanket of green grass and trees, that most important part of Ashford history at the center of it all.

Goodness, but Lady Tesh had thought of everything.

Lenora took up the smock and shrugged into it—only just realizing she could not do up the back herself. She turned Margery's way, intending to ask for help. But her friend had stepped away and was currently explaining the view to Mr. Nesbitt.

As she was trying to come up with a polite way to interrupt their exchange, Mr. Ashford spoke.

"Please, allow me."

He was at her back before she could react. There was a pause, the air heavy with anticipation. Lenora didn't so much as draw breath as she waited.

Suddenly the faintest touch, his fingers a whisper as he grabbed at the tapes on either side of her rib cage. The material pulled against her breasts, the gentle tugging as he did up the back a torturous friction. She drew in a shaky breath, closing her eyes, her head falling forward of its own accord. Soon the tugging stopped, his hands fell away—yet he stayed where he was. She could hear the faint rasp of his breath over the sound of the leaves rustling in the breeze, feel the warmth of it stir the hairs on the nape of her neck.

Heat pooled low in her belly, a warm rush that spread outward, filling her body with a heady need. She swayed back, straining for something, wanting his touch like she needed air to breathe.

With a soft curse, he stepped back and away. She felt it immediately, the loss of him. A chill wind seemed to sweep over her.

A light laugh reached her then. Jolted back to the present, she cleared her throat and managed a quiet "Thank you." Picking up a pencil, she sat on the stool before the easel. Shaken, she was unable to put pencil to paper for several moments, her hands trembled so. She knew what it must be, though she had never felt it herself: it was desire, plain and simple.

But why him, damn it? Why did she have to feel this for him, the very last man she should have wanted? A cold, unfeeling man who wore a scowl like others wore a ring or a watch fob.

She refused to want him. It would be as easy as blowing out a candle.

Looking at the paper once more, she straightened her shoulders. It should be as easy to paint without emotion. She had done it for the past three years, after all. Pressing her lips tight, she raised the pencil to the waiting paper and began to sketch.

* * *

Why in hell had he offered to tie that damn apron? The sight of the graceful curve of her neck had been torture. As it still was. He eyed it in a haze. How he longed to press his lips there, to run his tongue over the sensitive flesh.

He tugged at his cravat, turning away from the sight of

her. Her gown was a bit overdone and ostentatious, with the ridiculous flounces at the hem and the fussy puffed sleeves. Even so, she looked as fresh as spring leaves in the pale green concoction, her hair in cunning curls that danced enticingly against her throat. He would take a walk, he decided. He would take a walk, and not stop walking until he came to the sea.

Maybe not even then.

Before he could take a step, Mrs. Kitteridge, who had returned to her own easel, spoke. "Mr. Ashford, my grandmother bid me to tell you the history of the place, if you're amenable."

What could he do but acquiesce? With minimal grumbling, he moved closer to her, as far from Miss Hartley as he could manage. The shade was pleasant where they stood, the grasses green and fragrant. From here he could barely discern a rectangular-shaped indention in the valley below, several holes marking its perimeter. He settled in against an obliging tree and gave her a curt nod to continue.

She turned back to her easel. Beside her, Miss Hartley was already at work, her pencil scratching against her paper.

"You know, of course, that this island is called the Isle of Synne," Mrs. Kitteridge began, squinting out over the valley. "What you may not know is that it was named after our ancestor, an Anglo-Saxon maiden. She lived on this very spot; those markings in the ground below are the only thing left of her former home."

Peter had not felt an ounce of connection to this Isle since arriving. Yet he felt a tremor go through him at Mrs. Kitteridge's words. His eyes traced the depression, seeing now the outline of a house, the deeper holes no doubt the remains of where posts once stood.

"How long ago was this?" he found himself asking.

"Oh, I'd say nearly a thousand years ago. There are no official records, of course. Just stories passed down from generation to generation."

"A millennium?" Quincy whistled, even as he looked over Mrs. Kitteridge's shoulder at the sketch she was making. "That's an impressive lineage to be able to trace, even without the title."

"You think that because you've been in America for half your life," Peter drawled, "where everyone is as bright and new as freshly minted pennies."

"D'you think they dropped out of the sky then?" Quincy countered. "You've been there with me for the past thirteen years, old man. I'd think you would be better informed than that."

"Thirteen years? Is that when you left England?" Miss Hartley's musical voice broke through the good-natured banter. When Peter looked her way, there was a faint flush to her cheeks.

"Yes," he said. "My mother died and I left for America."

"You must have been very young. Just a boy."

"I was young, yes," he replied quietly. "Too young." A moment later, he wondered why he'd said such a thing. It was her eyes, perhaps. There was a compassion there that touched his very soul. That made him want to open up in ways he hadn't with anyone before.

Unnerved by the direction his mind was taking, he turned back to Mrs. Kitteridge. She had stopped to stare at him as well. "You were saying, madam," he prompted, eager to let the strange moment pass.

She jerked in surprise and flushed. "Ah, yes. Synne." She cleared her throat and turned back to her easel. "This was the time of the Viking colonization, you know, of

Danelaw. The Norsemen were not welcome here, though the land was theirs by right. The villagers had a long memory, and did not forget the raiding of their monastery a century before. And so, when the Vikings came to settle the island, they were met with barely banked hostility. Synne was no different. She despised the Norsemen. She might have gone the way of many others in history, forgotten over the intervening years, a mere stepping-stone in the grand scheme of it all."

Here she stopped, frowned, and erased a section of her drawing. Peter nearly growled his impatience. "What happened then?" he demanded, pushing away from the tree. Mrs. Kitteridge, however, was not listening. Instead she was talking quietly to Quincy as she attempted to fix whatever muddle her sketch had become mired in. Peter blew out a frustrated breath.

"One of the Vikings fell in love with her," came Miss Hartley's quiet voice.

He spun to face her. "I'm sorry?"

Her gaze darted to him for a moment before returning to her paper. "Synne dared to stand up to the Norseman Ivar. He resented being on the island, wanted to be sent to the mainland and the Jarldoms there, where the Danish political centers were located."

Now that was something he understood only too well, Peter thought acidly, being forced someplace you had no wish to be.

"But Synne captivated him," Lenora continued. "Despite himself, he fell in love with her."

Her voice had taken on a magical cadence, drawing him in. Without knowing he was doing so, he stepped closer to her. "How do you know the story so well?"

She shrugged. "I came to stay with Lady Tesh often

as a girl. This island is like a second home to me." Her lips quirked, softening her face. "Margery and I begged her to tell us the stories every chance we got. And how could we not be fascinated? The Viking warrior, a brave maiden, true love." Her smile wavered for a second, like a flame in a gust of wind, before it vanished, casting her face in shadows.

Was she thinking of Hillram and their doomed engagement? A sour feeling sat heavily in his gut at the thought. Confused—for it was unlike any emotion he had ever felt before—he slid his gaze from her profile to her drawing.

The valley was laid out on the paper, the minimal lines of her sketch imbuing a perfect—if strangely emotionless—sense of the place. Peter had the sudden desire to ask what had happened to Synne. Had she and her Viking lived happily together? At the last minute, however, he stopped himself. He didn't want to know. He didn't want to ruin this moment with the truth of it. For he knew, in his gut, that things could not have ended happily for the couple.

Perhaps there was a curse on this place if that was true. He looked at Miss Hartley's downcast profile. For wasn't she suffering through her own failed chance at love?

Again that sour feeling in his belly. Surely this wasn't jealousy. He could not be jealous of the hold some dead man had on Miss Hartley's affections.

Perhaps that walk wasn't such a bad idea after all.

Without a word, Peter turned and strode away, down the back of the rise. Leaving his confusing feelings back in the grass at Miss Hartley's feet.

Chapter 10

*P*eter kicked his mount on, needing the rush of speed. The horse obeyed immediately, lowering its head, its hooves pounding out a heavy, quick beat on the dry earth. Beside him Quincy's mount kept pace as they flew across the land.

He was going mad. That was all there was to it. He had been at Lady Tesh's home for a mere six days, and already he was going utterly mad. How else could he explain the complete disarray of his thoughts? Instead of revenge and anger filling his heart at every turn, instead of the constant burn in his gut to see Dane's legacy torn asunder, his mind was full of nothing but Miss Hartley. His eyes strayed to her when they were together; his thoughts strayed to her when they weren't.

Like now.

Peter growled and concentrated on the way the air hit his face, pulling on his hair and stinging his eyes. They crested a small hill, rounding a grove of trees. Heading for the next farm on his list.

It was this complete distraction from his purpose here that had prompted this particular outing. He was surrounded by people who loved the duke, who never spoke ill of him. Yet if anyone could attest to how miserable it was to be under Dane's thumb, it would be his own tenants. He'd decided then and there to interview the people who worked the land. Not that he needed proof that what he was planning was right. But some kind of confirmation that Dane was an unfeeling bastard and deserved what was coming to him would not be unwelcome.

But the people he had met thus far had proven to be a frustratingly happy lot. Not a one of them had an unkind word to say about the duke. Surely, he thought with growing frustration, someone despised the man as much as he did.

So anxious was he to get to the next property and find proof of Dane's cruelty, however, that he rounded the bend in the road much too fast.

And ran smack into a group of fat, freshly shorn sheep.

The animals rolled their eyes and bleated, scurrying away like so many bowling pins. Peter sawed back on the reins, his horse rearing. Over the noise he heard Quincy shout at his own mount and the accompanying yell of a third person. It was not until his stallion had all four feet safely on the ground that Peter could breathe and take stock of the chaos.

An older man in rough but neat homespun, his belly as round as that of his sheep, stood close by, his hands fisted on his hips. He glared at Peter and Quincy. "I'd ask you to take care when riding about these parts," he barked. "You near scared my flock to death."

Quincy touched a gloved hand to his brow. "Our pardon, sir. We meant no harm."

The man's eyes narrowed as he took them in. "You're not from around here. Visitors to the Isle don't usually come this far north. You're not up to any mischief, are you?"

"No more than usual," Quincy quipped with a grin. "But allow us to introduce ourselves. I am Mr. Quincy Nesbitt, and this is Mr. Peter Ashford."

The herder's animosity disappeared in an instant, his eyes widening as he took Peter in. "You must be the Duke of Dane's heir then." He sketched a bow, his face breaking into a delighted grin. "It's a pleasure, sir. My name's Hale Tunley, at your service."

The speculation and interest in the man's eyes were unnerving. Peter inclined his head. "Mr. Tunley." His eyes narrowed as he took the man in. It appeared he need not wait to reach the next house after all. "You are a tenant of the duke's?"

"Aye," the man answered with a smile. His chest puffed out like a cock of the barnyard. "My family has been a tenant of the Dukes of Dane for generations. They've always treated us good, they have."

"Surely not the current duke," Peter said.

But Mr. Tunley looked at Peter as if he'd lost his mind. "No, sir," he answered with unfeigned puzzlement, "His Grace is a wonderful landlord. Why, just last year my boy took ill, and he had the physician down and everything."

You're wrong, Peter wanted to shout. *The man is no better than a snake.* Quincy, seeing the outrage and frustration in him, spoke.

"I pray your boy made a full recovery?"

"Oh, aye," the man said, his eyes clearing as his attention shifted to Quincy. "That he did. He's right as rain now."

"Good, good. You say your family has lived here for generations?"

"Nigh on two hundred years now. Been raising sheep

on the same land as my grandfather's grandfather's grandfather."

"And you've never thought of uprooting?" Quincy asked. "Of settling somewhere else, with all the possibilities that are arising in this new age?"

Mr. Tunley could not have looked more horrified. "Never sir," he breathed. "My life's in this land. Why, I would rather cut off my right arm than leave."

A heavy ball settled in Peter's stomach. The man was so overcome by Quincy's suggestion that Peter had the notion that, had he been a Catholic, he would have crossed himself.

"Forgive my curiosity," Quincy said, placing a hand over his heart. "I've been in America half my life, you know, and I fear I've picked up some bizarre notions." Here he laughed, and Mr. Tunley joined in. "And now we must be off," Quincy continued, holding out a hand to the man, who shook it firmly. "So sorry again about your sheep."

"Not at all, sir. They need a good scare now and again. They get too lazy and fat otherwise." He laughed heartily at that before turning to Peter. "Mr. Ashford, it's been a pleasure, sir."

Shaken, Peter merely nodded before turning his mount back around. He gave the animal its head, his own too full of what Mr. Tunley had said.

Quincy soon caught up to him. They rode in silence for a short time before Quincy said, his voice low, "Are you certain your memories of the duke are right?"

The myriad emotions that had been rattling and tumbling about in Peter's head coalesced into pure anger. "You doubt me?" he snapped. "You think it's all in my head, that I fabricated a reason to hate Dane, that thirteen years of my life have been wasted in wishing for revenge over something that never happened?"

"Gad, no," Quincy said hastily, eyes wide. "But damn it, man, besides the mention of blackmail—which could be anything, for all we know—what we've heard so far doesn't match up to the bastard that turned you away. And not just from the tenants' mouths, either. The land is fertile, the houses clean and in good repair. That's not typically a sign of a cruel man who does not take care of what's his. Do you wonder at me questioning it?"

No, Peter thought grudgingly, he could not. For if their positions had been reversed, Peter would have questioned it as well.

"Despite all that, however," Quincy continued, eyeing Peter as their horses picked their way through a small copse of trees, "there is another far more pressing concern. If you go through with your plans to destroy the duke's title and lands after his death, you realize you will impact all the families we've met today, as well as countless others."

The fact that Quincy's words so closely mirrored his own tumultuous thoughts did not help Peter's peace of mind in the slightest. "I'd hoped to persuade the tenants to leave Danesford."

"With what, money?"

"Most men can be persuaded to do any number of things for money."

"Perhaps," Quincy allowed. "But there was a pride in the people we've met today. What if they refuse?"

Peter ground his back teeth together. "When the time comes, they will see what benefits them, and act accordingly."

Quincy gave a humorless chuckle. "I don't think it will be as easy as you hope."

Nor do I.

*   *   *

As far as dinner parties went, Lenora thought, tonight's was fairly tame. A dozen of Lady Tesh's closest friends were clustered about before the meal, talking quietly. It was nothing like London, where the guests outdid one another in dress and manners, where the assembled watched carefully for any perceived slipup to be reported to the rest of the *ton*. The whole affair was pleasant in the extreme, a gathering of people who were both kind and familiar.

Lenora eyed Mr. Ashford across Lady Tesh's vast drawing room. If one went purely by that man's face, however, one would think they were all being roasted alive. While having their toes cut off. While being stung by a swarm of bees.

She had the strangest desire to rescue him.

Which was laughable, really. Mr. Ashford looked like a warrior bent on conquest. He certainly didn't appear as if he could be laid low by a room full of smiling people. Yet there he stood, eyes burning. The very picture of a man being tortured.

Lenora frowned. The man was rude and abrasive. Not to mention he unsettled her in a very physical way. Even so, she could not sit idly by while he suffered.

Dinner was announced and everyone moved toward the door in natural pairings. Mr. Ashford froze, looking like a cornered beast. Before she quite knew what she was about, Lenora hurried to his side and tucked her hand into the crook of his elbow. "I believe, sir, you promised to bring me in to dinner."

He could not have looked more startled. For a moment, Lenora thought he would recoil. But then relief flared in his eyes. With a small incline of his head, they followed the rest out.

Dinner parties held by Lady Tesh were informal affairs. The guests sat where they would, so it was an easy enough thing for Lenora to maneuver herself next to Mr. Ashford.

The footmen came forward, placing the first course on the table. A muttered oath reached Lenora. She blinked and looked Mr. Ashford's way. He was staring at the spread as if he had never seen the like before in his life, his posture stiff and brittle.

Lenora leaned toward him. "I suppose it is a bit much."

"A bit?" he blurted out.

She laughed quietly. "Truly, this is mild compared to what you would see in London."

"You must be joking."

The look of horror and disbelief on his face was so comical, she nearly laughed again. But he would not appreciate her mirth at his expense. Instead she said, "Not at all. Why, on one occasion there were twenty-five dishes for the first course alone."

"Twenty-five," he muttered, eyeing the dozen or so dishes on the table and shaking his head.

Soup was served then. Out of the corner of her eye, Lenora saw Mr. Ashford taking in the myriad utensils at his place. With exaggerated care, she reached for the soup spoon, brandishing it above her bowl a moment before dipping it into her dish. Blessedly Mr. Ashford was quick as well as smart. He soon followed suit.

Lenora smiled to herself. "You must tell me about America, Mr. Ashford," she said in between sips of the creamy broth. "We've been occupying the same house for nearly a week, and yet I haven't heard a thing about it from you. Do you not have elaborate dinner parties in Boston?"

"I wouldn't know," he replied.

"But surely, with your success in business, you must have been out in society."

"I leave that to Quincy," he said, motioning with his spoon toward his friend, who was holding court at the far end of the table.

Yes, she could see how that man would be the face of the business. He had a gift for charming others. She had never seen anyone so in their element as Mr. Nesbitt surrounded by people.

He was the opposite of Mr. Ashford. How did two completely dissimilar men become such good friends?

"You are wondering," Mr. Ashford said, "how the two of us became acquainted, I suppose."

Lenora gaped. "Are you a soothsayer?"

For the first time in the days she had known him, Mr. Ashford's lips quirked in unrestrained humor. "It's a question we're asked often."

The soup bowls were cleared, and the guests began serving themselves from the surrounding dishes. Mr. Ashford froze a moment before he turned his gaze to her in question.

Her chest swelling, Lenora motioned surreptitiously to the nearest serving dish, then to her own empty plate. "If you would be so kind?"

The man took to his task with alacrity, soon filling both their plates to overflowing. Lenora could not help the laughter that bubbled up, even as she waved her hands for him to stop.

"What is it?" he asked, freezing, serving tongs dripping with asparagus extended over her plate.

"I will never be able to eat all this, much less the second course."

His mouth fell open. "There's more?"

"Quite a bit more, I'm afraid."

He dropped the tongs back into the serving dish, the metal clattering against the fine china. Attacking his cravat with nervous fingers, he seemed about to descend into his surly glowering once again.

"But not to worry," she hastened to assure him, "for I'm inordinately hungry. Now, you were about to tell me how you and Mr. Nesbitt met?"

"Was I?"

"Oh, certainly."

Again that small smile. Lenora stared at the curve of his lips, at the small dimple that appeared on his cheek beneath his short gold beard, at the small lines that radiated from the corners of his eyes. And here she had thought the man couldn't get any handsomer.

"I'm afraid it's quite a sordid story," he said. "When I left for America, I was thirteen, with little money and no prospects. As most boys, I believed that things would work out in my favor, even when the odds were stacked against me." The small light that filled his face suddenly dimmed, some remembrance clouding his eyes.

An ache settled in Lenora's chest. What he must have gone through. And at such a young age. She thought of the boy he'd been, alone in the world.

As a distraction from the sudden pall that had fallen between them, Lenora picked a fork from her setting and twirled it above her plate before taking a bite of partridge. As before, Mr. Ashford followed suit, the small act seeming to snap him out of whatever dark thoughts had taken hold of him. She would not question him further on it. Yet it was Mr. Ashford himself who continued their conversation.

"I didn't go to America immediately. London seemed the hub of everything to me, and I'd meant to make a name for myself there. But some ruffians quickly found an easy mark in me, beating me senseless and relieving me of the rest of my coin. After several days of going cold and hungry, I wandered down to the docks, where I saw *The Persistence*."

Her food forgotten in the drama of his tale, Lenora stared at him. "*The Persistence*?"

"A merchant ship, from America." A small smile played about his chiseled lips. "When I saw that glorious ship, its masts reaching for the heavens, its hull gleaming and full like the belly of a fat nobleman, I came up with the most incomprehensible, madcap plan."

His clear blue eyes focused on her, and a glimmer of almost boyish mischief lightened them. His manner was so completely different from what she was used to that her breath stalled in her chest.

"I would stow aboard, and make my way to America," he continued, that maddening smile once more drawing out a small indentation in his cheek. "Surely one as small as me—for though I'm a monster now, Miss Hartley, I was quite the scrawny, undernourished thing then—could go undiscovered in the time it took to cross an ocean."

Her mouth fell open. "You were a stowaway?"

"Indeed I was. Though my confidence in my ability to remain hidden was misplaced. We were barely out of port when I was discovered and brought before Captain Adams. He could have easily thrown me overboard. Instead he kept me on, even gave me a job. And he paired me with his newest crew member."

He looked at Quincy, a wry smile lifting his lips. "You would not know it, Miss Hartley, but my friend was not always the suave, debonair creature you see before you. At one time he was as gangly and awkward as they come. We quickly bonded. Later, when we might have parted ways in Boston, Captain Adams asked us to continue with him." He paused, staring at his plate. Then, with a shrug that said such things happened every day, he began work on the mound of food before him.

"You make it seem as if that's all there is to the story," she said, incredulous.

"Isn't it?" he asked around a mouthful of food.

"But what of your business? Surely that deserves mention as well."

He cast a dubious look her way and swallowed. "I was not aware," he drawled, "that young English ladies have any interest in such low talk."

Aggravation reared, that he would doubt her interest merely due to her sex and position. "I assure you," she said in a low voice, picking at a bit of salmon with the tines of her fork, "I wouldn't have mentioned it if I didn't wish to know."

He stilled beside her. "I'm sorry," he said, equally low. "You're being kind and I've offended you."

She stared at him. No one had ever apologized for such a thing before, not in all her time in society. It was on the tip of her tongue to put him at ease so they could go back to being pleasant with one another. At the last moment, she stopped herself. His gaze was earnest, and she found herself wanting to say what was on her mind. "You do not have a good opinion of English ladies," she said, her voice trembling for daring to speak her thoughts. "I would have you at least do me the honor of getting to know me before coming to conclusions about how I might feel about certain things."

He looked stunned, and she feared for a moment she'd overstepped. The look quickly passed, however, to be replaced with a grudging respect. "Forgive me," he said solemnly. "What do you wish to know?"

Pleasure curled through Lenora. It increased exponentially when he proved his words were no mere platitudes, placing his utensils down and turning toward her, waiting patiently for her questions.

The thawing toward him she'd sensed deep inside her chest increased. And for the first time, she welcomed it.

She took a deep breath. "You're in business with Mr. Nesbitt, correct?"

"Yes. And with Captain Adams and his family as well. After the English and French both made safely crossing the Atlantic an impossibility and the Embargo Act destroyed the rest of Captain Adams's business, we had to do something to help the family stay afloat."

"That is so kind of you, to care for them when they might have been ruined."

A flush stained his cheeks. "It was not kindness," he said, his voice endearingly gruff. "Anyone would have done the same."

"No, they wouldn't have."

"Yes, well," he hemmed, his face brightening even more, his eyes falling from hers.

Fighting back a smile, she searched her memories of the conflict to help ease his embarrassment. Finally she lit on something. "I overheard my father discussing how American ships were seized and their sailors impressed into the British Navy. Did you experience any of that?"

Her distraction worked. His face relaxed, his eyes finding hers again. "Yes. As a matter of fact, I was nearly impressed myself."

Her eyes widened. "How did you escape?"

Wry amusement lit his face. "Quincy hid me in a barrel of brandy."

She gaped at him, her hand unconsciously going to his arm. "Surely you're joking."

His lips quirked. "You may ask him later if you like. It was only half full, but I was quite waterlogged when I emerged some hours later. As well as stinking drunk."

A startled laugh escaped. "That must have been an interesting experience."

"It was, and the reason I don't imbibe in hard liquor to this day. A lurching ship and an aching head don't mix, I assure you."

They exchanged soft laughter, a moment of comfortable camaraderie passing between them. His eyes were warm on her face, wondering, as if he were seeing something in her that he hadn't noticed before.

She felt as if she were melting under the admiration in that gaze, her very skin tingling with awareness. The sound of utensils scraping plates, the murmur of voices, the low rumble of laughter all faded.

Suddenly his gaze shifted down. It was only then she realized she still had her hand on his sleeve. Every sense centered on the feel of his forearm, warm and strong beneath her fingers.

A laugh sounded close by, shattering the mood. She jumped and pulled away. Focusing her attention back to her plate, she picked up her fork and poked at the barely touched partridge. "How did you all survive then?" she managed in an attempt to return to the easy conversation they'd been having before she'd gone and pawed at him.

He didn't miss a beat, thank goodness. "The Adams children were too young to support their family. I talked the captain into letting Quincy and me oversee the running of their goods to Canada."

He spoke the history with such simplicity that it took her a moment to realize what he meant by such a statement. The fork she'd been maiming the partridge with stilled. "Surely you don't mean—"

He raised a brow. "Yes, Miss Hartley?"

She flushed, casting a surreptitious glance around before leaning in closer and lowering her voice. "Surely you're not implying that you became a smuggler."

He leaned in as well, lowering his voice to a mock whisper. "Aren't I?"

She blinked. "Oh."

His lips quirked at her shock. "It was that or starve, I'm afraid."

She shot him a cautious glance. "And do you and Mr. Nesbitt still . . . smuggle?"

"Fearful of being in company with criminals, Miss Hartley?" he drawled.

"Not in the least; fascinated, is more like it," she replied with utter honesty.

Again that warm, admiring look. "No, we're no longer smugglers," he replied. "A year or so after we began, we were nearly caught. Captain Adams would not hear of us endangering ourselves further." He took a sip of his wine. "And so I suggested real estate. The other merchants were leaving Boston in droves. We took advantage, bought up the property they wished to be rid of, and thereby found ourselves in a very lucrative business."

Lenora waited, but he took a healthy bite of fowl, seemingly content to finish his story in such a manner. She pursed her lips. "Why do I get the feeling that it was not as simple as you make it out to be?"

He smiled wryly down at his half-eaten meal. "You are very astute, Miss Hartley. Has anyone ever told you that?"

She smiled. "No, you're the first. Though you cannot get out of answering the question with compliments, sir. Was it difficult convincing the family to abandon everything and to start anew?"

"It was." He turned those incredible eyes on her, now intense with some emotion, as if he wanted desperately for her to understand something. "But I owed them everything. They saved my life. I couldn't let them lose their entire livelihood without trying to save them as well."

Something in his words struck her. Here was a man who did not take his debt to others lightly. She suddenly recalled the strange interactions between him and Lady Tesh. She had wondered if the viscountess had something over Mr. Ashford, something that was forcing him to do things he had no wish to.

Now she knew for certain she had not been imagining things.

Her musings were cut short as Mr. Ashford once again spoke. "It could just as easily have turned sour. I could have ruined them, and they might never have recovered. Thank goodness it paid off."

She tilted her head, considering him. How different he was from what she'd first thought. "You're a good man."

Once again embarrassment colored his cheeks.

"Nonsense," he said. But she did not fail to notice the faint smile on his lips as he turned his attention back to his plate.

The man on her right began to converse with her just then. But though she did her duty and gave her attention to him, she could not forget Mr. Ashford on her other side.

Nor did she fail to realize that, in her mind, he was no longer the glowering, acidic man who had taken Hillram's place. No, he was something much more.

Chapter 11

No matter his thoughts on the Isle or the people who inhabited it, Peter could not deny that the main thoroughfare was a beautiful place with its wide avenue and quaint shops all flowing right to the beach and the unending sea.

If only he wasn't distracted by thoughts of Miss Hartley.

Her arm linked with Mrs. Kitteridge's, they moved close to a shop window, peering at the array of richly bound books within. She laughed quietly, bending her head close to her friend's. Yet he did not fail to see the sideways glance she sent his way. Nor the way his heart pounded when their eyes met.

Just then Lady Tesh called to Mrs. Kitteridge. She moved away, leaving Miss Hartley by the window. Without thinking twice, Peter walked to her side.

"Miss Hartley."

She looked up into his face and smiled. "Mr. Ashford. How are you enjoying your first shopping expedition in town?"

Much more than he ever thought he would. But it had nothing to do with the town and everything to do with her.

Rather than admit that, however, he said, "I must thank you for last night. What you did for me was very kind."

"It was my pleasure," she said, her voice soft, her eyes glowing.

Overcome by that warm expression, he looked for Quincy. To his surprise, the rest of the party were already some way down the street. He offered his arm to Miss Hartley. Without hesitation, she tucked her hand in the crook of his arm and they started off.

The silence stretched between them. Each step made him more aware of the shifting of her grip, each gentle caress of salty sea air bringing with it her scent of summer berries. He cleared his throat, needing the distraction of conversation.

"I'm not easy around those I don't know."

"You make that sound like a failing, Mr. Ashford."

"Isn't it?"

"No."

He gave her a dubious glance. "You're used to society. Surely someone of my disposition wouldn't fit in."

"That's true."

Her admission hurt much more than he'd thought it would.

"But," she continued, looking at him, her eyes serious, "that doesn't mean you have a failing. One could also say that being cautious with whom you open up to is the more honest course, and therefore the more admirable quality."

A glowing started up in his chest, an entirely foreign feeling that left him dazed. Before he could make sense of it, Lady Tesh spoke.

"Let us delay the trip to the tearoom for a short while," she declared. "I'm in the mood for a new gown. What say you, Margery and Lenora, to indulging an old woman? We're to attend a subscription ball come next Friday, and

I would like nothing better than to deck you both out in something frivolous."

Peter nearly groaned. Shopping for gowns with not one but three ladies? The pleasant interlude of the past minutes disappeared in an instant. Surely the younger women would jump at the chance. They would be here for hours.

Miss Hartley, however, never failed to surprise him, even in this.

"I have no need of a new gown, Gran," she said, looking at the shop front they'd stopped before as if it were the gates of hell. "I brought a formal gown that will do quite well for the ball."

"And yet I still ask your indulgence in this," Lady Tesh said archly, "for I find I've become quite selfish in my old age." She shooed the younger women in the direction of the shop.

Miss Hartley sent Peter a pained look before she released his arm and disappeared inside. It warmed him, that glance, proof of their new camaraderie, something he had not expected with her. He had the mad urge to rescue her. Instead he squared his shoulders and made to follow, prepared to lend his silent support if that was what was needed. As he was about to step over the threshold, however, Lady Tesh turned to him.

"You may scurry yourself over to the tailor's, Peter. Don't think I haven't noticed the deplorable state of your own wardrobe. I'll not have you walking into the assembly rooms dressed in those rags you call clothes."

Behind him he heard Quincy stifle a snort of laughter. He might have laughed himself if he wasn't so offended at the woman's effrontery.

"There's nothing wrong with my wardrobe, madam."

The viscountess made a rude sound. "The only place your clothes are good for is the rubbish heap. I've been indulgent thus far, but you will not embarrass these young women by walking into the assembly rooms dressed as you were for my dinner party. Now off with you, and be back here within the hour." So saying, she slammed the door in his face.

Peter stood outside the shop for a moment, stunned. Quincy let out a hearty laugh. "By God, I love that woman," he proclaimed, clapping a hand on Peter's shoulder. "Let's be off then. No time to waste."

Peter turned incredulous eyes on his friend. "If you think I'll be browbeaten into dressing up in some dandy's frock, you're sorely mistaken. That woman has forced me to do much I have no wish to do; dressing up to please her will not be one of them."

"Come now, she isn't asking much. Only some formal wear."

"I won't renege on our bargain. But I will not dress myself in some society costume to appease her. Even I have my limits." He turned to storm off. And came face-to-face with the Ladies Clara and Phoebe Ashford.

"Oh! Good day, Mr. Ashford, Mr. Nesbitt," the elder of the two said. Her eyes lingered on Quincy a moment before she flushed and turned her attention to Peter. "How fortuitous to run into you. I'd thought to seek you out at Seacliff later, but now may save myself a trip."

He blinked. Surely he was hearing wrong. Dane must have said something to his daughters after their confrontation at Danesford. Peter should be the last person she would want to see.

But the woman was all smiles. "Well, you and Miss Hartley. Lady Tesh has told us of her commission of

Miss Hartley to paint the important places about the Isle, and that you were just learning of our family history. At Danesford we have a small piece of jewelry that may interest you. It's said to have been worn by Synne herself."

A current sizzled through Peter. Something survived of his ancestor besides the ghost of a foundation? Something she had touched with her own hands?

In the next moment, he shook off his excitement. It was of no interest to him. The family history stopped cold with him; after centuries it would wither on the vine. He had no need—nay, no desire—to view a thousand-year-old relic that would have no meaning after his death.

"I thank you for the invitation but I must decline," he said, chill dripping from each word.

The smile fell from Lady Clara's lips. She looked to her sister, who appeared equally distressed. In the next moment, the older woman dredged up a smile, but it was a mere shadow of what it had been. "I do hope you reconsider. Our father was most adamant about seeing you again; I know it would give him great pleasure to have you return."

"Your father wishes me back?" Peter asked sharply.

She nodded vigorously, no doubt seeing in his question a ray of hope that his refusal of her invitation would be reconsidered. "He's quite anxious to see you."

Why would the man wish him to return? Peter had left no opening for further discourse. He'd threatened the man's home and heritage. If the duke was in his right mind, he would never wish to see Peter again.

Quincy spoke before he could give the woman a firm letdown. "Thank you, Mr. Ashford will let you know when he's available. And if you wish to extend your kind invitation to Miss Hartley, she's currently within." He motioned to the modiste shop.

Lady Clara thanked him profusely, her eyes once more lingering on him. Then, seeming to recall herself, she flushed and, shooting Peter a wary glance, ushered her sister along and disappeared into the building.

Peter rounded on Quincy. "You had no right," he growled.

"I had every right," Quincy shot back in a rare show of anger. "Since we've arrived and I've gotten to know some of these people whose lives you'll be affecting with this mad scheme of yours, I can't help but think you're making a grave mistake."

"A mistake?" he sputtered. He was vaguely aware that people were slowing around them on the sidewalk, giving them curious glances. At the moment, he didn't give a damn.

Quincy took hold of his arm, dragging him to the side of the walkway. When he spoke, his voice was low and tense with frustration. "You can't see past the haze of your anger that your revenge against this man will throw everything out of balance. You won't just be affecting him, but everyone from his tenants to his servants to those two very sweet and very innocent women in there. I know," he said, holding up a hand when Peter meant to interrupt, "that you mean to take care of each and every person who would be affected. Yet you cannot deny that it won't be as easy as that. For in all your planning and plotting you didn't take into consideration one very important thing: that His Grace is loved by those around him."

Bitter gall rose in Peter's throat as his mother's ravaged face swam up in his mind. "And what do you expect me to do?" he rasped. "Do you think I should turn my cheek, to forget what he's done?"

Quincy stared at him mournfully. "I don't think you're capable of it. As much as I wish you were, you will never be able to let it go. And in the end, it will be your downfall." With that, he turned and walked away.

Peter could only stare after his friend, beyond words. They had fought in the past, but never like this. Regret settled heavily in his chest.

"Mr. Ashford?"

That now familiar voice was like a brilliant light, burning away his dark thoughts. He spun to face Miss Hartley. She stood only feet from him on the pavement, her pale green eyes wide with worry. She offered him a tentative smile. "I saw from the window that you and Mr. Nesbitt may have quarreled and I wanted to be certain you were well."

That peculiar glowing was back in his chest again. "You were concerned over my well-being?"

"Of course," she said.

The glow spread, surrounding his heart. He cleared his throat of the sudden lump that had formed there. "That's very kind of you, but I assure you, your concern is unfounded. I've never been better."

She didn't appear to believe him. As a matter of fact, she looked as if she believed he had spewed the biggest untruth she'd ever heard. "If you're certain," she said dubiously.

"Of course I am."

She gave him a long look before, with a nod, she turned to go back inside the shop.

He watched her, feeling a sudden loss. Without warning, he found himself calling out to her. "Miss Hartley, why don't you like to shop for dresses?"

She froze, her hand on the door, and turned to look at him. There was surprise in her eyes, which was quickly hidden. "I'm not certain such an answer would interest you."

"I believe it would," he said softly, stunned to find that he meant it.

She swallowed hard and, after staring at him closely for a moment, stepped back to the pavement. "My father is a very...exacting...man," she said with difficulty. "Don't mistake me. He loves me." Her features tensed for a moment, something like pain or uncertainty flashing in her eyes. Then she blinked, and it was gone. "Shopping for clothing, any clothing, tends to be a fairly tedious business, as he oversees every detail. Everything you see on my person, from my bonnet to my gloves to my shoes, has been chosen with care and precision by him."

His eyes traveled down her dress. Not that he knew the first thing about fashion, but even he could see the fine quality of the gown. It was made from some brown material that shimmered as she walked. Light blue braid decorated the front, from the high starched neck to the stiff hem. The sleeves were puffy, cinched tight at the wrists, and decorated with more of that braid. The hat was some monstrously huge confection with a wide brim and a tall crown, a pale blue ostrich feather bouncing ostentatiously from the band. The whole thing was too cold, too exact, containing not a bit of her warmth and kindness.

His sudden intuition into this woman's character had him reeling.

Shaken, he was tempted to murmur some platitude and excuse himself.

Yet when he looked into her eyes, he saw a vulnerability there that he could not turn from.

"Perhaps," he said, slowly and carefully, "now is your chance to do as you wish, to find your own style."

The look she gifted him with could only be described as dubious. "I doubt I have my own style, Mr. Ashford. I've certainly seen neither hide nor hair of it up till now."

"Mayhap you were never given the chance to find it."

She pursed her lips.

Peter had the ridiculous urge to laugh. What the devil was he doing, trying to encourage this young woman to enjoy herself in a shopping expedition?

But he could not forget the pained look in her eyes from moments ago. Nor could he forget the kindness she'd shown him the evening before at Lady Tesh's dinner party. Even now, he found himself struck at the remembrance of their shared conversation, at how she'd pulled from him what he shared with so few.

"Why not at least try," he said softly. "What have you to lose?"

She blinked. "Very well," she murmured bemusedly. "I'll try. Though," she continued with a sly smile, "if I'm to subject myself to something so distasteful to me, I think it only fair you do so as well." She motioned to the opposite side of the street and the tailor Lady Tesh had pointed him to.

He could not stop the chuckle that rattled up from his chest. She was a clever minx. "Very well. It's a deal then."

She smiled, and it was as if the sun had emerged from behind a cloud, bringing bright color to the world. Then she went inside, and the day seemed duller for it.

He stared after her for a time, unsettled. Then, with a frown, he turned and headed for the tailor.

* * *

Lenora pulled in a slow breath as they entered the Beak-head Tea Room. Small but cheerful, it was done up in bright blues and yellows, which made the interior a welcoming place even on the dreariest of days. Lenora could not count the times she had sat at one of the little round tables over the years with Margery and Hillram. So many memories crowded her mind, of laughing and gorging herself on sweets, sampling the lemonade the place was known for. And all the while the sea was a backdrop, its undulating waves licking at the fine golden sand of the beach beyond the chintz-bedecked bow windows.

She'd needed to come here, the place she'd first realized that Hillram's feelings for her were more than hers ever could be. His happy face flashed through her mind, eyes full of a love she couldn't return. She'd been worried then, over how his growing affection would affect their friendship. Now, however, the pain was sharp, so sharp she nearly gasped before firmly shutting the memory up tight again.

Just then the proprietress spotted them. The young woman smoothed her long braid over one shoulder and hurried through the throng of customers. "Lady Tesh, this is a pleasure."

Lady Tesh inclined her head. "Good afternoon, Miss Peacham."

"And you've brought your granddaughter and Miss Hartley, who we have not seen in an age. Though I have not had the pleasure of seeing these gentlemen about town." She eyed Mr. Ashford with a good amount of curiosity and trepidation. And no wonder, for the man looked like the proverbial bull in a china shop, surrounded as he was by small round tables topped with all manner of delicate china and glassware.

And he was glaring at it all in the most ferocious manner. As Lenora watched, he transferred his gaze, which had been fixed in an outraged fashion on the closest stool, to Miss Peacham. The proprietress took a step back.

"Oh, come now," Lady Tesh said. "You know as well as I that the Beakhead is the epicenter of information on the Isle. You could not have failed to hear of my great-nephew and his friend."

"Of course!" Miss Peacham exclaimed. "It's an honor, gentlemen."

Mr. Ashford merely grunted. Mr. Nesbitt gave an elegant bow. "The pleasure is ours, ma'am. Can't wait to taste the fine wares you sell here. The smell is divine."

As Miss Peacham flushed with pleasure, Lady Tesh cleared her throat loudly. "I trust you have my table ready."

"Of course, my lady," Miss Peacham said with a warm smile. She led the way to a table larger than the rest, surrounded by sturdy chairs instead of the cushion-covered stools the rest of the patrons sat on. Pressed up to one of the front windows as it was, the table gave a commanding view of the street and the beach beyond.

"You know what I like," she said to Miss Peacham. "Bring a selection of sweets, and your lemonade as well," she added. As the woman moved away, Lady Tesh turned to Mr. Nesbitt. "You shall not find finer pastries on the Isle. Isn't that right, Margery?"

As the three of them fell into easy conversation, Lenora took a quick glance at Mr. Ashford. He was staring out the window, seemingly lost in thought. Thinking he had no wish for conversation, she adjusted her skirts. The stiff material never did lie right. She thought briefly of the lovely burnt orange silk ball gown she had agreed to having made up while at the modiste's. As well as the pale green muslin, and the printed calico.

It seemed Mr. Ashford's gentle urgings had done what years of demands on Lady Tesh's part had been unable to do. And to her utter shock, she had enjoyed it.

Would wonders never cease?

Mr. Ashford's voice broke into her meandering thoughts. "You never drink tea."

She looked his way and blinked. "No. No, I don't."

"Why?"

Her lips quirked, for he looked utterly confused. "Is it a crime to dislike tea?"

"No, it's just..." His words trailed off, and he flushed.

Really, it should not be so adorable for a man to color so. On him, it was like a chink in the armor he constantly showed to the world, the soft underbelly.

It showed he was too human. Something that should not fascinate her as much as it did.

"You were going to say that most women like tea, weren't you?"

His lips twitched. "I admit, I was. And I'm generalizing again, aren't I?"

She didn't know it was possible to be made dizzy by the mere ghost of a smile. But that small quirk at the corner of his lips, the way his eyes crinkled at the corners, threw her completely off balance. For a breathless moment, she didn't know which way was up. Taking herself firmly in hand, she said with mock seriousness, "Yes, you are."

"I apologize."

She inclined her head in what she hoped was a regal fashion. "At least you're learning from your mistakes."

His eyes warmed with approval. "But why don't you like tea?"

She shrugged. "I haven't a clue, only that I can't stand the taste of it. But it seems it's quite unpatriotic of me, if the responses I receive are anything to go by. There are times I force myself to drink the stuff just to stave off comments."

"You should never force yourself to do other than what pleases you."

"Says the man who is staying with Lady Tesh against his will."

She had begun to grow so comfortable with him that the words tumbled out without her meaning to. She gasped, her hand flying to her mouth. "Oh, I'm so sorry. That was incredibly rude of me."

But he only shrugged. "My mother wished it."

Which wasn't an answer she expected. "Your mother?"

His shoulders stiffened, his features tightening. She thought for a moment he wouldn't answer. Which would only serve her right. She shouldn't pry.

Yet he barely paused before speaking. "It was my mother's final wish that I stay with Lady Tesh."

"I'm sorry about your mother."

He blinked as if not sure what to make of her condolences. "Why? She was nothing to you."

"No, but she was something to you. And I understand your pain."

He was silent, though disbelief was plain in his raised brow and pursed lips.

"Perhaps I don't know the whole of it, could never comprehend what you've gone through," she conceded. "But I, too, lost my mother when I was quite young. They would not let me see her, but I snuck in regardless." She swallowed hard, looking down to her lap. "I remember her thrashing in pain, remember the paleness of her skin...how she didn't even know I was there." She returned her gaze to his. "I would have given anything to have brought her relief."

Recognition flared in his eyes, an acknowledgment and understanding. "I'm sorry," he murmured.

She gave a nervous laugh, her gaze falling to her lap again. "I don't know why I told you that. I don't talk about her. To anyone."

His finger beneath her chin startled her, so much that she didn't object when he lifted her gaze back to his.

"I'm glad you told me."

She gave him a tremulous smile. "I'm glad, too."

He returned the smile. And for a moment, she felt as if they were in their own private bubble, the troubles of the world forgotten.

Just then the refreshments arrived. Platters of jellied fruits, custards, caramels, and small iced cakes were set before them, along with steaming tea and coffee, and the requested lemonade. And, of course, the ices. In nearly every color of the rainbow, they glistened in their little glass bowls, cool and sweet and tempting.

Lenora's mouth watered. Apparently Mr. Ashford felt the same way, for his eyes widened as he took in the glory of the spread. He licked his lips.

Lenora went hot all over. She longed suddenly for one of the ices to cool her heated skin, just barely stopping herself from snatching the closest one and gulping it down.

"This is magnificent," Mr. Nesbitt said. "I've never seen the like."

Margery spoke up. "Are you fond of sweets, Mr. Nesbitt?"

"I like them well enough. Though Peter here is mad for them."

All eyes swiveled to Mr. Ashford. Well, Lenora admitted ruefully, as her gaze had already been fastened quite firmly to the man, she didn't have to do any swiveling. And so she didn't miss the small tightening of his lips, nor the furious glare he shot his friend.

"I'm not *mad* for them," he growled.

"You are," Mr. Nesbitt insisted. "I've never seen anyone demolish a pumpkin pudding the way this man does. Or candied almonds. Good God, he gorges himself on the stuff."

Lenora was fascinated. If there was anything she had not expected, it was for gruff Mr. Ashford to be enamored of sweets. It was one more chink in the armor, one more piece of the puzzle falling into place, giving her a clearer picture of the true man behind the mask.

Though he'd begun to show her a bit of his true self in the past day, hadn't he?

Mr. Ashford, however, was not happy with his friend's teasing if his hands were anything to go by. Rough and tanned and scarred, so out of place in these delicate, feminine surroundings, they were balled up tight on the pristine white tablecloth until they nearly shook, the knuckles white.

"Mr. Nesbitt," she said hurriedly, cutting off whatever the man had been about to say, "I suspect you've had the pleasure of sampling foods we're unfamiliar with here in England. Won't you tell us of them?"

The distraction worked, for after a moment of surprise, the man smiled. As everyone helped themselves to the bounty of treats before them, he launched into a detailed recitation of all the wonders that America had to offer.

Beside her, Mr. Ashford's hand began to relax, the taut muscles loosening.

Lenora let out a surreptitious breath of relief. She tried telling herself that her intervention was merely to preserve Mr. Nesbitt's face, for Mr. Ashford had looked ready to dive across the table to pummel his friend senseless. Yet as she passed Mr. Ashford a bit of almond cheesecake and caught sight of the almost vulnerable look in his eyes as he murmured his thanks, she knew that was not it at all. Concern for Mr. Ashford had driven her, and nothing else.

Why did she feel the need to protect this man, someone who looked as if he could have bested Napoleon and his army with one hand tied behind his back? She hadn't the faintest idea. But as he took a bite of the creamy concoction, and his eyes closed in bliss, she found that she would do it again, and gladly.

Chapter 12

The following morning, Lady Tesh joined the small party for the morning meal. Normally, the viscountess preferred to breakfast in the comfort and solitude of her own room before joining them. So it was a sight indeed to see her, fully dressed in brilliant purple, a feathered turban perched upon her head, hands heavy with all manner of jewels, feeding small pieces of ham to Freya.

Lenora was an early riser herself, and so she found only humor in the colorful, energetic display the woman presented. As she looked across at Mr. Ashford, however, she could tell by the way he squinted at his great-aunt, his eyes tight at the corners, that he could well do without the added assault on his senses.

"Peter," Lady Tesh called out, eyeing the man's sparsely filled plate, "you simply must try the sausage." She speared one such plump item, the tines of her fork piercing the casing and sending juice streaming across the pristine table.

"Thank you," Mr. Ashford managed, lifting his steaming cup of coffee, "but I'm well supplied for my needs this morning."

"Nonsense," Lady Tesh declared. "A strapping man

like you needs sustenance. Lenora," she said in strident tones, "tell my great-nephew that he needs proper sustenance for today's expedition."

Lenora blinked, her fork suspended halfway to her mouth. The bit of egg on the end of it quivered as all eyes swiveled her way. "I'm sorry, where are we going today then?"

"Why, the Elven Pools, of course."

"The Elven Pools," Lenora repeated blankly.

"Certainly. You mentioned you wanted to visit your old haunts. And today is the perfect day for the Elven Pools. Just look at that sky." She pointed her fork at the window, the sausage still speared on the end. Lenora eyed it with fatalistic horror, certain it would go flying off the end any minute to pelt Mr. Nesbitt, who sat at her side, in the face.

The image was so ludicrous that she nearly laughed.

Margery spoke then, distracting her from her musings. "Oh, Gran, what a splendid idea. Lenora and I haven't been in an age. Not since..." Her voice trailed off, and she turned dismayed eyes to Lenora.

It took Lenora a moment to understand her friend's reaction. When she did, however, it hit her with stunning force. A loud clatter filled the room. She stared down at her fork blankly, the silver tines winking up at her beside the now chipped plate.

Quick as a wink, a footman was at her side, sweeping the damaged tableware away, replacing it with a fresh plate piled high with all her favorites. But at the sight of the steaming eggs, the scone, the plump sausage, her stomach flipped in protest.

"I say," Mr. Nesbitt spoke into the agonized hush, "are you ladies well? You both look as if you've seen a ghost."

An apt description. For the specter of that long-ago day hung over Lenora now, all the more powerful because of her forgetfulness...and her desperate wish to have kept it forgotten.

"I'm afraid," Margery murmured, "that when last we were at the Elven Pools, my cousin Hillram proposed to Lenora."

There was a thick silence, broken only by a low curse from Mr. Ashford.

Everyone looked his way, including Lenora.

"What was that, Peter?" Lady Tesh demanded.

The man flushed. "Burned my tongue," he muttered. "On the coffee."

Lenora could not fail to notice, though, that he was quick to down the rest of the beverage. Nor did she fail to see that his cool blue eyes were focused with disturbing intensity on her.

"Gran," Margery said low, "perhaps the Elven Pools can wait for another day."

"Nonsense," the older woman declared, feeding Freya some egg directly from her fork before spearing a second piece. "The anticipation of such a thing will only make the going worse."

"Then mayhap we might forgo the trip altogether," her granddaughter ventured.

Lady Tesh turned outraged eyes on Margery. "Forgo the Elven Pools? Do you forget the importance they played in the love affair between Synne and Ivar?"

"Of course not, Gran. And I know your records of the history of the Isle are important to you. Perhaps, in this case, I can take over the illustration duties—"

Lady Tesh slashed a hand through the air, cutting Margery off. Unfortunately it was the one holding her fork. Fortunately Mr. Nesbitt was quick, and managed to duck out of the way of the bit of egg that came flying off the end. This time, however, Lenora didn't have the slightest temptation to laugh.

"I won't hear another word about it. It's Lenora or nothing."

When Margery looked ready to continue the fight, Lenora held up a hand. "It's all right, Margery."

"Oh, dearest, are you certain?"

She forced a smile and nodded. "Of course. I *want* to go to the pools. We had so many lovely times there; it will be good to return."

Which was a blatant lie. She hadn't fooled Margery, if the dubious look she gave her was any indication, but her friend was too sweet natured to force the issue.

Blessedly the meal was quickly over. Lenora could no longer maintain an air of calm contentedness. She *knew* that she needed to visit the pools and face the memories of Hillram that were wrapped up in them. That was what she had come to the Isle for, after all, to face her guilt over his death. But thus far she'd done an abysmal job of it.

She pressed a fist into her midsection as she climbed the stairs to change. But ah, God, how she wished she never had to remember.

* * *

Of all the things Peter never expected to feel in his lifetime, jealousy over a dead man had to top that list.

He kept to the rear of their small party as they trudged through the copse of trees leading to the famed Elven Pools. Their footsteps were overloud on the well-worn dirt path, the sound echoing off the thick foliage. A crow called from the depths of the trees, the harsh cry echoed by its brethren overhead, an apt companion to their morose group.

In front of him, Miss Hartley stumbled on the path. He tensed, ready to drop his bundle of art supplies and jump to her aid. She quickly righted herself, however, and continued on after Quincy and Mrs. Kitteridge. Her steps, he noted, were slower than normal, her typical quickness made sluggish by her recent upset.

He would never, for the rest of his days, forget the look of shock that had etched itself into her face when her dead fiancé had been mentioned. He had at once wanted to comfort her and berate Mrs. Kitteridge and Lady Tesh for bringing it up at all.

There had been a time when Peter had resented Hillram. The boy had never been forced to come crawling for even the smallest scrap. While Peter had sat huddled in his cramped attic room, wiping sweat from his mother's clammy brow, Hillram had lived a life of ease and comfort.

Now, however, Peter was to have everything the duke's son had been destined from birth to receive. Yet even in death, the man was besting him. For in all the years that had passed, Peter had never felt as envious of Hillram as he did now, knowing he was the recipient of Miss Hartley's thoughts and tears and heart.

He breathed in deeply, the heavy saltiness of the ocean mingling with heady pine and rich earth. It made no sense that he should despise a man simply for being loved by Miss Hartley, for he certainly had no intention of loving her himself. He would leave the Isle free of entanglements, would never marry and carry on the Ashford name, would let the title die with him. He had never wished to marry, and so there would be no sacrifice in it. There was little he wanted less than the necessary closeness of such a relationship, or to bring a child into a union that would no doubt sour before the first year was through.

A strange ache started up in his chest. He frowned, fighting the urge to rub at the spot. That could not be regret he was feeling at the thought of leaving. He was determined in his plans, and would be happy to turn his back on the place when the time came.

Yet when a stray shaft of sunlight caught in Miss Hartley's golden hair, drawing his eyes and making his heart skip a beat, he rather thought it would not be as easy as he'd hoped. Mrs. Kitteridge spoke then, the only one who seemed inclined to do so. Or perhaps she was merely following Lady Tesh's orders to spoon-feed him every morsel of family history she could manage in some misguided attempt to make him feel a connection to the Isle.

"The Norsemen believed in the existence of elves, thus the name of the pools." She sounded like a governess addressing her charges, though her voice warbled with strain. "It's thought there were two types of elves. The darker ones were earth dwellers, quite possibly akin to trolls. The lighter ones resided in some elf world, though its name eludes me..."

Her voice trailed off, as if swallowed up by the very shadows that embraced them.

"Álfheimr."

Miss Hartley's soft voice drifted into the heavy atmosphere, the strange word rolling off her tongue, sending a shiver up his spine.

Mrs. Kitteridge looked back over her shoulder at her friend. "What was that, dearest?"

"Álfheimr," Miss Hartley said again, stronger this time. "That's the name of the elf world in Old Norse. Actually the name literally means 'elf home' or 'elf world,' as it derives from the Old Norse word for elves, 'alfar.'"

Just then the tree line opened up, a small valley spreading out before them of low, craggy rocks and lush vegetation. A wide river cut through it.

They stepped from the shadows of the trees, and it was as if the dark spirits that had held them in thrall through the morning fell away. Mrs. Kitteridge and Quincy walked a bit faster, heading for the river, their cheerful voices carrying on the air. Peter followed, yet kept his attention on Miss Hartley. The sun—or perhaps it had been the retelling of the old Norse history—had appeared to affect her as well. She stood a bit straighter, walked a bit quicker. So focused was he on Miss Hartley he didn't immediately notice that the rest of their party had stopped at the riverbed. The path ended there, taking up again on the far bank. And in between lay the river, fast moving and clear as glass. Large boulders had been placed across the width, their tops worn flat by centuries of use, though the faint gouges still remained of some long-dead craftsman's chisel.

"I do hope you gentlemen are not fond of your boots," Mrs. Kitteridge said as Peter and Miss Hartley joined them, "for this is where we cross. But take care, for the stones can be slippery, and your boots will be the least of your worries should you lose your footing."

Quincy grinned and leapt onto the first of the boulders before turning to assist Mrs. Kitteridge. That lady chuckled, accepting his hand as she picked her way across with more care. Soon they were safe on the far bank and heading up the gentle rise on the other side.

Miss Hartley contemplated the water as it gurgled merrily along. Peter briefly wondered if she was remembering crossing these very stones with her sweetheart, before he brutally squashed that thought.

"I'll be happy to assist you across," he said, in truth anything but. For he certainly had no wish to grasp that slender, graceful hand in his rough one, to feel that now familiar electrical jolt at the contact.

His suggestion seemed to jerk her back to herself. "Thank you, but no. I've made this trek a thousand times." She took her skirts in one hand, lifting the hem halfway up her calves before stepping with certainty onto the first rock.

Peter just stopped himself from staring at the slender bit of stocking-clad leg, the delicate ankle, the small feet encased in sturdy little half boots. To distract himself as he followed, placing his foot firmly on the smooth top of the boulder before heaving himself fully onto it, he said, "You seem to know a good deal of Norse mythology."

She gave him a wry smile before turning back to the task at hand. One arm held out for balance, she quickly moved to the next rock. "It's not something I was able to utilize while in London. I feared I'd forget it all. I'm glad to know such useless information is still rattling about in my brain."

Hefting her art supplies more securely under his arm, he eyed her back as he moved behind her, his steps shadowing hers as she found the driest portion of the stone. "Why wouldn't you need it in London?"

She was silent so long, he thought she would not answer. Finally they reached the opposite bank. She stopped in the middle of the path and turned to him.

"A gently bred woman is not expected to know such

information, much less flaunt it," she replied with a sad smile.

He frowned. "They don't allow a woman to speak with an informed mind in London?"

Her lips quirked at the corners, a spark of real amusement seeming to take shape in her eyes before disappearing like mist. "No, they don't, and any woman that dares would be labeled a bluestocking. Sir Alfred Hartley's only daughter would never be labeled as such."

His stomach clenched. That her own father would refuse to allow her to speak with any semblance of intelligence was a ridiculous notion. Yet he could see from the solemn surety on her face that it was only too true.

"Well," he said, "you don't have to worry about such antiquated ways of thinking with me."

Her face lightened at that, the delicate features transforming. And he nearly lost his breath.

Blinking to break the spell her smile had cast on him, he cleared his throat and indicated the path. "Shall we?"

Her cheeks flushed with color. "Of course."

They walked on together, following the meandering path up. "But you haven't told me how you attained your knowledge," he pressed, desperate to fill the silence and distract himself from his acute awareness of her at his side.

"You may have noticed that Lady Tesh has a deep interest in the history of the Isle."

"One might even call it an obsession," he muttered.

Miss Hartley chuckled. "She was born on the Isle, at Danesford, and moved to Seacliff after her marriage. She has spent her entire life here. In all that time, she's managed to acquire an impressive collection of books on the histories that have helped shape the Isle. Among those are several on ancient Norse mythology."

"You've read one?"

"No." She grinned up at him. "I've read them all. I'm afraid Lady Tesh's passion has proved to be contagious. I came here often as a girl, staying for months at a time. She would tell the most fantastic stories to Margery and me. I devoured all I could regarding the island's history, Norse mythology, anything really that kept the magic of it alive."

He stared down at her, transfixed by the sudden joy that illuminated her. It made her fairly glow, until he fancied for a moment that she was one of those elves of light she'd spoken of, come down from the elf world to bless him with her presence.

They crested the hill. He dragged his gaze from her, desperate to return to the ordinariness of the world once more. The sight that met his eyes, however, only pulled him further into the magical spell that had been cast over him.

"Mr. Ashford," she murmured softly, "welcome to the Elven Pools."

Chapter 13

*L*enora couldn't count the times she had visited the Elven Pools. There was a peace about the place that drew her time and again. It was here she had first found her passion for art, here she had strengthened the bonds of friendship with Margery over hundreds of picnics and imaginary battles and swims in the chill water.

And here she had found a friend in Hillram. Until he had gone and done the last thing she wanted and proposed to her.

Sighing, she started down the path that led to the base of the pools, only realizing after several seconds that Mr. Ashford didn't follow. She peered back at him, still atop the rise. The wonder on his face struck her to her very core. Of course he would be overwhelmed by the beauty of it. Hadn't she when first she'd clapped eyes on it, following like a duckling behind Lady Tesh, her hand clasped firmly in Margery's? She returned to his side, looking down at the scenery, trying to see it through his eyes.

Like steps, the pools were staggered down the hillside, each one bigger than the last, fed from the one before it by meandering trails of water that bounced and gurgled merrily over the rock. As lush as the vegetation had been on the way here, the area around the pools was craggy, pure stone with a smattering of plant life, the bowls of the pools carved into the rock over millennia of rushing water. Yet despite its sparseness—or perhaps because of it—the pools were things of heart-wrenching beauty. Every stone and rock that lay slumbering beneath the translucent surface was visible, colored in vibrant shades of turquoise, azure, emerald, indigo. The tinkle of a dozen miniature waterfalls sounded in the air, lovelier than the finest music, more melodic than a symphony orchestra.

"I didn't know anything like this existed in the world."

Instead of shattering the moment, Mr. Ashford's deep, rumbling baritone enhanced the magic of it.

"It's lovely, isn't it?"

"More lovely than I imagined."

She smiled. Here was the Mr. Ashford she was coming to know, without all his bluster. He looked at her then, his eyes warm, full of an emotion she had never witnessed in him. She took a hesitant step closer, overcome by the sudden urge to reach out, to place her hand on his cheek...

"Lenora," Margery's voice reached them, "where shall we set up the easels?"

Lenora gasped, stepping back from Mr. Ashford. He looked equally shaken. Clearing his throat, he gave a few deep *harumphs* and, holding her supplies in front of him like a shield, hurried down the incline with long, strong strides.

Her face hot, she fought for composure as she followed him. It took her some seconds to find her voice. "I do believe the best view will be up that small bluff," she called out to Margery, trying with all her might to keep her tone even—and her eyes from Mr. Ashford's backside. What in Hades was wrong with her?

By the time Lenora joined them, Margery was busy directing the men in the placement of the easels.

"So," Mr. Nesbitt said as he stepped back from his handiwork and looked out over the landscape, "these are the pools where fair Synne seduced a Viking lord."

"She didn't seduce anyone," Lenora said, shrugging into her smock and turning about so Margery could do up the tapes. "As a matter of fact, she wanted nothing to do with Ivar."

Mr. Nesbitt raised an inky brow. "Really?"

"Oh, yes." Lenora smoothed the front of the smock as Margery finished, then turned to help her friend on with hers. "You must remember, of course, that a mere century before, the Norsemen had invaded the island and stole from the monastery. People were killed, perhaps some of Synne's own ancestors. She wouldn't feel kindly toward Ivar and his ilk."

"Yet she grew to love him."

Mr. Ashford's voice was soft, almost contemplative. And it did strange things to her insides.

Lenora cleared her throat, focusing on unpacking her paints as she answered him. "Yes, she did."

A thick silence fell, broken only by the call of a bird and the soft clatter of their supplies as they finished laying everything out.

It was Mr. Nesbitt who spoke, his cheerful voice banishing the tension in the blink of an eye. "Come along, ladies. You can't keep us in the dark after teasing us with so little."

Lenora smiled, looking to Margery. "Do you think they can handle it? It is a love story, after all."

Her friend's brown eyes twinkled merrily. "It serves them right if we leave them squirming."

Laughing, Lenora peered over her shoulder at the men. Mr. Nesbitt had found an obliging rock and was lounging on it now, his long legs crossed at the ankles, his face full of good cheer. Mr. Ashford stood with his large feet planted wide, his thick arms crossed over his chest, looking as forbidding as he had when he'd first arrived on the Isle.

But what was that surreptitious little glance he gave her? Was the man waiting for her to speak?

Smiling to herself, she turned forward, adjusting the brim of her bonnet. "Synne snuck away from the village every chance she could. She came here to the Elven Pools often. It was her safe haven, and being hidden as it is, the Vikings hadn't found it."

"Until Ivar came upon her," Margery chimed in.

"And spied her bathing," Lenora added with a grin.

"Lenora!" Margery said on a gasp, laughter threaded through the shock.

"What? It's the truth. Your grandmother used to tell us as much when we were children."

"It's different now," her friend mumbled, her face flaming as she poked through her pencils. "You're an unmarried woman, and there are men present."

"Just think of us as one of the girls," Mr. Nesbitt called out.

Again Lenora's gaze found Mr. Ashford. *Not likely.*

"I daresay Synne was not pleased to be caught *in flagrante delicto*," Mr. Nesbitt prompted.

"She was furious," Lenora answered. "From all accounts, she pulled a knife on him."

"Where, I wonder, did she hide the knife?" Mr. Nesbitt drawled.

As Lenora and Margery choked on their laughter, Mr. Ashford growled low.

"Quincy." The warning in his voice was clear.

"Oh, don't tell me you weren't wondering."

"That's beside the point," he answered through his teeth. "There are ladies present."

"Very well." Mr. Nesbitt bowed his head in their direction. "My apologies, ladies. Please forgive me my barbaric Americanized ways. You were saying that Synne pulled a knife magically from the air...?"

Lenora fought back a grin. She had a feeling Mr. Ashford would not appreciate it in the least. "She went after Ivar, but he refused to fight back, though she drew blood. That tree there"—she pointed with her pencil to a tree not far from the largest of the pools, the only one that had dared to root itself on the craggy rock—"was said to have grown from the place where his blood was spilled."

"But he didn't die," Mr. Ashford said, his voice stern, as if he were berating her for the story taking such a turn. "You said yourself they fell in love here at the pools."

"No, he didn't die," Lenora assured him. Was it her, or did the man give a sigh of relief, his massive shoulders relaxing some?

Her heart twisted with...what? Affection? Flustered, she cleared her throat. "Synne realized her mistake in wounding him. If he died, her entire family would be made to pay. She quickly set about tending to his wound right there on the bank of the pool. Folklore says the magical properties of the pools healed him, bringing him back from the brink of death."

"By then, of course, Ivar was completely smitten with Synne," Margery added. "He never once revealed what she'd done, he was that in love with her." She smiled at Lenora.

"Yes, he was," she murmured. She was silent for

a moment, thinking of the great brute Ivar, his heart snagged by small, ferocious Synne, protecting her even as she hated him so. "She didn't trust that he wouldn't reveal her secret, of course. She visited him day after day, demanding he tell her what he wanted in exchange for his silence."

"And each day he told her the same thing, that he wanted only her heart," Margery said with a small, happy sigh.

"Only her heart?" Mr. Nesbitt mumbled. "Not even a kiss? Not sure those Norsemen were the most intelligent of creatures."

"Quincy," Mr. Ashford growled again.

"When he was well enough, he asked to join her at the pools," Lenora said, ignoring the small exchange. "She always refused. Until one day she didn't.

"And though you may think the worse of him for it, Mr. Nesbitt," she added, "he didn't so much as steal a kiss. He won fair Synne with his conversation and his company. And each day she grew to love him more than the last. Until finally she was the one to ask him for a kiss. And that, as they say, was that."

"He had a beautiful maiden begging him for a kiss?" Mr. Nesbitt stroked his chin. "Well then, perhaps Ivar wasn't such an idiot after all."

Mr. Ashford let loose another growl, like thunder echoing through the small valley.

"Lady Tesh did say late morning was the best light for painting the pools," he grumbled, shooting his friend a long-suffering look. "Perhaps we'd best get to it then."

Ah, yes, the painting. For a moment, Lenora had been so wrapped up in the story of Synne and Ivar that she had forgotten Lady Tesh's reasons for sending them there—and her own reasons for needing to visit the place.

Hillram. His face swam up through the murky depths of her memories, earnest, full of love as he'd proposed. Guilt flared with it, and a pain so acute, she nearly gasped. Shaking her head, she pushed the image away. First, painting, she told herself desperately. Once that was out of the way she could face her remembrances. Squaring her jaw, Lenora turned to her paper and lifted her pencil.

The lines came without conscious thought, the tip of the pencil flowing across the parchment with the same certainty of the water that flowed over the rocks below. Here was the fluid line of water meeting boulder, there the graceful arch of a waterfall. Soon a precise sketch was laid out.

But all the while she sensed Mr. Ashford behind her, watching her. And suddenly the image before her wasn't enough.

She saw in her mind what it could be: the swirl of movement under the water's surface, the mix of color like in a sorcerer's cauldron, as if the pools were alive with magic. There was a rock that resembled the craggy face of a troll. Beside it, a sparsely leafed plant, stretching up for the heavens, drinking in the warming rays of the sun.

The desire to capture that scene washed over her with frightening force, years of denying that part of herself quickly transforming it into a wave that crashed over her head, nearly drowning her in sensation. Fighting against the pull of it, she gasped and stepped back. Her pencil fell from her fingers to clatter to the stones at her feet, a harsh sound in the still peace of the place.

"Lenora, are you well?"

The familiar sound of Margery's voice grounded Lenora. She managed a wan smile.

"Of course I'm fine. Just a hand cramp is all," she lied.

Margery frowned. "Perhaps we'd best take a break for a few minutes before we add paint."

"Yes," Lenora mumbled, "perhaps you're right."

As Margery moved off to see to her things, Lenora hugged her arms about her middle and looked out over the pool. The force of her desire to draw what was deeper than the surface still thrummed inside her. And it frightened her witless. After three years of being denied, it seemed to have grown into a wild thing, a feral beast that demanded attention. She could not unleash it again.

"Miss Hartley, your pencil."

Again that electric jolt as Mr. Ashford's deep voice sounded in her ear. She looked down at the pencil he held in front of her, noticing the way his strong fingers gripped the thin wood, at the play of muscles and tendons beneath the sun-darkened skin. His knuckles were scarred, the nails blunt and painfully short.

She took the pencil from him, the remnants of warmth from his skin on the wood seeping into her and grounding her. "Thank you."

He stood at her side, silent. Finally he said, "Perhaps I'd best go after them."

Blinking in confusion, Lenora looked up. Margery and Mr. Nesbitt had walked off a way, no doubt to explore one of the many pools. As she watched, they kneeled down to inspect something, disappearing from view behind an outcropping of rock.

"Damnation, I told him to take care," Mr. Ashford bit out.

"You worry about Margery?" She gave a small, humorless laugh. "You may rest assured, Margery is quite safe with him."

"You don't know Quincy."

"No. I do, however, know Margery. And I can say with utmost certainty that she isn't affected in the least by your friend's charms."

"How can you be so certain?"

She gave a small sigh. "The love my friend had, and still has, for her late husband is uncommonly strong. She mourns him deeply, though you may not know it looking at her. She's as loyal as they come and will not betray his memory by allowing herself to be seduced by a rake, if you pardon my calling Mr. Nesbitt such."

"No offense taken, for that's just what Quincy is."

Lenora laughed softly.

Margery and Mr. Nesbitt popped into view again, working their way over the rocks to the next small pool.

"How did he die?"

"Margery's husband?" Lenora kicked at a small stone with the toe of her half boot. "At Waterloo. He wasn't supposed to have gone off to war. They'd been married a mere six months before he bought his commission. I never did learn why he insisted on going. Margery doesn't talk of it."

"And she won't love again?"

"No," Lenora said.

"And you?"

Lenora looked at Mr. Ashford, stunned by the soft question. He seemed equally shocked.

"Please," he muttered, "forget I asked that."

As if she could. The question preying on her mind now, however, was *why* he'd asked her. Flustered, she bent down, picked up a smooth rock from the ground, and chucked it out over the water. It fell with a splash, the pale blue of the disturbed water shining like diamonds in the sunlight for the briefest moment.

"And so this is where Hillram proposed to you."

She cast him a startled glance. He was frowning at the lone tree in the clearing, as if highly offended by its presence. When his eyes found hers, they were solemn, and almost gentle.

"You don't have to tell me about it if you don't wish to," he murmured low.

She was tempted not to. Mr. Ashford had known pain and would understand if she wanted to keep her own private.

Yet she found to her shock she wanted to tell him. Here was someone who didn't know Hillram, who wouldn't look at her with pity, thereby increasing her guilt tenfold.

But more than that, she felt a connection to this man, one much stronger than she'd ever expected.

She took a deep breath, letting the memory through, carefully probing it for pain, like a toothache. It was there, but so far bearable. "Yes, he did," she replied hesitantly, "by that rock. We'd come here for a picnic, the last one of the summer before the weather turned. He dropped to one knee on the bare stone. I was worried for his trousers but he laughed. He told me that starting our life in a place so dear to his family's history would guarantee our future happiness..." Her voice trailed off and she clasped her hands together tightly, vaguely aware of Mr. Ashford's warmth by her side. It gave her comfort, and the strength to look deeper into the memory.

She'd known the proposal was coming, of course, and had dreaded it. As the day of her departure approached, she'd begun to hope she would escape it. But then he'd asked her to go to the pools, and she'd known she wouldn't escape. She'd accepted him, seeing no other option, knowing it was expected of them, knowing it would make everyone, even her father, happy.

Everyone except her.

Mr. Ashford cleared his throat once, twice. "This place must inspire romance then."

She blinked. "I'm sorry?"

He waved a hand impatiently at the scenery. "The mythology surrounding this place, all that talk of elves, giving it a sense of magic. It certainly inspired romance between Synne and Ivar."

"I might have thought so, long ago," she murmured.

"You don't now?"

"No," she answered without hesitation.

His brows lowered. "Why?"

She let out a tense breath, wishing they were talking about anything but this. "Because, as much as I love the story of Synne and Ivar, what's romantic about it? He left her, with a small child to care for. And though she eventually married another, it's said she grieved for him the rest of her days."

He was silent for a moment, standing beside her, looking out over the pool. And then he observed, "Like *Romeo and Juliet*. People sigh over the love story. Yet it's the worst tragedy."

"Yes. Yes, exactly," she replied. "Mere children, in the throes of passion, acting without thinking. And they lost their lives because of it." She tilted her head, considering him. "But how do you know about such a tale?"

His lips quirked. "My mother insisted on it. She was a gentleman's daughter, though she fell far after my father lost nearly everything we owned."

His eyes closed briefly, as if in intense pain. Lenora longed to reach out, to lay a comforting hand on his arm.

Before she could, he straightened, seeming to physically shrug off the pall that had fallen around him. "But don't think you'll get out of it that easy," he said, spearing her with a stern glare. "You can't mention that Ivar left Synne and not finish the story."

She blinked. "Well, I can't tell you the story of his leaving when you're just learning how they fell in love."

He stared at her as if he couldn't quite believe she'd denied him. "Tell me what happened," he demanded, with all the officiousness of a Viking lord ordering a servant—Ivar come to life.

She managed to hide the smile that fought to break free. The man had spent the last week holding himself aloof. Yet now he was begging to hear the rest of it, like a child at bedtime.

"That, I'm afraid, is a story for another day."

He frowned. "You refuse to tell me?"

"Lady Tesh wouldn't approve."

"Hang Lady Tesh!"

She snorted in laughter, quickly clamping a hand over her mouth to hold it back. At his disbelieving glance, however, she lost the fight entirely. She doubled over, her arms going about her middle as she shook with the force of her mirth. She laughed as she hadn't in too many years, the sound of it rolling on and on, bouncing off the boulders and back at her.

Just as her laughter began to subside, he spoke.

"I don't see what's so blasted funny."

And she was off again. Tears streaming down her cheeks, she gasped for breath. Yet still the laughter came, the release of it incredibly freeing. It was as if something had been unlocked within her in the last minutes. As if, in sharing something of herself with

Mr. Ashford, a secret chamber of her heart had been opened.

As she wiped at her tears, clearing her vision, she noticed he was striding away from her.

Immediately she sobered and ran after him. "Mr. Ashford, I'm so sorry," she called to his retreating back. "I wasn't laughing at you. Well, I suppose I was, but it wasn't to make fun of you. Mr. Ashford, will you please slow down."

But the man made no indication he'd heard her. Frustrated—because, really, it wasn't as if she'd been able to control it—she reached out and grabbed hold of his arm.

He spun to face her. Her hand, firmly attached to his sleeve, went with it, throwing her off balance. She stumbled forward, landing with a soft exhale into his chest.

The wind seemed to hardly blow, the birds quieted their calls. Even Lenora's heart seemed to falter in her chest. She stared up at Mr. Ashford, her breath trapped. He stared back with wide eyes, so close she could see the darker blue outlining his iris, could hear the soft rasp of his breath. His arms came about her, bands of steel that anchored her to his chest. A chest that was amazingly firm and wide.

Her entire body flushed, awake with heat and life. Every inch of her thrummed, pressed from breasts to knee to his hard planes. So close, she could feel his heartbeat against the suddenly sensitive tips of her breasts.

Her fingers, trapped between their bodies, convulsed in the fabric of his coat. As if they could tether her against him, a port in the increasingly vicious storm of her emotions.

Though she feared that he was in truth the eye of the storm, the center of it all.

His mouth hovered above her own, his breath fanning warm over her face, drugging her senses until she could hardly see straight. She felt the mad urge to rise up on her toes, to press her lips to his…

He swallowed hard, his throat working. "Perhaps," he said, his voice quieter, more strangled than she had ever heard it, "it's time you returned to your painting."

Mortification reared up, blocking out the maelstrom of feelings that had momentarily overtaken her. She pushed away from him and stepped back. Feeling the loss of his arms as they fell away from her like a blow.

"Yes," she managed. "Of course."

Turning from him, she walked back to her easel. Forcing the doors closed once again on the Pandora's box of desire and tenderness—and mayhap something much more—that was churning inside her. Though she feared the lid no longer fit, and she would never be able to lock it again.

Chapter 14

"My dear Peter," Lady Tesh said several evenings later as they sat in her sitting room after dinner, "You're scheduled to revisit the tailor's tomorrow, correct?"

Lenora looked up from her embroidery quite against her will. Since the disturbing episode at the Elven Pools, she'd attempted to put some distance between herself and Mr. Ashford. For she couldn't shake the knowledge that she'd wanted to kiss him. If he hadn't spoken, she would have wrapped her arms around his neck, would have pressed her lips to his. Even now she felt the flush of need deep in her belly to do just that. She squirmed in her seat, praying not for the first time that her thoughts weren't written over her furiously heated face.

Mr. Ashford, too, seemed to be keeping his distance, seating himself far from her when possible, making sure they were never alone. A fact that should not have hurt as it did. But to her surprise, she found she missed the confidences they'd shared, the closeness they'd begun to have. The barriers he'd put up between himself and everyone else in the household seemed insurmountable.

Until now.

The man blanched. He dropped the book he had been

perusing, his hands going to his cravat, his long, calloused fingers mangling the fabric. "Er, yes. Yes, I am."

"Splendid," Lady Tesh said with a smile, her jeweled rings flashing in the candlelight as she scratched Freya behind the ear. "I look forward to seeing you in full formal wear."

Mr. Ashford's mouth tightened. It was plain as day he didn't feel the same.

Lenora frowned, looking down at her embroidery. She had forgotten about his trip to the tailor. It had been obvious that he'd been no more pleased than she by the prospect of buying clothing for the upcoming subscription ball. She recalled the night of Lady Tesh's dinner party, his discomfort in such a setting, his explanation that he left the socializing to Mr. Nesbitt. It occurred to her in that moment that he may have never attended a dance in his life.

Was it possible that he was nervous about having to attend such an event?

She glanced at him. Sure enough, a kind of panic had taken root in his typically cool eyes. His cravat hung limp now, but that didn't stop him from attempting to destroy it even further.

Forgetting her determination to stay as far from him as possible, she rose and went to him in his solitary corner. "Mr. Ashford, how are you liking your book? I'm looking for something new to read."

He jerked his gaze to her, no doubt startled by her sudden interest in a book he wasn't even holding any longer. "You're welcome to it," he said as she took a seat on the settee beside him, retrieving the book from his lap and handing it to her.

She looked it over as if it were the most interesting

thing she'd ever seen. In a soft aside, however, she said, "Do you know how to dance?"

"What?"

His voice was loud enough to carry. The other members of the group, all quietly immersed in their own pursuits, cast curious glances their way. Even Freya, who had been napping beside Lady Tesh on a plush pillow, opened one eye and gave them a censorious look.

"Please keep your voice down, Mr. Ashford," Lenora whispered, opening the book and holding it before them as if intrigued by the words on the page. "I don't want to inadvertently embarrass you. Do you know how to dance?"

Finally seeming to understand what she was about, he leaned close, his gaze fastened to the book she had brandished before them, and said out of the corner of his mouth, with obvious reluctance, "I do not."

"Would you like to learn?"

His eyes swung to her in shock. She indicated the book before them again with her eyes. He caught on, looking again to the open page. "I don't see that I have time to learn all the dances necessary. The ball is in three days."

"You don't need to learn them all, only one or two to get you by."

He snorted. "And who would we find to teach me at such a late date? You?"

"And why not?"

He stilled, then turned in his seat to look fully on her. She tried to motion again to the book, but he was apparently done with the ruse. "You would teach me to dance?"

She lowered the book to her lap. "Of course."

"Why?"

He seemed genuinely confused by her offer.

She smiled, hoping a bit of teasing would put him at ease. "Never fear, for you can pay me back later."

He didn't even crack a smile. But there was a definite change in his eyes, a slight crinkling at the corners, a warming of the cool blue that told her he acknowledged her ribbing, and even found it amusing. "And when are we to do these secretive dance lessons, Miss Hartley? For if you wish to keep from embarrassing me in front of the others, I don't know how we shall manage the lessons necessary to carry out such a thing."

She pursed her lips. That was a difficulty she hadn't considered. She either embarrassed him, or met with him in secret after the others went to bed.

The latter brought a sudden image into her mind, of them together in the concealing darkness of night, his arms about her, twirling to unheard music.

A tremor of pure heat worked over her skin, tingling along her limbs, condensing over the tips of her breasts. Pooling low in her belly.

He seemed to read her thoughts. His gaze fell to her lips, his eyelids growing heavy. "Will you meet me in the dead of night, Miss Hartley?" he murmured, the faint mocking in his voice doing nothing to hide the thickness beneath. "Will you risk your reputation to help me, a man who has taken your lost lover's place? Even you, for all your sweetness and light, cannot be that good."

The words stung. Yet beyond her hurt, she knew what he was trying to do. He was attempting to scare her off, to push her away. He might have succeeded, had she not noticed his tightly pressed lips, his clenched hands, all proof of the fear he was trying with all his might to hide beneath a rude façade. Though whether that fear was that she might accept or refuse, she didn't know.

But did it matter? She couldn't ignore the challenge of it, no matter that she knew better. Much better.

"Meet me tonight, Mr. Ashford, and you shall see what I dare to do."

* * *

That daring did not last the evening. In truth, it didn't last beyond ten minutes.

She should have told him to forget the whole thing. But he seemed to know she regretted her rash decision. The rest of the evening he cast her mocking glances, his golden brow raised, daring her to break and relent with her false show of bravado. That, and that alone, kept the steel in her spine, kept her resolve, however faltering, in place.

And now it was too late to back out.

She stood before the doors to the ballroom. The lantern in her hand shook, the light from the flame shivering, as if it, too, felt her trepidation.

Taking a steadying breath, she pushed against the door.

It swung open silently, revealing the great vastness of the space beyond, all bathed in pale blue moonlight. Except for the one patch of gold in the center, Mr. Ashford and his light shining like a beacon. He had placed the lantern on the ground, and it shimmered on the polished parquet floor like a pool of fairy dust.

As if she called out to him, he turned. His face was in shadow, though his eyes glinted in the faint light. He stood as still as a statue, waiting. And her body responded, like a puppet on a string, her feet carrying her to where he stood. Soon she was before him, so close she could have reached out and touched him. Her fingers itched to do so, her heart pounding in her chest, begging her to follow through.

"You came."

His voice was deep and rasping. A shiver ran through her and she nearly closed her eyes in pleasure. "I told you I would," she managed.

"I admit, I doubted it."

"You mean you wanted me to stay away," she shot back.

His lips quirked. "Perhaps." Suddenly his face darkened again. "It isn't wise for you to be here with me like this."

There was a flash of memory, that electric moment at the pools, her desire to kiss him nearly overwhelming her. She ruthlessly squashed it. But he was waiting for her reply. "You won't harm me," she finally said, surprised by the surety she felt. For all his size and strength and brusqueness, she had nothing to fear from this man.

Except your sanity, a small voice whispered in her head. *And perhaps your heart.*

Flustered, she took a hasty step back. He caught the movement, his eyes narrowing.

"Are you ready to start?" she asked with more bravado than she felt. "There's much to go over if you're to be at all comfortable dancing at the assembly rooms Friday. Unless," she continued tentatively, "you've changed your mind?"

"I have not," he replied.

She nodded brusquely, ignoring the surge of relief that filled her. "Very well then." Placing her lantern a distance from his, she stepped between the two glowing lights and beckoned to him. He came, though with obvious reluctance.

"The quadrille is made up of four couples in a

rectangular formation," she said, determined to keep this as businesslike as possible. "Your partner will stand to your right. We'll practice the part of the first couple."

He frowned down at her. "First couple?"

"Yes, the top couple."

"You're speaking gibberish, Miss Hartley."

She let out a sigh. "Your mother taught you Shakespeare. Did she never teach you dance steps?"

For the first time in the exchange, his stern expression faltered. "She did *try* to teach me. But I wasn't what you would call an exuberant pupil. Or even a willing one, to be honest." He cleared his throat. "I ran whenever she attempted that bit of my teaching."

Lenora felt the first stirrings of humor. "You ran?"

"Yes. Fairly bolted out the door, didn't return until well past nightfall. She finally gave up trying altogether."

"You didn't run from *Romeo and Juliet*, though."

"Yes, well, that's reading. And I quite like reading." When she continued to stare at him, he rolled his eyes heavenward. "It's one thing to immerse yourself in a book. It's quite another to be forced to hold your mother by the waist and twirl her around."

She couldn't help the smile that broke free, loosening something inside her, making her remember just why she had enjoyed spending time with him before the Elven Pools. Her mood vastly improved, she continued, "The top couple, or first couple, is the couple who begins the dance. The others follow. In this set, the couple across is the second couple. The one to your right is the third, and the one to the left is the fourth."

He nodded, his eyes traveling around the floor as if trying to see the imaginary couples in his mind's eye.

"First, face the inside of the square."

He took his place, staring forward, for all the world like a man facing a firing squad.

"Turn to me and bow." He did so while she curtsied. "Now bow to the lady on your left."

He turned and bowed to the imaginary woman, all the while mumbling, "This is the most ridiculous thing I have ever done."

"Then you're lucky I'm the only one here to witness it. For I assure you, I've had my share of embarrassments, and this in no way comes even close to them."

He looked at her, curiosity visible even in the dim light. He would welcome her confidence, just as he had before. Yet she couldn't. It was too fresh, that horrible sense of failure, the latest betrayal and her father's recriminations—and threats—hanging over her head.

Straightening her shoulders, she said, "Now we advance toward the second couple, then retire back to our positions."

He followed her instructions, moving at her side, his steps heavy and uneven.

"Do try to keep your steps light, and in time with the music."

"There is no music," he gritted.

"Ah, yes. Well, I can remedy that. Let's try it again, shall we?" She began to hum as they moved forward. His brow furrowed in concentration as he attempted to match his steps to hers, his head bobbing in time as they moved back.

And there he went, being adorable again. Did the man even realize he was doing it? But she couldn't let him distract her. "Now," she said, "you take my hand and we circle around the second couple."

He stilled, looking down at her hand extended in the air. "I take your hand?"

It was then she realized his lack of gloves. As well as her own. She thought of him taking her hand in his; of those large, strong, work-roughened fingers embracing her own, with nothing between them.

She swallowed hard. But she could not very well teach him to dance without their hands coming into contact. She simply had to deal with whatever sensations might bombard her.

"Yes," she said, a touch more hoarsely than before, "you must take my hand."

Was it her, or did a tremor run through him? No, certainly not. It must be the flicker of the lantern light.

Finally he reached out, took her fingers in a tentative grip.

Immediate heat shot through her, so intense she nearly gasped. His fingers tightened on hers. When she looked up at him, the flames from the lanterns burned in his eyes, doubling, until it appeared he was burning from the inside.

She swallowed hard, for a moment unable to speak. The darkness beyond their small pool of light made it feel as though they were the only two people in existence, nearly overwhelming in its intimacy.

Squaring her shoulders, determined to get this over and done with, she began her instructions. She ignored as best she could the urge to lean in closer as they linked hands for the double-handed promenade, tamped down on the desire to drag in the scent of him when they passed one another.

They ran through the dance several times, then shifted to a cotillion. At the end of nearly two exhausting hours, she guided him through the last steps of a minuet and stepped back, grateful for the distance between them.

"That dance is quite old-fashioned, but the master of ceremonies likes to do things right and start the ball with it." She moved toward her lantern, trying to keep her steps slow so she wouldn't betray her desperate desire to get away from him. "But it grows late, and I'm sure Lady Tesh will like us all to get into town bright and early tomorrow. Good night." Relief coursed through her as she curtsied and made to turn for the door. She was almost free, would be able to breathe again.

"What of the waltz?"

She froze, the lantern swinging in a wild arc as her feet skid to an abrupt halt. Without turning to face him, she said, her voice low, "You don't wish to learn the waltz."

"I assure you, I do."

There was something intimate in his tone. It worked over her skin, pimpling it with awareness. There went that tugging again, that invisible string that seemed to pull her to him no matter that her head didn't want to go. Desperate to escape before she lost the will to, she straightened her shoulders and tried once more, hoping that by imparting stiffness to her tone, he would understand that there would be no closeness between them— and that she would as well.

"I'm tired, sir, and it's late. I assure you, you'll do just fine with the dances I've taught you tonight."

"I wish to learn it."

But she was gaining control over herself now, tucking those errant, traitorous emotions back in their box. She took a deep breath, determined to leave.

Until…

"Please."

She could no more ignore that one word than she could stop the sun from rising in the morn.

As if in a trance, she turned to face him, moved toward him. In a few steps, she was before him again.

But though she longed to fall into his arms, there was still one small part of her that held on to logic, one bit that had not completely let go of all good sense.

"I don't know if this is wise," she whispered.

He stared down at her like a starving man, the fire in his eyes so much brighter than before, seeming to have been dredged up from the very depths of his soul. "To hell with wise," he rasped.

She drew in a shuddering breath as the last of her will evaporated like mist. But she couldn't move that last step, couldn't step off the edge and leap.

He did it for her, moving so close she could see the fine lines at the corners of his eyes. "Teach me."

She didn't know how the words came, her mouth was so dry. "Put your left hand at my waist."

He did as she instructed. His palm burned through the layers of her clothes.

"Now take my hand in your right."

In a moment, her fingers were in his grasp. "Like this?" he breathed.

She nodded, unable to look away from his face. "Yes."

His fingers flexed on her waist, tightened on her hand. He took a step closer.

She breathed in a deep, shuddering breath. His own scent of spice filled her, made her dizzy with longing. "That's a bit too close for this dance," she managed.

He moved even closer. "And this?"

This time the words barely emerged. "Much too close."

Closer again, until her breasts pressed into his chest, until she could feel the thrum of his heart beneath his linen shirt. "And this?" he whispered, before his mouth claimed hers.

Chapter 15

*H*e should have let her go. He'd known that from the second he'd opened his mouth to call her back. It had been torture enough being with her these past hours, wanting her and yet keeping himself aloof. It should have been a relief to be through with it all.

Yet when she'd turned to leave, he'd been filled by a panic so all-consuming, he'd reacted without thinking.

Now she was in his arms, and nothing had ever felt so right. Her lips were soft, giving beneath the pressure of his. She tasted of heaven, all sweetness and light, chasing away the darkness in his soul. Gone was the anger, the hate that had kept him going for so long. In its place was only need for her.

He cupped her cheek with his hand, felt the softness of her skin under his touch. The bones of her face were so fragile and fine, her hair like silk where it brushed his fingers. He deepened the kiss, urging her lips open, his every move careful, gentle, afraid to mark her with his roughness.

But she arched up into him, eager and frantic, and he felt the strength in her. Her fingers gripped tightly to his hair, the muscles of her back moved beneath his hands, lithe and powerful.

It was only when her tongue pushed through the barrier of his lips and touched his own, however, that the truth of her feelings came crashing down on him: she wanted him.

The realization drove him over the edge of sanity. He groaned and wrapped his arms about her, hauling her even closer, until there was not an inch of space between them. Their tongues sparred, clashed, her body pushing against his as if she couldn't get close enough.

But he needed more of her. He tore his mouth free, trailed his lips across her cheek to the sensitive spot beneath her ear, nipped her skin with his teeth before moving lower. She gasped, small sounds of surprise and pleasure escaping her lips. Her head fell back, offering him what he was so desperate to take.

But he couldn't. He pulled back, his chin dropping to his chest, his breath coming in hard pants. His hands crushed the delicate material of her gown and a soft curse broke free. What the hell was he doing? He was determined to remain unwed, to kill off the Ashford line, to destroy the dukedom. If he took Lenora as he so desperately wanted to, he would have to marry her. His honor would not let him do anything else.

A vision of that life rose up, being married to Lenora. Having her in his bed every night, enjoying her laughter and conversation every day. Raising a family with her, growing old with her.

The temptation of it stunned him. He might have jerked away from her, might have stumbled from the room with, if not his pride intact, at least with his heart unscathed.

If she hadn't whispered, "Peter."

He hadn't realized how much he wanted to hear his name on her lips, how desperate he was that she should see beyond "Mr. Ashford" to the person he was beneath. Proof positive that, no matter his wishes on the matter, she had already touched his heart.

But in this moment, with her in his arms, he couldn't bring himself to regret it.

His mouth came down open on the delicate place her neck met her shoulder. How could a woman taste like this, feel like this? She was like an angel come down from heaven, all stardust and sugar-spun clouds. He laved kisses over her collarbone, then lower, over the slight swell of her breasts at the edge of her gown. The skin there was so soft, he wanted to weep. She made a needy sound in her throat, rising up to meet his questing lips. He could so easily pull the bodice down, free her breast to his sight and touch.

He growled low, letting the sound of it ripple over her skin. She gasped in response, her fingers digging into the linen of his shirt, as if she would tear the material from him.

So much passion. He hadn't expected it from her, had never thought her capable of it. But it was here, boiling over in his arms, until he could hardly think straight.

"My God, I want you," he rasped, pulling back. Her eyes were closed, her face flushed.

It was then he saw the tears glistening on her cheeks. The trails of them winked in the lantern light, mocking him, berating him for his size, his roughness.

In an instant, he released her. She stumbled a step, righting herself. She was so damned beautiful standing there, her clothing rumpled, her mouth swollen from kisses. But his gaze was drawn to those tears. Proof that he should never have touched her, that he had no right to anything so lovely and pure and good.

Without a word, he turned and strode from the room, leaving the light behind him, letting the darkness of the house beyond swallow him up.

* * *

Lenora would never know how she made it to her room. Yet somehow she did, even managing to dress in her nightclothes, extinguish her light, and bury herself under her covers.

Sleep, however, wouldn't come. Nor would her mind pay heed to her demands that it not think of Peter. *Peter*. Yes, he could be nothing else to her now. No mere *Mr. Ashford* would do. In the space of an instant, his importance had shifted to something more. Much more.

But that wasn't true, was it? For the shift had begun before tonight, perhaps even from the first moment she'd stumbled into him and felt her world tilt even as he righted her. He had been working his way under her skin ever since, until it all coalesced into something hot and undeniable.

And with that came the memory of lips and hands, and the magic Peter had wrought on her.

Suddenly too hot, her skin too sensitive, Lenora threw back the covers. She focused on the sound of the waves outside her window, matching her breathing to them, trying to calm her body's reaction. But not even Mother Nature's power could dampen Peter's effect on her. His every touch, every caress, had pulled a response from her that had frightened her with its intensity.

More frightening, however, had been her willingness to surrender to him. She had wanted what he had to give— wanted it still—more than air to breathe. The emotions he had brought up in her were more powerful, more over-whelming, than anything she had felt before. Her body had not been able to contain it all, her tears falling with a sweet kind of relief.

Why he had turned from her, she would never know. But she could only be grateful. For she knew in her heart that she wouldn't have told him to stop. She would have given everything to him and more. A realization made all the worse knowing that she had never felt anything close to it for Hillram.

Eventually the sky began to lighten. By then her eyes were dry and itchy, the result of staring out the window all night long. Heaving a sigh, she rolled onto her back. Exhaustion sat heavily in her breast. She supposed she could close the drapes, bury herself under the covers, and claim a headache. She could stay in her room all day long.

And not have to face Peter and remember what they had done.

The idea was tempting.

But surely, with the coming dawn, the memory of last night would not have quite so much power over her. She would rise from her bed and face the day—and her feelings for Peter—so she could put it all behind her.

She threw back her covers, intent on finding a gown she could throw on quickly without having to call her maid. But after a cursory glance, she realized that the only dress that she could manage to do up herself was the one she had worn down to the ballroom the evening before.

The one she had kissed Peter in, which he had bunched his hands in while bombarding her with the most exquisite sensations imaginable.

She let loose a low growl, then stomped to where she had left her clothes draped over a chair. With quick, angry movements she donned them, then went to her dressing table to tug and pull her hair into a manageable braid. She refused to be cowed by what had transpired between them.

It was not until she had made her way downstairs and to the breakfast room, however, that she realized how early it was. The room had not yet been prepared for the morning meal, a lone chambermaid still sweeping the hearth. Hurrying out before the girl saw her, she chewed on her lip. What now? She was much too awake—and too determined to face what she had no wish to face—to return to her room.

Finally deciding that only a brisk walk would do, she pulled her shawl tight about her shoulders and made her way outside. The morning air was crisp, and heavy with moisture. She stopped on the front step, breathing in deeply, letting the faint mist of dew fill her lungs, taking in the scent of salt and sea. This Isle had been a place of refuge for her as a child, though she hadn't understood it at the time. Now, looking back, she saw how it had allowed her a freedom she hadn't had at home. There, she'd made sure to tread carefully, working hard every moment to be the daughter her father expected. On the Isle, however, she'd been encouraged to give her imagination free rein, and to explore that part of herself that she typically kept hidden away.

But though the place and the people in it were the same as ever, her youthful optimism was gone.

The realization sat heavily on her shoulders. She moved forward, heading across the drive and short lawn to the cliffs beyond. The wind came up from the ocean, made strong by the steep cliffs. It whipped her shawl about her, clawing at her hair until strands came free of her plait and slapped at her cheeks and neck. Stepping as close to the edge as she dared, she looked out over the roiling sea. It came up in sharp peaks, the white tops showing stark against the dark gray of the waters. A perfect accompaniment to the turmoil within her.

She wanted Peter. Even now, knowing he meant to leave in a little over a fortnight, she wanted him so badly, it hurt to breathe. For a moment, her willpower weakened, and she allowed herself to imagine him as he had been last night. When the maelstrom of emotions had carried her off, he had been the one thing grounding her. His arms about her, his lips on hers, had made her feel more alive, more herself, than she had in all the days and months before.

Sighing, she closed her eyes and raised her face to meet the wind, letting it carry the memory with it. The problem, of course, was that Peter was not a part of her world. No, he would eventually leave, and if she continued to care for him as she was, he would take her heart with him. And she would be left alone.

A familiar light step interrupted her thoughts; Margery had found her. She smiled. Perhaps not so alone after all.

"Dear heart, what are you doing out here?" Her friend stepped beside her and placed an arm about her shoulders.

Lenora opened her eyes and smiled into Margery's worried ones. "Just getting a bit of air."

But her friend didn't return the smile. "You couldn't sleep?"

"Not well, no."

"Was it Hillram?"

Guilt flared, that Margery's cousin had been the very last thing on her mind. She fought the urge to pull away. "No," she answered, admitting the small truth.

To her surprise, Margery nodded, as if she had expected such an answer. "Was it Mr. Ashford?"

Gaping at her, Lenora did pull back then. "What?"

"I've seen the way he looks at you. And you seem to like him as well. I didn't think much of it at first. But then last night, that strange conversation the two of you had in the drawing room. Now this morning he's gone and you're standing here by the cliffs, looking as lost as I've ever seen you."

"He's gone?"

She shouldn't have asked it. She knew it the moment the words left her lips.

The worried glint in Margery's eyes intensified. "Yes, he left not long ago, off riding, I believe. He appeared to be fleeing as if his life depended on it." She looked closely at Lenora. "Did something happen between the two of you last night after we all retired?"

"No!" Heat filled Lenora's face. She prayed Margery would attribute it to horror over the suggestion and not the true cause. "Why would you think such a thing?"

"I worry about you. Coming here hasn't been easy on you." She chewed on her lip, looking out over the churning sea below. Her body was tense where it met Lenora's, almost thrumming with agitation. "It was a mistake to come here. I shouldn't have suggested it. If I hadn't overimbibed on champagne, I wouldn't have even considered it."

Margery, usually so placid, so calm, was quickly working herself into a furor. Lenora placed an arm about her friend's waist, giving her a comforting squeeze. "You silly thing. There's nothing to regret. And you were not the only one in her cups that day."

"But I should have had the clearer head. You've spent

years avoiding any mention of Hillram. Then to go to the one place you can't help but think of him? And it's all my doing." She made an agitated sound in her throat. "And now this thing with Mr. Ashford. What if facing your memories of Hillram has left your heart open? I would be happy for you if you fell in love with someone, of course. There's nothing I want more than your happiness. But Mr. Ashford doesn't mean to stay. And if you fall in love with him, and he leaves at the end of his month, it will break your heart." She looked at Lenora then, her eyes brimming with misery. "You've suffered so much already. I'll never forgive myself if that happens."

Lenora was silent, stunned, Margery's fears so closely mirroring her own. And if Margery had so quickly seen inside her heart, then Lenora was beyond being in mere danger from Peter.

She was already in love with him, completely and totally.

As if a veil had been lifted from her eyes, she saw the truth in all its clarity. And she wondered how she had ever fooled herself into thinking she could prevent it. The future stretched out before her then, colorless and bleak. But though she might not be able to escape it, she refused to allow Margery a minute of guilt over it.

Knowing she wouldn't be able to hide the truth from her friend, she rested her cheek against Margery's shoulder, the better to avoid her anxious gaze. "Have no fear on that score," she murmured. "For my heart is no way in danger." And as she looked out on the landscape with weary eyes, she prayed for forgiveness for lying— once more—to someone who loved her so well. Though it seemed divine grace had been lost to her long ago.

Chapter 16

*P*eter stared hard at his reflection. "I want my damn boots," he growled.

Quincy looked up from adjusting his cuff and raised an inky brow. "Even you in all your stubbornness must know that you can't wear boots to a ball."

"But *pumps*, Quincy?" He pointed down to his feet in disgust. "Truly? And these pantaloons. I've never worn pants so tight. Are you certain the tailor didn't cut them too small? I wouldn't put it past the man to have shorted us on material to save some money."

His friend did laugh at that, though it was accompanied by a roll of the eyes that told Peter more than words that he was being an unmitigated ass about the whole ordeal. "Trust me," he drawled as he came to stand beside Peter, "you look perfect for an evening out."

Still Peter was not convinced. Especially as he looked on his and Quincy's reflections side by side. His friend was all lean muscle, and the snug evening wear fit his form perfectly. From the deep blue of his tailcoat to the tight white of his pantaloons, to the glint of the gold chain watch fob at his waist, the man looked every inch a London rake.

Peter, on the other hand, looked as awkward as he felt. The stark black of his coat and pants did nothing to hide the fact that he looked ridiculous. He was too large, too rough. Even with his beard trimmed neatly, his hair brushed and tied back in a queue, there was nothing debonair or elegant about him. He looked like the imposter he was.

Tugging at the edges of his coat, trying with all his might to keep his fingers from the intricate knot of his cravat, he turned from the sight. "Well, I hope Lady Tesh appreciates my efforts at least."

"I'm sure she will, old man." Quincy retrieved their gloves from the dressing table, handing Peter his before tugging on his own. "Now, shall we?"

Fighting the urge to look back one more time on the horror that was his reflection, Peter straightened his shoulders and stormed from the room. He may as well get it over with. And if his steps were a bit too quick, he would certainly not attribute it to wanting to see Lenora. He may not be the smartest man, but he wasn't stupid enough to pine for a woman who he would never allow to be more than his dead cousin's former fiancée.

Despite this, however, he found himself scanning the front hall as he descended the stairs. Lenora wasn't there. His fury toward himself for noticing her absence doubled as disappointment surged in him. He was a stupid arse.

"My goodness, Peter," Lady Tesh called out as he made his way to her, "I cannot believe the change in you. I would hardly know you if I saw you on the street. Though," she continued with a touch of sarcasm, "I do believe that scowl would reveal your identity right away. Do try not to scare all of the young ladies tonight."

"I've forced myself into this ridiculous costume," he

gritted, "and am attending the event against my will. I refuse to pretend to be happy for your amusement."

"You look as beautiful as ever, my lady," Quincy said with a bow. "And Mrs. Kitteridge, that color of amethyst on you is stunning. But where is our fair Miss Hartley?"

"She'll be down momentarily," Mrs. Kitteridge said. Was it Peter, or did the woman give him a worried glance?

Surely she didn't know what had transpired between him and Lenora. Though perhaps she did, for the women were thick as thieves.

In the next moment, however, that suspicion was laid to rest. Her face smoothed to its typical calm, a small smile lifting her lips. "And my grandmother is right; you look very handsome tonight."

He inclined his head, his face heating. His fingers twitched, itching to tear at his cravat. *Just get through the night.* Surely one ball wasn't going to kill him.

Though that may be a distinct possibility, he thought as he spied Lenora on the staircase.

He had done his best to keep his distance from her over the past three days. And so it only hit him harder, spying her for the first time in her finery. She was stunning. Gone were the stiff flounces and overly embroidered hems, and in their place was a vibrant orange gown that fell in delicate folds to the floor. The skirt was split, revealing a creamy satin underskirt that flashed and flirted as she made her way down the stairs. Cream-colored ribbon adorned the small puffed sleeves and the low curve of her bodice.

It was simplicity, and elegance, and a touch of inno-cence. Undeniably and completely Lenora.

She hurried to Lady Tesh's side. "I'm sorry I'm late,

Gran," she said as she gave the older woman a kiss on the cheek.

"Nonsense," the viscountess said, patting her arm, "for we've just been joined by Peter and Mr. Nesbitt. But you are a vision, child. That gown is becoming on you. Peter," she said, startling him, "don't you think our Lenora is lovely?"

Lenora had not looked his way once since her arrival. He should simply grunt an answer and turn away.

Instead he said, his voice thick and low, "She's beautiful."

She started, her gaze finding him. Her eyes widened, running down his body, her mouth forming a small oval of surprise as she took in the changes in him.

He felt that perusal like a physical caress. Heat shot through him, igniting what he had fought so hard against since their kiss.

It took every ounce of willpower he possessed not to take her in his arms and kiss her senseless. He shifted uncomfortably, hoping his thoughts weren't made obvious by his pantaloons. Which left *nothing* to the imagination, damn it.

"Thank you," she murmured. "And you look very handsome."

Polite words, no doubt, an automatic compliment that she had given a thousand times before. Yet he couldn't fail to notice the way her eyes lingered on him. Nor did he fail to notice the desperate hunger deep in him that her gaze dredged up. And not only to touch her. He had missed *her* over the past few days, her conversation and laughter, and the freedom from the bone-deep anger that had been his companion for so long.

Damnation, what was wrong with him?

A moment later, she seemed to recall herself. Blushing, she turned her attention to Quincy. "And you as well, Mr. Nesbitt. Why, you wouldn't be out of place in even the most discerning London drawing room."

Quincy grinned. "Miss Hartley, you shall turn my head."

Peter barely bit back a growl. "Shall we be off then? I wish to get this infernal evening over with."

"Oh, Peter, you're so gallant," Lady Tesh drawled as they turned for the door.

Once outside, Peter immediately strode for the box where the driver was perched, awaiting them. He would ride there tonight, and he didn't care if it was unseasonably chill, or that the drive would most certainly make a complete mess of the careful job he'd done on his clothing and hair. There was no way in hell he was going to be stuck inside a carriage with Lenora.

Lady Tesh, however, was not about to let him get away so easy.

"Peter, where do you think you're going?"

He ground his teeth together. "There won't be enough room for all of us inside the carriage. I'll ride up top with the driver."

"There will be plenty of room, for Mr. Nesbitt has graciously offered to ride his horse."

Peter cast an incredulous glance to Quincy, but his friend was already mounted up and looked sickeningly dashing. By the time he'd reined in his frustration and turned back to the others, they'd already been helped up into the waiting carriage. Grumbling to himself—for what else could he do?—he lumbered over, knowing even before peering inside that the only seat would be next to Lenora. Because what else could he expect, considering the joke his life had become?

Lenora, for her part, didn't so much as glance his way as he hefted himself inside. She fairly hugged the carriage wall as he settled onto the plush bench, as far away from him as she could manage. Even so, he couldn't fail to feel her leg pressing into his, to smell her faint scent of summer berries drifting toward him.

He swallowed hard, shifting in his seat.

"There now," Lady Tesh said with a contented smile. "Completely comfortable."

Peter would have disagreed, and loudly. If he had not been fully focused on controlling his baser urges. For the carriage started off down the drive with such a rocking jolt that Lenora instinctively reached out to steady herself. Unfortunately the closest thing was Peter's arm. She pulled her hand back as if burned, mumbling her apologies. Peter turned to look at the passing scenery and caught sight of Quincy prancing into view. The man had the gall to grin and salute him before kicking his horse off at a gallop.

If he didn't embarrass himself with the obvious proof of his desire showing in these ridiculously tight pants, or killing his best friend, he would count it a miracle.

Chapter 17

I admit, I did not expect that Peter would actually dance."

Lenora, standing against the wall beside where Lady Tesh sat, flushed hot. "Oh, is he dancing? I hadn't noticed." Which was a blatant lie, of course. She hadn't stopped noticing every move he made from the moment they'd entered the assembly rooms.

Like now, as he made his way with precise care through a quadrille. He was stiff as a poker, his brow furrowed in concentration. But he didn't embarrass himself. It seemed he had remembered every lesson she'd taught him with impressive recall.

A fact that shouldn't have sat sour in her stomach as it did.

As glowering and unwelcome as Peter was, he was proving himself to be a favorite with the local ladies. A moment didn't go by that he wasn't besieged by some flirtatious miss or another. As she watched, the young lady opposite him in the set batted her lashes, swaying a bit closer than was proper as they passed one another. And she wasn't even his partner.

Lenora fought the urge to gag. Not that she blamed the woman. In the stark black of his evening wear, the expert cut of it hugging every inch of broad shoulder, every sinew of muscle, Peter put the softer, weaker men about him to shame.

But Lenora's mumbled untruth was not enough to turn Lady Tesh off the subject. "You haven't noticed? How can you miss him? Not only is he the tallest man present, but he is quite the most good-looking one as well, even with his ridiculous beard and that horrendous glower of his. No offense to you, of course, Mr. Nesbitt," she said to the man who had just returned, hands laden with glasses of punch. "I mean, goodness, I knew the man would clean up well. But even I did not expect *that.*"

Lenora snatched at her glass, taking a deep draft of the punch in an effort to quench her suddenly parched throat.

"What I want to know," Mr. Nesbitt said, leaning against the wall, "is where he learned to dance like that in the first place."

Lenora, in the process of tipping her glass back to drain the rest of her beverage, promptly choked.

"I say, Miss Hartley," Mr. Nesbitt said, coming up behind Lenora and pounding her on the back with enthusiasm, "are you all right? I do hate it when that happens."

She gasped for breath, trying with all her might to tell the man to stop. The music must have ended just then, for within seconds Peter was at her side.

"Quincy, what the blazes do you think you're doing to Le—er, Miss Hartley?" Through watering eyes, Lenora saw him glare at Mr. Nesbitt and wave him off. Then he was there, his face close to hers, his eyes tight with concern. And Lenora found she could not breathe for quite another reason.

"Miss Hartley choked on some punch. I was helping her to clear it."

"Helping her? More like beating her to a bloody pulp." He leaned even closer. So close Lenora could see the dark ring of indigo in his ice blue eyes. He was closer than he had been since their kiss. "Can you breathe?"

No. "Yes," she croaked, wiping at her streaming eyes. "I'm fine, thank you." And then, because she couldn't stand to be this close to him and not throw herself into his arms, she took a hasty step back.

The worry that had softened his features faded away, to be replaced with a hard chill. "Yes, well, that's... good." He cleared his throat, his fingers twitching up toward his neckcloth before dropping back to his side. "If you'll excuse me." As he gave a small bow and made to turn away, Lenora did her best to ignore the desolation that swept over her.

"Just a moment, my boy," Lady Tesh said, thwacking him on the arm with her fan. "You've got me curious. Where did you learn to dance like that?"

Lenora blanched. Peter managed to keep his countenance much better than she; there was hardly a twitch on his stony face. Except for his eyes, which flitted to her for the briefest of glances. It was barely noticeable, yet it sent a waterfall of memories washing over her: of darkness and heat, open mouths and desperate hands.

"I've picked up a few of the more refined arts here and there," he mumbled.

"Where?" Mr. Nesbitt demanded. "I've known you for thirteen years, and can say with complete confidence that I've never witnessed you in any type of situation that required dancing."

"My mother was my tutor," Peter replied. A neat

attempt at deflecting. And one that didn't fool Mr. Nesbitt one bit if the predatory look on his face was any indication. Lady Tesh, too, seemed more intrigued than ever. Lenora could only be glad that Margery was off talking with a friend, for she didn't need another pair of sharp eyes on them.

But Peter would not be able to deflect them forever. And if the increasing tension in his face was any indication, it would not take long for Mr. Nesbitt to push him right over the edge. Her body wound tight as a top, Lenora stepped between the two men. "I hate to break up your conversation, but Mr. Ashford has promised me the next set."

Lady Tesh stared at her. "He has?"

"Yes."

The viscountess turned to Peter. "You have promised Lenora the next dance?"

His expression didn't change in the slightest. "Of course."

Lady Tesh looked about to say something more. Blessedly the music started up. The perfect escape.

Too late, Lenora realized it was a waltz.

She clenched her hands about the empty cup, her mind whirling now that she had effectively backed herself into a corner. For she could not dance the waltz with him, even had she managed to teach him the steps. Which she most certainly had not. She shivered in remembrance.

"Peter, you know the waltz as well?" Lady Tesh demanded.

"Er..." Finally a reaction from the man. He cast her a panicked look.

"No," Lenora cut in desperately, "he doesn't. But he has promised to walk the perimeter of the room with me."

She deposited the cup on a nearby table and, taking hold of Peter's arm, pulled him through the thickening crowd.

* * *

"You didn't have to do that."

Lenora stayed silent, keeping her gaze forward. She had dropped his arm like a hot poker once a safe distance from Lady Tesh and Quincy. Now they walked side by side, not touching, following the wall of the long assembly hall. The heat of her called to him across the small space between them, and his fingers itched to find the small of her back, to guide her to an out-of-the-way place, to take her in his arms...

He dug his blunt nails into his palm.

"I wouldn't have told them," he said.

"Can we not talk about it, please?"

Her voice was razor thin, full of her disgust for what they had done, cutting him as surely as if she had wielded a blade.

Hurt and fury welled up in him. It had been building up over the past days, until he thought he'd go mad with it. But after tonight, first being so close to her in the carriage without being able to touch her, followed by the attentions of the local ladies, as well as making certain he didn't embarrass himself on the dance floor, he finally snapped. Taking her arm in his grip, he pulled her to a stop. "I know what happened between us disgusts you."

She gasped, her gaze flying about wildly. "Now is not the time."

"There will never be a good time," he spat.

She rolled her eyes. "What I mean is, you stubborn man, we cannot discuss this in such a public setting," she hissed.

"Fine." Casting a look about the room, he took in the pale yellow walls with their white trim, the soaring ceiling and sparkling chandeliers. Yet there was not a single alcove to hide away in.

Just then the partygoers began moving as one toward the door beneath the musicians' gallery.

"What the devil is going on?"

"It's nine," Lenora replied. "Time for refreshments in the Tea Room." She grabbed at her skirts, obviously intending to follow the sea of humanity from the hall.

Peter, however, saw his chance to lay this matter between them to rest. Spying a door close by, he grabbed her hand and hauled her through it without a word.

The cool night air hit him as he stepped out onto what appeared to be a long colonnade that spanned the entire side of the assembly room. Carriages and sedan chairs lined the street. But beyond a few smoking grooms huddled in groups and their sleepy horses, there wasn't a soul in sight.

He turned her to face him. "Problem solved."

"You can't bring me out here," she sputtered. "If you had something to say, why couldn't you wait until we were back at Seacliff?"

"Because," he growled, "I can't trust myself to be alone with you again."

That stopped her outrage in its tracks. She let out a breath, her face falling slack.

"I know you have no wish for me to renew my . . . attentions." He cleared his throat, suddenly uncomfortable and questioning his wisdom in even bringing the subject up in the first place. "I merely wanted to tell you that I won't. That's all."

But she was frowning. "You mentioned before bringing me out here that your . . . ahem, attentions . . . disgusted me."

"Yes," he bit out. "Your point being?"

"My point is," she said, flushing so bright, he saw it even in the faint light from the street lamps, "they did not. Disgust me, that is."

Her attempts at appeasing him sat cold and bitter in his gut. "You think I believe that?"

Her brows climbed up her forehead. "And why shouldn't you?"

"Because I saw the proof of your feelings with my own eyes." When she merely frowned, he let out a harsh breath. "Most women don't cry when being . . . kissed."

Dawning understanding lit her face. "You think because I cried that I was disgusted by you?"

But he couldn't continue this conversation. Damnation, it had been the height of foolishness to bring her out here, and was only increasing his torment. "Forget I said anything," he mumbled.

"I shall not." To his surprise, she stepped closer, lowered her voice to a delicious rasp. "I cried because I was overwhelmed."

"Overwhelmed," he repeated blankly, trying not to think about how wonderful she would feel in his arms.

"Yes." She cleared her throat and looked down to her toes. "I haven't felt such strong emotion in . . . well, ever."

"Ever?" When she nodded, he couldn't help pressing, "Surely Hillram affected you."

When she remained silent, her expression turning almost miserable, the realization hit him: she had not felt these things even with Lord Hillram.

Something warm filled him, something he couldn't identify—and didn't want to.

"But it doesn't matter what I felt, or what you might have felt," she said. "For you aren't planning to stay."

It was not a question, yet her eyes found his in the dim light, asking him to deny it. And mayhap, begging for something else. Something he could never give her.

"No," he said, "I don't mean to stay. Nor," he continued, slowly and distinctly, a reminder to himself as much as a need to make her understand, "do I have any plans to take a wife back with me."

As she nodded and turned to go back inside, he wondered at the look of pain in her eyes. As well as the regret that filled his chest, so thick and cloying, he could hardly breathe.

Chapter 18

Lenora sucked in a sharp breath as her needle found her finger. She watched dully as a small drop of blood welled up before sticking the wounded digit into her mouth.

It wasn't the first time that afternoon she had pricked herself. No doubt it wouldn't be the last. To make matters worse, her efforts at embroidery were no better than a tangle of threads. Heaving a sigh, she tossed the pillow-case aside and looked out the sitting room window. From behind her, Margery's voice droned on as she read to her grandmother. Suddenly she stopped.

"Lenora," Lady Tesh called, "are you bored of embroidery? Would you like me to have your drawing things fetched?"

Lenora nearly blanched. If there was anything she didn't want to do in that moment, it was to draw. Since the kiss with Peter and the realization that she had foolishly fallen in love with him—a man who had bluntly stated he could never return her affections—it was more imperative than ever that she stifle her emotions. She could not again be tempted as she had been at the pools to draw what her heart willed her to. For if she opened herself up to the danger of that again, there was no telling what pain would follow.

"No thank you, Gran," she said, giving the woman a wan smile. "I think perhaps I haven't recuperated from the ball the other night, is all."

"Oh, pish," she scoffed. "We were home before midnight. I'm sure you've stayed out much later during your time in London."

She shrugged, trying—and failing—to keep her gaze from flitting to Peter. He seemed to be entirely focused on the card game he was playing with Mr. Nesbitt. She should be happy he managed to ignore her so completely.

So why did it cause such an ache in her chest?

"Yes, well," she said now, forcing her gaze back to Lady Tesh, "perhaps it's the weather then. It's quite gray outside."

"Hmmph. No doubt another storm," the older woman muttered. "It really is too bad, for I did so want you to go to the cliffs today."

Lenora sent up a prayer of thanks. She couldn't continue with the tragic tale of Synne and Ivar. Not today. Perhaps not ever.

Margery, who had been waiting patiently to continue reading to her grandmother, spoke up then, turning an understanding smile on Lenora. "Perhaps I should play something on the pianoforte."

But the thought of some cheerful tune filling the room made Lenora's skin crawl. "No, you'd best continue your reading. I'm sure Gran is waiting on tenterhooks. I'll write to my father; I haven't heard from him since we arrived."

Her attempt at deflection didn't clear the worry from Margery's face. But her friend did as she was bade, lifting the book and starting off again.

Lenora rose and made her way to the small escritoire

in the corner. She busied herself straightening the blotter, sharpening the pen nib, searching for paper. Finally she had everything precisely as she liked.

But the blank page stared up at her, mocking her. What could she say to her father? That she had fallen in love? That the man would soon be leaving? That her heart would be broken when he left?

On the heel of that thought came another: had her father begun the search for her latest betrothed as he'd promised to do? Her hands clenched until the knuckles showed white, misery pooling in her breast. Of course he had. Her father wasn't one to let moss grow when there was an opportunity to be had. And though the scandal surrounding her third failed engagement was dire indeed, Sir Alfred was clever enough to turn it in his favor. And she would once more be destined for a loveless match. Which was just as she deserved, after Hillram.

But how much harder would it be, now that she had tasted the possibility of something more with Peter?

She felt his eyes on her, burning into her back. Longing swept through her, making her want things she knew she could never have. She closed her eyes, dragging in a shuddering breath. She had to get out of this room before she went mad.

The click of small nails on the polished floor alerted her to her salvation. Freya had leapt down from her seat beside Lady Tesh and made her way to the sitting room door, where she stood with an imperious look as if to say, "I am ready for my walk, peasants."

Lenora stood so quickly, the chair scraped the floor, startling the other inhabitants.

"I'll take Freya out, shall I?" she blurted out.

"Nonsense, child. Let one of the footmen, for it looks about to rain."

But Lenora was already striding for the door. "There's no need for that. I'll be only a few minutes; the clouds look like they'll hold out for a good hour or more."

Before Lady Tesh could argue—and before Lenora's traitorous eyes could seek out Peter again—she was out the door and heading toward the front hall and freedom.

* * *

When he saw the bright flash of lightning and heard the low rumble of thunder, Peter realized Lenora had not yet returned.

No, that wasn't entirely true. He had been fully aware of her absence from the moment she had left with the dog. The storm only drove the fact home more fully.

"Lenora and Freya should have been back by now."

Lady Tesh's words, so closely echoing his own thoughts, snagged Peter's attention. She peered at the fresh drops of rain on the window, her brows drawn in a pucker of worry.

Mrs. Kitteridge wore a similar expression. "I hope she hasn't had an accident or gotten lost."

"Nonsense," Lady Tesh responded heartily. "Lenora knows this land almost as well as you do. No, she should be walking through the door any minute now with Freya in tow." Even so, the older woman didn't command Mrs. Kitteridge to continue her reading, instead keeping her gaze fixed to the window and the steadily increasing rain.

Mrs. Kitteridge's knuckles were white as she gripped the calfskin volume to her chest. "Lenora would have turned back immediately at the first hint of rain. No, something is wrong."

Without thinking twice, Peter stood. "I'll search for her."

Lady Tesh and her granddaughter looked at him as if he'd sprouted angel wings.

"Oh, Peter, will you?" the viscountess asked.

"Of course. And Quincy will help as well."

Quincy, who had begun the solitary pursuit of tossing playing cards into a large vase once Peter had lost interest in their game, started. He lost his grip on the remaining cards and they scattered across the floor. "What will I do?"

"You're accompanying me out of doors."

His friend looked to the window, his mouth falling open. "But it's *raining*."

Peter just kept his eyes from rolling. "Then I apologize in advance for the damage to your outfit. But Miss Hartley hasn't returned."

To Quincy's credit, he quickly redeemed himself, jumping to his feet and striding for the door. "Then let's be off. If she's out in this, there's not a moment to lose."

They made for the front door, donning their outer garments and retrieving umbrellas. Even as prepared as Peter was for the rain, the wind caught him completely off guard. It tore through his clothing, making his use of the umbrella impossible. His mind filled with images of Lenora, huddled wet and cold, maybe hurt.

Panic reared, nearly choking him.

Just then Freya came tearing up the steps. She bounded through the still open front door and stood on the pristine floor, looking as bedraggled and offended as any creature could.

As the butler scooped the shivering canine in his arms,

Peter spun back around. Surely Lenora could not be far behind. She would never leave the dog's side, loved the old lady too much to let anything happen to her pet.

Yet the seconds ticked by, and his hopeful scan of the horizon became a desperate search for even the smallest sign of her.

"Where did the damned dog come from?" Quincy asked.

"I don't know." Peter turned to his friend. "Make for the north and inland," he ordered. Desperation had turned his voice sharp and jagged, fear chilling it to ice. "I'll head south, along the shore."

Quincy didn't hesitate, nodding and starting off at a run.

Peter took off in the opposite direction. By now the skies had opened up completely, the torrent pummeling him, the wind turning the heavy drops to pebbles that stung his skin. Within seconds, his hair was hanging limp in his eyes, his coat was sodden.

Yet how much worse off was Lenora? With her flimsy dress and those tiny little slippers on her feet, she wouldn't stand a chance against the storm. He hurried his steps, sloughing the water from his eyes before cupping his hands around his mouth and calling out for her. But the wind carried his voice back to him, mocking him for thinking he could defeat it.

Where could she have gone? He'd seen her walking the dog along the path that curved along the cliff's edge. The thought of her taking that path on today of all days sent a chill down his spine. Every instinct warned him away from that ledge. But he had to look, had to know if she'd fallen to the rocks below. He went there now, testing each step before placing his weight down. When he was close enough, he peered over the edge.

No telltale pale yellow gown dashed to the rocks below, no broken limbs, no golden hair tangled in the jagged stone.

The relief that filled him was so great, he nearly sagged to the ground. But she was still out in the storm, so he hurried away from the danger of the ledge and began a sweep of the land. Far to the right, then back toward the cliff, then back inland again. His eyes scanned every rock, every hedgerow, searching for even the smallest sign of life.

He didn't know how long he searched; it could have been minutes or hours. All the while, as his boots moved swiftly across the saturated earth, his heartbeat pounded in his ears, a desperate accompaniment to his calls for her.

After traversing what felt like the entirety of the Isle, he came to a low fence. Beyond was a valley, large puddles forming in what he suspected was a field of wildflowers this time of year. Surely she wouldn't have come this far from Seacliff. Yet something called to him, propelling him over the fence, across the valley. The ground was soggy beneath his feet, the mud sucking at his sodden boots. "Lenora!" he called for what must have been the hundredth time that day.

It was then he saw it, the slight movement in the tree line ahead. A pale arm waving frantically.

His heart seemed to stall, then stop altogether, before starting up again at a gallop. He sprinted forward, his feet kicking up mud and water. And there she was, just inside the doorway of a dilapidated little hut. Her hair hung about her shoulders in bedraggled locks, her pale yellow dress soaked and muddied, plastered to her shivering form.

He had never seen anything so beautiful in his entire life. His feet ate up the distance between them. And then he was pushing into the hut, and she was in his arms, and he felt his world right as his lips found hers.

* * *

Lenora's fear melted away under the urgency of Peter's kiss. She clung to his shoulders, opening her mouth to him. She had never thought to feel this again, this roiling need that only he brought out in her, that only he could quench. How it had frightened her when it had first come crashing over her. Yet now she grasped onto it with both hands.

But she couldn't stop shivering, no matter how she pressed herself against him and tried to bury herself in his embrace. The violence of it seemed to break through to Peter. He pulled back and peered down at her in the gloom of the hut.

"My God, you're pale."

The warmth of his kiss was wearing off now, the chill reaching down into her again. She wrapped her arms about herself, rubbing hard at her upper arms. But no amount of friction could take away the bone-deep cold.

He came close to her, pushing her hands aside, replacing them with his own. As he tried to bring warmth into her limbs, he scanned the single room. "We have to get you warm."

She let out a shaky laugh. "You're no better off than I am," she admonished, the words coming out in a chatter of teeth.

He peered down at his drenched clothing as if just noticing them before shrugging. "Never mind that. I've been through worse."

He quickly pulled off his jacket, draping it over her

shoulders. Though it was soaked through, it still held his warmth. She pulled it tightly about her, willing that warmth into her, even as she said, "Now you'll be chilled."

He waved her concerns off. "Have you looked for any wood for kindling?"

She nodded as well as she could. "There isn't any." And she had looked, in every nook and cranny of the small cottage. But not a stray log or bit of kindling had been found, nor even a stick of furniture to break up and make use of.

Peter nodded grimly, eyeing the streams of water pouring in through the rotting thatch roof, the door that listed sideways on its hinge. "As horrible as it is outside, it will be infinitely more dangerous if we stay here. With no way to get warm or dry, we'll quickly fall ill." He looked at her, his grim expression sending his face into sharp shadow. "We need to get back to the house. Now."

She gave a cautious look out the doorway. She couldn't imagine going back out into that. "I don't know..."

He came closer, hooked a finger under her chin, forcing her worried gaze to his. "Do you trust me?"

"Yes," she said, without the least bit of hesitation. She was stunned to realize just how true that was. She would trust this man with her very life.

His eyes warmed. "Then let's be off." Without warning, he swept his arms beneath her and headed out the door. Immediately they were deluged with rain. It came down in buckets, making it nearly impossible to see.

"You needn't carry me, you know," she said into his ear. "I'm perfectly capable of walking on my own."

"The ground is soaked, and you have the most abysmal footwear possible for this," he replied without the least bit of breathlessness. His steps were long, eating up the distance to the house. "And," he continued, his voice darkening, though he tried to keep his words light, "your teeth are chattering so loud, I can hardly hear myself think."

His worry was palpable, his shoulders tense beneath her hands. A warm glow started up in her chest. She clenched her stiff fingers in his linen shirt, pressing her face into his neck, feeling safer than she ever had, though they were not yet out of danger.

He shifted her slightly, stepping over a low fence. "Why the devil were you out so far to begin with? Why didn't you return at the first hint of rain?"

Suddenly it all came crashing back down on her, the reason for her fear before Peter had found her, washing it away with his kisses. "It was Freya. There was a clap of thunder and she ran off. I looked for her as long as I could. Lady Tesh will be frantic. And that poor sweet pup. She must be frightened out of her wits, out here in this."

He snorted, shaking his head to clear his vision. "Oh, I wouldn't be overly worried about that dog. She's already back at Seacliff. By now she'll be warm and dry, and no doubt on a gilt-embellished cushion before a blazing fire."

Relief filled Lenora. "Thank goodness," she breathed.

Peter shook his head again. His hair, which had fallen out of its queue, was plastered to his cheek. Without thinking, Lenora reached up and smoothed the strands back, wiping the water from his eyes.

His arms constricted, his step faltering before starting up again. "Thank you."

"It is I who must thank you. You saved me, Peter."

His eyes shifted to her for the briefest moment, the tenderness in them taking her breath away. She studied his face as he trudged on, taking in the tense line of his jaw, his blue lips, the hair stuck to his temples, as if he were the most precious thing in the world. And to her, he was. That glow in her chest burned brighter, warming her from the inside out as no fire ever could.

She tightened her arms about his neck. "I'm sorry you had to come out after me."

"I'm not," he whispered, so low she almost didn't hear it above the sound of rain, the words going straight to her heart.

Chapter 19

The house was quiet, everyone in bed, when Peter made his way on bare feet to Lenora's room.

He shouldn't go to her. He knew that as surely as he knew the sun would rise on the morrow, bringing him one day closer to leaving the Isle for good. Yet he also knew that if he didn't see Lenora this instant, to verify with his own eyes that she was well and safe, he would go mad.

He stopped before her door. Everything was silent within. Perhaps she was sleeping. He should go back to his bed and try to fall asleep.

His toes curled in the plush runner, his entire body leaning toward the wooden panel as if it held all the answers to life. And perhaps it did. Taking a deep breath, he raised his hand and knocked lightly.

The door opened almost immediately. As if she'd been waiting on the other side, as if she'd expected him.

"Peter," she breathed.

It was as natural as breathing to take her in his arms, to claim her lips with his own. Her slender arms came about his neck, her fingers grasping greedily to his shoulders, digging into the fabric of his shirt. Heaven. She was absolute heaven in his embrace. Berries and sunshine and sweetness filled him. He walked her back into the room and pushed the door closed behind him.

"I had to see you," he murmured into her mouth. "I had to make sure you were well."

An understatement. These last hours, after they had whisked Lenora from him, closing her up in her rooms, had been the longest in his life. He'd paced the floor, sick with worry. Had he been too late? Had his decision to carry her through the pouring rain been the right one? Or had he merely made certain she would fall ill? The urge to see her, to make certain she was safe, had been more than a need; it had been a compulsion.

Now she was in his arms, safe and dry. And he couldn't stop touching her. He ran his hands down her back, over her hips, up her sides until his thumbs brushed the gentle swell of her breasts. She wore only a nightgown, a thin cotton affair. There were no layers upon layers of clothing, no stays to keep his hands from exploring every delectable inch of her.

"I was hoping you would come," she whispered, running her lips along his cheek to his ear.

"Were you?" He pulled back, looked down into her face. The fire had been banked, the faint orange embers sending barely enough light to where they stood half the room away. Yet the warmth, the hunger in her gaze, was as clear as if a thousand candles burned bright.

His breath caught in his throat. He had to leave before he did something they both regretted. "I'll let you rest," he said, his voice hoarse. "You need to sleep."

Her hands came up to cradle his face when he would have released her. She swayed against him, the tips of her breasts brushing his chest. He sucked in his breath, his body burning.

"Don't go," she whispered.

He shook his head helplessly. "You don't know what you're asking."

"I do." She smiled, her beautiful eyes clear of doubt. "I want you, Peter. I have from the start."

Her words sank in slowly. When their meaning penetrated the thick cloud his brain had become, his arms came about her, his hands clenching in the delicate material of her nightgown. He buried his face in her neck, pressing a desperate kiss to the soft skin there.

"I can't stay away from you," he rasped. "I tried. Damnation, but I tried."

"You don't have to stay away," she whispered into his temple. Her fingers threaded into his hair.

"But I can't marry you, Lenora." It was no more than he had said before. Yet one word stood out from the rest, adding a wealth of meaning: *can't*. Even so, his course in life suddenly sat heavy and wrong on his shoulders.

"I know. I never asked you to marry me, Peter," she murmured. And then, her voice dropping to a strained whisper, "I wasn't meant to be happily married anyway."

Was she thinking of Hillram? He expected jealousy to once more rear its ugly head. Instead he found only a deep grief, that she should have lost so much so young.

And that he had not been there first.

But if he'd kept his promise to his mother and stayed with Lady Tesh, he might have been. He sucked in his breath, regret such as he had never known crashing over his head. He would have been around for those summers she spent on the Isle as a young girl, might have been the one she fell in love with instead of his cousin.

Her fingers tightened in his hair, dragging him from the

hopelessness of could-have-beens. "But I'll have tonight at least," she whispered fiercely.

He swallowed hard and pulled back to look down at her, his heart aching at the determined light in her eyes. "I can't give you what you need, can't give you what you deserve."

She took his face in her hands, brought it down to hers. "Right now, all I need is you. In this moment, right now. Nothing else matters."

He should fight it, walk away. But then her lips were on his, and every care and worry, every doubt and fear, faded.

* * *

Lenora clung tight as Peter lifted her in his arms. He carried her with tender care, as if she were a treasure beyond worth.

Yet his lips were hungry, plundering her mouth with feverish intent. And when he lowered her to the mattress, laying her down amid the rumpled sheets, his body quickly followed.

He was everywhere, his hard weight pressing into her, the spicy scent of him filling her senses, the taste of his tongue and the rasp of his whiskers on her skin driving her nearly senseless with desire. She grasped him tighter, needing more.

"I won't ruin you," he vowed, the words hot as he moved his mouth down the column of her throat.

"I don't care," she panted.

"I do." He rose up on one elbow, stared down into her face, his gaze caressing her with infinite tenderness. "You're far too precious. And I won't leave you disgraced."

But she couldn't think of him leaving. There was only here and now. "I'll take whatever I can of you, Peter," she breathed, dragging his head down to hers.

He groaned, the tension transforming in an instant to a wild desperation. It mirrored her own, a silent acknowledgment of how fleeting this moment was.

He lifted his head from hers, and she cried out from the loss of him. But he didn't go far. His lips found the straining tip of her breast. Soon his mouth was open and hot over it, wetting the fabric that stood between them. His hand went to the hem of her nightgown, dragging it up her body, exposing her to the cool night.

This was no slow undressing. And she was glad of it, for she thought she might scream if he drew it out. All she wanted was his hands and lips on her. Finally her clothing was sailing through the air, his soon following. Then he was stretched over her and there was nothing between them.

He gave a low hiss of pleasure and buried his face in her neck. "My God, you're heaven," he whispered.

The words sent a shiver through her. She pressed her lips to the smooth skin of his shoulder, ran her palms over the muscles of his back. They bunched and shuddered under her touch.

Peter was the largest, strongest man she had ever known. Everything about him screamed power, competence. But hadn't she seen in the past fortnight that he was not as immune as he would like others to believe? Hadn't she seen the vulnerability in him, time and again? And now this, physical proof that just her touch had the power to render him helpless.

But in the next moment, he proved that his own touch on her was just as powerful. He began a slow slide down, his mouth and lips and teeth worshipping her skin. She gasped, arched up into him, as he showered kisses over her neck, her breasts, her quivering stomach. His hands followed, large and rough and calloused. They had seen grief and want, hard work and determination. They skimmed her skin, massaged into straining muscles, caressed with infinite care, bringing her to greater heights of pleasure.

When he reached the thatch of curls at the very apex of her, however, she froze. Margery had told her some of the mechanics of lovemaking, enough to whet her interest in what else could be involved. But Lenora had never in her wildest imaginings expected this.

"Peter?" Her voice warbled with uncertainty.

"Let me taste you," he breathed. His breath stirred the hair there, brushing what was hidden within. She shuddered.

"Please."

She would have given anything to him, such was the power of that one word from his lips.

"Yes," she whispered, letting her legs fall open to him.

And then his mouth was there, at the center of her. And nothing else mattered.

He started off gentle, the warmth of his tongue stroking her in slow, languid caresses. She gasped, her fingers digging into the soft white sheets beneath her, trembling as sensations rippled through her. She tried to remain still. Surely a lady didn't react in such a wanton way. Yet when his finger entered her in a gentle slide, filling her body, as well as her soul, she could no longer rein in the instinct to move.

Crying out into the dimness of the room, she raised her hips, pressing against his mouth. He growled low, and the vibrations of the sound, focused on that part of her that was quickly becoming the center of her universe, sent her spiraling further over the edge. His tongue worked faster, his lips closing around her, his finger working inside her until she thought she would shatter.

And then she did, into a million pieces that she thought would never find their way back together again.

Until he rose up over her, and pulled her trembling body into his arms, cradling her to his chest. It was then she felt it, her heart settling where it belonged, beating strong and sure against him.

* * *

Peter had never felt so content, so whole, so free from the pain and anger of his past, as he did in that moment. Lenora lay curled against his side, all limp softness. As much as she had surprised him with her passion before, her response tonight left him dizzy with pleasure. That she could trust him enough to open herself up in such a way humbled him. Would that he could spend the rest of his days bringing her such pleasure, that he could claim her for his own.

He immediately recoiled from the rogue thought. He couldn't abandon the plans of half a lifetime.

Regret, heavy and bitter, filled him. Yes, he would see his vow through. He tightened his hold on Lenora, paradise in his arms. Though it would not happen without a price.

"Peter?"

Her voice startled him. He'd thought her sleeping. "Yes?"

Her slender fingers played over his chest. "Is everything all right?"

He forced himself to relax under her. She didn't deserve his dark thoughts. She was innocent in all this, someone who had wandered too close to a flame. He prayed she didn't get scorched when it was over and done with.

He doubted he would be so lucky.

"Everything is fine," he murmured into the crown of her head. Dropping a kiss there, he rubbed his hand over her back, hoping to lull her to sleep.

But Lenora rose up on her elbow and looked down on him. Even in the dim light, he could see the worry that drew her brows together. "Tell me what's troubling you, Peter."

Damn but she was lovely. Her hair was in disarray, her lips swollen from his kisses. Unable to help himself, he cupped the back of her head and pulled her down for a kiss. "Nothing is troubling me."

"Liar," she whispered, though there was no anger in the word. She melted against him, splaying her hands over his chest. Suddenly a flush stole over her cheeks, even discernible in the low light. Her eyes lowered to his chin. "But you did not…uh…"

He frowned. "Did not what?"

Her cheeks went even darker. "When I…er…you did not…um…"

Was she asking him if he had finished? Despite himself, his lips twitched. "I thought you were more eloquent than that."

She shot him a glare, pushing against his chest. Immediately his arms tightened about her, his lips going to her neck to disguise the grin that had spilled over.

"You're asking if I reached satisfaction?" he murmured against her skin.

She shivered, and he could almost hear her eyes rolling

back in her head. She nuzzled his temple, nodding. "I want to know if you felt what I did."

The husky rasp of her voice, quickly building again to desire, nearly did him in right then and there. Taking firm control of himself—so he didn't spend himself like a young lad without even a touch, or roll her onto her back and sink into her warmth—he pulled back and looked her in the eye.

"Never mind me, Lenora. Tonight was for you."

Her lips parted, the breath leaving her in a soft rush. "But...don't you want to?"

He nearly groaned. "More than you know, sweet."

Her brows drew together again in a frustrated little dip. "Then why?"

Cupping her cheek, he ran his thumb over her soft skin. "I told you I wouldn't ruin you. I won't break that promise."

Instead of being grateful, she glowered at him. "I don't recall asking you to make that promise."

He stared at her, stunned. Suddenly a laugh welled up, breaking free. His head fell back against the pillows as his mirth washed over him.

"And what is so funny?" she demanded.

Her voice held hints of aggravation and frustration. His chuckles died down, but he couldn't erase the smile from his face for anything. He had never been so blasted happy in his life. "Are you angry at me for not ravishing you?"

"No, of course not."

She tried once more to rise. He rolled them over, so he was half on top of her, the truth finally sinking in that she was serious.

"You wish for me to ravish you?" he asked.

"Would it be so terrible?"

Her voice was so small, he could tell it had taken everything in her to ask that simple question. Leaning down, he took her lips in a gentle kiss. "It would not be terrible," he whispered. "In fact, it would be the single most amazing event in my entire life. But," he continued when she would have opened her mouth to argue, "I cannot. I'll keep what I can of my honor; I promised not to ruin you, and I won't go back on that."

Her fingers dove into his hair, increasing both his pain and his pleasure a thousandfold. "You're the most honorable man I know."

"I'm not. If I was, I wouldn't have come to you tonight."

She was silent for so long, he thought she wouldn't answer. Then, in a quiet voice, "I'm glad you did."

"I'm glad as well," he said through a throat thick with some emotion he could not—would not—name. As he claimed her lips again, he ignored the small voice in the back of his mind that said that, as glad as he was now, the pain of leaving would only be worse.

Chapter 20

*M*iss Hartley," Quincy said the next morning after they had all sat down to breakfast, "you look none the worse for your ordeal yesterday. As a matter of fact, you appear to have a fresh bloom on your cheeks."

Peter, transfixed by that very same blush—and knowing the reason for it—nearly choked on his coffee. Blessedly Margery spoke up, drawing any attention he may have attracted to himself.

"Oh, goodness, Lenora, I hope you're not feverish."

"Of course not," Lenora said in a perfectly normal voice. The blush staining her cheeks, however, didn't help matters in the least.

Margery rose from her seat and went to Lenora, placing her wrist against her forehead. She frowned. "You're not warm," she murmured. "Quite cool, in fact."

"I told you I wasn't feverish."

She bent down to peer closely at her friend. "But there is something different just the same."

Lenora's fingers worked at the triangle of toast she had been eating, turning it to crumbs. She cast Peter the briefest of glances, but it said volumes.

Ah, God, those eyes. But it wouldn't help matters if he were caught staring at her like a lovesick calf. He straightened and placed his coffee cup down. "It was quite an ordeal she went through last night." Then, hoping to distract Margery, he asked in an offhand manner, "I wonder what Lady Tesh has planned for us today? Now that the storm has passed, she no doubt has something up her sleeve."

Giving Lenora one last confused glance, Margery returned to her seat. "She mentioned something about the cliffs, but I talked her into letting Lenora rest for the day."

From the pained look on Margery's face, he assumed that conversation hadn't been an easy one. But it was soon replaced with her typical calm demeanor. She took a small sip from her steaming cup and smiled at Lenora. "Which means we shall have the entire day to laze about."

Lenora smiled back. "That sounds divine."

Peter's stomach flipped, watching that small curve of lips. Lips he had kissed just last night. Lips that had trailed hungrily over his skin.

He poked at a piece of ham, then quickly returned to his coffee, taking a deep swallow and letting the rich, bitter brew seep into him. Last night would have to be their only intimate memory together. He shouldn't have gone to her in the first place; he couldn't make that same mistake again.

His gaze drifted back to Lenora, and despite his intentions, he felt a decided softening in the region of his chest when their eyes met. She gave him a small smile before she returned her attentions to Margery.

That curve of lips, that warm gaze, obliterated in seconds what he had been attempting to build all morning: the strong will that would be needed to keep away from her the duration of his stay, and to leave her at the end of his month here.

For he couldn't fool himself any longer. It was not his estranged family he would be leaving. No, it was her. She had become the center of everything to him.

He had a flash, a vision of them in the future, seated across from one another over the breakfast table, sharing meaningful glances as they remembered the passion from the night before. He would have spent the night in her arms instead of sneaking from her bed before dawn, would have woken to find her curled warm and soft against him instead of opening his eyes to the cold loneliness of his borrowed room.

And he wanted that, more than he had ever wanted anything before.

An ache started up in his chest, the need for that possible future squeezing until he could hardly breathe.

He could ask her to be his wife, bring her back to Boston, set up a household.

Have a family.

He drew in a deep, unsteady breath as the idea flashed hot and desperate through his mind. No, he had never wanted a family. It was the one thing he had known with certainty all these long years that he *didn't* want.

And yet it did not seem to be a new need, but something dredged up from the very depths of his soul. Had it been in him all this time then? A foolish question, perhaps; he saw with painful clarity it had been.

For so long it had been just he and his mother. They had been everything to one another. When he had lost her, he had lost the safety and security of knowing he was loved, that he was part of a family.

And he had not wanted it again. Not with Lady Tesh, not even with Quincy, or Captain Adams and his brood, though they had all been more than willing to accept him with open arms. Every one of them had treated him like family, had let him know what he meant to them.

Yet he had kept every single person at arm's length, not wanting the pain of loss to destroy him again. Even Quincy, who had saved his life on more than one occasion, who was closer to him than anyone else had been since his mother's death. And so it had been easy to make the decision to remain unwed and childless in order to thwart Dane and destroy the family line. He never imagined that anyone could breach the walls he had put about himself.

Until Lenora.

Now that future he had planned seemed cold and lonely. He could not imagine life without Lenora in it, bringing light and love such as he had never felt.

He froze, his cup halfway to his lips. Love? Where the devil had that come from? Surely he didn't love Lenora. He cared for her, of course. But love was beyond him, his heart too petrified for that soft emotion.

But as warmth spread through him, like a spring sun melting the frost of winter, he knew deep down he was fooling himself. He loved Lenora. He sucked in a breath, stunned, as the realization coursed through him.

Dropping his cup to the table with a clatter, he shoved his seat back and rose. The pleasant chatter that had filled the room stopped abruptly, every eye turned to him in shock.

"Peter, you're pale as a sheet," Margery said, her brows turning down in worry. "Are you all right?"

"I'm fine," he said, perhaps a touch louder than he'd intended, for Margery's eyebrows flew up her forehead. He tried to focus on her and not Lenora. He needed to clear his head, but he knew if he caught sight of that sweet face, it would be impossible to leave.

"I'm going for a ride," he said.

Quincy stood. "I'll go with you."

"No." Again his voice carried through the room, startling its inhabitants. And now, dash it all, Quincy looked suspicious. As well he might, for he was acting like a madman.

"That is," he continued, trying for a more normal tone of voice, "I need to clear my head. After last night."

Which was as true as he could make it without telling his friend exactly what part of last night had him so out of sorts.

Quincy, however, wasn't fooled. "If you're certain," he said, his voice dubious.

"Of course I am."

When Quincy, after a pause, finally lowered himself to his seat and nodded, Peter turned to go.

"You'll be back in time for dinner, won't you?"

That voice. It skidded down his spine, washed over him, sending heat to every part of his body. Finally he looked at her. Her expression was tight with concern. The flush that had so worried Margery was still there, staining her cheeks a becoming pink. As he watched, it darkened and spread down over her neck, toward the high bodice of her gown. For a split second, he faltered, nearly returning to his seat so he didn't have to spend a moment away from her.

No. He had to think, and he couldn't do that when she was near. "Yes," he replied, "I'll be back for dinner."

Her features noticeably relaxed, a small smile lighting her face. A jolt of desire rushed him, so intense it took his breath.

Before he could rethink matters, he spun about and hurried from the room as fast as he could manage.

* * *

The air was clear and crisp, filling Peter's lungs as he urged his horse over the sodden fields away from Seacliff. The rain of the night before had washed clean the dust and dirt and made everything shine like a new penny. Droplets sparkled like gems on the grass, flying through the air in glorious rainbows under his mount's hooves.

He blanched. What drivel was this, that he was likening mere drops of water to gems and rainbows? All the more proof that this solitary ride had been necessary. He focused on the feel of the horse beneath him, on the way the wind tugged on his unbound hair. Focus was needed to help him decide what it was he wanted for his future. And what he couldn't live without.

He came to the crest of a gentle rise and pulled the horse to a stop, looking down into the low valley.

Danesford lay before him, elegant and sprawling, nestled in the valley. The dark brick exterior, the stone dressings, the windows winking in the sun, made it appear as if some lumbering mythical beast had come to slumber between the rolling hills. His eyes scoured the mansion. It was precious to the duke. Everything about this land was, from the carefully trimmed gardens to the smooth expanses of lawn. It screamed wealth and status and privilege. Everything the Duke of Dane held dear.

It had long been his desire to see it fall into ruins. But if he married Lenora, those plans would be destroyed. She loved this land, loved the duke's family. She wouldn't allow him to lay waste to them.

He had to choose between everything he had wanted for so long, and his love for Lenora.

He tried to dredge up the memory of Dane as he had been that day, the cool cruelty that had twisted his face as he'd turned him away. To his frustration, he saw only the abject misery of the duke as he was now, a sick, broken man begging for forgiveness.

Peter growled low in his throat. His horse stepped sideways, agitated by the sound. He quickly brought it back under control, patting its quivering neck absentmindedly. He had to remember just what it was he was doing here, and why he had to make Dane pay. His mother's face swam up in his mind, haggard and pale, drawn with pain. He let the familiar fury settle under his skin, welcoming it like an old friend. How could he forgive that? How could he let that remain unpunished?

Yet if he didn't, he would lose Lenora. And he wanted her, more than air in his lungs.

Blowing out a frustrated breath, he cast a furious glare at the mansion before turning his horse's head and thundering away. He was no closer than he had been to making a decision, was even more mired in doubt. And he could see no clear path to what was right.

He had not gotten far, however, when a small, grizzled man came into view. The man whipped his hat off his nearly bald head and began to wave it cheerfully in the air.

"Mr. Ashford, so nice to see you!"

Peter groaned, his wish for solitude effectively destroyed.

"Mr. Tunley," Peter acknowledged as he came closer, his voice cool and unwelcoming. The man would see he didn't wish for company, surely.

But Mr. Tunley was either thick as a stump or quite the friendliest man in existence. He stopped in the middle of the path, grinning at Peter as if he could not think of a person he wanted to meet more.

"Out for a ride this morning, are you?" He breathed in deeply and peered up at the cloudless sky, replacing his worn cap back on his head. "Mighty fine day for it. That was some storm we had last night, eh?"

"Yes, it was." Perhaps if he simply answered the fellow and didn't engage him in conversation, he might be able to escape him the quicker.

But the man showed not the slightest hint of leaving. He seemed rather to settle more firmly into the road. "I myself love a good storm. It cleanses the earth, makes everything new again."

"Yes."

"Do you have storms such as these in America then?"

"Yes."

He nodded as if Peter had imparted something interesting. "Wonderful. Always love learning about new places."

Goodness, the man wasn't going to stop, was he? Peter drew breath, intending to extricate himself as quickly as he was able. Mr. Tunley, however, launched on again.

"I don't suppose you'd like to share a bit of food with me, would you?" The man held up a small bundle.

Peter blinked, utterly confused by the lightning change in topic. So much so that he quite forgot he was trying to keep the man at arm's length and escape. "You wish me to share your breakfast?"

"Certainly. Though it's not my breakfast I'll be sharing with you. No, I've been up since long before dawn." He brought the bundle to his nose, sniffing experimentally, before grinning. "If I'm right, and I usually am, my Mrs. Tunley has packed me some meat pasties and a quantity of early apples. And if I've been good, I suspect I shall find a hunk of hard cheese within as well. And I'm always good. At least as far as Mrs. Tunley is concerned." He chuckled.

To Peter's mortification, his stomach rumbled. Lady Tesh served up elegant food, delicious yet far too fancy for Peter's tastes, with intricate flavors that only palates much more refined than his could appreciate. What Mr. Tunley described was good plain fare, food to nourish the body. It was food he had grown up eating, food he had preferred even in Boston.

But though his stomach cried out for sustenance, rebelling at the meager diet of black coffee he had consumed at breakfast, he shook his head. "I wouldn't wish to take away food from your plate, Mr. Tunley."

"Oh, 'tis no trouble at all, my boy," the man said. "Mrs. Tunley always gives me much more than I can eat. As my girth can attest to." Here he patted his rounded middle, letting loose a laugh that could not fail to wring an answering smile from Peter.

"If you're certain."

"Of course! It would be my pleasure."

Before Peter quite knew what he was doing, he dismounted and fell into step beside Mr. Tunley, leading his horse behind him.

Chapter 21

I was headed for that small beach there," Mr. Tunley said, all joviality, pointing to a small copse of trees ahead and the endless blue sky beyond. "Nothing like looking upon the majesty of God's creation, a nourishing of the body, as well as the soul, eh?"

Peter said nothing. He couldn't remember a time he'd thought about such things. Eating had been a way to feed his body and nothing more. He thought of Lady Tesh's picnic, all formality and pomp, or the elegant meals he had shared with that lady where too much focus had been on the beauty of the setting and the elegance of the dishes. He hadn't enjoyed those occasions, not even a bit.

They picked their way through the small stand of trees, and the beach came into view. And Peter knew that this meal would win over all the others by far.

The sand was pale beneath his boots, stretching to the water's edge, where the waves played a coy game, coming in to caress the shore before retreating with a hush. Mr. Tunley led the way to a fallen log. Doffing his cap, he dusted the surface, then laid his worn jacket over the damp bark before easing himself down with a happy sigh. Bemused, Peter followed, tying up his horse and removing his own jacket, nearly as worn as Mr. Tunley's,

before seating himself. As his companion busied himself opening his bundle, murmuring his approval of each
item he pulled from the cloth, Peter took the chance to
look about.

Yet again the Isle surprised him in the best possible
way. There were no buildings lining the beach, no bathing machines being pulled out into the sea. Instead all
was quiet and still, the only movements the gentle lap of
waves, the rustle of trees in the faint breeze, the hop and
scuttle of birds chasing the tide. And Mr. Tunley, ever
cheerful, creating a makeshift tablecloth with his hand-
kerchief, prouder of his simple fare than Lady Tesh had
been of her footmen and tents and furniture and expensive
delicacies.

"As you can see," the man said, gesturing to the food
he had laid out with such care, "my Mrs. Tunley does
spoil me so. I'm glad you joined me today. I do hope you
don't mind such simple food, Mr. Ashford. I know you
must be used to much better."

Was that a hint of uncertainty in the man's voice? Sure
enough, when Peter looked closer, he saw a faltering in
the perpetually cheerful smile.

"This to me is better than anything in the world,
Mr. Tunley," he replied with utter seriousness, eyeing
the spread. And indeed it was. Plump pasties with flaky
golden crust, thick chunks of pale cheese, fine red apples
that shone in the dappled sun. His mouth watered.

Mr. Tunley beamed. "Well, I hope your praise is as
heartfelt after you've sampled it. Though I haven't a
doubt it will be, for I've been told my Mrs. Tunley is
quite the finest cook on the Isle."

"I shall be the judge of that, shall I?" Peter said with
a grin as the man handed him a pasty. Peter took a bite

under Mr. Tunley's anxious eye. The crust crumbled, the flavor of fresh mutton and gravy and vegetables filling his mouth. He closed his eyes in appreciation.

"You may tell your Mrs. Tunley," he said after he'd swallowed, "that she has another admirer in me. I've not had anything half so good since my mother passed."

The man's chest puffed up so, Peter was surprised he didn't pop a button. They ate in companionable silence, the stress and strain and uncertainty of the morning melting away in the simple setting.

Sometime later, as the last morsel of food was devoured, Mr. Tunley spoke again.

"I'm glad to see you so relaxed, Mr. Ashford. You looked earlier as if the devil himself was trailing your heels."

"Did I now?"

"Aye."

Peter nodded, looking out to the horizon. "I didn't think I was such an open book."

"Well now, I don't know about you being an open book. But when a man has trouble in love, it tends to show in certain ways."

Peter started. "Love?"

"Oh, aye. You're having women troubles, I'd bet my best hat on it," he said.

The food that had sat so warm and comforting in Peter's belly suddenly turned sour. He rose from his seat and walked toward the gently churning sea. Bending down at the water's edge, he picked up a rock and threw it out over the water, watching it disappear beneath the surface.

Perhaps it was the constant hush of the waves caressing the shore. Mayhap it was simply that his mind was back at Seacliff with Lenora. But he didn't hear Mr. Tunley until the man was at his elbow.

"You're thinking I'm an old man, what do I know about affairs of the heart." He chuckled. "I was young once, too, lad. I've known my share of heartbreak."

Heartbreak. Yes, his heart was breaking. For no matter what choice he made regarding Lenora, he would lose something dear to him.

But he could feel Mr. Tunley's knowing gaze burning into him. To distract the man, he asked, "You've experienced a broken heart?"

"Oh, aye." He chuckled. "My marriage to Mrs. Tunley is a happy one now, but we had our problems. Why, it took me years of being a stubborn, prideful arse before I finally wised up and married her." He paused. "But you wouldn't be distracting me from your own problems now, would you?"

Peter smiled wryly, glancing down at him. "You're an observant man, Mr. Tunley."

The man grinned. "I'm also one to know when I've stuck my nose where it doesn't belong. Though, lamentably, it's usually after I've done the sticking." He chuckled before reaching into his waistcoat pocket and pulling out a dented but lovingly polished pocket watch, giving it a quick look.

"Well then. I'd best be off. My Mrs. Tunley will be waiting for me, and I've learned long ago not to keep a good woman waiting." He chuckled again. "Do you wish me to show you the way back?"

"No need," Peter said. "I've a mind to stay a bit longer. I thank you for your hospitality, Mr. Tunley. It was most appreciated."

"It was my pleasure. I wish you happiness, Mr.

Ashford." Touching the brim of his hat, he was off, gathering his things and trudging back through the copse of trees, the cheerfulness of his whistle melting into the soft cries of seabirds. Leaving Peter with the same dilemma he'd had before the strange interlude. Though wasn't it a bit clearer, the answer a bit more within reach?

Happiness. He mulled over the word, tried it on. It felt strange to him, like a pair of new shoes not yet broken in. Happiness had never been a consideration to him when planning his future. His focus had been on surviving. Happiness had been a myth, something only a select few could hope to attain.

Now, however, wasn't it within reach? Lenora could give him that. She could chase away the demons, bring a peace and contentment into his life he would have never dreamed possible just a week ago.

A strange sensation stirred inside him, and it took him some moments to realize it was hope. But still there was that deep shudder of rebellion tarnishing it. What of Dane? How could he let his empire stand? He brutally pushed the thought aside. He would deal with that when the time came. For now, wasn't it worth seeing what he could have with Lenora?

Anxious now to return to Seacliff, he strode to his horse, quickly untying it and mounting up. It seemed to sense his mood, for it was off like a shot at his slightest touch, racing away from the beach, over the hills, unerringly making its way home.

Finally the house rose into view. The sun bathed the façade in golden light, glinted off the mullioned windows. As if calling to him.

He reined in his horse, wishing his thoughts were as easily controlled, and purposely turned toward the stables.

As anxious as he was to get to Lenora and see what kind of future they might have together, he had never run blindly into any decision and he would not start now. No matter what happiness might hang in the balance.

He took his time at the stables, seeing to his horse's care, though there were grooms aplenty, making sure it was rubbed down and fed and watered before, unable to delay it any longer, he headed to the house. Yet despite his attempts to maintain some semblance of control over himself, his heart had other ideas. It pounded out a fierce beat the closer he got to Lenora, just the idea of that bright future with her enough to make joy surge in his chest. When he made the front drive, it took every ounce of self-control to keep from breaking into a run. Just a few more steps. A grin started up, quite of its own accord.

Just then a horse and rider pounded up the drive. Peter faltered, then stopped altogether at the sight of the beast. It was magnificent, even to his untrained eye. An inky coat that had been brushed to a sheen, muscles quivering and bunching under sleek horseflesh. Its rider pulled it to a practiced stop and it responded beautifully, slowing to a graceful canter before coming to a halt, tossing its head, tail swishing.

The rider dismounted in a fluid motion, then turned. Peter expected a nod of the head, a greeting. What he did not expect, however, was what came next.

"Ho, man. Come and get this horse, will you?"

Peter stiffened. "I'm sorry?"

The man grinned, patted the horse's neck. "Don't be nervous about taking Hades's reins. He may be named after the lord of the underworld, but he's as docile as they come."

As if to give lie to his owner's words, the creature

tossed its head and pranced sideways before the man brought it under control.

"Come along then," he continued. "I've come all the way from London and am eager to complete my journey."

Peter's face heated. It had been years since anyone had made him feel the lowliness of his origins. But in that moment, he felt every smear of dirt that had ever soiled him. The man standing before him was everything he never had been and never would be. Slim and elegant, with features that would put the finest Renaissance painting to shame, he wore his confidence as well as he wore the finely tailored clothes that graced him.

Fury boiled up, that this man should reduce him to the uncertain boy he had been. "You mistake me," he growled, bringing himself to his full height. "I am Lady Tesh's great-nephew, Mr. Peter Ashford. What I would like to know is your identity, sir, and your business here."

Instead of turning haughty, as so many men of station did when brought to task, the man looked utterly abashed. "Goodness, now don't I feel an utter arse. My apologies. I certainly never meant any offense. I would blame the long trip from London and my own exhaustion, but those would be poor excuses. Please permit me to start again. I am Lawrence Watford, Lord Redburn." He held out a hand.

Peter took the proffered hand only with great reluctance. He had hoped to find the man's grip weak. But to his frustration, it was firm and hearty. "And what is your business with Lady Tesh?"

"Lady Tesh?" Lord Redburn laughed. "Never met the woman in my life, though I'm eager to do so."

A groom ran up then, interrupting further conversation.

Frowning, Peter waited with barely concealed impatience as Lord Redburn greeted the groom, giving him instructions for the horse's care. Finally the beast was led away. As he and Lord Redburn walked up the front steps, Peter was quick to pick up where they'd left off. An uncomfortable premonition had settled under his skin that he could not shake.

"If you're not here to see Lady Tesh, who is it you wish to see? Mrs. Kitteridge?"

He knew he was grasping at straws. In the next moment, those final straws were dashed to the ground.

"No, I'm here to see Miss Lenora Hartley."

"And what do you want with the young lady?"

Lord Redburn stopped before the great front doors of the mansion and turned to Peter. "Why, to see my fiancée." He grinned. "Miss Hartley and I are to be married."

Chapter 22

*L*enora. Goodness, child, I've never seen you so inattentive."

Lenora started, her cheeks warming as she glanced at Lady Tesh. Her face grew hotter when she spied the salver piled high with letters that graced the low table between them. The butler must have just brought it in; she'd been so wrapped up in her thoughts, she hadn't heard him enter. "I'm sorry, Gran."

Margery lowered her embroidery to her lap. The worry in her eyes had been growing stronger since breakfast. "You've been incredibly distracted all morning. Perhaps you should return to bed, dear. No one would begrudge you more rest after your ordeal."

Which was the exact opposite of what she should do to calm her roiling thoughts. She could imagine the state of her mind if she went back to bed, curling up in sheets that still carried Peter's scent, remembering what he had done to her mere hours ago. How he had brought her such pleasure, made her feel much more than she had ever thought to.

And how, despite knowing better, she had allowed him into her heart. Frustration and dismay reared up, that she could be so careless. But despite all that, she couldn't regret what they'd shared.

She cleared her throat, trying to control thoughts that were quickly veering off course again. She had to put him from her mind as best as she was able. For, as he'd warned her, he was leaving at the end of his month.

And she could not handle the heartbreak.

"No, I'd much rather stay here with you." She looked down at the slim volume in her hands. She had forgotten she was even trying to read the thing. "Though," she continued wryly, "perhaps I'd better give up on this book. It's not holding my interest at all."

Just then the sound of footsteps sounded in the hall, accompanied by masculine voices. Lenora turned her attention to the sitting room door, her heart skipping a beat as Peter's deep baritone stood out from the others. Anticipation ran along her skin, and she found herself straightening, waiting for the moment he strode into view.

Suddenly he was there, and the breath left her. *This is not good*, a small voice whispered. She could not hope to survive his leaving if she could not control her reaction to him. Yet that did nothing to stop the smile of pleasure from lifting her lips, from the greeting that formed on her tongue.

That greeting died a quick death when she caught sight of the stormy look on his face. But she had no time to process what it might mean. In the next instant, a second man entered behind him. It was not Mr. Nesbitt, however, though a person still known to her.

"Lord Redburn!"

"You know this man?"

Lenora pulled back at the darkness in Peter's voice. "Yes, we became acquainted in London." She smiled at the other man. "It's a pleasure to see you here on the Isle, my lord."

The earl bowed low, flashing her the smile he was renowned for, the one that had set half the female hearts in London to fluttering. "My dear Miss Hartley. You are even more beautiful, if that is at all possible. And Mrs. Kitteridge," he continued, turning to bow Margery's way, "so wonderful to see you."

Margery shot Lenora a confused look before she turned a kind smile on the man. "You as well, my lord. But I don't think you're acquainted with my grandmother."

As Margery made the necessary introductions, Lenora snuck a glance at Peter. He wasn't looking at her, which she supposed shouldn't bother her as it did. But it was the *way* he wasn't looking at her that was troubling. As if he was trying with all his might to ignore her very presence in the room. Instead his narrowed gaze was fastened to Lord Redburn, as if the very devil were in his midst.

Which was ridiculous. Peter had been in America half his life and couldn't know Lord Redburn. And anyway, the young earl was one of the nicest men she had ever met.

What he was doing in Lady Tesh's sitting room, however, was a mystery. Almost as much as Peter's peculiar reaction.

"Lenora," Lady Tesh said, eyeing Lord Redburn with interest, "why don't you call for a tea tray."

"Certainly." She made her way to the bell pull, trying to catch Peter's eye as she did so. Still the dratted man wouldn't look at her. By the time she rejoined the rest of the group, Lady Tesh was ordering everyone into seats. Lenora took hers, trying not to show her hurt when Peter pointedly ignored his great-aunt's suggestion and positioned himself as far from her as he was able to.

"Lord Redburn," Lady Tesh said, her fingers running

through the mop that topped Freya's frazzled head, "what brings you to the Isle?"

Ignoring the frustrating man across from her, Lenora focused on the earl. Finally one mystery would be solved.

But to her further confusion, he looked her way and smiled. "Oh, I'm sure Miss Hartley should be the one to tell you, my lady."

Frowning, Lenora looked to Margery, who appeared even further in the dark than she did. "I'm sorry, Lord Redburn, but I haven't a clue what you're referring to."

The man's smile faltered. "Have you not received word from your father?"

"I have not heard from him since I arrived."

"Oh, dear." Lord Redburn gave a weak chuckle, his expression turning apologetic. "This is an unfortunate turn of events. He assured me he would write with alacrity, that his letter would prepare you before my arrival."

A roaring started up in Lenora's ears. She gripped the arms of her chair with suddenly numb fingers. She could imagine only one reason why her father should write to her with haste, only one reason why Lord Redburn was in Lady Tesh's drawing room.

In a flash, she recalled the salver of letters. She dove for it, scattering the myriad correspondence in her search for one particular missive. Finally, at the very bottom, she found it. Her father's sparse, methodical writing glared up at her like a scold.

She reached for it with shaking fingers. "It appears it did arrive before you," she said through numb lips. "Though only just." She drew in a slow breath, fighting back the mounting panic that was quickly taking over her. "If you will all excuse me?" she managed as she rose.

The two men rose as well, drawing her eye. She

looked at Peter, and nearly gasped. For the first time since
he'd entered the room, his gaze had settled on her. And
it burned.

She must have paled considerably, for Lord Redburn
stepped to her side in an instant. "Perhaps it would be best
if I accompany you, Miss Hartley. In case you have any
questions regarding the contents of your father's letter."

Again a glance at Peter. His gaze had slipped from her
and was now fixed with barely banked hostility on Lord
Redburn. Lenora cringed. She certainly had no wish to
be alone with the man, especially if her father's missive
disclosed the information she feared was in its folds.

But the thought of leaving him with Peter, who looked
as if he were plotting the man's demise, made her break
into a cold sweat.

"Yes," she replied to Lord Redburn, "mayhap that
would be for the best."

The young earl held out an arm to her. She stared at it
for a moment, panic rearing up again. Fighting the urge
to run, she placed her fingers on the fine material of his
coat and let him lead her from the room. Trying with all
her might not to turn and run back to Peter's arms.

From his expression, she didn't think he wanted her
there again.

* * *

"Miss Hartley," Lord Redburn began when they had
ducked into the small, seldom-used sitting room down
the hall.

Lenora held up a hand, praying the man would heed
her silent entreaty. Blessedly he understood at once and
fell silent.

Turning her back on him, she made her way to the far side of the room. With trembling hands, she broke the wax seal and carefully unfolded the paper. Her father's letter wasn't long; in a matter of seconds, she would be able to determine if her suspicions were founded. Even so, she couldn't bring herself to focus on the neat lines of script.

Finally, when she thought she might either scream or faint from the horror of anticipation, she took a shuddering breath and began to read.

Lenora,

I have managed in short order to find a husband for you. It seems your unfortunate history has not destroyed your chances. That the man is an earl is a damn miracle. You will treat Lord Redburn with all the civility and encouragement necessary to hold his interest until the vows are said.

I don't have to remind you what will transpire should you fail in this.

Yours,
Sir Alfred Hartley

A hard ball settled in the pit of her stomach. She read the letter again, searching for any hint of affection. Yet, as before, the words were stark, to the point—and so chill she thought she might never be warm again.

She didn't know how long she stood there, staring down at the letter. It was only when the words began to swim in her vision that she recalled herself. She blinked and drew in a breath. "I must say," she said, her voice overloud

in the silence of the room, "this is quite...unexpected."
Which was such a glaring understatement, it might have
been funny, had there been even a morsel of humor in
the situation.

Her voice seemed to unfreeze Lord Redburn from his
patient watching. His boots sounded on the floor, coming
closer, until he stood at her elbow. Lenora fought the
urge to pull away from him. An unfair reaction. He was a
good man; it was not his fault his timing was so abysmal,
that his suit was the last thing she wanted. That she had
already given her heart to another.

"I'm sorry for the shock. It wasn't my intention to
distress you. I believed your father's letter would arrive
well before me." There was a pause and a soft chuckle. "I
suppose I was a bit eager to get here. I should not have
traveled on a Sunday. My mother would have my head,
were she to find out."

She looked at him then. "Why?"

A puzzled frown drew his inky brows together. "Why
did I travel on Sunday?"

"Why were you eager? You must know my history."

Lord Redburn appeared taken aback. As well he might,
for the words were harsh even to her own ears. But
she couldn't bring herself to care. Her world, which had
finally begun to come together after so long, felt as if
it was unraveling again, and she was only beginning to
realize the impact this would have on her.

He was quick to recover, his features falling into his
perpetually cheerful expression. "You must know, Miss
Hartley, that you're an attractive woman; in fact, you're
one of the most beautiful women of my acquaintance. But
that is merely the surface. It may be presumptuous of me,
but I believe I've gotten to know some of your character

over the past years. And I do believe you are one of the kindest persons I have had the pleasure to know. I have long thought you would make an exceptional Lady Redburn. I would have secured your hand sooner had Landon not gotten the jump on me." Here another soft chuckle before he quickly sobered. "Ah, but how unfeeling of me, for it must pain you still, what happened between you."

It was more question than comment; no doubt he expected some kind of answer. How would he feel to know she could not remember the last time she'd thought of Lord Landon? That her thoughts had been taken over by quite another entirely. She shook her head, too numb to do more than that.

He let out a relieved breath. "Good. That is, I'm glad. For, though I know you cannot care for me as I care for you, I do have hopes that you might one day."

When she remained silent, merely looking at him with a confusing mixture of shock and grief, he smiled sheepishly. "Which, I suppose, was putting the cart before the horse. And here I haven't even asked you properly, though your father assured me when he had the contracts drawn up that you would be only too willing to enter into a union with me. I'm sure it is not a dream young ladies have to let their fathers choose their future husbands for them and have the papers signed before they can voice their acceptance."

The papers signed? Did he mean to say the thing was as good as done, that her father had not waited until the end of summer as he'd promised, but had instead signed her future away without even a warning?

Lord Redburn moved closer and took her hand in his. She was too stunned to react. "I am only too eager to court you, of course," he murmured. "I would dearly love to get down on bended knee and do the whole thing up proper."

He looked so sincere. For a moment, regret overrode the rest of her emotions. If Lord Redburn had come a week ago, she would have been all too willing to do as her father wished and let this man court her. But that was before.

Before Peter had taken her in his arms and loved her body.

Before he had touched her soul.

Before she had fallen in love with him.

Pulling her hand from the earl's, she turned her back on him, pacing to the empty hearth. Her hands found the cold marble of the mantle, her fingers pressing into the hard stone as she fought to right the world back to one that made sense. Every instinct in her screamed to break the thing off now. The words settled heavily on her tongue, begging to be let loose and release her from this hell.

But her father's missive, still clutched in her hand, crinkled then as she gripped the marble tighter. She stared at it, seeing in her mind the final line of that damning letter.

I don't have to remind you what will transpire should you fail in this.

If she refused Lord Redburn and turned down his suit, her father would disown her.

Her stomach lurched. Bile rose in her throat, sharp and acidic. With effort, she forced it back down.

Her father loved her—he must; they were all they had for family in the world—yet she knew he would make good on his threat. Sir Alfred Hartley was shrewd, but he was also almost painfully honest. He was not bluffing in this; she was certain of it.

There was silence behind her. And then, "I'm sure this must all be quite a lot to take in, especially so soon after your last engagement. Please just give it some time. I'm certain you'll find as much happiness in the arrangement as I before long."

He was being far too kind and understanding. And it was doing nothing at all to ease her mind, only making her feel a keen guilt on top of her stunned confusion.

"I need to speak with my father," she mumbled through numb lips.

"Of course. He mentioned he would arrive on the Isle after he concluded some business. We shall await him, talk to him together. I would have you at ease with this decision."

She choked on a manic laugh. There was not much chance that she would ever be easy with this. For while Lord Redburn was by far the most palatable fiancé her father had found for her, he was not Peter.

"And until then," he continued, moving closer, taking her by the shoulders, and turning her gently to face him, "perhaps you might allow me to court you properly? We're to make a life together; I would show you, if I could, how well we will suit."

He took her hand up and brought it to his lips for a gentle kiss. Just then a noise sounded in the hall. Lenora gasped, tearing her hand free from Lord Redburn's grasp, and turned to the door.

Peter stood in the hall, his eyes cold and shuttered. And centered on her. As she watched, helplessness coursing through her, he turned and strode away.

Guilt flared, sharp and hot. But what did she have to feel guilty for? The man had proclaimed there could be nothing between them. He was set to return to Boston. And her place was here, in England.

Yet a small voice whispered that, if he asked, she would go with him to the ends of the earth.

She turned to Lord Redburn. "If you will excuse me for a moment, my lord?"

Before he had a chance to answer, she bolted from the room. Her slippers were silent on the runner as she ran down the hall after Peter's retreating form. Goodness, his legs were long. He was striding across the front hall, his boots sharp on the polished floor, when she caught up with him.

"Peter." She reached out, grasping his arm.

He jerked back as if burned. When he turned to face her, she reared back from the glacial look in his eyes.

She nearly turned tail and fled. This was not the man who had kissed her senseless the night before, who had treated her with such tenderness, who had brought her to such heights of pleasure.

But she would not run. That man was inside somewhere. And this was her future, after all.

"Do you have a moment?"

"I am headed out, Miss Hartley."

The breath left her. His voice told her what his eyes hadn't, that he wished to be gone from her presence with all haste.

But there was a chance that this new attitude was due to Lord Redburn's arrival. If that was true, then perhaps he cared more than he was letting on.

"Could we go someplace private to talk?"

"I don't see what there is to talk about."

Frustration boiled up. Maddening, stubborn man! Couldn't he see she was trying to explain? But losing her temper would only push Peter away. And there was too much at stake for that.

Stepping closer, she lowered her voice. "We didn't have a chance to talk about last night."

If anything, his eyes grew colder. "Have no fear, I won't tell anyone."

"I didn't think you would. But that's not why I wish to speak with you."

"Please stop prevaricating, Miss Hartley. I have places I need to be."

She sucked in her breath. "I am asking for five minutes of your time."

"Are you certain you should keep Lord Redburn waiting so long?"

Aha! Excitement bubbled up. The curl to his lip when he said the other man's name, the clipped words, all spoke of deep emotion. He cared, damn it. Now if he would only admit as much. "If you're concerned over what Lord Redburn is to me—"

"Why should I be concerned?"

He was making no attempt to lower his voice. She glanced hastily about, noting the footman across the hall who was trying his best not to look their way. Face heating, she turned back to Peter and whispered, "Please, if we could speak in private."

His lips pressed tight. Finally, after a moment so long she began to count the ticks of the hall clock, he gave a sharp nod and spun about, heading for a room off the side of the front door.

Lenora hurried in his wake, nearly colliding with his back as he stopped just inside the door.

"There, you have got your privacy, Miss Hartley."

"You did not call me Miss Hartley last night, Peter."

She tried to impart some of her feelings in her tone, to

force him to remember what had been between them. It could not have meant so little to him.

His next words dashed that to bits. "No, I did not. But I think we can both agree that what happened between us was a monumental mistake."

"A mistake?" A ringing started up in her ears. "I assure you, I don't see it as a mistake, Peter."

"I'm sure your fiancé would think differently." His eyes pierced her with sudden intensity. "He is your fiancé, is he not?"

She opened her mouth to deny it, that she had made no promises.

But the contract had been signed. Lord Redburn had said as much. Of course her father would have had everything tied up nice and tight before Lord Redburn left London. Which meant that, for all intents and purposes, she was engaged. Hopelessness coursed through her.

She could deny it, of course. It would be easy enough to do. But she couldn't lie, not to Peter.

The truth sat heavy and bitter on her tongue. "He is." When Peter's features tightened and he made to leave, she hurried to step in his path. She braced her hands on his chest and looked up into his face, beseeching him to understand.

"It was not of my doing, I swear it. My father had the engagement contracts drawn up without my knowledge. He normally would not do such a horrid thing, to go against my wishes in such a way. Or at least not so blatantly. But I have not had the best of luck in engagements, and he knew I wasn't keen on another, and no doubt wanted to make certain this one did not fall through. I'm afraid Lord Landon's abandonment bruised his pride much more than I initially thought—"

"Lord Landon?" Peter's voice sliced through the air. "You mean Hillram, do you not?"

Lenora went cold. "Er, no. I was set to marry Lord Landon not long ago. He…um…did not quite make it to the church the morning of the wedding. It's why I came to the Isle, to escape the scandal."

Beneath her palms, Peter's heart pounded out a fierce beat. Finally he spoke again. His voice, however, was far from kind.

"And so you were engaged to a Lord Landon after Hillram."

Again, she could not lie. "Not exactly."

His eyes narrowed. "Not exactly?"

For the first time in the encounter, Lenora was the one to put distance between them. She stepped back, letting her hands fall from the tense wall of his chest. She had thought to save herself embarrassment by not telling Peter the whole truth of her history. Now, however, that seemed laughably pathetic. She swallowed hard. "Before Lord Landon there was Lord Fig."

He went so still, she wouldn't have been surprised to find pure stone instead of flesh if she'd reached out to touch him again.

"Tell me," he said, his voice a deadly calm she had never heard from him before, "are there any more fiancés? Or have you exhausted your list?"

Her face went hot, an equal mix of mortification and anger. "Three engagements is hardly cause for me to feel shame over." Or so she kept trying to tell herself.

"Four. One mustn't forget Lord Redburn."

Lenora nearly blanched. "He was not of my choosing."

"And the others were?" He crossed his arms, the muscles bunching beneath the material of his coat. "I nearly pitied Hillram for dying so young. Now I wonder if the boy did not have a near miss, as your affections are so fluid."

Her breath left her in a harsh exhale. Tears rushed hot behind her eyes. "And you, Peter?" she asked, her voice barely a whisper. "Did you have a near miss?"

It was as close as she would get to asking if he cared for her. She was bruised from the inside out; she could not let herself become more vulnerable than she already was without losing the very last shred of her pride—and her heart.

And thank goodness she hadn't, for his answer was like a death knell to whatever hopes had reawakened in her breast.

"I was in not the least bit of danger, Miss Hartley. You may ease your fickle heart on that score."

With a curt nod, he strode from the room. Lenora stood staring at the place he had been. For a second, she could not breathe, the grief was so great.

She had been a fool to fall in love with Peter.

How could she have allowed it? He had never left any doubt that there was no hope for a future between them. Yet she had been only too eager to accept his kisses, even to ask for more.

She clenched her hands into fists, feeling the bite of her father's letter in the soft skin of her palm. It would not happen again.

Straightening her shoulders, she marched back to where she'd left Lord Redburn. She half expected to find the man gone.

Yet he was still there, standing in the middle of the small, seldom-used room. When she walked through the door, his face lit up in a smile.

There was not enough left of her heart to twist in guilt. No man should be so happy to see a woman who had given her heart to another.

"Lord Redburn," she stated, stopping before him, "I have thought about it, and would be open to your courting of me."

He grinned that dazzling smile of his and took her hand up again for a kiss. But as she looked down at his dark head bent over her fingers, she felt not a thing.

Chapter 23

*L*enora had just seen Lord Redburn from the house, had barely stepped foot over the threshold of the drawing room, before Margery was hurrying toward her, a half-eaten biscuit still gripped in her hand. "Is Lord Redburn the man your father has chosen for you then?"

Peter's face, cold and unfeeling, swam before her tired eyes, until she managed to banish it. She nodded, allowing Margery to link arms with her and lead her back to her seat. With a sigh, she sat, resting her head against the back of the couch.

A small, warm body settled in her lap. She looked down to find Freya gazing at her with large, solemn eyes. A tiny pink tongue darted out to lick Lenora's fingers before the dog curled up and drifted off to sleep.

"She's not one to worry overmuch for people's feelings," Lady Tesh remarked, "so you must be troubled indeed. I take it you're not happy with Lord Redburn's suit."

What could she say to that? Who wouldn't be happy with the man? He was handsome and kind, titled and rich.

But he wasn't Peter.

No! She would not think of him. He had made it abundantly clear that he didn't care for her. It didn't matter who she married now. It wasn't as if she would give her heart to another.

That didn't stop the grief from welling up in her chest, however.

"Perhaps if I were to have a choice in the matter," she mumbled, more to herself.

"Don't you?" Margery pressed a cool glass of lemonade into her hands.

Lenora drank deeply, letting the cool sweet and sour of it work its way into her weary body before shaking her head. "I knew it was to happen, of course. And it could just as easily have been some aged reprobate."

"And that Lord Redburn is the furthest thing from an aged reprobate as I've ever seen," Lady Tesh said. Her eyes went distant, a small smile flitting over her face. "Why, if I were fifty years younger...Hell, if I were twenty years younger."

"Gran!" Margery exclaimed.

The older woman waved a hand in the air. "Don't tell me you didn't find that man attractive."

Margery's face went scarlet. "That's neither here nor there. It doesn't matter if Lord Redburn has the beauty of the angels—"

"Who wants an angel?" Lady Tesh muttered.

Lenora nearly choked on her lemonade.

"The earl's looks don't matter in the least if Lenora doesn't wish to marry him," Margery stated loudly. She turned to Lenora. "Do you want to marry him?"

"It hardly matters. My father has decreed I marry him or—" She swallowed down the lump that had formed in her throat, tried again. "Or I shall be disowned."

Both women stared at her, aghast. "I know he threatened

as much, but he can't possibly have meant it, Lenora," Margery breathed.

In answer, Lenora handed over the creased letter. The other women read it together, their faces leaching of color as their gazes traveled down the page.

Margery's eyes found hers, wide and stunned. "He couldn't be so cruel."

"I have given him enough heartache in the past years with three failed engagements. He merely wishes to ensure this one is a success."

"But they were not your fault," Margery cried. "Not a one of them."

The first had been. If she had only kept on pretending, Hillram might be alive even now.

Margery, however, was blessedly unaware of Lenora's dark thoughts. "It must be a bluff."

From the expression on Margery's face, however, she didn't believe her words any more than Lenora did. Margery had known Sir Alfred long enough to recognize that he didn't say or do anything lightly. And his threats were never hollow.

Lenora's heart, which she did not think would feel again, nevertheless lurched with a pitiful ache. To know that he would cut her from his life, as easily as if he were removing a splinter from his thumb, hurt her more than she could have thought possible.

Self-pity, however, would not do her a bit of good. She straightened. "He's to come to the Isle. I'll talk to him then. In the meantime, I have told Lord Redburn he may court me, so we may get to know one another better."

Lady Tesh started. "But I thought..."

"Thought what, Gran?"

The older woman seemed to struggle for a moment

before letting out a breath that made her appear to deflate. "I thought it would be much too soon for you to enter into another engagement. The last one ended less than a month ago, after all. There will be a terrible scandal."

Lenora's lips twisted. "No more a scandal than actually being left at the altar, I believe."

"Yes, well." She colored before falling silent.

Suddenly Lady Tesh straightened. Her piercing gaze settled on Lenora with almost frightening intensity. "If he's courting you, I expect he'll be around quite often?"

"I suppose. Though if you have any qualms about his presence, Gran, I understand." For a moment, hope flickered that she might be able to get out of seeing the man at all before her father arrived. A silly wish, for there was no good reason to spurn the man's suit. The signed contract and the threat from her father aside, he was one of the nicest, handsomest men she had ever known.

But he isn't Peter.

The voice whispered again through her mind, desperate now. Grasping her hands tightly in her lap, she tried with all her might to push back the encroaching panic at the lack of control she had over her own fate. Not that she had ever had much control over it before.

Lady Tesh's next words crushed whatever small, silly hope she might have had in getting out of seeing Lord Redburn.

"Of course I don't mind. In fact, I think having Lord Redburn around will be positively wonderful."

The sly look on Lady Tesh's face was quickly replaced by a look of polite interest. It happened so quickly, Lenora thought perhaps she had imagined the whole thing.

"As a matter of fact," Lady Tesh continued, "I believe

you should send a note off to him, to invite him to dinner here tonight."

Once again a vision of Peter's face flashed through her mind, the coldness in his eyes, the cruelty in his voice as he crushed the remains of her heart to dust.

She swallowed hard. "I'm not sure that's wise."

"Nonsense," Lady Tesh declared. "It's perfect. Now off you go." She made a shooing motion in Lenora's direction, dismissing her.

Confused, Lenora lifted a sleepy Freya, placing her on her embroidered cushion at Lady Tesh's side before walking from the room in a daze.

* * *

Peter considered leaving the Isle. For one mad moment, he stood at the edge of the cliffs surrounding his great-aunt's estate and dreamed of booking passage on the next ship, leaving his belongings and even Quincy behind, escaping the heartache that was this blasted island. Why should he stay? To court more pain?

But even as the idea slinked with temptation through him, he knew he would not. His mother's face took shape in his mind, her beauty a mere shadow after the ravages of want and grief and illness. He had ignored his promise to her to his detriment these last thirteen years, had suffered from the guilt of not seeing it through. Her presence had haunted him all that time. Now he had a chance to put her soul to rest once and for all. He couldn't turn his back on it.

That didn't mean, however, that he need return immediately. So he stood on the edge of the rock that was the Isle, looking out over the vast expanse of seemingly unending sea. Feeling as if he were at the edge of the world. But even here he was reminded of Lenora. The breeze tugged at his hair as her hands had done last night. The sun warmed his skin as her slumbering body had done, curled against his. She was in the sigh of the branches, in the call of the seabirds.

He tried with all his might to recall why she didn't deserve his thoughts. She was engaged to another. Worse, she'd been engaged thrice before. All this time he had thought her pining over Hillram. Instead she'd given her fickle attentions to a parade of others. He had merely been last in a long line of them.

There should be nothing but rage within him. He had nearly abandoned the plans he'd spent so long forming in order to be with her.

Yet he still wanted her. More than anything.

Furious with himself, he bent and scooped up a rock from the ground, sending it sailing in a wide arc through the air to plunge into the sea far below. A litany began in his head, a list of names repeated over and over. Lord Hillram. Lord Fig. Lord Landon. Lord Redburn. All men she had been promised to, all men she had been ready to bind her life to. He found, however, that the more he focused on that list, the less power it held. Who was he to expect that she should have sat waiting for his arrival all these years? He was no saint, after all, had certainly not been without companionship. And she was a woman from a good family; marrying well was expected of her. He had heard some of her father. No doubt she had not had much say in the matter.

He punished himself with the image of Lord Redburn bowing over her hand. The two had looked to be in their own world in that moment, the very picture of romantic love. And how well she had looked with him, her dainty blonde fragility only enhanced by the other man's dark elegance. Redburn's looks complemented her in every way.

Bile surged into his mouth, bitter and jarring. Damnation, he couldn't do this. Bracing his hand on a nearby tree, he dug his fingers into the bark, breaking off bits to fall to the still damp ground.

He stood that way for a time, breathing in deeply of the salty sea air, letting the heaviness of it fill his lungs. It was only when the sky began to darken, when the breeze pushed up by the churning waves began to force a chill into his bones, that he heaved a sigh and pushed away from the tree. He would return to the house and attend the blasted dinner party Lady Tesh had planned for this evening, would finish off his time here with as little further emotional entanglement as he could manage. And when he finally left this hellhole, he would not look back.

Chapter 24

*T*hough she knew a trip to the cliffs was imperative, not only to complete her promise to Lady Tesh but also to continue facing her memories of Hillram—which she had regrettably forsaken since Peter had begun to take up so much of her thoughts—it was the very last thing Lenora wished to do. Not when she knew what was coming, and how it so painfully mirrored her own heartbreaking story with Peter.

Yet here she was, with both Peter and Lord Redburn. At the most tragic place on the Isle.

She rubbed the back of her neck as the carriage wound its way toward their destination. Last night's dinner party had taken a toll on her. She was used to donning a mask for public events, to smile and converse when she would rather hide in the corner. Her father had expected no less from her.

But nothing had prepared her for the pain of pretending everything was right with the world when in reality she wanted nothing more than to bury herself under her covers and cry until her heart was wrung of tears. She had done it, however, and had used every ounce of strength to keep her gaze from straying to Peter, keeping her attentions focused on Lord Redburn and the future he hoped to make with her.

No, not hoped, she reminded herself. For it was all too certain. She reached into the pocket of her gown, crushing the already abused letter from her father. She had known after the torment of last night that she would need a reminder of why she had to go along with this arrangement. She had thought her father's threats would be just the thing.

It seemed, however, they did not hold the power over her that she'd thought. Her heart still cried out that this was wrong, that she could not go through with it. She withdrew her hand and clenched her fingers in her lap. Her heart could protest all it liked. If Peter didn't want her, what was the point in fighting the inevitable?

The carriage slowed, then rocked to a halt. The door opened, and Lenora braced herself to descend from the conveyance and face Peter in all his scowling splendor.

Margery, however, startled her by murmuring a few words to the waiting groom and closing the door. She faced Lenora, her countenance grave.

"Are you certain you're up for this?"

"It's just sketching, Margery."

"That's not what I was referring to and you know it." Her friend paused, then said in a rush, "What's going on with you and Mr. Ashford?"

Lenora fought against reacting to the stab of pain in her chest. "Nothing at all," she managed with what she thought was impressive calm.

But Margery was not about to be fooled. "Lenora, don't lie, not to me. I know there's something going on between you." She reached across the carriage, placing a hand over Lenora's. "If you prefer Peter, you can break it off with Lord Redburn. You made no promises, after all—"

"You know I cannot," Lenora exploded, pulling back

from Margery's touch. Guilt bloomed hot; she'd never talked to Margery thus. She pushed it brutally aside. Her very sanity was at stake.

"I'll be disowned," she continued more gently, unable to look at her friend's face, knowing the hurt that would be there. "You saw the contents of my father's letter. I cannot escape this fate, even if I wanted to."

"But you don't want it!" Margery burst out. "Lenora, you must know, my grandmother and I would provide you with a home."

"And am I to live on your charity for the rest of my life?" She looked at Margery, willing her to understand. "When Aaron died, and your father decreed you should live with him, did you do it? Or did you insist on living on your own terms?"

Margery sucked in a breath, pain flashing in her normally mild brown eyes. "This is different," she replied. "None of this is on your terms. But..." She seemed to struggle, before blurting out, "But if Mr. Ashford were to marry you, you wouldn't have to worry about your father's threats—"

"Peter will not have me!" The words burst from her. She clapped a hand over her mouth, desperate to hold back anything else that could give away the secret agony of her heart. But it was too late, for Margery understood only too well what those words meant.

"So you do love him," she whispered.

Lenora nodded miserably.

"Why didn't you tell me? Why did you lie to me?"

Tears sprang to Lenora's eyes at the pain in her friend's voice. "You felt so guilty over suggesting our trip to the Isle. I'd hoped to protect you from more."

"Protect me?" Margery gave a disbelieving laugh,

grabbing Lenora's hand. "You silly, misguided thing, you've no need to protect me." She paused and frowned then. "But what do you mean, he won't have you? He's said as much?"

Defeated, Lenora slumped back against the plush squabs. "Yes, Margery. I practically begged him to admit there could be something between us. And he was very adamant that there was nothing."

Margery stared at her, stunned. "Then he's a fool," she whispered.

"I'm the only fool in this." When Margery made to speak again, Lenora held up a hand. Her emotions were hanging by a thread as it was; if Margery continued worrying away at it, Lenora feared her control might snap.

"Let's talk of it no more. Please."

Margery must have heard the barely banked desperation in her voice, for she pressed her lips tight and, squeezing Lenora's hand, gave her a look of utter sadness before nodding and opening the carriage door.

Right away Lord Redburn was there, holding out his hand to help them down.

"My dear Miss Hartley," he murmured as she placed her fingers in his, "you are looking a trifle pale. Are you certain you're well enough for this outing?"

The man was far too kind, far too good. He deserved a woman who could care for him. Not Lenora, whose heart was a fractured thing.

Just then Peter stepped into view. She had a brief glance of his hard features before he turned away.

Setting her shoulders, she attempted a smile for Lord Redburn, who was waiting patiently for her answer. She would make certain the man never had cause to regret chaining himself to her.

"I'm well enough, my lord. There's nothing a bit of fresh ocean air can't cure."

He laughed, his dark eyes crinkling at the corners, and waved an arm out at the sea, where it crashed far below the cliffs. "That you have got in abundance." Then he bent his arm toward her, his gaze warm and affectionate on her face. "Shall we?"

She nodded, placing her fingers on his sleeve. Ignoring the pang in her chest that wished it were quite another arm she was holding.

Chapter 25

*P*eter followed far behind the rest of the party as they made their way to the formation of rock that rose up near the cliff's edge. He tried his damnedest to keep his gaze from Lenora and Redburn, but thus far had been an abysmal failure. Which was doing absolutely nothing to improve his mood.

Thank goodness he hadn't been relegated to pack mule again. No, Redburn, gallant fellow that he was, had been more than happy to take on the carrying of Lenora's supplies. With Quincy helping Margery, Peter was left to his own devices.

Which was as he liked it. He wouldn't even consider how his lack of a task left him with too much time to think about Lenora and her fiancé.

The night before had been utter torture. Lenora had appeared content, happy even, guiding Redburn around the room to introduce him to the other guests with a natural ease that spoke volumes of where she belonged. Was that what she was like in London, a glittering diamond, in her element? That was the Lenora he didn't know, the one who had a place in the world that he could never be a part of.

But Redburn was a part of that world. He would give her

all she deserved and more. And Peter had been the greatest fool in creation to think he could have made her happy.

They came to the formation then. From the road, it had appeared to be solid stone. But upon closer inspection, there was a wide opening tucked in the rock. They slipped through, one by one. A short walk through a tunnel into a wide, open-ended cave, and suddenly the whole of the ocean was before them in all its splendor.

Beyond the cave a sturdy shelf jutted out over the sea, and it was here they stopped and took in the view. As with the Elven Pools, Peter stood for a moment in wonder. He had looked out over the sea during his time here, of course, had stood at the cliff's edge and studied the churning waves. But there was something different here, dredging up an inscrutable kind of recognition that Peter felt to the very depths of his soul.

He frowned, studying the surrounding scenery, trying to make sense of the emotions awakening in his breast. The wind caught in the bowl of rocks, whipping the sparse vegetation, twisting it into fanciful shapes, a hollow lowing moving through the protected grotto. It sounded eerily like distant sobbing, bridging the distance of a millennium. He shivered, though the air was so warm today as to be nearly uncomfortable, his wonder transforming to a keen sorrow as that recognition became clear: it was grief calling to grief, of a loss so profound, he felt it in his very bones.

Quincy spoke then, pulling Peter from the dark depths of his musings. "This is quite the place," he said, moving tentatively toward the edge to peer down. Peter couldn't blame him his caution. The wind tugged at his hair and his clothing, so that he felt as if it were trying to drag him over the edge.

"It's disconcerting, I know," Margery said. "But quite important to Synne and Ivar's story. I do hope it's not too much for you gentlemen."

Redburn let loose a weak chuckle. "Certainly not," he said with false bravado.

"Of course not," Quincy echoed. Despite his brave words, however, he was quick to step far back from the edge.

"And you, cousin?"

"I assure you," Peter said, "I cannot be frightened away."

She gave him a long, considering look before turning to Lenora. "Shall we begin?"

Lenora nodded and took a seat on a flat rock close to the wall, adjusting her skirts. Redburn was at her side in a trice, handing over her sketch pad, asking her if she needed her pencil sharpened. When she murmured her thanks, the man immediately went to work, using a small knife to trim the tip.

Peter fought the urge to gag. Did she truly like that fawning attention? She was certainly welcoming it readily enough.

As disgusted as he was, however, he couldn't fail to recognize the desire deep in him to be the one beside Lenora, trimming her pencils and seeing to her comfort, the one receiving her smiles.

Margery spoke then. "You remember, of course, that Synne and Ivar fell in love at the Elven Pools," she began, settling beside Lenora and accepting her own sketch supplies from Quincy with a smile. "They lived happily for a short time. Synne even gave Ivar a son."

She looked out over the water. "Ivar was often at sea. Every time he left, Synne would keep vigil here during the day, waiting for his return." Her fingers drifted over the rock wall between her and Lenora. "It's said she carved this symbol into the rock to protect him while he was away."

Despite his determination to remain aloof, Peter found himself transfixed. The carving was rough, a circle made up of what looked to be runes, surrounding a figure that branched into eight spokes. He stepped closer, the better to see it.

Lenora, who was bent over her blank page, tensed. Too late he realized he had stepped too close. A breeze blew into the alcove, stirring the tendrils of hair that curled against her cheek, and he was assailed by her sweet scent of berries. It wrapped around him, making him remember things he shouldn't. Of a dim room, pale limbs against white sheets. The taste of her on his tongue. Her moans of pleasure filling his ears.

He jerked back as if burned. Even so, he couldn't tear his eyes from her. She wouldn't return his gaze, instead staring at her blank paper. But her beautiful green eyes were wide, her face pale. Was she remembering as well? He longed to reach out for her, to skim his fingers over her cheek, to see if she turned her face into his palm in silent plea, or if she pulled away. Her lush lips parted as if she heard his thoughts. His hand twitched, and he felt himself leaning toward her...

"A symbol of protection," Redburn said in his jovial tone, breaking Peter from the spell he'd been under. "That's quite romantic, wouldn't you say?" He smiled down at Lenora.

Peter recoiled, striding to the far side of the alcove. The more distance he placed between him and Lenora, the better.

"I'm afraid," Margery murmured, "it doesn't have a happy ending. You'll recall, Ivar never meant to make this island his home. He had ambitions that went far beyond a mere outpost. And so, when he was offered a position in one of the Five Boroughs, he took it. And left Synne and their child behind."

There was a stunned beat of silence. And then a voice, ringing through the grotto: "You cannot be serious."

Every eye turned his way, all save Lenora's. And Peter realized that *he* had been the one to speak.

His face heated. "That is," he continued, "I'm surprised it ended in such a way."

"I agree," Quincy jumped in. "We were under the assumption it was a romance you were telling us. But he left. That's not a romance. A romance should end with a happily-ever-after. This is a tragedy, like *Romeo and Juliet*."

Lenora did look at Peter then, her eyes wide with the pain of remembrance. And he recalled with stunning clarity the conversation they'd shared at the pools, and how close he'd been to kissing her.

Blessedly the others were too engrossed to notice their tense exchange. "I do apologize, Mr. Nesbitt," Margery drawled. "I should have warned you."

"Yes, you should have," he grumbled.

She laughed. "But does that mean you don't wish to hear the rest?"

Quincy threw up his hands, leaning against the stone wall. "You may as well tell us. I don't see how it can get any worse."

Margery grinned but continued. "Synne remarried soon after and is thought to have had a long and prosperous life, though she never bore another child. Perhaps she wasn't happy in that life, however. For when she died, she asked that her ashes be brought to these very cliffs, to be spread over the sea so she might find her beloved Ivar in the afterlife."

"I was wrong," Quincy muttered. "It got worse."

Margery shrugged. "Love does not guarantee a happy ending, I'm afraid."

There was a small sound from Lenora's direction. It mingled with the lowing of the wind, until they appeared to be one and the same. How Peter kept from looking at her, he would never know.

Suddenly she spoke. "We should get started, Margery. It unsettles me to be out here."

Strange wording. Peter could see her being nervous. The height, as well as the concentrated wind, had even Quincy looking a bit green.

But no, she had specifically said "unsettled." Did she feel it, too, the eeriness of the place? As if there would never be happiness here again?

As Quincy and Redburn moved off to the side, conversing quietly, Lenora and Margery bent their heads over their paper. Several minutes passed, the faint sound of pencil scratching parchment breaking through the low sounds of wind and conversation. Eventually Peter realized that only one pencil was moving across the page. A quick look at the women, and he could see he was right on that score. But it was not Margery whose pencil was still. No, it was Lenora.

* * *

Peering down at the pristine paper, Lenora frowned. The simple mechanics of art had always come easily to her, even when she had refused to put her heart in it. Now, however, the image wouldn't come. By sheer will, she lowered the pencil, scratched out a few hesitant lines. She glanced up at the view, returned her gaze to the beginnings of her drawing, tried adding a bit more.

Blowing out a huff of frustration, she erased the image. She would try again. And this time she would succeed. No matter her determination, however, only disjointed lines came from her pencil. Tearing the sheet free, she crushed it in her hands and tossed it across the stone floor. It bounced along, caught up in the wind, until it was launched over the side of the cliff and fell out of view. But there was no satisfaction in it.

She returned her attention to the paper in her lap and bent her head to try again. And again. Yet no matter how many times she attempted it, the image wouldn't come. Finally she was out of paper and she sat there, lost.

"Lenora."

Her name on his lips. She closed her eyes, feeling it flow through her, a tingling that worked its way through her limbs to her very heart. Taking a deep breath, she fought against her longing with everything in her.

But he wasn't through tormenting her. She felt him lower to his haunches beside her. "Are you well?"

Damn the man for choosing now to be kind. And damn her traitorous heart for clinging so desperately to it, for trying to find hope in it. Things were over between them, and she'd best remember it.

She opened her eyes and looked out over the cliff's edge. For she knew, if she looked at him, she would be lost. "I'm fine."

He paused. His breath stirred the wisps of hair that had come loose at her temple. Lenora gripped her pencil tight, feeling the aromatic cedar begin to bend in her grip as she fought against the desire to lean into him and feel his strong arms close about her.

Peter spoke again. "Is there anything I can do?"

Leave me, she wanted to cry out. *Leave the Isle, let me heal from this and find peace again!* The words clamored at her lips, begging to be released. As long as he remained on Synne, she would never be able to put him behind her.

Desperate, she pressed her lips tight and shook her head. Still he stood there, hovering over her. Pulling her nerves so taut, she thought she might snap in two. *Please go away.* The thought whispered through her head in an endless litany.

Finally he seemed to sense he was not wanted. He rose and moved to the far side of the grotto. And Lenora thought she would suffocate from the crushing loss that washed over her.

She stood, the remainder of her supplies falling to the stone floor with a clatter. The conversation beside her paused. Margery peered at her, concern darkening her eyes.

For a moment, she feared her friend would ask if she was well. Because she was not. She was the furthest thing from "well" there was.

Instead her friend forced a smile that didn't reach her eyes as she rose from her own seat. "I've had enough for today as well. It's not the easiest place to sketch, is it, dearest?"

Immediately she set about gathering their supplies with a busy cheerfulness. Lenora let her direct the men, her mind too full of Peter and Ivar and Synne and tragedy and her own broken heart to help. When they were ready to depart, she took a deep breath and turned to join the others. Only to find that Peter was not there. His mount, too, was gone when they emerged. The only indication he had even been there, the distant pounding of his horse's hooves in the air, and the ache in Lenora's chest.

Chapter 26

*H*ow was it possible a week could seem so long?

Redburn's laughter reached Peter, setting his back teeth on edge. Ah, yes, that was how.

He had tried his damnedest to ignore the man's presence. But Redburn spent more time at Seacliff than he did outside of it. And Lenora seemed only too happy to have him about.

Lenora. The same ache that had plagued him since Redburn's arrival settled in his chest. He rubbed at it, sinking more deeply in his chair by the window, and looked out at the bright blue of the sky over Lady Tesh's rose garden. In three days' time he would be free of this place, and he could leave all of this behind.

Which only made the ache worse. He let loose a soft curse. He was miserable here on the Isle. He was miserable about returning home. It seemed nothing about this could make him happy. Even worse, the knowledge that he would not have to forgo his revenge on the Duke of Dane gave him no comfort, either. Where was the burning desire to see the man suffer? What had happened to the rage that had fueled him for over a decade?

A stupid question, really. He knew what had happened. Lenora had happened. Working her way into his heart,

making him want things he had refused to consider before.
Revenge had been all he had ever wanted, the impetus
that drove him, the fire in his blood. Now it was a bitter,
hollow thing. It wouldn't warm him at night, wouldn't
bring comfort and contentment to him in his old age.

"Peter." Lady Tesh's voice crashed into his morose
thoughts with all the finesse of a glass shattering. "The
tea has arrived. Come here, Peter."

Heaving a sigh, he closed his eyes and took a steadying breath. He would not fail in finally keeping his last
promise to his mother. He'd sat through countless hours
biting his tongue as Lady Tesh baited him, had donned
that ridiculous formal suit, had traipsed all over this
blasted island learning about the love affair—and subse-
quent tragedy—that had shaped it. Surely he could suffer
through another three days to see it realized.

He rose and made his way to where the group was
sitting. As had become his habit in the past week, he
eschewed the sturdy, comfortable, ugly chair he'd placed
there that first night, instead easing himself down on a
delicate, spindly excuse for seating as far from Lenora as
he was able. What care did he have if the damn thing
splintered to bits under him? If he had to sit close to
Lenora, to smell her and watch how she allowed Redburn
to cater to her, he would vomit.

Margery was already busy with the tea tray. As the
beverage steeped, she poured a glass of lemonade from
the pitcher, handing it to Lenora.

"I still don't understand how you can prefer that to a
bracing cup of tea," Redburn said. The words were spoken
with his typical joviality. Yet it rubbed Peter wrong. As
it had every time the man had commented on Lenora's
beverage choice.

"It's a silly quirk, I know," she replied with a small smile.

Peter expected Lenora's comment to be the end of it, as it had been every other time her drink preference had been brought up. After all, the two were amazingly cordial with one another.

They would have years of happy politeness ahead of them.

But Redburn was not quite ready to let it go today.

"Truly, though, you can't mean to never drink tea."

"If I can manage it."

"But surely, when you're hostess in your own home, you'll drink what your guests do. Otherwise they might be made to feel uncomfortable."

There was a pause in the conversation, Redburn's words hanging like a challenge in the air. The meaning was subtle but clear: Redburn didn't wish for Lenora to embarrass him in front of their guests once they married.

Margery, ever the peacekeeper, broke the strained silence as she busied herself with the tea, asking everyone their preference, though she had been serving the same cups of tea to the same people for weeks now.

"And Mr. Nesbitt," she asked, "how would you like your tea?"

Peter didn't hear Quincy's reply, for Redburn chose that moment to speak again.

"Perhaps if you were to *try* to like tea, you might find something to recommend it," he said with an encouraging smile.

Lenora stared at Redburn, the only movement her hand as it tucked into the pocket of her gown. Surely she would fight back against such high-handedness.

But in the next moment, she nodded. "Perhaps" was all she said.

Outrage rose up in him. Where was the spitfire who had put him in his place, who had never backed down from a fight with him? He had the urge to lurch to his feet, grab Redburn's cravat, and beat him to a bloody pulp. Instead he turned to Margery.

"I would like a glass of lemonade."

Margery, in the process of adding a splash of milk to some tea, blinked at him, which caused considerably more milk to be added if her horrified expression was anything to go by.

"Oh, Mr. Nesbitt, I am so very sorry. Here, let me prepare you another cup."

"No need," Quincy said with a smile. "I was actually hoping for a bit more milk today." He took the cup, casting Peter a hooded look.

It took Margery a moment to regain her calm demeanor. "Let's see," she fretted, looking at the tea tray. "Oh! Peter, of course I can give you a glass of lemonade."

Peter accepted the glass she offered him, refusing to look Redburn's way as he did so. Despite his determination, however, he could not keep from glancing at Lenora. Her face was impassive, a blank mask. But there was something deep in the pale green of her eyes, an emotion he couldn't fathom.

Conversation turned to innocuous things, the weather, the quality of Miss Peacham's biscuits at the Beakhead Tea Room versus the ones made by Lady Tesh's own cook, the assembly ball that evening that they all expected to attend.

At the next lull in conversation, Lady Tesh, who had been silent until then, spoke up. "Have you decided when to return to the cliffs? It's the final painting I require for my records, you know."

"Yes, we know," Margery said with the patience she had used in fielding the very same question for days now. "But Lenora is not ready to draw."

"And when will she be ready?"

Peter chanced a glance at Lenora. She had fallen silent at Lady Tesh's question. While the other women talked about her as if she were not there, she gave no indication of having heard them.

Save for the slight tightening of her lips, the convulsion of her fingers on her untouched glass. In a flash, he remembered the frustration on her face as she'd struggled at the cliffs to draw, her unexpected failure to sketch anything. He'd been unable to stand by silently and do nothing then, though she had not appreciated his concern in the slightest. He could not stand by now.

"She will return to the cliffs when she's good and ready to," Peter growled.

That seemed to break her from the fog she was in. She looked at him fully, for what felt like the first time in over a week.

Oh, she had glanced at him, her lovely green eyes with that maddening fringe of thick lashes skimming over him like a ladle taking the thick cream from the top of a bucket of fresh milk.

But she had not allowed her eyes to settle on him, to take him in. No, the last time she'd done that, she'd been begging him to understand about Redburn, claiming he was not of her choosing. Asking Peter if he'd had a near miss with her.

He'd been a fool, a damn fool, for turning away from her.

He took a deep draft of his lemonade, trying to shock the ridiculous regret back into the ether where it belonged.

Redburn was her match in every way. He would give her the life she deserved.

But did he understand her? Would he make her happy? For the first time, doubt settled in Peter's gut. And all over a damn glass of lemonade. It was an overreaction on his part, surely. The two had been nothing but pleasant with one another over the past week, to the point that Peter had been nearly physically ill watching it. One small disagreement did not indicate their future unhappiness.

Mundane talk buzzed about him for a time. It was interrupted by the butler entering.

"Lady Clara and Lady Phoebe are here to see you, my lady."

The two women sailed into the room, their faces wreathed in smiles as Peter, Quincy, and Redburn rose from their seats.

"My dears," Lady Tesh said with a wide smile, "what a splendid surprise. Is your father feeling better today then?"

"He is, thank God," Lady Clara replied. Just then her gaze snagged on Quincy and her steps faltered. With seeming effort, she tore it away, turning a bright smile on the rest of them.

"When he ordered us out of the house, we could not think of a better place to come than here," Lady Phoebe chirped happily, moving forward to kiss Lady Tesh's cheek.

The two sisters headed for seats. Suddenly Quincy lurched away from his chair next to Peter. "Here's a fine seat, Lady Clara."

The woman appeared startled by the offer. Coloring, she nodded her thanks and moved to the chair in question. "And how are you, Aunt?" she asked as she sat. "You seem well."

"How can I not be well, when I have such company to keep me young?"

Happy greetings commenced. Finally they came to Peter.

"Cousin," Lady Clara said warmly, "it's good to see you."

Peter grunted a response, turning back to his drink in the hopes they would leave him in peace.

But it was not to be. As the others fell into easy conversation, Lady Clara, seated at his side, turned her full attention on him. "I had hoped you might take me up on my invitation to visit Danesford," she said, accepting a cup of tea from Margery with a smile. "My father is most eager to see you again."

Peter didn't think it possible for his shoulders to tense further than they were. But he felt it, the tightening of the muscles, spreading up over the back of his neck, making his head pound. "I don't know that I will have the time," he muttered.

Lady Clara laughed. "Not have the time? You're here for another few days at least, are you not? I'm certain you can manage an hour or two."

"I cannot."

"Goodness, is our great-aunt such a taskmaster?" Again that laugh. "I must have a talk with her then."

"It will not do any good, my lady."

"Oh, pish. She's not a difficult woman; she will understand it's something you wish to do."

"I do not wish to visit the duke," he growled, unable to take one more minute of her rambling.

The words hung in the air between them. Lady Clara stared at him, the pleasant smile that had curved her lips faltering.

"You don't wish to see Father?"

He should retreat. This woman had done nothing wrong, did not deserve his ire.

Yet now that the beast of his frustration and anger had been released, he couldn't close it back up again.

"I've said all there is to say to your father, and if I never see him again, it will be too soon," he snapped. "Your father is a heartless monster who deserves nothing from me."

As Lady Clara stared at him in stunned horror, Peter gradually became aware of the silence in the room. Every eye was trained on him, with expressions running from shock to pity to anger.

A ringing started up in his ears. Good God, he had to get away from here. Rising, he strode from the room, realizing only as he reached the front hall that the glass of lemonade was still in his hand. He slammed it on a nearby table and hurried out into the bright summer day. He would ride, until the riot of his emotions was tamed, until the devil on his shoulders was appeased.

He had not gone twenty paces when a hand on his arm spun him about. Quincy stood there, his face tense with anger.

"What the devil was that about, Peter?"

He threw off his friend's hand, continuing on the path to the stables. But Quincy's boots sounded behind him, angry and quick on the crushed shell path.

"I'm talking to you, damn it."

"It's no business of yours," Peter shot back over his shoulder.

"Isn't it? I followed you halfway across the world. I think that makes it my business. You're still going through with it, aren't you? You still intend to ruin their lives."

"Did you think I would give it up? You know me better than that."

"You damn, idiotic fool," Quincy spat. "Stop and face me."

It wasn't the insult that caused Peter to do as he was bid. It was the pain in his friend's voice. The fury that twisted Quincy's normally cheerful countenance, however, stunned him.

"Even after getting to know these people," his friend said, his words low and furious, "you will still go through with your revenge?"

What could he say to that? "Yes."

The one word, clipped and tense, hung in the air between them. "You bastard," Quincy breathed.

Peter drew himself up. "He deserves to pay for what he did."

"The duke?" Quincy let loose a humorless laugh. "The man is dying. Your revenge, for what it's worth, doesn't have to go beyond the end of his life."

"Are you suggesting I forget it all after he's dead?"

"And why not? He'll be dead; he'll never know."

Fury snaked through Peter. "So I'm to pretend the debt is settled, just because the man is dead?"

"It will be," Quincy insisted. "Don't you see? Your revenge will be complete."

"My revenge will not be complete until everything he loved is destroyed." He shook his head. "It matters not that he's not here to witness it. *I* will know his empire is intact. *I* will know that I'm the reason his bloodline lives on."

"This is madness," Quincy cried. "You would ruin countless lives because of your mother's death? It's just as well she's dead, for she would be ashamed of you."

Peter's fist met Quincy's jaw. Pain exploded in his knuckles, the skin splitting from the force of the impact. He stood, breathing heavily, the sudden blossom of red in his vision fading as Quincy fingered his bloodied lip.

"Forgive me," his friend murmured, his eyes focused on something over Peter's shoulder. "I should not have brought your mother into it."

Peter wanted to howl. The apology, sounding so hollow, so defeated, only managed to expand the guilt that had begun to work under his skin. He opened his mouth, desperate to mend the breach between them. Quincy, however, cut the words off before they could take shape.

"I think it's best if I return to Boston as soon as possible. I can no longer support your efforts here. And I can't sit by and watch while you destroy these people's lives and your own."

Pain stole the very breath from Peter. "You would leave?"

Still his friend would not meet his eyes. "I can see no other way. For what you've been to me, I can't watch the damage you would willingly cause."

The pain intensified until it was all he could see, all he could feel. He fought against it, transformed it, turned the burn of it into the cleansing fire of anger.

"I will bid you goodbye then," he said, before turning and stalking away.

Chapter 27

*I*t really is too bad Mr. Nesbitt had to miss the ball," Lady Tesh lamented for what felt like the hundredth time that evening.

Peter closed his eyes and fought the urge to curse. Though whether it was from Lady Tesh's reminder, or the sight of Lenora twirling about on that popinjay Redburn's arm—or even from the ridiculously snug evening clothes that he continued to abhor—he wasn't certain. For the first time in his life, he wanted to drown himself in drink, to muddle his brain with all manner of alcohol. And of course, in the Isle of Synne's luxurious assembly rooms, there was not a drop to be had.

Quincy would have known where to get the stuff. Hell, he would have secreted a flask of it in his tails.

For a single, glorious moment, the hurt that had sat on Peter's shoulders since that afternoon lifted and he felt his lips curving into a smile. In the next instant, however, he remembered the violent argument, the one he wasn't sure he and Quincy could come back from. He closed his fingers into a fist, the burst of pain in his damaged knuckles an even more potent reminder of what he had lost.

Lady Tesh, oblivious to his distress, cheerfully added

to it. "My, but Lenora and Lord Redburn look well together. I have never seen a couple so well matched."

"Except he's a pompous arse who doesn't deserve
her," Peter muttered before he could think better of it.

"What was that, Peter?"

"Nothing, nothing at all." He grabbed at his cravat,
yanking hard at it, and cast a desperate look around the
vast room. "Isn't it time to leave yet?"

The viscountess laughed. "My boy, we've been here
less than an hour. Would you take the ladies away from
such merriment before the evening has even begun?"

Against his will, his eyes found Lenora. She smiled
up at Redburn as he guided her into a circle. *Yes.* The
fierce—and foolish—need to get her away from Redburn
pounded in his temples. He'd better get it through his
head, and quick, that Lenora was bound to the man.

"And anyhow," she continued, "you've not danced
once this evening. I expect to see you out on that floor for
the next set."

"Then you shall be disappointed, for I don't intend to
dance tonight."

"I beg your pardon?" She gaped up at him from her
spot on the bench. "You would refuse to stand up and
dance when there are so many females without partners
here tonight? That is not well done of you, Peter. I must
insist you do your gentlemanly duty and dance."

"I am no gentleman, madam," he gritted.

"Poppycock. You are the most gentlemanly man I
know."

He could not help the harsh laugh that escaped his
chest. "Do you need spectacles then? For I assure you,
Redburn is much more a gentleman than I."

Too late he realized his mistake. Lady Tesh's too-knowing eyes narrowed on him. "Fine manners are all well and good, Peter. But it is the things that lie deeper in a man's heart that determine a true gentleman."

He couldn't help the question that tumbled from his lips. "Such as?"

"Such as a man who would make it a point to put a young woman at ease and take lemonade instead of tea. Or a man who would wander over hill and dale just because a sentimental old woman wishes it. Or an even greater example, a man who would run out into a storm to save a young woman's life with no care or concern for his own."

Heat suffused his face, his gaze sliding away. "You read too much into small things."

She was silent for some time. "No," she murmured, "I don't think I do."

The music ended then, the wave of bodies exiting the floor preventing him from making a response. Which was just as well, for he hadn't a clue what to say.

Lenora, Redburn, and Margery returned to their side. "I vow," Redburn said with a jovial smile, "I have not had so much fun in longer than I care to remember. The idea to come to this subscription ball was genius, Lady Tesh."

She chuckled. "Coming from such a worldly man, who has seen his fair share of elegant London balls and soirees, I shall take that as the highest compliment."

Lenora, Peter noticed, was silent throughout the playful exchange. She seemed to watch them happily enough, a small smile curving her lips. Yet there was something off about it. She looked like a china doll, with nothing behind the cheerful expression.

"Miss Hartley," he said, taking a step closer, just

stopping himself from reaching out for her arm, "do you require a beverage?"

She blinked, appearing as if she were awakening from a dream. She flushed, her smile faltering. "I'm well, thank you," she murmured, not looking at him.

Her dismissal shouldn't sting, yet it did. But if it was space she wanted from him, he would give it to her. Clenching his hands into fists, he retreated a step. Redburn's attention, however, had been snagged by their quiet exchange. "I do think Ashford is right, my dear. Allow me to fetch you some punch."

Before she could reply, he was off, threading through the crowd.

Peter stared after the man, a haze of red obscuring his vision for a moment. *My dear?* When the blazes had that started? A moment later, he dragged in a deep, steadying breath. They were to marry. What was it to him what the man called her?

Redburn returned in short order, carrying not only the promised cup of punch, but matching cups for Margery and Lady Tesh as well. *Of course he would.*

The four of them talked and laughed, while Peter did his best to ignore them. Soon a new set began to form. Redburn held out his arm to Lenora. "Shall we, my dear?"

"Of course." She smiled, placing her fingers on Redburn's arm, and he made to lead her away.

"Just a moment there, Lord Redburn," Lady Tesh called before they had taken even a step. "You cannot mean to dance again with our Lenora."

He smiled that sickeningly cheerful smile at the viscountess. "How can I not, when Miss Hartley looks so fetching tonight? She quite outshines the rest—"

"Yes, yes," Lady Tesh interrupted, waving her hand in the air. "But that is neither here nor there. The fact of the matter is, you cannot monopolize her time all evening long. It isn't done. Even in such a small place as the Isle."

Peter's smug satisfaction was cut short as she turned her sharp eyes on him. "You can take her out, Peter."

Peter gaped at her before looking at Lenora. She was staring back at him, her expression a mirror of the horror that was coursing through him. And in a flash, he remembered a dark ballroom, her hand in his, the feel of her waist as he guided her to unheard music. And then her mouth hot under his, her soft gasps echoing in the cavernous room.

"No." The word came out harsh and desperate. "That is," he continued in a much more controlled tone, "I don't plan to dance at all this evening."

"Nonsense," Lady Tesh scoffed. "I've seen you dance before. There's no earthly reason why you cannot do so again."

"I cannot."

"Why?"

"Because…" His gaze flew about, searching for a reason, any reason, he could give. Finally he settled on, "I injured my shin. Against a low table."

The viscountess pursed her lips. "I don't recall hearing about such an injury."

"I didn't wish to worry you. It's minor, after all. But," he said, a tad louder as the older woman opened her mouth to argue again, "it's enough to prevent me from dancing."

Margery intervened, giving him an apologetic smile before looking at the viscountess with mild reproach. "Gran, don't force the man to dance if it pains him."

Peter could have kissed his cousin. Instead he gave them a jerky bow, and keeping his gaze from Lenora, he hurried off, remembering a dozen paces away to favor his leg. His completely hale and hearty—and uninjured—leg.

Oh, he was going to hell. But he would accept that gladly if it meant he did not have to dance with Lenora.

* * *

Peter stood just outside the side door of the assembly hall, ignoring the muffled sounds of merriment from within and trying his damnedest not to think of Lenora inside. That was why he had come outside in the first place, wasn't it? He was certainly not going to remember how soft her skin was, or how her voice turned husky calling his name, or how eager her mouth was...

He sucked in a gulp of sea air, shaking his head to clear it. Damn it all to ever-loving hell, he had spent the past hour or better freezing his bollocks off in the unseasonably cold weather in a quest to forget her, yet his thoughts were even more uncontrollable than they had been before.

It was painfully obvious that no amount of clear air would help him. He should go back inside. Lady Tesh would be furious at him for disappearing for as long as he had.

But he suddenly didn't give a damn. For he knew that, with the increasing unruliness of his thoughts, if he caught sight of Lenora smiling up at Redburn while dancing in his arms one more time, he would lose his mind entirely.

He peered past the glow of the street lamps into the dark night beyond, squinting, as if he could make out

Seacliff from here. He could walk back to the manor house. It was just a few miles, surely no more than five. If he kept up a brisk pace, he could be there in an hour or two.

Purposely ignoring the glaring fact that his dress pumps were not made for such a hike—perhaps if he destroyed them to a respectable degree, he would never have to wear the damn things again—he set his shoulders and made to walk off.

Just then he heard a familiar voice on the other side of the door. He froze.

Redburn.

"...surely it's not as horrid as you say..."

Instant fire burned under his skin. He tried to ignore it. But in the next minute, he had no wish to as he learned what Redburn was discussing—and with whom.

"I assure you that, to me, tea is every bit as bad as you can imagine and worse."

Lenora.

The bastard was still on her about the damn beverage.

It mattered not that it was an asinine subject, that in the grand scheme of things, it was so ridiculously minor as to be laughable. His frustrated musings of the past hour had brought him closer to the precipice of losing control than all the days before it; this simply tipped him over the edge. Rage reared up, nearly choking him. Without thought, he threw the door open. It crashed against the pale yellow walls of the ballroom. Several women gasped, stepping hastily back. But he had eyes only for Redburn.

"She's told you she doesn't like the stuff, Redburn. I suggest you leave her be."

Redburn's dark eyes widened. "I beg your pardon?"

"Leave Lenora alone about the damn lemonade."

The man gaped at him a moment before sputtering on a laugh. "You must be joking."

"I am not." Peter clenched his hands at his sides and took a menacing step forward.

Lenora stepped between them then. "Mr. Ashford," she said, her voice low and tense, "now is not the time or place. Perhaps we might speak later, at Lady Tesh's."

He peered down at her, into those incredible green eyes of hers. Damn, but she was beautiful. He felt himself soften, was about to reach for her.

Redburn's voice broke through the moment.

"That's a sound plan." He came closer and placed an arm about her waist, smiling down at her. "Brilliant idea, love."

It wasn't the endearment that turned Peter's vision red, or even the way Redburn looked at her with that nauseating mixture of concern and affection. No, it was the way he touched Lenora as if he owned her. The sight of Redburn's gloved hand curling over Lenora's hip snapped something Peter had too long held in check.

With a roar he lunged for Redburn, grabbing his lapels. The man released Lenora, gripping onto Peter's wrists as he was slammed back against the wall. The plaster cracked from the impact.

"You bastard," Peter hissed.

"Damn it, Ashford," Redburn cried, "what do you think you're about? Unhand me at once."

"If I ever see you touch her again, I'll snap you like a twig."

Suddenly two small but surprisingly strong hands were on his arm. "Peter," Lenora cried, breaking through the haze of fury that pounded through his blood. "Stop, Peter."

Her voice anchored him to sanity, bringing him crashing back to earth. He blinked, looked down at her. Her face was white, pain imprinted in every line and curve.

He stumbled back, away from her touch. His fists loosened on Redburn's lapels and the man crumpled to the floor, gasping. Peter watched, dazed, as Lenora rushed to his side. She looked him over, her graceful hands skimming the man's crumpled jacket, before she turned her eyes to him. "Peter, please go."

The small hitch in her voice was the thing that finally cleared his head. He cast a desperate glance around at the crowd of partygoers. Their faces were alight with shock and horrified glee.

But the sight that destroyed him the most was the horror and disappointment in Lenora's eyes. Ah, God, what had he done?

Sending her one final, agonized glance, he pushed through the tight group of onlookers until he was outside again in the cool sea air. But even then he couldn't escape the reality of the monumental mistake he had made.

Chapter 28

*L*enora hurried on bare feet down the hall, pausing only a heartbeat before quietly rapping on Peter's bedroom door. She refused to think about the wisdom—or lack thereof—of what she was doing. After all, the last time they'd been alone in a room, they'd wound up in each other's arms.

But that would not happen this time. She was too furious to let it.

He opened the door. Before he could react, she pushed past him. His room was dark, not even a fire in the hearth, a single lamp beside the bed the only light. And it smelled of him, dark spice and utterly male. She closed her eyes as memories assailed her, fighting against the pull of them.

"Lenora—" he began.

"No." She steeled herself and turned to face him. Too late she noticed what she had failed to upon entering: that he was shoeless, shirtless, his hair unbound. He looked like a Viking lord with his feet planted wide, his shoulders a tense line, face hard and hands in tight fists at his side.

But she would not let herself get distracted. She focused on the hurt and anger that had been burning in her breast since the debacle of a scene at the assembly hall.

"What did you think you were about, accosting Lord Redburn like that?"

He flinched at the tightly wound fury in her voice. "It was badly done of me," he said through stiff lips.

She gaped at him. "Badly done of you? That's all you have to say?"

The sigh that escaped him sounded agonized, pulled from the bowels of his soul. "What do you want me to say, Lenora?"

"An apology would not be remiss," she gritted.

"Very well." He lifted his arms, as if offering himself to her. "I apologize. With every ounce of my being, I apologize. I never meant to create a scene, to embarrass you as I did."

She slashed a hand through the air, her anger mounting—and her heart aching—with every word that spilled from his lips. Damn him. Why couldn't he just leave her in peace?

And why did she still care so very much?

"I think Lord Redburn deserves your apology much more than I," she snapped.

He looked like he might explode, so tense had he become. Then, in the space of a moment, he seemed to deflate. His shoulders dropped, and he looked more haggard than she had ever seen him. "Yes, you're right. I will apologize when next I see him."

She gaped at him. Surely he wouldn't stand there and take whatever she had to give. He was stubborn, and overbearing, and never couched his words. This wasn't Peter at all.

Fury flared hot, that he would deny her a fight when

she was fairly itching for one. "One moment you declare you will not have me. The next you're attacking a man— my intended, I might add—for touching me. Why, Peter? What do you want from me?"

Finally emotion flared in his face, yet it was dark, and desperate, and called to something deep inside her. He drew in a ragged breath but remained silent.

So this was how it was to be? He would stand there in silence while she railed at him? Fury pounded through her, for all she wanted and could never have. And for all she loved him still.

She advanced on him. "How dare you! How dare you come here and crash into my life and turn everything on its head. I was fine before you came along—"

"You were not fine," he exploded, the words sounding as if they were ripped from him. "You were a shell, hiding every ounce of emotion you could manage. Do you think I didn't see how it pained you to draw? How you refused to open yourself up to it?"

He was the one to advance then. Lenora gasped as his hands closed over her arms, hauling her against the hard breadth of his bare chest. "Imagine my surprise when I uncovered the passionate woman beneath." His voice turned husky then, his gaze falling to her lips. Heat pooled low in her belly, her breath coming in short gasps, the fury in her transforming to a dark desire.

In the next moment, his face contorted. He let her go so unexpectedly, she stumbled back. She watched, stunned, as he retreated to the far side of the bed. The lantern light caught in the planes of his muscles as he ran his hands through his hair. "Forgive me," he muttered. "It's no business of mine. Redburn is your future now."

"Yes," she whispered, "he is." She swallowed hard,

forcing down the regret that sat like a stone in her chest. The anger that had fueled her into coming here had already fallen away, like dead leaves in winter, leaving nothing but a stark, barren landscape of her heart. "Just leave me alone, Peter. Please."

Before she could think better of it, she hurried for the door. But she found she could not leave, though her hand gripped the knob, anchoring her to sanity in the storm of emotions battering her. Letting loose a weary sigh, she closed her eyes and pressed her forehead to the wooden panel, unable to hold her head up a moment longer.

"Why did you come back, Peter?"

"I told you why."

But she was beyond hearing the pained undercurrent in his voice. Behind her closed lids, she saw him as he had been earlier that afternoon in Lady Tesh's drawing room, the anger that had burst from him when he'd lashed out at Clara.

"You said you returned to the Isle to pay Lady Tesh back for helping your mother," she managed, her rasping voice echoing back to her against the door. "But that wasn't the only reason, was it?"

A short, heavy silence followed. And then, "No."

"Judging from the way you fairly attacked Clara about her father, shall I assume the other reason was His Grace?"

"Yes."

She remained silent and still, waiting. Finally he continued.

"When I was thirteen, I went to Dane, begging him to help my ill mother. She was dying. I had no money, no connections. He was my last resort." He pulled in a deep, agonized breath. "He refused me, turned me from the house. She might have lived if not for him."

"And so you would make him pay for not helping your mother."

"Yes."

Her fingers tightened about the doorknob. A harsh laugh escaped her lips. "At least I know now why you intend to never marry. You mean for the line to die out with you, don't you? As punishment. That's the debt he must pay to you for destroying your mother's life, for destroying your life."

The silence was so great, she thought he would never answer. Finally his voice reached her, a whisper in the heavy air. "Yes."

One word that proved what a fool she had been even to consider making a life with him. Her heart, already fractured, shattered. Any chance for a happily-ever-after between them had been doomed from the start.

Without a word, she opened the door and slipped from the room.

* * *

Peter stared at the place she'd been, the devastation left in the wake of her departure making mere minutes seem like hours. He had thought he could not feel any lower after the subscription ball. But this left that in the dust.

He couldn't stay at Seacliff any longer. He should have left as soon as Redburn arrived. It had been pure stubbornness that had kept him from leaving. He was the only one affected, he had told himself. Once the promise to his mother was seen through, he could leave, and never give this island and the people on it another thought.

Lenora had made him see in mere minutes how wrong he had been.

The agony on her face would haunt him the rest of his days. By acting the animal and attacking Redburn, he had brought her grief.

He could not hate himself more.

Again a flash of the agony in her eyes, the fury in her voice. Lenora did not deserve the heartache Peter had brought into her life. He would leave tomorrow, and never return. And she would never have to suffer from his presence in her life again.

But by leaving, he would once more be breaking his promise to his mother. The guilt from ignoring her final wishes had haunted him all these years. By seeing them through, he could finally lay his mother's ghost to rest.

He sank down on the edge of the bed, his head dropping into his hands. But how could he stay here knowing he was hurting Lenora? Her face swam up behind his tightly closed lids, white with strain, and he knew in a flash he couldn't. To hell with how this affected him. He'd lived with the guilt for half his life. What he could not live with was giving Lenora even a moment's more pain.

He surged to his feet, pulling a shirt over his head, striding through the door. Making his way down the hall on silent feet, he paused only an instant outside Lenora's door before moving off to the room at the far end.

He rapped on the polished wood. She might be sleeping given the late hour, he told himself, preparing to move away and return to his room—coward that he was.

A faint voice called from the other side, "Enter."

Taking a deep breath, he opened the door.

Lady Tesh was sitting up in bed, an open book on her lap, looking like a wizened fairy surrounded by rich brocade fabrics that glinted like jewels in the faint light. Her hair hung in a thin white plait over one shoulder, and she wore a lacy nightgown that came up to her chin. Beside her, a frizzled white mop rose up, two beady eyes peering sleepily at him. Then Freya yawned and dropped off to sleep again.

Lady Tesh blinked owlishly at the sight of him. "Peter. I admit, I did not expect you."

No recriminations in the carefully modulated tone. Didn't he deserve them? He had come into her home, fought her at every turn, though she had welcomed him with open arms, even including his friend, a stranger to her. And how did he repay her? He had attacked her guest in public, embarrassing her in front of the entire town. He deserved her anger, just as he had deserved Lenora's.

Yet she looked on him with patient, sad eyes. It was the same expression she had worn when she had come to him all those years ago to help his mother.

God, what he owed this woman. And here he was, about to refuse her the one payment for her kindness she had requested from him.

He steeled himself and stepped closer to her bed. "And yet, I think you know why I'm here."

A look of ancient sadness flitted through her eyes. "Yes." She sighed. "Is there nothing I can do to entice you to stay? You have a mere three days, after all, until you make good on your promise to your mother."

His lips twisted. "I find I don't care about that now."

She nodded, understanding sitting heavily on her frail shoulders. "When will you leave?"

"Before daybreak. I don't want…That is, I cannot…"

She smiled, though it was a dejected thing. "I know, my boy."

He blinked back a sudden burning in his eyes. "Well then. Goodbye."

"Goodbye, Peter."

He spun about, so quickly the fine wool rug burned the balls of his feet. In a moment, he was out the door, his mind already on the journey ahead. Trying his damnedest not to think about what he was leaving behind.

Chapter 29

*T*he last thing Lenora wanted to do the following morning was to go downstairs and pretend that everything was as it should be. Goodness knew the last week had been torture enough, feigning happiness with Lord Redburn and her lot in life when all she wished to do was weep.

Today, however, made the past sennight seem laughable. She rubbed at the muscles in her neck, wincing as her fingers massaged at the proof of a tense, sleepless night. Fighting to ignore the aching in her chest that seemed a permanent part of her now. Gone was the fury at Peter for attacking Lord Redburn; in its place was a burning anger that he had made her care when all along loving him had been an impossibility, when pride and revenge had been more important than her. She wouldn't cry, wouldn't weep for him. He didn't deserve that from her.

Nor would she give him the satisfaction of seeing her affected. And so she strode from her room, hoping the outer shell of her did not show the wreck within.

Margery caught up with her as she was taking a stroll in Lady Tesh's rose garden. "My dear, how did you sleep last night?"

The question was not a mild one. Lenora gave her a

sad smile and linked arms with her friend. "Not well," she admitted. "But I managed to get some rest. And you?"

"I didn't sleep a wink." She paused, letting her hand trail over the delicate bloom of a summer rose. "If you want to talk about last night, I'm here for you, Lenora."

There was a cautiousness to Margery's voice that made Lenora's battered heart ache. They were not as easy with each other as they had been. And Lenora could blame no one but herself. She'd been so consumed with keeping the tragedies of her heart private that she'd effectively put up a wall between herself and her dearest friend. And though she had finally opened up some to Margery regarding her true feelings for Peter, she still held back the truth about Hillram. She should confess everything; goodness knew it was long overdue. And what a relief it would be to finally open her heart, not to feel so very alone anymore.

Yet to do so might cause her to lose the best friend she had ever had.

And so she smiled when she would cry, and shook her head. "It was distressing. But I'm quite over it, I assure you. Now I only need hope that Lord Redburn was not frightened away."

Margery looked infinitely sad, and Lenora feared her ruse had been seen through. But soon her friend was smiling wryly. "I doubt he could be, dearest. He seems quite smitten with you."

Lenora smiled along with her, for all the world as if she were a happy bride-to-be and not brokenhearted with grief. And she should be happy. Lord Redburn had proven himself to be attentive, affectionate, and all any woman could hope for in a husband. Yet she could not help being aware of a kernel of unease within her, a spark of misgiving regarding the man. She shook her head sharply, doing

her best to ignore the whisper of a thought. No doubt it
was due to Peter's hold on her heart, which was proving
to be as strong as ever. For her own sanity, she needed
to find a way to free herself of that hold, to go into her
marriage unencumbered by the past.

But how could she let Peter go when she hadn't been
able to let go of her guilt and grief over Hillram? And
what would be left of her if she succeeded?

* * *

Upon their return to the house, they made their way to
Lady Tesh's rooms to determine the plan for the day. What
they did not expect, however, was to find that lady still
abed. Though she typically kept to her rooms most of the
morning, she was nevertheless up with the sun, working
on her correspondence, conferring with the housekeeper,
and generally running a tight ship at Seacliff.

This morning, however, they found her bundled under
her covers, looking older than she ever had.

"Gran, what is it?" Margery rushed to her bedside and
took the woman's hand in hers. "Are you unwell? Shall I
call for the physician?"

"Goodness, an old woman decides to sleep in and
she's suddenly at death's door?" Lady Tesh waved off
Margery's hovering, pushing herself straighter.

"Is anything amiss, Gran?" Lenora asked, coming up
beside Margery.

For a moment, Lady Tesh's gaze flickered to her, and
Lenora shivered, for it was bleak indeed.

The mood was short lived. "Only that you both are
making me feel my age. And if there is anything that's
dangerous for someone of my advanced years, it's to

actually feel every day of it. Now get back, the both of you, while I rise and ready myself for the day."

She threw back the covers. Freya, who had been sleeping peacefully beside her mistress, gave an irritated growl as she was buried in brocade. As Lady Tesh hobbled to her dressing table, the dog worked her way free and, with an offended sniff, pranced from the room.

"Margery, choose something for me to wear. And none of your dismal, dreary colors. Give me something bright and brilliant. I've a mind to be outrageous today."

"When are you not?" Margery replied with an affectionate smile as she disappeared inside Lady Tesh's dressing room.

Lady Tesh peered at herself in the mirror before holding a brush out in Lenora's general direction. "You may as well make yourself useful, child," she said.

Lenora went to her at once, untying the ribbon from the viscountess's plait and using her fingers to loosen the strands. Soon she was pulling the brush through the shimmering white hair, her long strokes going from the top of the woman's head to nearly her backside.

"That is lovely, child." Lady Tesh closed her eyes. "I vow, your touch is much lighter than my maid's. Half the time, I think she's got a vendetta against me, for all she tugs and pulls."

Which would not have surprised Lenora one bit. Though never cruel, Lady Tesh was not the gentlest taskmaster. But now was as good a time as any to ask about their plans; as much as she dreaded the day, she would get it over and done with.

"Do you have any errands you wish us to run for you today, Gran?"

"Not errands, no. Though seeing as you did not have a

chance to complete the drawings I wanted of you, perhaps you can make a visit to the cliffs again."

Lenora's hand faltered in its brushing as she remembered her last trip there, how she had struggled to sketch the simplest drawing, her recent heartbreak with Peter preventing even the instinctual mechanics of the act. But she could not avoid the place forever. Schooling her features into polite acceptance, she said in a bright tone, "Of course."

"Splendid." Lady Tesh sighed. "I'm only sorry Peter shall miss it."

Lenora focused on keeping her hand steady, though her stomach lurched. "It's for the best, I suppose. He cannot want to follow us about when he could be exploring the Isle on his final days here."

Lady Tesh looked as if she'd been struck. "But didn't you hear, child? Peter left this morning before daybreak. He has returned to America."

The brush dropped from Lenora's numb fingers, clattering to the floor. "What?" *He's gone?* No, he couldn't be.

The older woman nodded sadly. "He came to me last night. This morning I had him checked on. His room was empty, his horse gone."

Lenora did not realize she had ceased to breathe until spots swam in her vision and she swayed on her feet. Lady Tesh's fingers on her arm jolted her back to herself.

"Lenora, you look as if you'll keel over on the spot. Sit and I'll call Margery back to help you to your room."

"No." The one word came out loud and desperate, stunning Lady Tesh into releasing her. She had to gain control of herself. It was for the best that he was gone, after all. Now she could concentrate on her future, unencumbered by his effect on her.

She felt a mad laugh bubble up and quickly suppressed it. Unencumbered, indeed.

"That is," she continued, struggling for a calm she didn't feel, "I only need a bit of fresh air. Tell Margery I've gone out, will you?"

Before Lady Tesh could respond, Lenora was out the door. But once out in the hall, she couldn't fathom where to go. The only thing in her mind was Peter, and that he had left without saying goodbye.

That mad laugh finally broke free then. There was no need for goodbyes when she had practically driven him from the house the night before. *Just leave me alone, Peter*, she had begged him. *Please.* And he had done as she had bid him.

Her chest grew tight, her breathing labored. It was as if she were being pulled by an undertow and didn't know which way was up. She had to get out of this house.

She collected her drawing supplies and headed out to the stables. In no time, she had a horse saddled and was on her way. The wind was in a furor today, whipping her hair loose from the simple twist it was in. It was not the type of day Lenora would have liked to come to the cliffs. She was never easy out there, though the grotto was fairly protected from the elements. Besides that, there was always a melancholy atmosphere in the place, as if it would never see happiness. Now, however, that only drew her more, grief calling to grief. She hurried out to the cliffs, securing her mount before rushing through the hidden crevice and into the grotto.

It was as it had ever been. Seemingly carved by ancient giants, looking out over the great sea. Making one feel they were at the edge of the world.

She made her way to the boulder, next to the Viking

symbol Synne had carved into the stone. Laying her bag on the ground, she took a deep breath and closed her eyes. *Forget him*, her mind whispered. *He's gone, and will never return.* Even as she fought to purge him from her mind, however, her heart had quite another idea. As battered as it was, it insisted on holding on tight when she so desperately wanted to forget.

The tears came then, a torrent of them. They fell unchecked down her cheeks. And she realized in that moment that there was no way on earth she could release herself from him. Her heart would belong to him always. She would always regret losing him, would always mourn him, until her dying day.

Hopelessness filled her. And with it came a grief she had never felt before. Grief for a life she had desperately wanted, though she had known all along that her part in Hillram's death had made that an impossibility. She had been too cowardly to face her guilt over that tragedy, and this was her penance.

She gasped, her hand finding the stone wall, her fingers digging into Synne's carving. She could not handle this pain. It would destroy her. She'd held back as long as she could, but she was tired, so damn tired, of fighting what was in her heart. Heaving a deep breath, she squeezed her eyes shut and did what she had never allowed herself to do: she let go.

Like a wave, it crashed over her head, filling her up until she thought she'd drown from it. The force of it ripped an uncontrollable sob from her aching chest. She let it come, dropping to her knees, falling to the cold stone floor.

She cried as she hadn't since her mother's death. Her arms came about her middle, holding tight as the grief wracked her body. As if she could hold herself together by sheer force. But nothing could stop it now that it had started. On and on, it rolled, the tears falling until there was nothing left to give. And still it demanded more from her, turning her inside out with the pain of it. And all the while images flashed through her mind: Peter's cold eyes when he'd turned her away, the pain in Hillram's face when she'd told him she didn't love him, her father's disappointment as she failed him once again, Peter attacking Lord Redburn. Hillram's eyes closed forever, his blood soaking her skirts.

Finally, after what felt like an eternity, her sobs subsided and then stopped altogether. She lay there for a time, breathing deeply, her cheek pressed to the dirty stone floor. When her body started to ache, she rose, her limbs stiff. She stood there, looking down at the damp patch her tears had left on the ground, then to the wide-open ocean beyond the grotto. She had come to the Isle hoping to free herself of her guilt over Hillram's death by forcibly remembering the most painful memories of their time together. But she was going about it all wrong. She had been from the start.

Because it all came back to her how much she *had* cared for him. He had been one of her closest friends. They had been playmates when young, confidants as they'd gotten older. Yet she hadn't been able to love him. Not as he'd wanted, not as he'd needed. Not as he'd deserved. She rubbed her aching chest. That final truth had overshadowed all the good that had been between them. And because of that, she hadn't grieved for him as she should have.

Weary beyond belief, she stumbled back, to the rock she had been sitting on. As she sat, her foot hit something hard.

Her bag.

She stared at it uncomprehendingly for a time. For three years, she had thought that by refusing to paint from her heart, she was somehow serving a necessary penance. Instead she had managed only to stifle emotions that she needed to properly come to terms with Hillram's death. She had not realized that truth until her growing feelings for Peter had begun to awaken the part of herself she had brutally repressed.

It was time to face her memories, and the emotions that came with them, now. Or she would never properly heal. Frightened but determined, she reached down with shaking fingers, pulling her drawing pad and a pencil from the bag.

She balanced it on her knee and looked out over the grotto. And then, putting pencil to paper, she began to draw.

The lines came haltingly at first, her fear still holding her back. Soon, however, her fingers found their rhythm. She expected to draw the grotto. Yet it was Hillram that appeared on her paper, his face youthful and carefree as it had been when they'd first become friends. When that sketch was done, she pulled out a fresh page. Again her fingers went to work, this time sketching Hillram at the Elven Pools, a tricorn hat perched atop his head, holding a stick aloft as his sword. Another sketch of Hillram, and another, until she had a small stack of them, remembering all he had been to her. When her pencil finally stilled, she stood, holding the pages to her chest, and moved to the edge of the shelf. Then, giving the drawings a gentle kiss and a whispered "I'm sorry, my dear friend," she let them go.

They sailed off on the wind, twisting and dancing in the

air as if to bid her farewell before falling from view. She felt it then, the loosening of the band around her chest. But she wasn't done yet, though exhaustion pulled at her.

Returning to the boulder, she took up her supplies once more. Now, however, instead of Hillram, she drew Peter. Image after image blossomed from her pencil, each one coming faster than the one before: Peter glowering and angry on that first day, Peter vulnerable at the dinner party, Peter kissing her in the ballroom, Peter coming for her in the storm. She did not stop until every page had been covered with sketches of him. At the end of it all, she looked down at her work and smiled. Though she missed him, though she would always miss him, she could look back and remember the happiness of the time they'd shared.

The idea that she could feel joy through her pain so stunned her, a laugh soon followed. She'd thought to return to who she had been before Hillram's death. But that young girl was no more. This was who she was now.

And she was glad of it. She felt stronger than she had ever been in her life.

But she had best be getting back to Seacliff. They would be wondering where she'd gone and must be worried sick. Packing up her supplies, she started off for the house.

Her contentment, however, was short lived, for there was a familiar carriage in the drive.

Lord Redburn.

Goodness, but she had forgotten about him completely all the morning long. Her steps faltered, reality crashing down on her. She had felt as if she were a new person. But nothing had changed in her life. Peter was gone and on his way back to America, and she was still engaged to a man she did not wish to marry.

Frustration and anger pounded through her. She had punished herself these three years, thinking she was worthy only of a loveless marriage, believing she didn't deserve to follow her heart.

But that wasn't true. She had her passion for her art back now, and a new lease on life by finally embracing both the bad and the good in her past. She had not deserved to be made to feel she must marry Hillram, though she had loved him only as a friend, had not deserved to be foisted off on Lord Fig or Lord Landon or Lord Redburn. And she had not deserved to be second in Peter's life, overshadowed by a revenge he could not let go of. Like the water of the Elven Pools, determination and persistence bringing about unimaginable beauty, she deserved to cut her own path in life.

But what could she do to claim her independence? As a woman of good breeding, she had neither skills nor experience.

The bag holding her supplies bumped into her leg. She had forgotten about it. In a flash, she remembered the fever that had overtaken her to draw, and the relief she had found in it.

Her fingers tightened on the strap. Perhaps there was something else for her, after all.

She marched inside and straight on to Lady Tesh's sitting room. Her gaze immediately fell on Lord Redburn seated close to Lady Tesh and Margery.

"My lord," she said without preamble, "I am most anxious to talk to you. Alone."

"My dear," he said, a warm smile lighting his face as he rose, "I'm glad you're here, for I have brought you a surprise."

"I am most appreciative, but perhaps that had better wait until we've spoken."

"Er, Lenora?" Margery ventured.

Lenora did not take her eyes from Lord Redburn. "I am sorry, dearest, but I really must insist on speaking to Lord Redburn now."

"But, Lenora—"

Frustration reared. If she didn't do this now, she would never have the nerve. "Not now, Margery," she bit out.

"I did not raise you to be rude, Lenora."

She gasped and whirled about. "Father, you're here."

He stood by the window. His face was as it ever was, craggy and stern, no softness marring the harsh lines. He lifted one eyebrow. "I see you are still stating the obvious."

She clasped her hands in front of her. "I didn't expect you."

"No doubt, or you would not have been running wild like some hoyden. If I'd known this is what becomes of you when you're here, I never would have agreed to send you."

Lenora flinched at the blatant rebuke, her cheeks burning.

"She was doing a favor for me, Alfred, so you may remove that stick from your posterior," Lady Tesh drawled.

"Damn it, Olivia," Lenora's father snapped, "you always were too soft on her, letting her do as she wished, giving her too much independence. If you had kept better control of her when she was younger, she would be readying herself to be a duchess now."

Lady Tesh took hold of her cane and rose, leveling a glare on Sir Alfred that was positively chilling. "His Grace is not yet in his grave and you dare say such things?"

Lenora had never heard such a frightening tone from the viscountess. Even during the few times she had truly railed at Lenora and Margery, she had never sounded so terrifying. Sir Alfred's lips tightened, and though he offered no apology, he nodded, once and sharply.

He leveled that cold stare at Lenora. "Well, I see you have not mucked things up yet with Redburn here. It's time we talked about the wedding. I've brought a special license with me from London. We will have this done and settled before the day is out."

There was a moment of stunned silence before the room burst into noise.

"Alfred, you cannot mean to marry her off so quickly, and in such a shabby manner."

"Sir Alfred, our dear Lenora must have more time."

"I say there, Sir Alfred, I'm all for moving things along quickly, but this seems a trifle hasty."

Lenora, for her part, remained silent, staring at her father in disbelief. It was all so cold, so calculating. A mere business transaction. Was that all she was to him? Was that what she had been to him all this time?

Sir Alfred raised a hand for silence. "Enough. We will have a wedding today and see this done with."

"No, Father, we won't."

Again that imperious brow rose, though this time it was accompanied by a flare of anger in his cold eyes. "You have no say in the matter."

"I do. And I say I will not marry today. Nor," she continued, turning to Lord Redburn with an apologetic look, "will I ever. I am sorry, my lord, but I cannot marry you."

His expression, ever kind and considerate, turned puzzled. "I'm sorry, Miss Hartley, I don't believe I heard you right."

Placing her bag down on the nearest chair, she walked to him and took his hand in hers. "You're a wonderful man. And any woman would be happy to have you for her husband." She drew in a deep breath. "But I cannot marry you."

His brows drew down in the middle. "But the contract has been signed."

She squeezed his fingers. "I cannot in good conscience continue on with this engagement. Forgive me. I know you will find someone else to care for, and who will care for you in return."

He continued to stare, dumbfounded, at her. Lenora's heart ached, that she must hurt this good man.

In the next instant, however, his face twisted into harsh, ugly lines. He yanked his hand free. "Are you truly so simple that you believed this was about affection?"

As Lenora recoiled, stunned speechless, he spun to face Sir Alfred. "I did my part, and would have even gone through with this travesty. I will be cleared of my debt to you."

"The wedding was never finalized," her father bit out, shooting her a furious glare. "Your debt still stands."

"You old reprobate," Redburn snarled. "It was bad enough you foisted me off on a woman who has the stain of three failed engagements on her. I was not happy to have such damaged goods. But I was ready to take that on. My debt is cleared, or I will have all of London know what you've been about, selling your daughter to the highest bidder."

With that, he stormed from the room.

Lenora, mouth agape, watched him go, before turning slowly to look at her father. A man she had known and loved all her life yet appeared a stranger to her in that horrifying moment.

"You would have given me to him in exchange for a debt?"

His lip curled. "Did you think the man was in love with you? Damnation, girl, you really are as simple as he says."

She stared at him. "How could you?"

A harsh laugh burst from his lips. "It's no different than what I did with Fig, and that idiot Landon. D'you think they wanted you for your sparkling personality?"

The breath left her. There was not an ounce of affection in his expression. And she realized in that moment that he didn't love her, and probably never had. She was a piece of property to him, something to be used for gain and nothing more.

A kick to the gut could not have hurt more.

Lady Tesh stepped forward. Her voice shook when she spoke. "Alfred, I have always known you were a cold man, but this goes beyond what I believed you capable of."

"Do you honestly believe interactions like this don't happen in Society? Please, Olivia, you cannot be so naïve."

The viscountess drew herself up, leveling a furious stare on Sir Alfred. "I am fully aware that many families trade position for fortune, using their daughters as leverage. But I never knew a man to use blackmail to force his daughter into a union. You are a—"

Whatever vile name Lady Tesh was about to say was lost as Lenora laid a gentle hand on her arm. As touched as she was by Lady Tesh's passionate defense of her, she needed to stand on her own two feet now. "I need to do this myself, Gran."

The quiet words dampened Lady Tesh's ire in an instant. She searched Lenora's eyes before, with a sad nod, she patted her hand. "Margery," she called to her granddaughter, "let us be off." She glared at Sir Alfred, one last rebellion. "We have to see that a carriage is made ready for our guest, after all."

The two women left, closing the door behind them.

Lenora took a deep breath and faced her father. "How could you do it?"

"How could I try and marry you to a rich and titled gentleman?"

"You didn't do this for my benefit," she said, her hands shaking. "It was for you and you alone."

Anger suffused his face. "Do not turn this on me, girl. You should have done your duty and married where I willed you. Lord Redburn was your last chance. I warned you I would not look kindly on this union dissolving. Or have you forgotten?"

"I've not forgotten." Her heart twisted, for all she loved him still.

But now was not the time for a faint heart. She would have this out with him now, and learn her fate for good or ill.

"You said you would disown me if my next engagement fell through. And it has."

"Yes," he spat.

For a moment, a single fragile moment, he appeared so much older than before, his face ashen, the fine lines about his eyes and mouth deeper than she remembered. He had always seemed beyond the frailty of mere mortal men, had been larger than life to her. But he was not a young man, having been so much older than her mother. He would surely not want to end his days alone.

Taking her chance, she stepped toward him and laid her hand on his sleeve; it was something he never would have permitted before, yet she could not be fearful now. Their entire relationship, her entire future, rode on this moment.

"You cannot mean to cut me from your life, Father," she said quietly. "I'm your daughter. We're all the other has."

She thought she saw him falter, and hope bloomed bright. But in the next instant, he shook her hand from him. His face turned openly hostile, a furious flush coloring his cheeks.

"You think that means anything to me, girl?" he snapped. "You have always been a burden, and now you're an embarrassment as well. I'm done with you."

He stormed out the door, leaving Lenora alone in the middle of the room, her heart breaking for the second time that day.

Chapter 30

Almost immediately, Lady Tesh and Margery hurried in, worry clear on their faces.

Lenora tried for a smile but couldn't manage one. "Were you standing at the door listening?"

"Yes," Lady Tesh said baldly.

"Oh, my dearest," Margery cried, rushing to her. "I knew Sir Alfred was a cold man, but I never believed he could be so cruel."

Lenora sank into her friend's embrace, the events of the day crashing down on her head. Hot tears threatened as she pressed her face into Margery's shoulder.

"That damned idiot," Lady Tesh spat, glaring at the door as if she could incinerate him at a distance through pure intent. "Well, my dear, you are well rid of him."

"Poor Lenora," Margery cooed into her hair. "You've had so much heartache. If only Hillram had lived and you had married. You would even now be living a happy life with him."

Her friend's well-meaning words, spoken in that painful moment, finally broke Lenora. "But I did not want to marry Hillram!" she cried, tearing away from Margery.

The two women stared at her in openmouthed shock. Lenora's shock was just as great. What had she done?

She had spent so many years pretending, for the sake of everyone else, for the sake of Hillram's memory. Now the words were out and she could not call them back.

But did she want to take them back? As horrifying as this moment was, she felt lighter now that the truth was finally out.

"Whatever are you talking about?" Margery demanded. "You loved Hillram."

"I did," Lenora said, slowly and carefully. "As a friend, and nothing more."

Margery stared at her in stunned incomprehension. Lady Tesh, looking no less shaken, placed a hand on her granddaughter's arm when she would have spoken. "Margery, perhaps you'd best ring for tea. Or better yet, go into that sideboard there and pull out the sherry. I do believe we may have need of it."

Margery did as she was bid, and they were soon seated in a small circle, overlooking the rose garden. As Lenora settled into a chair, she had a flash of memory, of Peter hefting this same piece of furniture and placing it here their first night at Seacliff. Her fingers curved around the arm.

They sat in silence for a time, drinking, each of them seemingly more than happy to put off the coming conversation. Finally, their glasses drained, Margery turned wary eyes on Lenora.

"I believe now is as good a time as any, dearest."

Lenora swallowed hard. Her relief that she no longer had to pretend did not make the telling of it any easier. "Next to you, Hillram was my dearest friend. But that was all he was to me. I didn't love him. Not in the way you loved your Aaron."

Margery was shaking her head. Her fingers, clenched

tightly on her empty glass, turned white. "Why did you agree to marry him?"

Lenora shrugged helplessly. "It was expected. And I thought I would grow to love him. How could I not? He was kind and loving, sweet and charming."

"But you did not."

Lenora shook her head, her eyes falling to her lap. "No," she whispered. "And each day it grew harder and harder to pretend." Tears burned and she squeezed her eyes shut. "He wanted so much more from me than I could give him. It killed me inside to smile when he talked of love, to welcome his kisses when inside I felt nothing. I knew I could never reciprocate his feelings. The day of his death..."

Her throat closed tight. She swallowed past the grief. "He'd begun to grow frustrated with me over my lack of...enthusiasm." Her face heated, remembering the hurt in his eyes when she'd flinched from his touch. "I don't know what made me finally snap. But I suddenly couldn't take the pretending a moment longer. I told him—" Her throat closed again. She cleared it and forced herself to finish, needing to purge it after so long. "I told him I didn't love him in that way; that he was my friend and nothing more. That I only accepted him to please our families. He was so hurt, so angry. He left without a word. And then he tried to make that fool jump on the way home. When I think of his face when I was called to Danesford, the pain in his eyes, how he held my hand as if he would never let go—" A sob broke free. She pressed her knuckles to her lips. She had no right to cry over him. She had broken his heart.

But Margery was at her knee, tears tracking down her pale cheeks. She grabbed Lenora's hand and held tightly, though Lenora tried with all her might to pull away. She did not deserve the compassion of this woman, Hillram's cousin, who had loved him so well.

"No, Margery..." she choked.

"You listen to me," Margery said through her tears, her grip strong. "You are not responsible for my cousin's death. Hillram was wonderful, yes, and I adored him. You know as well as I that he was maddeningly optimistic and the most forgiving man in existence. I'm certain that before he had even made it down the drive, he'd already forgiven you and made plans to win your love. That's who he was."

"Margery has the right of it, Lenora," Lady Tesh said, her voice quiet and yet strong with her conviction. "It was a tragic accident, nothing more."

Lenora's stunned gaze swiveled between the two women. "Don't you understand that I broke his heart? If I had stayed quiet, he would not have been careless on the ride back home, and he would still be alive. How can you not hate me for it?"

A watery smile flitted over Margery's face. "All you did was tell Hillram your true feelings. I knew my cousin, and he would rather you were honest than to stay silent for his sake. Besides, I could never hate you, dearest. You're like a sister to me and always shall be."

Shaking her head in disbelief, Lenora pulled her friend close. "I don't deserve you. I don't deserve either of you."

"You deserve every happiness, Lenora," Margery murmured into her hair.

They stayed that way for a time. And as she held on tight to her dearest friend in the world, Lenora felt the guilt she had carted about like a loadstone melt away. She breathed in deeply, freely, for the first time in too long.

They broke apart, hands going to cheeks to wipe away the wetness there. "What shall you do now, dearest?" Margery asked quietly.

What would she do, indeed? Before Lenora could answer, however, Lady Tesh's hand, its paper-thin skin smooth and cool, landed on top of hers. "Well, my girl, you shall just have to stay here with me."

Lenora's chest swelled with love. But she knew deep down that would be the easy way out, going from being dependent on her father to being dependent on Lady Tesh. She could not do it. She had to stand on her own two feet.

Somehow.

"I do love you, Gran," she said with a smile. "Though I think you know I cannot do that. And no, Margery," she continued, "I cannot live with you, either. Your portion is barely enough for you to live on as it is. I will not be a burden to you."

"You could never be a burden," Margery declared fiercely.

"Well, if you will not stay with Margery, and you will not stay with me, where will you go?" Lady Tesh asked.

Unerringly Lenora's gaze found the drawing bag she had left half the room away. "Gran, how much would you say my paintings are worth to you?"

Confusion clouded the viscountess's brow before, with a suddenness that completely transformed her, understanding bloomed. "I would say," she said with a grin, "that they will just about pay for the first year's rent on the small dowager cottage that has been sitting empty on the far side of the property. Wouldn't you?"

Lenora clasped the woman's hand and grinned. "That sounds splendid, Gran. Absolutely splendid."

* * *

It had not taken Peter long after arriving in Liverpool to learn that Quincy had not yet sailed for Boston. He'd located the inn easily enough—the most luxurious one in the port city, naturally; Quincy was not one to deny himself the comforts in life.

What took much longer was locating the man himself.

He searched every pub and house of ill repute he could find, and yet not a one remembered seeing Quincy. Finally, frustrated and heartsick, he made his way through the narrow alleys to the docks.

The place was bustling with humanity as he walked the worn boards. The sights and smells of the place had him remembering better times. Life aboard Captain Adams's beloved *Persistence*, Quincy at his side. The wind in his hair, the lurch and sway of the ship beneath his feet. Revenge had driven him, keeping him going when most men would have given up, propelling him to move up in life, to succeed, to thrive. The world had been full of possibilities then.

Now he didn't know where to go, what to do. Everything seemed duller now for the loss of Lenora.

"Peter."

He started, turned. Quincy stood behind him, looking as forbidding as Peter had ever seen him. A bruise stood out in stark contrast on his jaw, already turning a sickening green. Peter clenched his fist, felt the pull of newly healing skin on his knuckles, and nodded. "Quincy."

"What are you doing here?"

"I'm returning to Boston."

His friend's brows drew down in the middle, confusion breaking through the barely banked animosity. "But your promise to your mother—"

"Broken."

There was a pause as Quincy searched his face. "Your mother meant the world to you. That love drove you all these years."

"You're right" was Peter's quiet answer. "And I will never stop loving her. But it's time to move on."

A careful hope flared in Quincy's dark eyes. "And Dane?"

Peter heaved a sigh, looking out over the bustling docks. "I find," he replied slowly, "that I don't have the stomach for it any longer."

The tension left Quincy in a moment, and in its place was the old friendliness. He clapped Peter on the shoulder, and as one, they turned and began walking down the length of the docks. "And so you won't let the line die out?"

Peter's relief was quickly tempered by regret as Lenora's drawn face swam up in his mind. He gave a humorless chuckle as he sidestepped a thick coil of rope. "I don't know that I have any control over that. I cannot see myself marrying, having a family..." He swallowed hard at the lump in his throat and pressed on. "But I will do everything in my power to ensure the land does not go to ruin, that the tenants don't suffer, that the duke's daughters are well provided for."

He prayed Quincy would leave it at that. But, as ever, the man could not keep his nose from where it did not belong. "And what of Miss Hartley?"

The quiet question nearly undid him. He shrugged. "What of her? She's to marry Redburn—"

"That arse?" Quincy scoffed. "He doesn't deserve her."

"No one deserves her," Peter muttered.

"You do."

Peter stopped dead in his tracks and gave his friend a somber look. "I especially don't deserve her."

Quincy rolled his eyes heavenward. "God save me from thick-skulled bastards. You blasted idiot, you're perfect for her. Did you think I didn't see how she lit up when you were around? You made her *happy*."

Peter gaped at him. "You're delusional."

"Delusional to think you might finally get your large head out of your arse. You care for the girl, don't you?"

Peter flushed. He should deny it all, claim there had never been anything between them, tell his friend his imagination had run away from him.

But he couldn't. This was Quincy, the man who had been there for him for over a decade, who had saved his life in so many ways. And he was done hiding from his best friend.

"Fine," he spat, "yes, I care for Miss Hartley. Hell." He ran a hand over his face before yanking hard at his limp cravat. "I love her. I love Lenora. Are you happy now, you meddling bastard?"

He expected anger, shock even. Instead Quincy was grinning from ear to ear. "You're damn right I'm happy."

"I'm not!" Peter exploded, his hands flying in the air. "How do you think it's been, seeing her with Redburn, knowing she's to be his wife, to bear his children, to grow old with him? A knife to the gut could not have hurt worse." He lost his breath from the pain that sliced through him. Dragging air into his lungs, he plowed on. "And to make matters worse, I went and lost my temper, attacked the man—"

"You attacked Redburn?" Quincy gaped at him.

"Yes," Peter groaned, closing his eyes briefly as mortification filled him. "At the damn assembly hall."

"Oh, I would have loved to see that," Quincy muttered. "Mind telling me what finally set you off?"

"He was badgering her about her penchant for drinking lemonade. Again."

One inky brow rose. "*That's* what did it?"

Peter's cheeks grew hot. "It was not my finest moment," he muttered.

"No doubt." Humor colored Quincy's words. Peter was too miserable to feel more than a hint of annoyance.

"But what I want to know," his friend continued, "was what Miss Hartley's reaction was to your display."

"What do you think?" He looked Quincy full in the face. "She was aghast, embarrassed, outraged."

"And so you left." Peter nodded. "Because you love her," Quincy continued. Again another nod, this one more wretched than the first.

Silence stretched between them, made all the more obvious by the bustle and commotion around them. Unable to look his friend in the eye a moment longer, Peter gazed out over the chaos. He followed a stringy youth as he hefted a crate up the gangplank of a merchant vessel, remembering a time when that was him. Life had been so much simpler then.

The lad came down for another load, yet still things remained quiet between him and Quincy. He squirmed, unused to such uneasiness with his friend. Finally, when he couldn't take it a second more, he asked, "And so when do you leave?"

"Tomorrow at first light."

Peter cleared his throat. "Tell me the name of the ship and I'll book passage with you."

A pause. And then, "No."

Peter looked at him, stunned. Here he thought they had gotten past the rocks their friendship had nearly been wrecked on. Yet Quincy was serious, his eyes pained, his mouth a thin, firm line. "Perhaps I didn't apologize as I should have," Peter stammered. "I am sorry, Quincy, more than you know—"

Quincy slashed a hand through the air. "I know you are, you daft man. And I forgive your idiocy, fully and completely."

Peter blinked in confusion. "Then why...?"

"Because you're not going back to Boston. At all."

It was Peter's turn to frown. "I have to. My place is there, the business—"

"Will not collapse without you. The Adams children are grown, and are more than capable of handling things now."

"But my home is in Boston. You, Captain Adams, his family—"

"We will miss you, with all our hearts."

Peter shook his head, utterly confused. "I don't understand."

Quincy's fierce expression finally softened. "You always were a dumb bastard. You're not coming back to Boston with me because your place is back on the Isle, at Danesford." He smiled. "With Miss Hartley."

Peter was already shaking his head. "She's marrying Redburn."

"Yes, she will. If you don't put a stop to it."

Anger ran hot under Peter's skin. "You make it sound easy."

"It is easy. You love her, Peter. And I know she cares

for you. Do you think she wants to marry Redburn when you hold her heart?"

He'd seen her face that day when Redburn arrived, her eyes shining with unshed tears, her voice a mere whisper as she'd asked him, *"And you, Peter? Did you have a near miss?"*

He cursed. "She will not have me now. Not after the arse I made of myself."

"Oh, I'm sure she already knew you were an arse, Peter," Quincy drawled.

But he could not be waylaid so easily. "I'm not right for her. I'm too rough, a brute, an uncultured swine who brawls with men in public. She would be miserable with me."

The humor only increased in Quincy's laughing dark eyes. "Hmm, yes, miserable being loved by the man she loves herself. What a horrid fate."

Aggravation surged, that his very real concerns were being so easily dismissed. "Stop patronizing me," he growled.

"Then stop being a stupid prick!" When Peter gaped at him, he launched on. "You've always taken the helm, helping me and Captain Adams and his family, making the decisions, pulling us from the brink of poverty more than once. And we are so damn grateful to you for it." He put a hand on Peter's shoulder. "But for once in your life, you need to take a chance on more than our finances. You need to take a chance on trusting someone else, and let Miss Hartley make her own decisions. You cannot take that away from her, or you will be no better than her father and Redburn. Besides," he continued, his expression more serious than Peter had ever seen it, "do you really want to be like that fool Ivar? He left Synne, broke her heart, and she married another. All because he was too damn stupid to stay with the woman he loved. Would you follow the same path he did? Or will you learn from his mistake, and hold on to happiness with both hands?"

A spark lit in Peter's chest, a tiny flame in the darkness that was his heart. It took a moment to realize it was hope.

He rubbed at his aching chest, trying to snuff out the longing Quincy's words were bringing to life. "She will say no," he replied gruffly.

Quincy shrugged. "Perhaps. And she might say yes, and give you both lifelong happiness. Isn't the possibility of her rejection worth the chance of loving her for the rest of your days?"

Yes. The word, silent in his own head, nevertheless filled him. The spark of hope burst into a raging flame. Yes, the chance of loving her, of making her his wife, was worth any amount of pain. And this time, he would not let anyone, be it Redburn or her father, stop him from trying.

Damn, but he loved her. And if she accepted him, he would do everything in his power to make certain she never, not for one minute, ever doubted it.

"Quincy?"

His friend grinned. "Not booking passage with me back to Boston then?"

"Not on your life." Peter returned the grin, then sobered. He held out his hand. "I will miss you, my friend."

Quincy took it in a bone-crushing grip. "No more than I will miss you." His eyes glistened, and for a panicked moment, Peter feared he would cry. In the next instant, his grin was back in full force, the shimmer turning to wickedness. "But don't think I won't be visiting you, and often. I find I have a taste for English beauties and will not be able to stay away for long. You just may grow sick of me."

"Never," Peter managed through a tight throat. He threw an arm about Quincy's shoulders. "Now, let's see about finding the fastest horse Liverpool has to offer. For I've a proposal to make."

Chapter 31

*B*y the time Peter returned to the Isle of Synne, his momentary fever of hope and excitement was long gone. Nearly three full days of riding hell-bent for leather had effectively cured him of those foreign emotions, leaving only soul-sucking anxiety and a vague kind of panic. What the hell was he doing? He still wasn't convinced he was good for Lenora, that she could be happy with him. And he sure as hell didn't deserve her.

Regardless, here he was. Ready to be kicked in the groin by love for the chance to claim her for his own.

He pulled his horse up when he came to the crossroads between Danesford and Seacliff. She was so close, he could almost feel her in his arms. Every bit of him ached to close the distance between them and put himself out of his misery once and for all.

But for the first time since he was a lad, sneaking aboard *The Persistence* in a desperate attempt to survive, fear reared up, almost choking him. This was nothing like the fear he had felt when Lenora had been lost in the rain. Then, it had only honed his focus and determination to find her and bring her home safe. No, this fear had him wanting to turn tail and run, to return to his old life, where everything was planned and prescribed. Where the only danger to him was to his bank account and there was no chance of having his heart dashed to pieces.

He frowned. No, that wasn't right. For his heart wasn't whole to begin with. Lenora had it, held in her small hands, with those talented, graceful fingers. And so there was nothing to lose and everything to gain.

Still he couldn't urge his mount forward. There was something else holding him back, something unfinished. As his gaze swung to the left, and down the path to Danesford, he suddenly knew what it was. How could he possibly go to Lenora, asking her to make a life with him, when things were so unfinished with Dane?

For too long he had let hate and revenge abide in his soul, to drive him in every decision he made. He had to go to Lenora with no encumbrances, no anchors holding him back. Without giving himself time to think it through, he turned his horse's head toward Danesford.

As he rode up the drive, he realized with a start that, though this place had been such a huge part of who he was now, this was only his third time traveling up the long, straight drive. The first time he had been a lad full of fear and a desperate hope. The second time he had been a furious man with a cold, hateful heart. Now he had come full circle, for he was once again filled with fear and desperate hope. He only prayed he came away this time free of the past.

He did not expect, however, to be turned away at the door.

"I am sorry, Mr. Ashford, but His Grace cannot see anyone."

There was a quiet grief in the stoic man's eyes that chilled Peter to the bone. "Is he...that is, has he..." He could not finish the thought. As much as he had hoped for

the man's demise, that he would end his days in fear over
what Peter would do to all he held dear, now the very idea
filled him with agony. No, it could not end like this.

The butler's next words had him nearly collapsing in
relief. "No, sir. But he is close."

He should depart. The duke might even now be insen-
sible to the world. Such had been the way his mother had
passed, incoherent, not even able to return the pressure of
his hand as he'd begged her to come back to him.

But he had to try.

"Please," he rasped. "I have come all this way. I must
see him."

"I am sorry, Mr. Ashford—"

"I will take him to see Father."

Peter looked up sharply and spied Lady Clara on the
stairs. Her face was haggard, and thinner than it had
been. The rosy blush that so often stained her cheeks
was gone, and a dull pain suffused her gentle eyes. She
nodded to him, and his heart ached from the coolness
there, when before she had been all warmth and welcome.
It was not only her father's coming death that had put it
there, he knew. He had done that, had put the wall up
between them.

"Mr. Ashford," she said now as the butler bowed and
moved off in quiet respect, "if you will follow me, I shall
show you to Father."

He rushed after her as she made her way back
up the stairs. Immediately upon passing the threshold,
he sensed it, the still and hushed atmosphere of the
house, heavy with the impending death of its master. It
was cloying, seeping under his skin, bringing with it
that same panic he had felt thirteen years ago. Once
again he was that young boy, watching his mother pass

into the next world. Once more hopelessness crashed through him.

He shook his head sharply and peered at Lady Clara's back, her posture brittle and ramrod straight. He longed to tell her all would be well. Empty words, he knew, when her father was about to be ripped from her.

The family quarters were shrouded in silence. She brought him to the door at the far end. Once her hand was on the latch, however, she paused. She bowed her head, and he thought he saw a trembling in her limbs. In the next moment, however, she pushed open the door on silent hinges.

"Father, Peter Ashford is here to see you."

There was a rasp of sound from the depths of the room, unintelligible to where Peter stood out in the hall. Lady Clara stepped aside and, keeping her eyes on the floor, indicated with a nod of her head that he was to enter.

Taking a deep breath, Peter moved past her and entered the Duke of Dane's private apartments.

The space was brighter, much brighter than he'd expected a death room to be. The curtains were open, light streaming into the space. Yet a feeling of dismal grief permeated the air. Death was close; he could feel it in his bones. Shivering, he turned toward the huge four-poster bed that dominated the space.

If he had been shocked at Dane's appearance upon their last meeting, he was doubly so now. In the space of a month, the man had withered away to mere bones. His skin appeared almost translucent, pulled tight over the harsh planes of his face. With pale, cracked lips, he spoke, and the sound of his voice chilled Peter's very core.

"You have come."

Peter swallowed hard and nodded. "Yes." After a

moment's pause, he moved into the room. A set of chairs sat next to the bed, no doubt for his daughters to keep vigil over him. Peter took one. Now was not the time for stiff manners and social niceties. His gaze swept the sunken form beneath the pile of blankets, regret sitting heavily on his shoulders. "I am sorry I did not come sooner."

Dry lips lifted in a shadow of a smile. "But you are here, my boy. That is all that matters." The smile fell then, as if the will was strong but the body too weak to hold it. "I am sorry, Peter, so sorry about your mother."

Tears stung Peter's eyes. The old fury tried to sputter to life, remembering the day the duke had turned him contemptuously away. But it was a weak thing and shriveled before it could find purchase. "I..." The words stuck in his throat. He cleared it and tried again. "I forgive you."

The man seemed to deflate in relief. His hand twitched, reaching for Peter. Without hesitation, he grabbed it, holding the frail bones gingerly in his own. "But," he continued through a throat thick with emotion, "only if you will forgive me. It was cruel of me to threaten you. And I promise, here and now, I will not let Danesford go to ruin. I will take care of your tenants, your family, and make certain they do not want for anything."

The old man nodded, tears spilling over onto his withered cheeks. His skeletal fingers convulsed in Peter's own. Peace descended, such as Peter had never known. Lenora had done this, he knew, had brought him this healing. His heart swelled, thinking of her and the possibility of a life with her.

But he had forgotten Lady Clara.

"What do you mean, you threatened him?" She stood at the far side of the bed, facing Peter, her hands fisted at her sides. "He's dying and you threatened him?"

"Clara," her father tried, his voice a weak whisper.

"Have you no shame?" she hissed, her eyes filled with outraged fire. "It was not my father's fault. If anyone deserves the blame, it's me. If not for my actions, he would not have turned you away all those years ago."

"You?" Peter rasped. He released the duke's hand and stood. Tension threaded through his body. "What do you mean, you're responsible?"

For the first time, uncertainty flared in her gaze. "But surely..." She looked to her father, then back to Peter in confusion. "Surely Father told you *why* he turned you away."

"Clara, don't," Dane tried again, his hand rising toward her.

"Yes," Peter answered, his gaze darting back and forth between father and daughter, a horrible premonition rising like a floodwater in him. "He told me my father was blackmailing him, that he thought I had come to do my father's work."

"Did he not tell you the reason for that blackmail?"

"No."

Lady Clara sat on the bed heavily. "Papa, why didn't you tell him?"

The duke only shook his head. With a tearful smile, she leaned forward and kissed his forehead. "You silly, stubborn, wonderful man," she whispered. "You cannot protect me forever, you know."

He gave her a wan smile. "I shall, as long as there is breath in my body."

She patted his hand, then sighed. "Mr. Ashford, you may as well take a seat. We have much to discuss, you and I."

Uncertainty coiling in his stomach, Peter did as he

was bid. Still it was some moments before Lady Clara spoke.

"I suppose I must start at the beginning, for you to understand fully what was at stake," she began. "Mr. Ashford, have you heard of the rivalry between the previous Duke of Dane and your paternal grandfather?"

"Peter," he said.

She smiled wearily. "Peter."

"I only know my grandfather was cut off without a cent. That when his father died, and his brother, your grandfather, took the helm, there was a falling-out and he was banished." It had been a favorite topic when his father was in a drunken rage—which had been a good portion of the time before he'd abandoned them to an even more desperate poverty. All their misfortune could be traced back to that one moment.

Clara nodded. "Yes, that's true. But do you know why they fought?"

Here Peter could only shake his head. His father had conveniently left that bit out when cursing the duke.

"From all accounts, your grandfather refused to take the living that was offered him, instead expecting to be supported in every luxury and extravagance. When my grandfather cut him off, hoping it would force him to take responsibility for his own life, he stole a quantity of jewels and coin and fled into the night."

Peter nodded, sensing there was more, dreading the telling of it with every fiber in his being.

"Years later..." Here she faltered, looked to her father. But that man had his eyes closed, weary sadness mingling with the subdued pain creasing his gaunt features. She took a deep breath, plowed on. "Years later, your father came to us, begging for help for his family. Despite my grandfather's misgivings and distrust, my father encouraged him to open his heart, to not put the sins of the father on the son. And so he offered him a generous sum, a place to lay his head that night, and the promise of more help to come. It seems your father was not happy with what was given, however. Like his father before him, he, too, took what he could and disappeared before dawn."

"When?" Peter demanded. "When did he do this?"

"Nearly twenty years ago." She smiled sadly. "I know, because I was there and witnessed the entire thing. It destroyed my grandfather, bringing back all the old hurt. He fell ill after that, and never recovered."

Twenty years ago. *After* his father had abandoned them. The bastard had used them for personal gain, with no intention of helping them.

If he could strangle the man with his bare hands this second, he would, and gladly.

But the story wasn't done. For didn't he already know that his father returned to blackmail the duke?

Seeing the tight lines of pain marring Clara's gentle face, however, he had no wish to learn what followed.

"You needn't tell me the rest," he said, his voice gruff in the heavy silence that permeated the room.

She gave him a small smile. "No, I need to say this. If we are to move past this, I need you to understand."

There was a fire in her eyes, a determination he recognized all too well. With reluctance, he nodded.

She drew a deep breath. "When I was a young girl, I allowed my head to be turned by a young man who promised to marry me." She chuckled darkly. "No, it was more than my head, for the rest of me turned right along with it. You are a man of the world; I think you understand what I'm implying."

Grasping the seat beneath him, Peter gritted his teeth and nodded.

"Unfortunately, his promises were as insubstantial as mist. He abandoned me." She clasped her hands tightly in her lap, her knuckles showing white. "I became quite ill as a result of it and was near death's door when your father reappeared, in need of more funds. I don't know how he learned of my . . . situation. Perhaps he coerced my maid, for she left soon after, never to return. All I know is he used his knowledge of my transgression to bribe money from my father."

"Dear God," Peter breathed.

She nodded. "His Grace thought you were in league with your father, and wouldn't help you as he would have had not my idiocy put us in such a situation. When he learned from Lady Tesh the truth of the matter, he tried to track you down. But by then it was too late. You were gone." She looked at him full in the face then. "Peter, it has sat heavy on his soul all these years. No act could be more regretted."

It was an echo of what Lady Tesh had said to him when he'd first come to the Isle. He shook his head. "Why did no one tell me?"

"No one, not even Lady Tesh, knew of your father's blackmail or my shame."

Fury filled Peter, for what this woman had endured. "It's not your shame," he growled, "but the shame and dishonor of the man who used you, and my own father for using that shame against you."

A ghost of a smile flitted over her face. "You're kind." She drew in a deep breath. "And so now you know. Though," she continued, giving her father a mock stern glance, "you should have been told long ago."

The duke gave her a smile full of love. As father and daughter murmured quietly with one another, Peter was aware of a gradual falling away of the old hurt. Though he had determined to shrug off the last of the shackles of his past days ago, it was only now that he was set free. He took a breath, for once his chest unburdened by the bands of hate and revenge that had so long held him prisoner. And suddenly the future looked bright, and full of a hope he'd dared not ever dream of before.

Over the next hour, he talked in quiet tones with Clara and the duke. The man had seemed to rally some, and listened with bright eyes as Peter talked of the future, his smiles showing more than words ever could of his gratitude that Danesford and all that he loved would be cared for. When it was time for his laudanum, and he fell into a peaceful slumber, Clara guided Peter from the room.

"Thank you," she said as they walked side by side down the hall.

"I should be thanking you. You've entrusted me with a painful truth to bring better understanding of a horrible situation." He looked down at her. "I had already offered him forgiveness. You didn't need to, you know."

"It was the least I could do." She looked at him then. "I'm sorry, more than you know."

She still held the burden of her mistake, and would not soon let it go. "It's in the past," he said now, his voice gentle, hoping it would give her some peace.

She nodded, seemingly no more convinced. As they reached the top of the grand staircase, however, she paused, her face brightening. "But I've forgotten. I have promised to show you something." With that, she turned about and headed down the west wing. Puzzled, he followed.

They stepped into a long, open room. Portraits graced the walls at intervals, each one grander than the last. "This is the portrait gallery," she explained as they walked its length. "These, Peter, are your ancestors."

He gazed at the paintings as they passed them. Centuries of Ashfords stared back at him, and he found himself looking for something identifiable in their faces. It was then he saw it, the cool blue eyes of one, the stubborn chin of another, the pale hair of a third. He saw bits and pieces of himself in all of them. As before, when he'd first learned of Synne and her history, he felt the golden thread connecting him to these people, all dead and gone now. And he the last male of the line. Would he and Lenora keep it going? Would their portraits, and the portraits of their children, and their children's children, grace these very walls as well?

His musings were short lived, however, as Clara stopped before a small glass cabinet. Small daggers encrusted with jewels, elaborate gilt crosses, small miniatures, all crowded the interior. But one item stood out from the others, though it was the plainest by far. The dull gold ring, roughly hewn, shouldn't have drawn his attention. Yet he could not keep his eyes from it.

"You've found Synne's ring, I see," Clara said, a hint of humor in her voice.

He gaped, unable to take his eyes from it. "That belonged to Synne?"

"It did." There was a pause, and then, "Would you like to hold it?"

Before he could refuse—for he felt if he held such an ancient, brittle-looking piece in his rough, too-large hands, he would destroy it—she opened the case and pulled the ring from its velvet bed. In the next instant, she had hold of his hand and was placing the band in his palm.

The metal should have been cool to the touch, but it felt hot against his skin. It filled him up, erased who he had thought he was, grounded him to where he truly belonged. And he saw that what he had thought to be delicate and in need of protection was, in fact, enduring and strong.

Like Lenora. Like his love for her.

His chest ached. "Thank you," he whispered. He watched with reverence as the ring was placed back on its bed, and soon he was saying farewell with a promise to return.

He mounted up and turned his horse for Seacliff. There was nothing holding him back now. Soon Lenora would know his heart, and he would do everything in his power to make her his.

Chapter 32

"Peter!" Lady Tesh exclaimed as he was shown into her sitting room not half an hour later. "You have not returned to Boston."

His lips quirked as he strode toward her. "Obviously." And yet, despite the sarcasm in his drawl, he could not help scanning the room. Lenora was not there. Damn and blast, he'd been so certain she would be. But perhaps that was for the best, for if she had been, Redburn was certain to be as well. And he could not stomach the thought of the man just then.

"You're looking well, Aunt," he said, bending to kiss her cheek. Freya lifted her head, and he scrubbed at her messy mop with his fingers before seating himself beside Lady Tesh.

Still the viscountess gaped at him. He tried for a mocking smile, though his insides churned with impatience. "I see I have rendered you speechless. One might think you were not happy to see me."

Lady Tesh seemed to recall herself at once. "Of course I'm happy to see you, my boy. Goodness, but I've been lonely. It is good to have you back."

Uneasiness settled under his skin for a moment. He laughed, but it was strained. "Lonely? I would hardly call having the company of two young ladies a lonely thing."

To his shock, Lady Tesh appeared stricken. "But you don't know? Lenora and Margery are no longer here. They've been gone several days now."

He straightened, leaning forward. "Gone? What do you mean, gone?" The dread that had been simmering beneath the surface exploded into a choking fear. "And Redburn?"

She shrugged. "Gone, too. Back to London."

Shock pulled at him and he slumped back in his seat. There was only one reason for them to return to London: marriage. He was too late. She was lost to him. He ran a hand over his face. To be so close, and still to have lost her.

But the fire of hope was not yet extinguished. She had been gone only a few days. Even if Redburn managed to obtain a special license once they reached the capital, they would be traveling by carriage; if Peter rode hard, he might make up the time.

He surged to his feet. He must have appeared a madman, for Lady Tesh stared at him as if he had lost his mind.

"Peter, what the devil are you about?"

"I have to get to London," he muttered, hurrying for the door.

"Why?" she cried.

"For Lenora," he bit out over his shoulder. "She can't marry Redburn. I have to stop her."

Nothing on God's green earth could have stopped him in that moment. Except for the sound of Lady Tesh's laughter.

He wheeled about, gaping at her. "What is so damned funny?"

"Oh, Peter," she gasped between guffaws, "you needn't travel all the way to London for that."

He frowned. "You make no sense, madam. Speak plainly or let me be off."

Her laughter fell away, yet her eyes still glinted in amusement. "It is a fool's errand to go to London for Lenora, because she's not there. She's still here, on the Isle."

He stared at her in disbelief. Was the woman losing her mind? But no, she appeared in full possession of her faculties. In fact, she appeared much saner than he did in that moment, seemed to find him absolutely hilarious, in fact. Brows drawing down in warning, he demanded, "If Lenora is not here, yet still on the Isle, where is she?"

Lady Tesh pursed her lips, her eyebrows rising in a considering arch. "She was devastated when you left, you know. She did not voice it, but Margery and I saw it all the same."

Nothing could have destroyed him more. Nor given him more hope. For if she had been hurt by his abrupt leaving, it meant her heart was engaged.

Perhaps, just perhaps, she loved him as desperately as he loved her. Though he had been a complete arse and deserved her disgust until the end of time.

He shifted forward in his chair. "Please," he begged, something he had never allowed himself to do, "I will do anything to win her back."

A spark flared in her sharp gaze. "Anything?"

The old woman looked almost feral. But Peter didn't care what she was plotting in that disturbingly agile mind of hers. "Yes," he answered without hesitation.

She studied him for a long moment, as if taking his

measure. In the end, she nodded. "She will attend the subscription ball this evening."

"I'll be there." He stood and strode for the door, his mind already whirling with the possible outcomes, fear and hope warring for dominance in his chest. Lady Tesh had asked if he would do anything to win Lenora. In a heartbeat. He would walk through fire, would face a dragon.

Would don that ridiculous formal suit every day for the rest of his life.

But how to prove it to her?

He stilled, his hand on the latch. How indeed. Storming the assembly hall and glowering in the corner, as he had on his last two visits, would not be enough. He had to show Lenora just how committed he was to loving her the rest of his days. No matter what.

"Peter, you have not changed your mind, have you?"

His grip on the latch tightened, determination roaring through him. "Not in the least, madam." He turned to face her. "The ball is not for several hours."

Again that white brow arched up her forehead. "Correct."

He grinned. "You've called me a gentleman before. What say we make that official?"

* * *

Lenora frowned, peering up at the ochre stone façade of the assembly hall as their carriage slowly made its way down the long line of equipages. "I told you, Margery," she grumbled, tugging her glove smooth, "there's still too much to do at the dower cottage for me to even consider attending a ball."

"Nonsense," Margery declared with a bracing smile. "You've been working yourself to the bone day and night to make the cottage habitable. Between that and your painting, you've not had a moment to relax."

I hardly call a ball relaxing, she nearly said. At the last moment, the words stuck in her throat. The echo of Peter was in them, and she would not allow herself to think of him. Not now. Those painful moments were relegated to the quiet dark of her bedroom, her tears kept private from all but the pillow beneath her head as she tried unsuccessfully to find peace in slumber.

Not that her life was all heartache. Her determination to carve out this new and wholly unchartered path in her life had seen to that. The dower cottage had been unused for years, and while it was in fairly good repair, it still needed hard work to bring it back to the glory it had been. Between the physical labor of painting and dusting and polishing, and the very emotional labor of her art, she had found a purpose she'd never thought to have. And it had surprised her that, though her father had disowned her, though Peter had left, she was able to claim a contentment and satisfaction in this new life of hers.

But there was still much to do. Which was why this ill-timed trip to the subscription ball rankled so.

Margery laid her hand over Lenora's, dragging her attention back to the present. "I'm happy you've come tonight," she said softly. "I've missed you, dearest."

The quiet words struck her mute. While it was true the last week had seen them much in each other's company, Margery insisting on helping where she could in the start of Lenora's new life, there had been no time for sitting quietly together as they used to do. Lenora realized in that moment how much she had missed her friend, missed their walks and easy affection, missed the way she felt grounded after time in her presence. And as she looked into Margery's gentle brown eyes, she recognized an answering need for reconnection.

Lenora slumped in her seat, her heart twisting. "I've missed you, too," she said, sandwiching Margery's hand between her own. "And you were right, I need this. *We* need this."

The carriage rocked to a halt, the door opening to reveal a bewigged footman. The two women descended to the pavement, linking arms as they entered the assembly hall. From the echoing strains of music that drifted out to them, to the gentle roar of laughter and conversation that made the dances on the Isle so much more palatable than those stiff, starched affairs she had grown accustomed to in London, it sounded as if the ball was already in full swing.

Lenora eyed the crush of people as she and Margery worked their way through the portico and toward the wide double doorways leading into the ball. "Has Gran arrived yet, do you think?"

"Oh, you know Gran," Margery said, pressing closer to Lenora as she sidestepped a group of young women loitering near the entrance. "She will have wanted to be first in the door. No doubt she's been watching for us this past half hour or better."

Lenora let loose a small sigh. "The blame for our tardiness is mine. I've been so anxious to have everything just right, I have not given her the attention she deserves. I do hope she can forgive me for being so distracted these past days."

"Oh, I don't know," Margery murmured, a smile in her

voice as they made their way into the long ballroom. "I do believe she would forgive you for anything tonight."

Lenora frowned at that peculiar statement. Before she could ask Margery about it, the crowd opened up, and they spied Lady Tesh seated at her typical place along the wall. And beside her, his back to them, was...

"Peter," she breathed.

He stilled, then turned, as if heeding the call of his name on her lips. A silly thing, really, considering the noise that filled the place. And yet his eyes found hers unerringly, the heat in them nearly buckling her knees. Only Margery's arm linked with hers kept her on her feet.

"I—I don't understand," she managed through stiff lips. "He left, set sail for America."

"He came back," Margery said in her ear.

Lenora swung her gaze to her friend. Margery smiled at her, not an ounce of surprise on her face.

She blinked in incomprehension. "You knew?"

Her friend merely smiled wider before she released Lenora's arm, with a comforting squeeze, and stepped away, melding back in with the crowd. Lenora stared after her for a moment, utterly confused, feeling lost in a rough sea.

Until a familiar deep voice anchored her.

"Lenora."

Peter stood silent and still, a great stone monolith in the midst of the chaos of revelry. And yet he looked as if he belonged. Garbed again in that expertly tailored formal suit he so despised, he was nevertheless the epitome of a noble. He stood straight as an arrow, his hair brushed and tied back into a neat queue, his beard trimmed close. He would not have been out of place in a London ballroom, surrounded by the cream of society.

But this was not her Peter. She ran her gaze over him, searching for the man she had come to love, hidden somewhere in this impeccably dressed swain. She wanted to weep that he seemed gone—until she came to his eyes. They were the same, wild and untamed. And burning.

The urge to fling herself into his arms nearly overwhelmed her. But she resisted. He had made himself clear; his revenge on his cousin was too important to him. He would never abandon his carefully laid plans. Most especially not for her.

She hugged herself about the middle, painfully aware of the crowd of people surrounding them, the happy sounds of celebration that bounced jarringly off the tense bubble she and Peter seemed to be encased in. "You were returning to Boston. You should be on the ship this very moment."

"I couldn't leave."

Three words, so simple, yet full of some hidden meaning. Her heart ached to know: was she the reason he had come back? But she would not ask. She *could* not ask.

His gaze didn't leave her face, his blue eyes lacking the defenses that had so filled them before, a fragile longing shimmering from their depths. "May I have the honor of this dance, Lenora?" He held one pristine gloved hand out.

In the next moment, her hand was in his. It was as if her heart had taken control of her body, doing what her mind willed her not to. He led her to the floor with careful, stately steps. She should remove her hand from his grip, should refuse him. Yet she could not. *It would cause a scene*, she told herself. But even as the words whispered halfheartedly through her mind, she knew they were a lie. She did not pull her fingers from his grip for one reason, and one reason only: it felt right to have them there.

It was only as he stopped in the center of the gleaming

floor that her befuddled brain caught the familiar strains of the music: a waltz.

She shook her head helplessly as he bowed low, his eyes never leaving her. "You don't know the waltz, Peter."

In answer, he grasped her right hand, placing his free hand along the curve of her spine.

She dragged in a deep breath as longing washed over her, his scent of spices and black coffee and horse and leather bringing tears to her eyes. She dropped her gaze and blinked them away, desperate that he not see how much this pained her, how he affected her still.

He was the proper distance from her, his posture perfect, nothing scandalous in the way he touched her. Yet he filled the space between them, overpowering it with his sheer presence. He began to move, and she helplessly followed his lead. *This is a mistake*, her mind whispered, even as her heart pounded out quite another rhythm. Ignoring them both as best she could, she found herself focusing on the way he moved, on the elegance of his step, on the masterful way he guided her. Which only brought about more confusion to her dazed mind.

"You waltz," she blurted out.

"Aunt Olivia was most obliging in my schooling."

She blinked, taken aback not only by his formal speech but his address of Lady Tesh. Since when had he called the viscountess by anything other than her title? He swung her in a turn, and she caught sight of that woman and Margery, heads bent close together, watching them with beatific smiles lighting their faces. She narrowed her eyes, remembering the lack of surprise in her friend when they'd first spied Peter. And even before that, her uncharacteristic stubbornness in insisting that Lenora attend the ball.

"And Margery?" she asked tightly. "Did she have a part in your lessons?"

"My cousin was very helpful."

His overly proper manner snapped her frazzled patience in two. "And did she also teach you how to talk like a pompous arse?"

He blinked, his steps faltering before he quickly recovered. "I'm only conversing as any of the men you knew in London would."

"And does it look as if I care for all that?" she exploded before recalling they were surrounded by couples. Spying more than one set of curious gazes on them, she closed her eyes and breathed in deeply. Trying not to focus on the feel of his hands or the gentle swaying as his large body conformed to the tight, square pattern of the dance.

Weariness filled her, until she thought she might burst into tears. She could not do this again, could not work past the grief of him leaving her.

Or rather, she could. She had learned in the past week that she was stronger than she had ever thought. But the very idea of having to battle her way through the pain again had her heart breaking anew.

"Why are you here, Peter?" she whispered, too exhausted down to her bones to manage more.

He seemed to sense the brittleness in her, for when he spoke, his voice was gruff, back to what it had been. Back to what she loved. "I had to see you."

"Why?"

He blinked, seeming at a loss. Then, "You did not leave for London with Redburn."

"No."

"You did not marry him."

Lenora frowned. It was not a question, yet there was

an undercurrent that seemed to beg for an answer. "No. I knew we would not suit. I broke off our engagement."

Immediately she wanted to bite her tongue. Why had she told him as much? He would not care that yet another of her engagements had failed.

Yet his shoulders, tense up until then, sagged with obvious relief. "I'm glad," he said in a voice that barely reached her ears for all the noise surrounding them, yet seemed loud to her hungry heart.

"Why?"

The one word, harsh, tearing from her throat, finally broke her from her weary grief, replacing it with a deep anger. How dare he come here and undermine the foundation she was trying to build her new life on? She stopped in the middle of the dance floor, not caring that she was making a spectacle of herself, pulling herself from his arms. About them, couples twirled and spun, a dizzy array of bright colors that made her feel as if she were the center of a riotous kaleidoscope.

"Why are you glad, Peter?" she demanded. "By all accounts, you were more than happy to let me marry Lord Redburn, were more than happy to leave without a word of farewell."

"I was never happy to leave you," he rasped.

"Then why did you?" she cried. The words burst from her, startling her with their vehemence. There had been a time she would have curled into herself and apologized for making a scene. But she was through holding in her emotions. And she refused to give any more time to this man who had not wanted her.

She fought back the tears that threatened and glared at him with all the anger that simmered in her before storming across the floor for the side of the room. The dancing couples parted for her like the Red Sea. "Never mind. It doesn't matter."

He let loose a low curse. "Of course it matters." He followed her, grabbed her arm. "Lenora—"

She threw her arms up, breaking his tentative hold. Panic rearing that, even now, she wanted nothing more than to fall into his arms. "Don't," she managed.

His lips pressed together in frustration, but he nodded, his hands curling into fists at his sides. "I never wanted to leave you. But it was the only way I could see."

"See what?"

"For you to be happy."

The confession knocked the breath from her. "You thought that by leaving, you were making me happy?"

He didn't answer, but she could see from the pain that flashed in his eyes, the way his fingers twitched up to his pristine cravat before dropping heavily again to his side, that was exactly what he'd believed.

She felt a softening in the general region of her heart, his unintentional vulnerability affecting her as it always had. She longed to caress the side of his face, to kiss away the self-recrimination that sat heavily on his brow. She swallowed hard, trying to hold herself together by sheer force of will.

Yet she couldn't sit silently by and watch his torment. "You did not make me happy by leaving, Peter," she said in a low, pained voice.

Hope flared in his eyes. A dangerous thing, for she was beginning to forget why she should hold him at arm's length.

Her resolve was decimated by his next words.

"I was a fool, Lenora. I should never have left. I should have fought for you. No matter that I'm big and rough and uneducated. No matter that I don't deserve you. I should have never let you go so easy."

As she stared at him, shocked, he moved closer, his movements slow and careful, as if he feared she would bolt. As if she could leave him in that moment.

"The second Redburn arrived at Seacliff, I should have told him the truth of the matter," he said in a voice thick with emotion, "that you had stolen my heart, and I could not imagine my life without you."

"Peter," she whispered.

A small, tender smile curved his lips as he reached her. His hand came up, his fingers caressing the curve of her cheek. "And I should not have allowed him to prevent me from telling you one very important thing."

Her heart pounded, her fingers trembling as they found his chest, pressing over his heart, a heart that beat as fiercely as her own. "What is that?"

He sank to his knees. Peter, the strongest, proudest man she had ever known, kneeled before her in front of everyone in that overheated, crowded assembly hall.

He took her hands, held them tight in his own. "That I love you. With all my body, all my heart, all my soul. I love you, Lenora."

She let out the breath she had been holding on a soft "Oh."

His smile faltered, doubt creeping into his eyes. "Is that a good *oh* or a bad *oh*?"

In answer, she dropped to her knees, flung her arms about his neck, and pressed her mouth to his. It seemed to unlock something in him, and he let loose a low moan of pure longing that vibrated through her. He held her with a tenderness that belied his rough past, with arms banded from years of manual labor, hands scarred with the trials and tribulations of a hard life. His mouth worshipped hers, every bit of the love he professed to have for her displayed in the achingly gentle kiss. She nearly cried out when their mouths separated, when he placed his forehead against her own.

The noise about them, which had faded away to nothing, intruded once more. The music had stalled, but gasps and horrified laughter rang through the space. Out of the corner of her eye, she spied faces lax with shock, people whispering.

Lenora had experienced her fair share of embarrassments and scandal. This time was not one of them. How could it be, when she was so happy?

Letting loose a giggle, she lurched to her feet, pulling Peter right along with her. Holding hands, they hurried through the crowd and out the side door. Her last glimpse before the door closed behind them was of Lady Tesh and Margery at their places against the wall, faces beaming.

And then she was back in Peter's arms, and everything else was forgotten.

"I know I'm not one of the polished gentlemen of the *ton*," he whispered, the coarseness of his beard a heady contrast to the feel of his full lips against the bare curve of her neck. "I'm rough and crude and ill-mannered."

Heart aching, she pulled back and placed her hands on either side of his beloved face. "Is that what this was all about?" she asked, not a hint of humor in her voice. "The way you've dressed, the proper manners?"

"You deserve a gentleman," he said, voice thick, his eyes begging her to understand. "And I can be that for you. I'll go to London, put on this ridiculous suit every evening, polish my speech until no one can find fault with it."

She shook her head even as her heart fractured. "Do you think I want that?"

He pressed his lips tight, pain flashing in his eyes.

She smiled, a watery thing. "If that was all I wanted, I would have been happy with Redburn. I prefer my men to have hair wild as any Viking's." She reached for the strip of silk holding his hair, pulling it loose until his golden locks fell in disarray about his shoulders. "To listen to a woman with respect and interest." She ran her finger over the swirl of his ear. "To say what they mean instead of mere platitudes." She caressed the softening line of his lips.

"And," she continued with a smile, her fingers going to the starched, careful folds of his cravat, destroying what had no doubt taken much work, "to wear their heart on their sleeve. Especially if that heart is covered by a limp cravat."

Love and joy flared in his eyes. He took her hands, pulling the gloves from her fingers and pressing his warm mouth to her palm. "I know your heart will always belong to Hillram. But do you think you might come to care for me, Lenora?"

"You silly man," she managed through a throat tight with unshed tears. "Yes, I loved Hillram. But only as my dear friend, nothing more."

His eyes searched hers, hope a living thing in their depths. "Truly?"

"I told you that night when you came to me, I never felt with anyone else what I feel for you. That includes my heart." She smiled. "You are one of the most giving, caring men I have ever had the honor to know. You wonder if I could come to care for you? Peter, I have loved you almost from the moment you caught me up against you on Lady Tesh's front steps."

He searched her face, more than golden lantern light glinting in his eyes. "Say it again," he demanded gruffly.

She blinked in confusion a split second before understanding washed over her. Smiling, she caressed the sharp curve of his cheek with her thumb. "I love you, Peter."

The words were hardly free of her lips before he claimed them again. "Marry me," he said into the dark recesses of her mouth.

She longed to accept. But a tinge of doubt polluted the haze of happiness that enfolded her. "What of His Grace?"

He would know what she asked: Would he be able to give up his revenge? Would he be happy with her when making the duke pay his debt was so important to him? She tensed, waiting for his answer.

She did not have long to wait. He smiled, his hands stroking loose tendrils of hair back from her face with an expression amazingly clear and free. "Dane and I have reconciled."

As shock swirled through her, and more questions than she could wrap her head around, he turned serious. "Marry me, Lenora. Be my wife."

And then, "Please."

That one word banished any lingering doubts in her heart. He wasn't telling her what she should do; he was asking, begging, with every ounce of his soul. He was giving her the choice to accept or reject. "Yes," she said without hesitation.

Relief flared in his eyes. His kiss was tender, reverent. But she wanted so much more of him. She wanted all of him. Her fingers tangled in his hair, her body arching up into his.

He did not misunderstand what she was trying to convey. "Lenora," he gasped. "Are you certain?"

"Yes."

The desire that flared in his eyes was brighter than any flame. Anticipation shivered through her as his gaze zeroed in on her mouth—

A rumble of laughter interrupted them. And not muted through the assembly room door but much closer than anticipated. Peter must have heard it as well, for he stilled, his hands tightening protectively on her before he raised his head.

A small group of grooms stood close by, grinning. One of them saluted Peter with his flask.

"If I may say, sir, you're a right lucky one," the man quipped.

To Lenora's surprise, a deep chuckle rumbled up from Peter's chest. "Luckier than you know. You may be the first to congratulate me, for this lady has just consented to be my wife."

As the men burst into a rousing cheer, Lenora peered up into Peter's face—and nearly lost her breath from the happiness shining there. Never had she seen him so utterly content. Knowing that she had been the one to put that joy there made her heart swell.

Another man stepped into the pool of lantern light under the colonnade, this time Lady Tesh's own groom. "Mr. Ashford, sir? Are you needing the carriage then?"

In no time, they were being herded to the waiting equipage, the cheers of the men fading behind them. "To Seacliff, sir?" the groom asked as he saw them inside.

Before Peter could assent, Lenora spoke, a smile curving her lips. "To the dower cottage, if you please?"

Chapter 33

*P*eter gave her a curious look but said nothing as they settled themselves inside the carriage. His arm came about her shoulders, pulling her into his side. She went happily, her arm going about his waist, her head resting on his chest. It was just where she wanted to be.

They rode in silence, the moment too precious, the anticipation too great. She hardly saw the moonlit landscape outside the window for all her focus was on that precious heartbeat beneath her ear. Soon the carriage slowed, then stopped. Before the groom could dismount from the box to open the door, Peter was in motion, throwing it wide, leaping down to the drive, helping her down beside him. In moments, she had her key, opened the door...

It closed behind them with a soft click. And they were alone.

The front hall was dim. Yet there was enough moonlight shining through the mullioned windows to see the wonder that suffused his face as he gazed down at her. As he turned to glance about the space, however, his expression changed to one of confusion. "What is this place?"

In answer, she went to the small side table and lit a lamp. A faint golden glow filled the hall. Suddenly unaccountably nervous, she watched as he took it all in:

the narrow hall, the door that led to the small parlor, the simple flight of stairs.

"It's mine," she explained, unable to keep the hint of pride from her voice. "Or rather, it is Lady Tesh's, and mine to lease."

His gaze swung to hers in shock. "Lease?"

Uncertainty crashed through her. She was a lady who had gone into trade. It wasn't done.

In the next minute, she ground those feelings down to nothing. There was no shame in it. And this was Peter, after all. If anyone would understand the importance of this, it would be him.

She nodded. "Paid for with my paintings."

Understanding lit his features then. And a pride so fierce, she thought she would cry from the joy it gave her. Before she knew it, she was in his arms, his mouth covering hers with a desperation that took her very breath. His fingers grabbed at her hips, pulling her against the hard length of him, leaving no doubt as to her effect on him. His mouth was hot on hers, more demanding than it had ever been. She met the demands with joy, showing him with grasping hands and writhing body that she was no delicate flower he need fear bruising. Her fingers were busy, working at the disheveled folds of his cravat, pushing his jacket from the massive breadth of his shoulders, fumbling at the buttons of his waistcoat. Every brush, every tug, seemed to make him wilder. Until, finally, his mouth ripped free.

"Bed," he gasped.

She pointed up the stairs. And then she was whisked up into his arms, secure against the hardness of his chest as he pounded up the treads. In mere seconds, he burst through the narrow doorway of her small room, the door closing behind them. Then there was no time to breathe, no time to think, as their lips met in a fiery kiss that fairly melted her shoes from her feet.

This time, she knew, there would be no holding back, no stopping for fear of being caught or what tomorrow might bring. He would be hers before the night was through.

And he loved her.

The realization sang through her as he lowered her to the bed. This man, who had known so much heartache, who had survived by sheer will, clinging to control and balance in every aspect of his life, had given it all up in coming to her and asking for her love. He had entrusted himself to her. Tears burned her eyes at the realization of what that must have cost him, this proud man who had kept walls up about his heart since childhood.

His rough hands felt wondrous on her skin as he undressed her, peeling off the fine silk of her clothes. It was when she was fully bared to him that he paused. Uncertainty clouded his gaze.

She understood at once. Grabbing up his hand, she placed it on her aching breast, squeezing his fingers around her. "I will not break, Peter," she whispered into the dim light of dusk, gazing up with trust into his beloved face. "I promise."

He groaned, his fingers convulsing. She gasped, pleasure coursing through her, and arched up into his touch. "Peter."

The desire coating that one word, her body's untutored reaction, seemed to snap his tightly held control. He tugged at his clothing, his hands clumsy in their desperation. Her fingers joined his, and soon the fabric lay in an untidy heap beside her own. He stretched out beside her on the ancient bed. But Lenora would have none of his caution. She tugged at his shoulders until he lay atop her, the incredible strength and weight of him pinning her to the mattress.

"I'm too heavy," he insisted.

"And I have told you before, I am stronger than I look."

He searched deep into her eyes before relaxing, his gaze turning infinitely tender. "I know you are," he whispered. His mouth found hers, and there was no more room for words.

The rasp of his beard drove her wild as his lips trailed down her body. This time there was no shock when he claimed the sensitive buds of her nipples, no surprise when he moved lower, across her belly, and buried his face between her legs. She opened up for him, welcoming him, reveling in the way he adored her body, bringing her to the pinnacle of pleasure, nearly sending her over the edge. She grasped his hair, pressing him into the core of her, almost coming apart when he growled in approval, the sound filling her up until she thought she would burst.

But this would be no one-sided coming together this time. With a yank, she pulled him away from her, though her body cried out for completion.

"I need you now, Peter," she gasped. "Inside me."

He needed no further urgings. Moving up her body, he settled his lean hips between the cradle of her thighs. But even then, as he positioned himself at the throbbing center of her, he held back.

"Are you certain?"

And she had not thought her heart could be any fuller, any more his. This incredible man, who would deny himself in that very moment if she asked him to. In answer, she wrapped her legs about his hips and brought him home.

The twinge of pain hardly registered in her pleasure-infused mind. Her entire focus was on the heat of him as he entered, his hiss of breath as he eased himself into her folds, the way he filled her up, body and soul.

His brow rested against her own, his breathing ragged. "Are you well?"

She smiled up at him. "More than well. But…"

He stilled. "But what?"

"Is there more?"

A hoarse laugh escaped him. "Ah, love, so much more."

He began to move in her, slowly at first. Pleasure filled Lenora, bringing her to where she had been and beyond. Yet still he kept such control over his movements. The silly man, always so careful. But words would do nothing just then. Lenora knew the only thing that would release him was the reaction of her body.

So she let him know, with every dig of her nails into his sweat-slicked back, every lift of her hips, every gasp into his ear, that he could let go. But it was only when her teeth closed over his shoulder that he seemed to fully understand what she needed from him. The jerk of his hips grew more desperate, his breathing growing harsher. Lenora pressed her heels into the bed, meeting him thrust for thrust. The pleasure built, swirling in eddies, the wave growing in strength until, with one final thrust, it crashed over her head.

She heard Peter's shout echo her own cry of completion, felt him shudder. And then he collapsed to the bed—beside her, of course, the wonderful man—and pulled her into the crook of his arm. The last things she remembered were his lips on her hair and the steady beat of his heart under her ear.

* * *

It was the sunlight on her face that woke Lenora. She
yawned, stretched, and peered blearily around the room,
utter contentment making her limbs weak and lazy. She
could lie like this forever, she decided with a small smile,
replete after a night of lovemaking, next to the man
she loved. She reached to the side, searching for Peter's
warmth—and her heart stuttered in panic. For the sheets
were empty and cold.

Had he left? For a moment, the fear rose up, hot and
desperate.

But reason was quick to reassert itself. Peter loved her.
There was nothing to fear.

Just then she heard footsteps on the stairs. The door to
her bedroom opened, and there he was.

She drank him in. He had wrapped a blanket about
his hips, and his chest was bare, his hair loose. He
would have been at home on the bow of a Viking ship.
But instead of a fearsome blade cradled in his hands, he
held...breakfast?

She blinked. "You cook?"

He smiled sheepishly at her. "Not well. But enough to
survive on."

She grinned, lurching to her knees on the soft mattress.
Only realizing when his eyes dropped to her chest and turned
molten that the sheet had slipped to reveal her breasts.

"Then again," he murmured, "I do believe eating is
overrated."

Which was just fine with Lenora. The next hour was
spent quite happily pursuing activities other than food.
Finally, spent, ravenous, they pushed aside the tangled
sheets and brought the tray onto the happily rumpled bed.

"Oh, this is wonderful," Lenora said around a mouthful of eggs—cold after their interlude but delicious nonetheless.

Peter grinned. His smile quickly turned to something wicked, however, when she bit into a piece of buttered bread and let out a low moan. "You'd best not make that sound, love, or the food shall have to be put aside again."

She laughed, and they ate in companionable silence. Finally the last morsel had been devoured and they lay back in each other's arms.

His hand stroked over her hip languidly. "I saw your painting."

Lenora trailed her fingers through the pale gold hair dusting his broad chest. "Did you?" she murmured.

He nodded, his beard rasping in her hair. "It's beautiful. And the other sketches, the ones laid out on the table...they're incredible, Lenora."

These were no mere words. This man, who so often hid his feelings behind a stoic mask, was trying to convey to her the importance of what her art meant to him. She rose up on one elbow, gazing down into his face. "You helped me unleash that part of myself, you know."

He flushed, tried looking away. She put her hand on his face, brought his gaze back to hers.

"It's the truth. You were right, when we fought before you left. I did try to bury anything that gave me happiness, including my talent. I didn't believe I deserved it." She took a deep breath. "You helped me to see that the good in life is worth the pain of the bad. And that I should embrace both. Otherwise I'm not living."

His hand came up, the rough calloused palm cupping her cheek with infinite gentleness.

"I was no better," he admitted. "I clung to my pain, let it drive me, until it was all that I was. Not realizing that it was a life, but no way to live." He smiled, his eyes shimmering. "You made me see that, Lenora. You gave me peace, and happiness." His throat worked as he swallowed hard, his voice gruff as he said, "A day will not go by that you will not know how much I love you, Lenora."

Tears blurred her vision. "I love you, Peter," she whispered. As their lips met, she wove her fingers with his, as surely as their hearts were bound.

Epilogue

*L*enora rinsed her brush out in the water, the tinkle of the wood handle on the glass a beautiful accompaniment to the faint pianoforte music playing in the distance. It had taken time for the atmosphere at Danesford to lighten again after the duke's passing. Yet now the laughter and happiness that rang through its halls were natural, lovely things, sweet memories beginning to take the place of their grief.

Focusing again on the work before her, Lenora turned to her paints. A quick dab of blue, a hint of purple, a splash of green, and she swept the bristles across the page, melding and combining in a rich medley of hues. Another rinse, and this time she worked the naked brush through the still wet paint, lifting and blending until the depth was just right.

She lowered her hand, tilted her head, looking over the newest portion. Yes, that was it exactly. Already thinking of the next section to tackle, she dipped her brush again into the water—and stilled as a pair of warm, firm lips found the nape of her neck.

She smiled, embracing the arms that stole around her waist, and leaned into the solid wall of chest at her back. Then, with an impish grin, she asked with coy innocence, "Who is it?"

He growled, giving the sensitive skin under her ear a playful nip. "You know well and good who it is, wife."

She giggled, then sighed as his clever lips did wonderful things to the side of her neck. "And how was your lunch with Mr. Tunley?"

"Wonderful," he murmured against her skin. "He had the most ingenious idea for a mill, one that would revolutionize weaving techniques. I recall seeing something similar during my time in Boston. It could prove to be quite lucrative and would bring an amazing increase in revenue for the Isle."

Lenora fought to focus on Peter's words as his lips continued to play along the side of her neck, amazed that he could make something so dry sound so very seductive. Just as she was thinking of ways she could coerce him into an interlude on the small couch that graced the corner of her studio, he raised his head. "Nearly finished with Mrs. Harris's painting, I see."

"Yes." She studied the watercolor critically. A fae creature, ethereal and delicate, sat at the pond's edge, dipping her fingers in the water. About her, branches reached for the heavens, mist swirled, and small creatures peered out from the leaves. "I do hope she likes it. I admit, I did not expect such paintings to become so popular."

"Why wouldn't they?" Peter murmured, his arms tightening about her midsection. "You have an uncommon talent, and people could not fail to be charmed by your work."

She flushed, pleased beyond words by his defense of her. Even so, she could not help saying, "It is certainly not Royal Academy worthy, though."

"Their loss, then. I would much rather you paint what's in your heart than conform to the stuffy parameters set by that illustrious place. Besides, the good people of Synne don't seem to think there is anything lacking in your work." He paused to kiss the top of her head, and when he spoke again, she could hear the smile in his voice. "You are a success, my love. Not that I ever had a doubt you would be."

Lenora's heart swelled. Peter had been incredibly proud that long-ago night at the dower cottage upon learning she had not collapsed with fear or grief upon her father disowning her, but had instead been planning a career as an artist to support herself. Nor had he batted an eye when she had broached the idea of continuing to work toward that goal after they were wed. With his support and Lady Tesh's patronage, she had seen that dream realized, accepting commissions of her fanciful watercolors from the Isle's longtime residents and visitors alike, even starting instructions for those that would learn.

"I did seek you out for a reason, you know," he said into the companionable silence.

She turned in his embrace, twining her arms about his neck. "Besides kissing me, you mean?"

His gaze heated at her husky tone, a low groan escaping his lips as she pulled him down to her. The kiss was hot, and hard, and stoked the fire that had sparked to life as soon as he'd entered the room.

His hands were doing wicked things to her breasts, and her fingers were working at his perpetually limp cravat, when they heard the distant barking of a dog. Peter lifted his head and gave her a rueful, regretful look. "Ah, yes. Lady Tesh and Margery have arrived."

She chuckled. "And with Freya in tow, I see."

"Naturally. Though fear not for the footmen, for Clara and Phoebe are seeing to them and are more than capable of entertaining my great-aunt and keeping her from mischief."

A bittersweet sadness stole through Lenora as Peter helped her off with her apron. "Our trip to London is but a week away. I have a feeling that one, and perhaps both, will not return to Danesford with us at the end of the season." She gave a small sigh. "I shall miss them when they marry."

His hands found her arms and squeezed reassuringly. "As will I," he said gently, working at the knot at the back of her apron. "But it will be good for them, to take steps toward their future happiness. It has been difficult for them since their father's death." He finished and came to stand before her. "I know a bit of what they're experiencing, I think. It's not easy to be a caretaker for a person who is leaving this world, especially when their illness is a long and painful one. I do believe they've felt adrift since Dane's passing. This will perhaps help them move past the pain and heal."

She cupped his bearded cheek, tears prickling at her eyes. "You have been so good to them. Their path would have been much more difficult had you not shown them such kindness and love."

He shrugged, clearly embarrassed by her praise. "Enough," he said gruffly, planting a quick kiss on her lips before offering her his arm. "Let us go down to our family."

Our family. Those two words sat warm and glowing inside her as she tucked her hand in the crook of his elbow and let him lead her downstairs. For it was true, the ladies below were her family now, not of her blood, but of her heart, something that was infinitely more important.

They stopped outside the drawing room door, listening

to the happy, chaotic sounds from within. Lenora squeezed Peter's arm, met his loving gaze, her heart lurching at the small smile he gave her. She did not think she would ever grow immune to that tender look.

"Happy, Lenora?"

"Oh, yes," she whispered, just before he took her lips in a kiss.

Don't miss

Someday My Duke Will Come,

the next lush historical
romance from
Christina Britton!

Coming Winter 2021

See the next page
for a preview.

Chapter 1

1818

*M*r. Quincy Nesbitt had suspected his return to London would be painful, that riding down streets that were at once foreign and familiar would be like tearing open an old wound.

It brought him not an ounce of pleasure to know just how right he had been.

He took a deep breath as he made the turn down Davies Street from his hotel, trying to rein in the sensation of being suffocated under a wet blanket. But no matter his attempts, the feeling persisted, increasing with each clip of his horse's hooves on the cobbles. Damnation, but this had been a mistake. He had thought it the ideal plan while setting sail from Spain. Being so close to England, and not knowing when he might be back this way again, he could not pass up the chance to visit his closest friend, Peter Ashford, now the Duke of Dane. And with Peter in London for the season, it gave Quincy the push he needed to finally reveal truths too long buried—and to confront the ghosts of his past. It was something he should have done long ago.

Now that he was here, however...

His mount tossed its head in protest. Quincy took a

deep breath, relaxing his iron grip on the reins, silently reproaching himself for his distracted ham-handedness. There was no reason for his anxiety, he told himself stoutly. Though his family's townhome was but two streets up in Berkeley Square, though he was closer to that place than he had been in fourteen long years, he was not headed there just yet. He would see Peter first before bearding that particular lion.

As he thought of his friend, however, and how he might react to what Quincy must now reveal to him after so many years of concealment and outright falsehoods, he broke into a cold sweat.

And why shouldn't he worry? Peter had become more of a brother to him over the years than his own had ever been, had stayed by his side through every high and low. This was a meeting long overdue, a tale too long untold. But he just might lose his dearest friend in the bargain. Panic whirled through him, sending his stomach tipping in the most dangerous manner. Nevertheless, he turned down Grosvenor Street, headed for Peter's townhouse. He would finally make things right.

Though his friend's home had a quiet elegance, blending in with its surroundings in an understated way, it was still an impressive specimen. Quincy gazed up at it as he dismounted, a low whistle escaping his lips. Egad, but the filthy orphan he'd met shortly after running away from home all those years ago had certainly come up in the world. Then, Peter had been reeling from his mother's untimely death and running from an uncertain and abhorrent future. It had bound them, that fear, a lifeline for two young boys.

Now Peter was a duke. Quincy grinned, anticipation overriding his anxiety for the first time since stepping foot off the ship and onto English soil. Damn but he had missed his friend. The past year had been a long one; he had not been without Peter's companionship for more than a day or two at a time since that first meeting. Their time apart had brought forcefully home just how much the other man meant to him. Securing his horse, he strode up the front stairs to the imposing black door.

His knock was answered with alacrity by a stoic-faced butler. "May I help you, sir?"

"Is His Grace in?"

"Who may I ask is calling?"

Quincy grinned. "Oh, now, don't spoil the fun."

The man blinked. "Pardon me, sir?"

"I shall, and gladly," Quincy said, pushing into the front hall, "if you play along and show me to the duke immediately."

The butler's mouth fell open. "Sir, I must insist—"

"Have no fear," he declared, holding up a hand, "for His Grace will not bring down fire and brimstone on your head; though he can be a grim fellow at times, I promise he will be happy to see me." He smiled his most charming smile. "Now do a man a favor, for I've traveled long and hard to see my friend and I cannot wait a moment longer."

The man, dazed by the barrage of charm Quincy was piling on his head, nodded and mumbled, "If you'll follow me?"

Quincy's grin of victory quickly faded as he took in the interior of the cavernous house. Though the place had been impressive from the street, he hadn't expected such a behemoth to be hiding behind the elegant facade. They'd lived a comfortable life in Boston, yes. And he had not been a stranger to these places of elegance and excess in the past. But this put that all in the dust. Soaring ceilings painted with heavenly landscapes of cavorting cherubim basking in their divinity, black and white marble tiles glistening at his feet, the walls a buttery yellow and covered with all manner of paintings. He just managed to swallow down a chortle. Best to save his mirth for Peter, when it would annoy the most.

The butler stopped before a closed door. Instead of opening it, however, he looked at Quincy with a healthy dose of uncertainty. "Sir, if you would only let me introduce you—"

In answer, Quincy clapped the man on the shoulder, winked, and threw open the door. It hit the wall with a resounding thud as he strode within. "His Grace the Duke of Dane, I presume," he bellowed into the silence.

Peter, seated behind the desk, jumped a foot, nearly falling out of his seat before catching himself on the edge of his desk. "What the ever-loving... Quincy?"

He grinned. "Surprised to see me, old man?"

When Peter only sat there, mouth hanging comically open, eyes like saucers, Quincy laughed. "Damn, but that expression there was worth the hassle of diverging from my travels. Now come and give me a proper greeting, for I've missed you like the devil."

Peter, it seemed, needed no further urgings. And Quincy soon learned he had made a fatal error, for his friend was quite the largest man he had ever known. Surging from his chair, a grin breaking over his face, Peter rushed to him. Quincy barely had time to brace for impact before his friend's bulk hit him like a veritable wave. The breath was knocked from his body, meaty arms surrounding him in a crushing embrace preventing even a single gasping breath.

"Damn me, but you're a sight for sore eyes," Peter exclaimed.

"Air!" Quincy managed.

Peter merely chuckled, squeezing a bit tighter—how was that even possible?—before releasing him. "When last I'd heard from you, you were just setting sail for Spain. What are you doing in England, man?"

Quincy's exuberant mood took a stumble at that. He held on to his grin by pure will alone. It was the opening he needed, the perfect time to reveal all. And yet...

He had not realized until this moment just how lonely he'd been over the past year. Though he'd had Captain Adams and his family back in Boston, though the months of travel following his leaving that city had brought him into contact with more people than he'd ever dreamed of, he always felt as if he were searching for something, some unidentifiable need that he couldn't quite attain.

Now that he was with his dearest friend again, however, he felt the ache in his chest begin to ease. Surely he could not be blamed for postponing his mission just a few minutes longer.

Ignoring a pang of guilt, he grinned. "Do you think I could sail this close to England and not visit you?"

Though Peter rolled his eyes, Quincy could not fail to see the smile tugging on his lips. "I'm sure my charms pale in comparison to the wonders you've seen. But how has it been, traveling and seeing the world? I know it's a dream long held."

"It's been incredible," he replied softly. "If only my father had been alive to see it." A vision of his father's face swam up in his mind then, that long-ago grief tempered now by the distance of time, and by the knowledge that he was finally seeing the man's dreams realized. He had worked hard over the years, surviving, building an empire to be proud of with Peter. Now, however, it was time to return to that promise he had made so long ago when leaving his family's house.

He gave Peter a considering look, only half teasing as he said, "You made a pretty penny in the liquidation of our assets. I don't suppose I could ever tempt you to join me? Even for a short while?"

Peter grinned. "There's not a chance of that. But I do plan on enjoying your company while you're in town. How long before you're off again?"

Quincy shrugged. "Not long, a week or two at the most."

"You will stay here at Dane House, of course."

Quincy's chuckle was strained. For there was one reason, and one reason only, he had made certain to find lodgings before coming here: he did not think he would be welcome after the truth was revealed.

"Not on your life," he said. "I'm a bachelor in London. If you think I'm going to miss out on cavorting to my heart's content, you are sorely mistaken. But Mivart's is just a street away, and so you may see me much more often than you'd like. Though," he said, casting a glance about him, taking in the richly carved bookcases, the deep blue silk-covered walls, the towering windows looking out onto a verdant garden, "I admit to feeling more than a bit of regret now that I've seen your London residence. The place is amazing, man. Is Danesford even half as incredible?"

"Even more so." A quiet pride shone from Peter's eyes. "I thought I would forever despise the place, that I would be glad to see it fall to ruins. Yet now my feelings could not be more different."

"And I suppose having Lenora by your side has not aided in that about-face," Quincy murmured with humor.

"Laugh all you want, for I can only heartily agree with you." Peter chuckled.

Quincy shook his head, grinning. "I cannot believe the change in you, man. After all, when last I was here, you were in the throes of despair for love of Lenora. And now look at you, happily married, master of all this." He swept his arm out. "And a damn *duke*. Don't tell me I have to start calling you *Your Grace* now."

"Arse," Peter muttered. "If I hear those words from your lips, I'll gladly trounce you. Sit, while I pour a healthy dose of something to celebrate this visit."

As Quincy settled himself into an overstuffed chair before the hearth, his friend went to the small cabinet in the corner. "Never tell me you're drinking strong spirits now."

Peter chuckled. "I've not changed that much. Though," he added, his tone turning rueful as the sound of clinking glass echoed about the room, "there are times I wish for a small dose of something stronger than lemonade or wine."

"Has it been much of an adjustment, then, taking over the dukedom?" Quincy asked, stretching his long legs out.

Peter's lips twisted as he turned and made his way to his friend, a glass of whiskey in one hand and something that looked suspiciously like ratafia in the other. "Transitioning from commoner and self-made man to a duke has been...different," he said. "There are so many people whose well-being and livelihood I'm responsible for here, it boggles my mind. Without Lenora by my side, I don't know that I would have taken to the position with any grace."

Quincy snorted as he accepted his glass and Peter

settled across from him. "Grace. That is one word I would have never associated with you. But how is our dear Lenora? I look forward to seeing her again after so long."

At the mention of his bride, Peter's face lit up. That was the only phrase to describe it, for it fairly glowed from within. It was an expression Quincy had never witnessed before in his normally stoic friend, a softening of features typically held tight against the rest of the world.

"Lenora is wonderful. She's out with Clara and Phoebe just now."

At the mention of Lady Clara Ashford, Quincy started. Just barely; the whiskey hardly quivered in his grip. But inside he felt the shifting of something. He recalled Lady Clara well. He had not met much with her when last he was in England; her father had been quite ill, keeping her close to home. But he recalled each meeting with her as if they had been etched on his brain.

What had it been about her? Even after all this time, he still didn't have the slightest clue. She had been pretty, yes. Most women were to him. He always found something lovely to admire in every female he came into contact with.

With Lady Clara, however, it had been more. A calling to something inside him that he had been hard-pressed to understand.

And apparently he was still just as affected. He should have known such would be the case, of course. Whenever Peter had written to him, Quincy had been incredibly aware of any mention of her. And so he knew she and her younger sister, Lady Phoebe, had stayed on at Danesford at Peter and Lenora's insistence after their father, the previous duke, passed on, and that Lady Clara was in the party that had made their way to London for the season and Lady

Phoebe's come-out. He had told himself it was merely a healthy interest. Lady Clara was, after all, Peter's family.

Which, of course, did not explain why the lady's sister, or any other member of Peter's family, had not garnered as much attention.

Blessedly Peter spoke then, breaking him from thoughts of a freckled, round face and dark blue eyes. Unfortunately, it was to ask about the very last thing Quincy wished to discuss.

"Doesn't your family hail from London?"

How Quincy didn't blanch outright, he would never know. He brought the glass to his lips, taking a healthy swallow, followed by a second, letting it burn all the way to his gut. "They do."

Peter regarded Quincy over the rim of his glass, worry clouding his eyes. "Do you plan to see them while you're in town?"

"I had considered it, yes," he admitted gruffly. He gave a nervous laugh as his friend continued to look at him soberly. "It worked out so well for you, after all, I thought why not give it a chance."

His sad attempt at humor only made the worry in Peter's eyes grow. "I could come with you if you'd like," he said, his voice quiet. "For moral support."

A mad laugh threatened, only barely held in check. "Ah, no, I'm not sure that would be wise," he managed.

But apparently his attempts at deterring Peter only made him suspicious. He narrowed his eyes. "What is it, man?" Before Quincy could think of a suitable reply that would allay the situation, an understanding light dawned in Peter's eyes. "You needn't be embarrassed, you know," he said, his tone gentler than Quincy had heard it before. "I grew up poor, too. You know that."

Quincy did blanch then. Ah, God, if Peter only knew.

The alcohol sat sour in his stomach. This had been a mistake. He should never have postponed telling Peter; he should have been up front from the beginning instead of trying to wring out one last bit of closeness with the man.

He knew in a moment it was time. He looked to his drink, noticing as if from far away the trembling liquid, realizing only then how much his hands shook. Placing his glass down with care on the table beside him, he dragged in a steadying breath. "Peter, there's something I must tell you—"

A commotion in the hall just then interrupted him. In the next moment, Lenora sailed through the study door.

"Peter, darling," she said, tugging off her gloves, "your aunt has bid me to tell you—Oh! Mr. Nesbitt, what an absolutely wonderful surprise!"

Quincy, his heart pounding in his chest from dredging up the courage to finally tell his friend the truth, wanted to simultaneously howl that the moment had been snatched from him and kiss Lenora for postponing this thing he dreaded so very much. He surged to his feet, plastering a stiff smile to his face. "Your Grace."

"Oh, none of that. Lenora, please," she said with a warm smile.

"Lenora," he repeated, some of the tension melting from him. "I do hope you don't mind me dropping in unannounced."

She laughed, accepting a kiss from her husband before taking Quincy's hand. "Why, you make it sound as if you were merely in the neighborhood and did not have to sail for weeks across an ocean to get here. But we never received word that you intended to visit. Did you not write?"

"I admit, I had hoped to shock this fellow here." He jerked a thumb in Peter's direction.

"I do wish I had seen that. For though I try my hardest, not much surprises my husband." She sighed happily. "But this is just splendid. I'll have Mrs. Ingram prepare a room right away."

Before he could lay waste to that generous offer, a sweet voice carried in from the hall. "Prepare a room for whom, Lenora?" And then Lady Clara was there, filling the doorway and his vision.

The breath caught in Quincy's chest. Damn, but she was just as lovely as he remembered her, if not more so. Rich brown hair in a riot of curls so soft his fingers itched to dive into their depths. Pale skin with a smattering of freckles across the bridge of her nose. A willowy figure, accentuated by the light blue of her dress.

And those eyes. Damnation, those beautiful clear blue eyes that widened when she saw him. Her full lips parted on a soft gasp of air.

He bowed a second later than was polite. "Lady Clara, it is an absolute pleasure to see you again."

The delicate rose of a blush spread up her neck and settled, bright and warm, on her cheeks. She gave a quick, shallow curtsy. "Mr. Nesbitt. How lovely to have you back in England."

Quincy, please. The words echoed through his head, aching to be let loose. He just managed to hold them back. To hear his name from her lips would be the most exquisite torture. And if there was anything he did not need right now, it was more to tempt him with this woman. Not taking into account the fact that he would be gone in a matter of weeks, she was Peter's cousin and under his protection. There was no way in hell he could ever act on whatever this was he felt for her.

Her blush deepened as his silence crept on. She looked to Lenora. "Shall I go to Mrs. Ingram to have that room made up, then?"

Before Lenora could answer, Quincy stepped forward, his hand raised. "No need, my lady. I'm staying at Mivart's, you see."

Was that relief in Lady Clara's eyes? Or disappointment? And why did he want so badly to know which one ruled her? Thankfully he would never know, for it was there and gone in a moment, her face taking on a pleasant if blank expression.

"Oh, but we have more than enough room," Lenora said. "And Lady Tesh will be ever so disappointed. She always speaks so fondly of you."

Quite an accomplishment, that. Peter's irascible great-aunt, the Dowager Viscountess Tesh, was as plain spoken and opinionated a woman as he had ever had the pleasure to know. And he adored her.

But as much as he wished to stay here with these people, he could not. Not just yet. Not until everything was settled.

The remembrance of just why he was there in London hit him then, coursing through him in a wild panic that was especially potent after the pleasure of being with people he loved so well. Which just proved what he had known all along, that he would never be free until he put the past behind him once and for all.

"That is because she has wonderful taste," he teased, desperate to rein his anxieties in. "But I shall be about so much, you'll no doubt grow sick of me. Speaking of which." He turned back to Peter. "I don't suppose you have a moment, old man, before I head out?"

"Of course," Peter was quick to say. Until Lenora placed a hand on his arm.

"I'm so sorry, but can it wait for this evening? We're expected for tea at Lord and Lady Crabtree's, and are already running behind schedule. Phoebe is recently engaged to their son, and this shall be our first informal meeting with them. And they are quite the sticklers for propriety," she added ruefully.

Peter groaned. "I had forgotten." He gave his wife a pleading look. "I don't suppose I can stay behind?"

Quincy might have laughed at his great beast of a friend, who looked more the part of a Viking than a duke, begging his wife for a respite from a tea, if his disappointment wasn't so sharp. For this meant he would have to postpone revealing the truth to the man. And it had been difficult enough to build up the nerve for today.

Any hope he had that Peter might stay behind died a swift and thorough death as Lenora leveled a stern look on her husband. Which was an impressive thing, being as small and delicate as she was.

"Peter, you know you must attend. This meeting is important." She turned to Quincy. "You are, of course, welcome to join us. You're family, after all."

That warmth in his breast was back, and he very nearly relented. Especially when Peter gave him a look that fairly begged for his company.

But he knew, having stood on the edge, muscles tensed to take the leap and reveal all to his friend, that he could no longer pretend that everything was well. He could not converse and smile without betraying the turmoil in his breast. Nor could he return to his rooms and sit and wait for the axe to fall. No, he had to take action, to move forward. And that meant it was time to visit his family.

The very thought had him breaking out in a cold sweat. But underlying it was a sense of relief. In short order, it would be over and done with. And he could move forward.

Filled with a new determination, he smiled at Lenora. "Alas, I have an errand to attend to."

"You will return this evening?"

That it was Lady Clara who spoke shocked him. And by the look on her face, she was equally stunned. Once more she colored. "To make certain we have enough places set for dinner," she explained. "And to mollify Lady Tesh. She'll be livid she missed you."

He should have looked upon his return to Dane House with nothing but dread; though it would be later than he wished it, there could be no postponing telling Peter the truth of the matter tonight.

Instead he felt an odd kind of anticipation. "Yes," he replied, unable to look away from the deep blue of her eyes, "I'll be back."

He saw it then, the slight tightening of the corners of her mouth, a smile suppressed. As he made his farewells, he wondered why it pleased him so.

About the Author

Christina Britton developed a passion for writing romance novels shortly after buying her first at the tender age of thirteen and spent much of her teenage years scribbling on whatever piece of paper she could find. Though for several years she put brush instead of pen to paper, she has returned to her first love and is now writing full-time. She spends her days dreaming of corsets and cravats and noblemen with tortured souls.

She lives with her husband and two children in the San Francisco Bay Area.

You can learn more at:
ChristinaBritton.com
Twitter @CBrittonAuthor
Facebook.com/ChristinaBrittonAuthor

Looking for more historical romances?
Forever brings the heat with these sexy rogues!

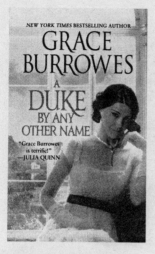

A DUKE BY ANY OTHER NAME
by Grace Burrowes

Lady Althea Wentworth has little patience for dukes, reclusive or otherwise, but she needs the Duke of Rothhaven's backing to gain entrance into Society. She's asked him nicely, she's called on him politely, all to no avail—until her prize hogs *just happen* to plunder his orchard. He longs for privacy. She's vowed to never endure another ball as a wallflower. Yet as the two grow closer, it soon becomes clear they might both be pretending to be something they're not.

FOREVER AND A DUKE
by Grace Burrowes

Eleanora Hatfield knows from experience that dealing with the peerage can lead only to problems. But she reluctantly agrees to help Wrexham, Duke of Elsmore, sort his finances. What starts out as an unwanted assignment soon leads to forbidden kisses and impossible longings. But with scandal haunting Ellie's past and looming in Rex's future, how can true love lead to anything but heartbreak? Includes a bonus story by Kelly Bowen!

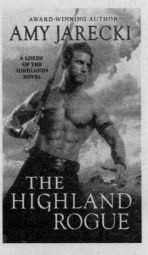

THE HIGHLAND ROGUE
by Amy Jarecki

Abandoned on a deserted Scottish island by her family, Divana Campbell is both terrified and relieved when Highlander Sir Kennan Cameron drags himself from the surf. Trusting Kennan is her only chance for survival—and by the time they escape the island and arrive at his home, she can barely imagine life without him. But as the heir to a powerful chieftain, Kennan could never marry the likes of her.

A GOOD DUKE IS HARD TO FIND
by Christina Britton

Next in line for a dukedom he doesn't want to inherit, Peter Ashford is on the Isle of Synne only to exact revenge on the man responsible for his mother's death. Yet when he meets the beautiful and kind Miss Lenora Hartley, he can't help but be drawn to her. Can Peter put aside his plans for vengeance for the woman who has come to mean everything to him?

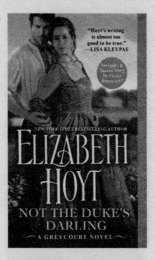

NOT THE DUKE'S DARLING
by Elizabeth Hoyt

When the man who destroyed her brother appears at the house party Freya de Moray is attending, she does what any devoted sister would do: plans revenge. But the Duke of Harlowe is already being blackmailed—by someone else. Freya knows all Harlowe's sins, but her fierce tongue and bold sensuality are a temptation he can't resist. When it becomes clear Freya is the one in danger, he'll have to earn Freya's trust to keep her safe...by any means necessary. Includes a bonus story by Grace Burrowes!